PRAISE FOR THE SCEPTER AND THE ISLE

The Scepter and the Isle is the second book in the World War II Pacific Theater 'The Islands Series' written jointly by Murray Pura and Patrick E. Craig. It continues the journey of three Mennonite boys (Bud the Corpsman, Johnny, and Billy) who become young men under the harshest of battle conditions as the Marines continue to Island hop to Tarawa, through Saipan, and finally Tinian Island. This book is not for the 'faint of heart'. It very accurately depicts the gore, and brutality of this kind of warfare; squad level and individual Marines fighting a determined Japanese enemy that welcomes death and believes surrender is abhorrent.

I particularly appreciated their stories being told through the multiple points of view; each experiencing the horror of the same vignette with varied emotional responses. With great acumen, these authors weave the complex elements of the human dimension into a very accurate, however shocking view of actual close combat. As a retired professional veteran, I appreciate that the book accurately dispels the myth that wars garner great glory for the victor. In fact, these Marines like those before them, fight for each other with the hope of ending the war and returning home to loved ones and 'normality' (a condition these Marines wisely question will ever return given the horrific visages they have experienced.)

Further, a related theme that many infantrymen experience is the desire to secure freedom for a brutalized populace; this was clearly evident in the battle for Saipan. For these young Marines, they also experience the conflict between their Mennonite belief system, and what they must do to accomplish their combat missions. I found it summarized with this quote from 'Bud the Corpsman' after he had to kill or be killed: "—there are no pacifists in foxholes." Still some hope of returning to their belief system once home and immersed in the civilian populace. This book is an excellent read and provided insights, and induced unanswered questions to ponder that no purely historical account can elicit. Highly recommended. I enthusiastically give it Five out of Five Stars. I am anxiously awaiting the next in 'The Island Series'!

— COLONEL STEVEN L. CRAWFORD (USA, RET.)

I only finish novels with entrancing characters and gripping plots, and even so, when the book is finished, I typically am as well. But at the end of the first in this series, *Far on the Ringing Plains*, I wasn't finished. I wanted to experience more of their well-drawn characters, their realism and grit and hearts, how they interacted, the caliber of writing that captives. Craig and Pura delivered in *The Scepter and the Isle.*

So, I heartily recommend Book Two. You'll enjoy the journey, and a journey it is. But read it with a warning—expect some unexpected twists and turns. Let it speak to you. And then wait. For Book Three.

— TIM RITER, AUTHOR OF *GOD, A MOTORCYCLE, AND THE OPEN ROAD* AND *NOT A SAFE GOD.*

The Scepter and The Isle is the riveting sequel to *Far on the Ringing Plains*, the story of three Mennonite boys, Bud,

Billy and Johnny, who become men very quickly as they serve together in the United States Marine Corp during WW II.

This story is well researched with very graphic battle scenes of blood, guts, gore and language not intended for the faint of heart. War is Hell.

My father was a Marine. He was there. He once told us that he watched his two best friends blown apart on a beach landing. He said war was Hell and we were never to ask about it again. We always stood to salute the flag. ALWAYS even when it was on TV. After reading The Scepter and The Isle, I am even more proud of the fact that I am the daughter of a Master Tech Sergeant who often said, "It would have killed an ordinary man."

"And Johnny knew he wanted Billy to live, and he wanted Bud to live, and he wanted to go home to the US of A with his friends, because he knew that for the rest of his life he would need someone to call in the middle of a sweat-filled night with the friggin' Movietone running over and over in his head. Someone who knew, someone who cared, someone who had been to hell and back with him."

I learned numerous things about both Tarawa and Saipan. I had never heard of the Chomorro, the horrible persecution they suffered, the courage they displayed or the sacrifices they made for their independence. The Serpent was an intriguing character that caused me to do some fact checking. This may be a novel, but it is very educational and full of actual facts wrapped around the experiences of the three main characters. Guts, gore, blood and language aside, I want to know what happens to these three Marines. Patrick Craig and Murray Pura are masterful authors. I hope I don't have to wait long!

— MARIA WEEKS

The Scepter and The Isle by Murray Pura and Patrick Craig, the second novel in the Island Series, moves this historical fiction tale wonderfully onward. The writing is superb and friendly to the reader, a riveting page-turner. The authors progress their coming of age tale forward by masterfully developing the characters from Book One, Johnny, Billy and Bud, to maturing adults as World War Two's island battles swirl around them, shaping and forging them. The last chapters are so well introduced and written that their effect is stunning.

— SPEC4 REB BLAKE II FIRE CRASH RESCUE
1ST INFANTRY DIV PHI LOI ARMY AIR BASE
REPUBLIC OF SOUTH VIETNAM 1967—1968

THE SCEPTER AND THE ISLE

MURRAY PURA

PATRICK E. CRAIG

Copyright © 2021 by Murray Pura and Patrick E. Craig

Islands Publishing P.O. Box 73, Huston, Idaho 83630

Library of Congress Cataloging—The Scepter And The Isle / Murray Pura / Patrick E. Craig

ISBN 978-1-7347635-5-3 (pbk.)

ISBN 978-1-7347635-6-0 (eBook)

Printed in the United States of America

ACKNOWLEDGMENTS

The authors would like to acknowledge William Manchester for his brilliant book, *Goodbye Darkness* and it's importance to the writing of the Islands series.

ISLANDS

A series by Murray A. Pura & Patrick E. Craig

Three friends, three years, six islands and a war that demanded from all three the ultimate in faith, courage, honor & sacrifice.

THE ISLANDS SERIES

Book 1: Far On The Ringing Plains
Book 2: The Scepter And The Isle
Book 3: Men That Strove With Gods

Book 1: Far On The Ringing Plains
—Guadalcanal—
Book 2: The Scepter And The Isle
—Tarawa & Saipan—

CONTENTS

Preamble   xvii

Part I
NEW ZEALAND
1. Goodbye, Cactus   3
2. A Rock and a Hard Place   9
3. Winter Hunt   17
4. In Love With Kalasia   25
5. A World of Hurt   33
6. An Island Named Helen   41

Part II
TARAWA
Day 1 — D Day   51
7. The Dark Land   53
8. A Hero's Reward   61
9. The Spider   69
DAY 2 — D+1   77
10. Firefight   79
11. Hell's Kitchen   87
12. The Tipping Point   95
DAY 3—D-Day + 2   103
13. The Dragon's Teeth   105
14. San Juan Hill   111
15. Ten Thousand Years!   119
DAY 4 — D-Day+3   127
16. Slaughterhouse   129
17. Johnny in The Pocket—0700 D-Day+3   137
18. Thanksgiving Day   143
19. Charon's Barge   151

Part III
HAWAII

20. Christmas Cards   161
21. Silver Star   169
22. Shorelines   177
23. The Red Road   185
24. Island X   193
25. How Much More...   209

Part IV
SAIPAN

DAY 1 — D-Day   219
26. Once More Into The Breach, Dear Friends—0400 D-Day Saipan   221
27. The Serpent Strikes   229
28. The Chamorro   243
29. You Can't Go Home Again   257
30. The Sugar Cane War   265
31. The Nature of The Enemy   283
32. The Lady and The Tiger   289
33. Delight of Battle   299
DAY 16 — Garapan   315
34. Casualties   317
35. To Hell and Back   327
DAY 22 — Banzai   335
36. The Rocket's Red Glare   337
37. The Last Roundup   345
38. If I Had Wings   351
39. The Weight on his Back   361
40. The Things We Leave Behind   369

Murray Pura   377
Patrick E. Craig   379
Also by Murray Pura   381
Also by Patrick E. Craig   383

PREAMBLE

BUD, THE CORPSMAN

THE WORLD HAS CHANGED—at least for the men of the 2nd Division. Back in the States, life goes on. St Louis celebrates a cheap World Series title and America's newest heroes have names like Harry Gumbert, Johnny Hopp and Max Lanier. Out here, it's different.

Here the heroes have names like Hotchkiss, Malena, Sharples, McKeever, and Kramer. I know them, Billy knows them, Johnny knows them, but back home they are not and never will be known—except maybe on a Christmas night when a young wife looks at the empty chair and comforts a crying child, or a mother walks out to the barn and stands beside the hay mount where her little boy broke his arm.

Now they are bones, and we are the sepulchers. The flesh is rotting beneath the terrible jungle mud, but the bones are alive inside us. Bones named friendship, bones named grief, bones named horror, bones named love.

For the love of men in war is great and men with the immensity of such love become a force. When death comes seeking prey, the force meets it head on—men die horribly, blown to bits, shot, stabbed, gutted, drowned... And afterwards men live on, sick with the loss, shaken with fear, ravaged by disease and hunger, in the rain, in the mud, fearing the enemy, tired of living but afraid to die... nameless.

When the sun paints the weary west with golden light and the ship sails into safe harbor, we will disembark, but we will not leave the bones behind. We will carry them—rattling mementoes of another time.

If I live to be an old man, on the day I die, I will still have the bones.

Corpsman

I

NEW ZEALAND

GOODBYE, CACTUS

BUD, THE CORPSMAN

January 31, 1943. Early in the morning, the order came down, and we picked up our bags and started walking to the coast. Most of us were in sad shape, so it took a while to get down there, but we finally got to the beach while maintaining a semblance of order. The big grey transports lay off Lunga Point and the small LCPs were waiting to take us out. I watched the boys as they loaded—scarecrow thin from repeated bouts with malaria, skin cracked and furrowed, faces gaunt, and eyes full of memories of awful days and worse nights. Some guys were so bad they had to be carried on. I kept busy for a while, making sure that the sickest guys got on board.

Thank you, Jesus, we are leaving this God-awful dung-hole. For six months we had kicked Hirohito's butt and now, with the Army guys in control, the Second Div was getting out. Johnny Strange and Billy Martens showed up at 0800 hours, and we had a Mennonite farewell ceremony of sorts on the beach. What I mean by that is we looked back at the jungle and cussed that frigging island from the depths of our souls. After I rattled off a particularly good string of Gyrene imprecations, Billy smiles. "Say, Bud, that's dang fine cussin' for a devoted Christian."

I smiled. "I've been hanging around you boys too long."

"What would your pop say, Bud?" pipes up Johnny.

"My dad was never on this hell-hole. If he was he'd be cussin' it worse than me."

I watch Billy as he walks toward the boats. He's still limping, but he's doing better since we got that foot rot under control. I worry about Billy. I think he's the one who changed the most. When he first got here, nothing seemed to bug him. He was the sniper, our go-to-guy when the going got tough. He could shoot a rat out of a tree at five hundred yards, and the eye out of a Jap Colonel from even further. But towards the end, after he'd blow away some Jap, he'd wander off and puke his guts. Then, when he found out the KIAs were staying here to rot in the jungle, he got a little shook up. It was like the dead were talking to him. He came to me one day with his gripe.

"Bud, it ain't right. Maybe these guys don't want their bones left here to rot. Maybe they want us to take them away. Hell, Joseph had his bones carried out of Egypt."

"What are we supposed to do, Billy? Half these guys are just bits and pieces. Most of the dead are already dirt. You can't take them all back."

"We could try to find their bones, Bud..." And then he realized how dumb that was and he left off. But it got me to thinking about the bones. I guess the only way to take them home is in our hearts and our memories. Half of the guys who climbed into the Higgins boats with us on D Day died, blown to bits, beheaded, eaten by sharks, sucked into bottomless mud-holes. Billy was right to feel bad. These were our friends, our buddies. I can't count the number of times I'd be dead if it wasn't for one of my squad shoving me down and taking a bullet for me. All we can do is remember them and keep going.

Johnny Strange? Well, he's just Johnny. He's been twisted up since I met him. His girl, Marjean, having his little boy back in the states, kinda gave him a window of grace, but during those

last battles I saw the old crazy look come back in his eyes. It's
going to take a lot of killing to fix what's broken in that boy's
head. But other than he's bat-shit crazy, he's a great guy, and he's
my friend. It was Johnny who took a bayonet meant for me after
the Japs captured me and tied me up in a hut during our little
sojourn up to Aola Bay. That was the day I helped Johnny kill a
guy and to tell you the truth, I didn't think another thing about it.
That sonofabitch had been slappin' me around and putting out
cigarettes on my chest, so when I got a chance to knock him down
so Johnny could choke him to death, it just came natural.

We're going home. Well, not home but away, out over the
water. Some boys are thinking Australia or Hawaii, but I think the
ships are headed for New Zealand. The Sixth has already been
there on the way out and the 4/10, too. They built some camps
while they were there, so I'm thinking, "Why reinvent the wheel?"
New Zealand, here we come.

THE TRIP down was a big readjustment. After wallowing in mud
in the steaming jungle for six months without a hot shower, your
shorts get a little stiff. Shaving with a Bowie knife is an adventure,
and you never knew what was swimming in that muck the cooks
called chow. Forget about socks, they rot off in three weeks. And
forget about sleep. Every Marine I know could sleep standing up,
so we didn't worry about beds, because if you laid down in that
muck you could get sucked straight down to hell. When we
crawled into those iron bunks on the ship, it was like heaven. You
knew when you woke up, that steel plate would still be there
under you and the dead hands that reached up out of the mud in
your dreams could never get through all that metal.

Hot water! Did I tell you about the hot water? Man, on the
ship you could just stand there with the water burning your skin
off, take a bar of soap and wear it down to a nub in one shower,

and then grab a clean towel and buff yourself off like a shoeshine boy on a Seattle street. And the food? Hot food that you could recognize, in sterilized containers with no critters doing the backstroke in them. We sailed back on the old "Unholy Three," the Hayes, the Jackson and the Adams, the same ones that took us out to Cactus, but now they seemed like floating palaces.

You could get anything you wanted on the mess deck. Me, I craved milk. Tall, frosty glasses of milk, I couldn't get enough. I think I emptied every bottle of milk they had below decks and the cookies were glad to give it to me. Steaks, potatoes, eggs, bacon, hot coffee with plenty of sugar and cream—boy, I tell you, I could have stayed on that boat for the rest of the war and been just fine.

But then we got to New Zealand and the ship and Cactus and everything that went before became just a dark memory. If I live to be a hundred, I'll never forget that wonderful place. Every Marine I know will tell you that except for some special spots in the good ol' U.S. of A., there's nowhere like New Zealand in the entire world. If I walked into a bar today and saw a Marine, I know if I sat down next to him and ordered up a couple of Blue Ribbons, and then asked him what his favorite place in the whole war was, he'd say Wellington, New Zealand.

I'm standing on the deck with a Gyrene from the Sixth when some little green hills pop up out of the water miles ahead of us. The sun had been coming up on the port side of the ship for five days, so I knew our direction was due south. That could only mean one thing...

"New Zealand, that's New Zealand!"

My first sight of NZ is Mount Edgemont. It's a big old rock that sits on the western side of the North Island. It comes right down to the water and makes a giant headland. You sail around the promontory and there's Wellington Harbour. It's beautiful and big and you could put a fleet in there.

The Gyrene is getting excited. He points to a little island.

"That's Taputeranga. I got to sail out there and go snorkeling when we stopped here on the way to Cactus. Man, there's crazy fish down there and kelp, big ol' octopuses, cod, and dolphins."

Having grown up on the flat dry dirt of Ritzville, Washington, I don't have the faintest idea what he's talking about. We spent six hellish months way inland on Guadalcanal and never saw the ocean unless we got in boats to run up the coast. And even then, I never saw an octopus.

After we sail by Octopus Island, the ship takes a left turn into the prettiest little bay you ever saw. As we get closer, I can see wharf-lined waters, with hills rising as steep as the ones we saw in Frisco on our way down to Dago. A fresh wind hummed in the rigging, and I see snow-capped mountains in the distance. The ship drifts toward the dock, and it looked like we would walk ashore. The docks are filled with… women; red-haired women, blondes, brunettes, white-skinned women, dark skinned, man, oh man, oh man.

I hustle below deck and fetch Billy and Johnny, and we join the boys lining the rails to watch the greeting these wonderful New Zealand women are giving to our friendly invasion. They got a brass band playing some marching music and "Big Band" brings his trumpet up. He starts with some Harry James riffs on top of the Souza march, and pretty soon the guys are jitter-bugging on the deck. I tell you there was never a happier bunch of guys. Even Billy is doing this strange kinda' western tango with his gimpy feet. All the guys are checking out the dames and I nudge Johnny.

"Just sight-seeing, Johnny?"

Johnny smiles and nods. "Someday you'll get to meet Marjean, Bud, and you'll see why I would never even think of going off the reservation."

Now Billy, he could use some cheering up, and I hope he gets to enjoy a little female companionship while he's here. Me, I left my heart in Tonga.

Then there are a lot of whistles and horn blasts and the boat is tying up at the dock. They run a gangplank down, a gangplank, of all things. I can't even remember how to walk down a gangplank, I'm so used to cargo nets and Higgins boats. We all fetch our gear and start down to the dock. I'm looking at all these lovelies and looking left and right, and then a face swims into my field of vision. It's a beautiful face, brown skin, long dark hair, beautiful lips, deep eyes like bottomless pools, a face I've seen a thousand times in my dreams. It's the face that launched a thousand ships in my heart. Kalasia.

2

A ROCK AND A HARD PLACE

JOHNNY STRANGE

Johnny Strange stood at the railing with Bud and Billy and looked down on the teeming crowds waiting on the Wellington dock. Girls, hundreds of them, were waving and shouting. A band was playing a Souza march and American flags were waving everywhere.

Bud nudged him and nodded toward the girls below. "Just sight-seeing, Johnny?"

Johnny let his eyes run over the eager faces below. A picture came to his mind—A lovely girl, the prettiest he had ever seen, corn-silk hair that peeked out from underneath a ski cap, an oval face, full lips and startling green eyes...

Marjean!

He smiled at Bud. "Someday you'll get to meet Marjean, Bud, and you'll see why I would never even think of going off the reservation."

Bud slapped him on the back. "She's a lucky girl, Johnny."

The gangplank swung out and down. The speakers mounted below the bridge crackled to life and the Boatswain's call sounded Officer of the Day. Johnny could see a naval officer making his way to the gangway. A familiar figure accompanied him.

"Look, Bud, Billy, it's Red Mike."

Johnny's thoughts went back to the battle of Bloody Ridge, where he watched as Colonel Edson rallied the men to fight off overwhelming Japanese forces. Red Mike's arm was beckoning to men on both sides and Johnny could hear him yelling. "Raiders, parachuters, engineers, artillerymen, I don't give a damn who you are. You're all Marines. Come up on this hill and fight!"

Johnny grabbed his kit and followed Bud and Johnny to the gangway. Red Mike was greeting every man that passed. When the three Mennos got to the head of the line, Red Mike smiled.

"Hey, I remember you fellows. Bloody Ridge. X-Ray Platoon." He put his hand on Billy's shoulder. "You're the one they call Sniper. I saw you doing some terrific shooting from that hill." He glanced at Bud. "And you're the corpsman who kept going down the hill to bring our Company B boys up. Outstanding work, son." He smiled at Johnny. "And you're Johnny Strange. I remember that name. Seems like you got a rep on Cactus—you'd do anything or go anywhere to kill Japs. Might be a little calm for you here, eh Strange?"

"Could be, Colonel. I'll try to stay out of trouble."

The Colonel laughed. Just then a Marine with silver Lt. bars on his shoulders went by. The Colonel hollered after him. "Hey, Lieutenant Burke!"

The Lieutenant turned around, saw the Colonel and snapped a salute. "At ease, Lieutenant," Red Mike smiled. "Say, I hear you're planning on putting together a boxing squad."

Lieutenant Burke grinned. "Yes, Sir. I've already got some matches lined up."

Red Mike nodded at Johnny. "You need any tough guys?"

"As many as I can get, Sir."

Red Mike turned to Johnny. "How about it, Strange? Interested in the manly art of boxing?"

Johnny shrugged. "I have done little boxing, Sir, but I did well in hand to hand in basic."

"And on Cactus, son, from what I heard. What about it, Burke? Need another hand?"

"If the Colonel is recommending, I'm good with that."

Edson nodded. "Yep, I'm recommending. You hook up with Burke, Johnny."

Burke looked at Johnny. "Get in touch with me when we get to Paekakariki, and I'll get you set up."

"Sounds good, Sir. Thank you."

Red Mike slapped Johnny on the shoulder. "That should help you work some steam off and keep you out of that trouble you were talking about."

THE TRAIN to Camp Paekakariki wound through green hills and then down onto a flat coastal plain. Johnny sat next to a window and watched the waves rolling in toward the shore.

I wonder if any of those waves hit Cactus before they got here...

Billy leaned over. "I was thinking about the guys we left behind, Johnny."

Johnny grimaced. "Is that still eating you, Sniper? One of these days you will have to let it go."

Billy shrugged. "I can't help wondering if we'll ever go back there, you know, like when Ulysses visited the land of the departed dead?"

"Man, Billy. That Ulysses stuff is wearing thin. You still on that?"

"Look, Johnny, you may brush it off, but I think it's important. We're on a journey, we went to Troy and now we are trying to get home, Just like Ulysses. I'm telling you, the dead speak to me. Eddie Kramer, Tony Malena, Jake, Teacher... they're out there, Johnny, and they speak to me. They advise me, like when Ulysses went to the end or the world and met old Agamemnon and that seer who told him how to calm Poseidon down after Ulysses killed his son, the Cyclops."

Johnny just shook his head. "Billy, I think you need to talk to somebody, or get yourself a woman. You're scaring me. Or maybe you just need to get out in the woods and hunt something that won't shoot back."

Billy looked at Johnny for a long minute. "Okay, Johnny, maybe you're right. Maybe I need some clean air mountaintops where the stink of the jungle never comes. Maybe I need to follow some deer tracks down through a white field of snow, clean white, no friggin' damn mud. Maybe I need to sit by a fire and look up at the stars and not have anything in my head but me, and God. No voices, no pictures, no screams, no gunfire, no bombs... Maybe I..." he blushed.

"What, Sniper?"

"Maybe I just need to go home and see my mom."

THE DAY after they settled in, Johnny went to look up Lieutenant Burke. Burke took him to a makeshift gym they had set up in an old Quonset. There were some punching bags, some weight racks, and a ring. Burke issued Johnny some gear. "You ever boxed before, Strange?"

"No, Sir. I grew up in a church that didn't allow fighting, so I got no formal training. But I beat the crap out of a few guys who thought I would be a pushover in high school. Nobody messed with me after that."

"Well, Strange, the word is out that you are pretty tightly wrapped."

Johnny scowled, but Burke smiled. "That's just the scuttlebutt. Don't get bent outta shape. Maybe we can use some of that to turn you into a boxer. Get dressed and meet me in the ring in ten minutes."

When Johnny showed up ten minutes later, Burke was waiting. He helped Johnny get his gloves and his helmet on. Then they climbed into the ring. Burke showed Johnny the stance, and how to hold his hands. He put up both hands and motioned to Johnny. "Come and get me, kid, and don't pull any punches. My bars are still on my shirt."

So Johnny bored in and threw a left that Burke just went away from. He threw a right that Burke went under, and then Burke slammed Johnny with a right to the heart. Johnny backed off, but Burke smiled and motioned him in again. This time Johnny led with a right to Burke's head, but Burke just shook it off and let Johnny have two jabs that snapped his head back. Then, before Johnny could clear his head, Burke came in and slammed away with both hands at Johnny's ribs. Johnny pushed him away and hooked a short right to Burke's head, but Burke caught him with a long overhead right and Johnny went halfway across the ring and landed on his tail.

Burke grinned and motioned again. "Come on, Strange, let me have it."

Johnny got up and moved in. His left hand flashed out in four quick jabs that caught Burke like a machine gun. Burke tried the overhand right again, but this time Johnny was ready, slipped it and landed a brutal right hook that put Burke flat on his back. Burke lay there for a minute, shaking his head, and then smiled. He put up his hand and Johnny pulled him up.

Burke just nodded. "You'll do, kid, you'll do."

JOHNNY STRANGE LOVED BOXING. The demons inside him stopped their yammering after an hour at the heavy bag. Burke worked with him at first, but Johnny improved so quickly, he turned him over to a Filipino boxer name Manny Escobedo. Escobedo had been boxing a long time, and he knew what to do. "You got a lot of strength, Johnny, but you got no ring smarts."

"Whadda'ya mean, Manny?"

"It's like this, kid. Every fighter has his own way of winning. If you know how he scraps, you can use it against him. Dempsey was a rusher who liked to get in close and work on the body. So Tunney held him off and tied him up when he got too close. Tunney finally wore the guy out before he could do any damage. Or Max Schmeling versus Joe Louis. Schmeling spent a long time watching films of Louis, and he figured him out. The first three rounds he used his jab, while sneaking his right cross behind his jab. He caught Joe flat-footed. In the fourth round, Max landed a snapping right on Louis' chin, and Louis went to the canvas for the first time in his twenty-eight professional fights. Schmeling continued to use this style, and Joe couldn't figure it out. Schmeling took him out in the twelfth, Louis's first knockout."

Johnny nodded. "So Schmeling played it smart and beat him?"

"Yeah, kid. But the next year Joe won the heavyweight championship. Then, two years later, he met Schmeling again. This time he didn't let Max jab him to death. He came straight out and put a world of hurt on Schmeling in the first round. He landed 31 solid punches and beat him in two minutes and four seconds. That's what I mean by ring smart."

"Can you show me that, Manny?"

"Sure, kid, sure. We'll start our tour with some local matches, and I know the guys. I'll ask Burke to put me in your corner." Manny tapped his head. "What you got in strength and speed, Manny will make up the difference with what I got up here."

IT WORKED out just like Manny said. Johnny's first match came against a guy called "Butcher" Bennett. He was a heavy-muscled two-hundred-pounder with a face like a piece of brick, all bones and skin like sandpaper.

Manny talked to Johnny before the fight started. "This guy looks tough, but he's a plodder. No spring in his legs. He'll want to back you into a corner and nail you. Stay away from his right and make him chase you around the ring. After two rounds work on his belly, he's soft and you'll hurt him. And he's got a weak point—dead center on his chin. He knows it and he'll be guarding it. Use that against him."

When the bell sounded, Johnny took his time. Just like Manny said, the "Butcher" plodded after him, trying to connect with a big lazy right hand. Johnny kept slipping away, and at the end of the first Johnny could tell he was tiring Bennett out. He used the same tactic in round two, and by the third, Bennett was good and winded.

"Start working the gut and look for him to drop his right to protect himself."

When the bell rang, Johnny went out fast, closed on Bennett, and began a series of lightning left jabs to the midsection, followed by hammer blow rights. Bennett grunted in surprise and put the right in Johnny's ear, but he was too close and there was nothing behind it. Johnny went back to work and this time Bennett dropped his left to defend. He let go with a wild right swing that sizzled but missed. Johnny lunged and got a solid left right on Bennett's ear. Bennett jerked back in surprise, but Johnny bored in and worked on the midsection again. This time the "Butcher" dropped both hands. It was the opening Johnny was waiting for and he sent a straight, hard right to the point of Bennett's chin. The big man did a half turn and dropped on his face, dead to the world.

"Atta boy, Johnny, that's the way," Manny yelled as Johnny went to a neutral corner. The ref could have counted to a thousand—Bennett was not getting up.

Manny came out and held up Johnny's hand.

Johnny looked around at the crowd of appreciative gyrenes who were whooping and hollering.

I could get to like this...

3

WINTER HUNT

BILLY MARTENS

There were only a few hundred feet to go. Billy would have been sweating more, but May was the beginning of winter and the temperature was less than fifty. Especially in the mountains of New Zealand's North Island. His first hunts in February and March had been a lot warmer. That had been the Island's fall. Everything was upside-down. Billy didn't mind. He wanted to be mixed up. He wanted to be disoriented. That way he forgot Guadalcanal. At least for a while.

He was at the summit, rifle strapped across his back. He stood straight. The sky was a powerful blue. So was the Pacific, far below his feet. The sun blazed in the sky and in the sea. He thanked God and prayed. Then he sat on a smooth rock, unslung his bolt action firearm, drew a thick roast lamb sandwich out of his pack and ate. He closed his eyes. The light was so bright, but he wasn't complaining. The more of that light God sent his way, the better. When he thought back to the jungle everything was darkness.

He chewed slowly. He was in no rush. He had already potted the day's elk farther down and the New Zealanders had field dressed it and taken it down for the troops. There'd been a lot of that. Bagging game for the Marines, which they ate for their lunches and suppers. The New Zealanders had given the Corps the green light to hunt to feed the men. They had handpicked Billy as one of the deerslayers. That's how he liked to think of it. He was part of James Fenimore Cooper's frontier tales and hunting for wild meat alongside Hawkeye in *The Last of the Mohicans.* Most days he brought down two or three elk or red deer.

The red deer had the most incredible antlers, so large and spreading out so far. Some racks ended up in Wellington homes and others graced the Marines' barracks. It made no difference to Billy. He had never been a trophy hunter. His rifle was for meat in the pot, and the hunts were for clearing his mind and soul. He felt more complete in May than he had in February. Prayer and sharp mountain air and unstoppable vistas from the North Island's mountain ranges had accomplished that. New Zealand was freeing him.

Billy opened his eyes and squinted into the glare coming off the ocean. This was his way of finding the Montana boy again. The high hills of the South Pacific. His pal Johnny? Johnny was getting into boxing. Fighting was where Johnny found Johnny. And Bud? Bud had his little miracle. They had transferred the gal that brought him to his knees on Tonga to the military hospital in Wellington, where she could do more good.

He smiled. More good all around. Kalasia was a hit with everyone. Her and the other smart, sassy, confident Tongan nurses that they transferred to New Zealand with her. The Marines tried their luck with all of them. But so far as Kalasia went, she only had eyes for Bud. And he was definitely head over heels for her. So much so that when she'd been called a "tar baby" by one of the locals he swung his right fist.

Billy had been at a table near the bar nursing a Coke and he couldn't believe his eyes. It must have been a trick of the light. But no. Bud swung a second time. Both times he broke noses and busted heads and left three men unconscious on the floor. Good

Lord. What? When the three men's pals got involved, shoving Kalasia around and calling her worse names, and pinning Bud to the wall, Billy reckoned it was time he did the Montana thing. He jumped up and went in, fists flying. Johnny was right behind him, in his element, smacking heads and pounding flesh and breaking bones. More Kiwis piled in. More Marines piled in. It took a while, but in the end, it was another USMC victory right up there with Guadalcanal.

The weird thing was, Bud didn't feel any remorse. Neither did Billy. And Johnny Strange sure didn't. No wonder Johnny had taken to boxing like a shark to bodies in the water. He would've liked a bar brawl every day. And having a good excuse, like men insulting Bud's woman, was ice cream on cherry pie for him. Billy kept chewing his sandwich and shook his head, continuing to take in the magnificent view. Some Mennonite boys they were.

"I don't get it," Billy had told Ty Jackson, the Protestant chaplain. "It's like I don't have a conscience anymore."

"I'm sure you still do, Marine," the chaplain responded.

"Yeah? Where is it? Back in the States?"

"You can't expect to come out of six months of combat unscathed. Things are going to change. Your way of thinking is going to change. You have to harden. Your heart has to harden. Or you'll crack up."

"I don't dream about the Island. I don't have nightmares."

"That's good."

"I didn't think twice when I beat men up in that bar," Billy went on. "It didn't just seem like the right thing to do because Bud's gal had been treated like dirt. It seemed like the natural thing to do. It felt as good as breathing or eating. My fists busted men up and I liked it. It felt sweet to feel my punches hit home and watch my opponents fall to their knees. I loved a knockout better than anything. To send them flying and see their eyes roll back white. That solid crunch of my hams cracking into their bones and skulls."

"It'll wear off," Jackson promised.

"Yeah? When?"

"When you've got it out of your system."

"Got what out of my system?" demanded Billy.

"All the killing on Guadalcanal. Not just the killing you did. The killing that was done to men you knew and cared for."

"So, one day I won't feel like punching someone's lights out anymore?"

"You won't even want to squash a fly."

"Then I'll be a good Mennonite again?"

"You're a good Mennonite now."

Billy had laughed at that. "Yeah? I can guarantee you that my dad and his church wouldn't agree with you in a thousand years."

So, Billy realized the only remorse he felt was remorse at not feeling any remorse over the barroom fight where he'd laid out a dozen men. Heck, he could've killed one of them he'd hit so hard. But neither Bud nor Johnny moaned and groaned about it. A woman had been insulted, a woman had to be respected, the locals had to be taught a lesson, justice was served, end of story. Bud refused to apologize for decking the men that had harassed Kalasia. But he'd avoided bars since, and so far as Billy knew, there hadn't been any more confrontations.

He took a swig from his canteen. Ice cold lemonade. He was about to take a second drink when barking exploded on the trail he'd come up. The dog was still a good way off, but its barking grew louder and more insistent. Billy smiled. It wouldn't take Rugby long. He knew Billy's scent, and he'd come for him now like a bullet.

WOOF! WOOF! WOOF! WOOF!

A large black and tan dog, with short ears that hung down, barreled up the last stretch of trail while Billy watched, and jumped into his lap, licking Billy's face eagerly. Billy laughed and rubbed the dog's ears. "Hey, Rugby, it's good to see you. What kept you? Where's the rest of the crew?" The dog weighed about eighty pounds, but Billy didn't mind. He liked big dogs, and he liked Rugby. They play wrestled, and it felt wonderful. Rugby was a New Zealand breed the Kiwis had created in the 19th century to herd sheep in rugged country. They called them Huntaways. Billy loved the name they'd given the breed. Everything in New Zealand was better than anything on Guadalcanal. "Where's everyone, hey? Where's the Kiwis? Where's Tonga?"

Rugby galloped back down the trail. Voices erupted. "Did you find him, boy? Where is he? Where's the mighty hunter?"

In a minute, several men reached him and he got to his feet and shook hands all around. His first Sunday at church in February, he'd met a family with five sons, the youngest fourteen and the oldest twenty and twenty-two. The older boys he'd never seen, they were fighting with the New Zealand Army in North Africa. The others had swept him up and taken him under their wing. He spent Fridays, Saturdays and Sundays at their vast sheep ranch. They'd guided him on his first hunts, even given him the bolt action he was using to harvest the elk and red deer. Now they'd decided to pay him a visit on the mountaintop. He knew they were coming.

"Heard you got one early, is that right, Billy?"

"How big was it? How many points?"

"I think most of your mates must be getting sick of elk steak by now."

"Did you hear the news, Billy? Did anyone tell you the news?"

The three boys were short and husky like their father, freckled and red-haired like their mother, always full of good cheer and a lot of chat like both their parents. The father spoke up, "I'll be telling our Yank the news." He offered Billy a cigar and a flask Billy knew had Scotch. "Our boys aren't in the casualty lists in the papers, thanks be to God."

"I'll drink to that," Billy replied, taking the silver flask and unscrewing the top.

"But wait. There's more. The news just came through the

radio a few hours ago. The Germans and Italians have surrendered. The Afrika Korps has surrendered. On May 13th, it was. Isn't that grand? The fighting in Africa is over."

Billy grinned and clapped Mr. Williams on the shoulder. "Congratulations! That's swell! I'll smoke to that!"

They laughed as he used his USMC Zippo lighter to get his cigar going. Mr. Williams smoked with him and permitted the oldest of the three boys, Ryan, who was seventeen, almost eighteen, to join him and Billy and take a drink of Scotch too. The other two boys, Frank and Scott looked on in envy, their faces screwed up in a pair of pouts, but Mr. Williams shook his head. "You'd just get sick and spoil your appetite and your mother's cooking up a grand victory meal. You won't want to miss that. There will be plenty of opportunities for you to toast victories before this war's over."

"I'll hold you to that, dad," said Scott, who was sixteen.

"Hold me to it all you like. I wish it wasn't so, but there's plenty more fighting to do."

"And not just against the Nazis either."

The group quickly grew quiet, and Billy could see Scott wished he could take back what he'd said. He knew Billy wanted to forget about the war while the Marines were in New Zealand. Billy reached over and put his free hand on the boy's shoulder. The other held the flask while the cigar puffed away in his mouth. "Forget about it, Scott. You Kiwis take care of the krauts and the Marines will take care of the Japs. Deal?"

Scott kept his head down, but nodded. "Deal."

WOOF! WOOF! WOOF! WOOF!

Rugby raced off down the trail. In a moment, he reappeared, herding Bud and Kalasia and Johnny Strange up the track to join the others. Billy waved his cigar. "Hey! Did you hear the news?"

Johnny laughed. "About the German surrender in Africa? That's all the Kiwis have been talking about. You can't go two steps without someone offering to buy you a beer or give you a smoke. But, hey, I'm not complaining. Who can blame them? That's a big win."

Mr. Williams offered cigars to Johnny and Bud. "It is indeed. There will be a celebration at the town hall tomorrow evening. I hope you all can make it. There will be a band. There will be dancing. Mind, there will be quite the celebration at our own digs tonight. Mrs. Williams is cooking up a storm that includes several racks of lamb and her own mint jelly. It's not to be missed."

"Count me in," said Johnny, stretching and taking in the view. "Lord, it's beautiful up here."

"That it is, mate."

"Not just beautiful," enthused Kalasia in an accent distinctive from the New Zealanders and from the Americans. "It's spectacular. I've never been up this high before."

Bud hesitated a moment, but finally put his arm around her waist. Grateful, Kalasia snuggled into him as they stood gazing at the bright Pacific waters.

"It was worth the climb, wasn't it?" Bud asked her.

"Oh, infinitely. Thank you for coaxing me up here. I was a lazy bones before our climb. Now I feel I could fly off the peak here and soar. Just soar."

Bud didn't smoke his cigar, just placed it in a shirt pocket, but Billy knew, to be polite, he'd sip the Scotch, and he was right. Johnny, of course, had no problem with Scotch or cigar, and lit his Cuban right after taking a good pull from the flask. "I can taste the peat in that, Mr. Williams," Johnny remarked.

"You can. Do you enjoy the flavor?"

"I do."

"Well, then, that would make you a connoisseur. Like me."

"That sounds like a good word, sir."

Mr. Williams extended the flask to Johnny again. "It's a grand word. Drink up. There'll be plenty more where that came from tonight at the Williams's table. The Lord knows we've had little enough to celebrate. But with Guadalcanal behind us and

Rommel's Panzers coming to a halt in Tunisia, I'd say we have more than enough to be grateful for."

Johnny saluted him with the flask. "For sure, we do, Mr. Williams."

Billy bent to rub Rugby's ears and face, the dog licking his hands while his tail thrashed. He looked past the dog and out over the ocean like everyone else, but he saw more than blue water and sunlight. Far away, he saw an island. It was a small island, but it oozed the same menace the Canal still oozed into his mind. It sent a warning his way, the same way a rattler would, only there was no sound, just the image in his mind of beaches and palm trees and, in his heart, a cold, hard feeling of death.

4

IN LOVE WITH KALASIA

BUD, THE CORPSMAN

don't think there ever was a time where I was "falling for Kalasia." I fell right away. There was none of this gradually liking her more and more. It was a lightning strike from the first moment in Tonga.

Not that I knew what to do about it. I didn't write often from the Canal and what I did write I had to get coached through by my platoon commander, Lieutenant Jamison Crandall. "He was the one that got you cooking with gas," Johnny told me. Okay, he pushed me where I needed to go. And even when she showed up in Wellington in all her radiant, sun-kissed beauty, I still had a hard time getting the engine in my Chevy started. Johnny would shake his head. "Can you believe your luck, Bud? She gets transferred right into your lap with all those other Tongan nurses. There must be a God, right? Heck, she's already thrown the first pitch. But what do you do? Sit there in the cheap seats and eat Crackerjacks. Geez, man, get in the frigging ball game."

Johnny wished his girl had shown up in Wellington instead because he'd know what to do about it. Billy told me to take it easy and take my time and ignore Johnny. But Billy didn't have a girl, and he didn't go out of his way to find one either. So how helpful was his advice? One thing I knew, I was head over heels when it came to Kalasia and I didn't want to lose her. I didn't want to fly solo anymore.

So, bit by bit, I got there. A kiss. A hug. An arm around her shoulders. An arm around her waist. Letting her lean into me and snuggle. Letting myself go and leaning into her. My head in her lap. Her fingers playing with my hair. It was so hard not to hold back and keep it formal and polite. But she cupped my face with her long brown fingers one evening, the setting sun making her dark eyes flash gold, and said, "Listen. I don't want you at a distance. I don't want you at arm's length. I want you right up against my heart. Stop being afraid of me, American man. Stop being afraid of us being a couple. We're good. Now. Make it better."

That was The Kiss. Sure, we'd kissed a lot before, but after she said that, I gathered her in and kissed her like I never had. I lost myself, I lost my head. It's like she took me down into a deep, dark dive and there was no need to surface. We both had plenty of air. I doubt we broke off in under two hours. Just kept kissing and diving into our hearts, kissing and diving. When we finally came up for oxygen, the sun gone and the stars shining big over our heads; she smiled and did an old-fashioned Polynesian nose rub with me. "That," she whispered, still catching her breath, "was more like it. You act as if you love me."

"I do," I said, resting my forehead against hers. "I do love you."

"Yes? Then say it again."

"I love you."

"Say it better. I know you can say it better."

I kissed her again, and I felt woozy, like I'd had too many beers, because she laced her arms around my neck and brought me in tighter. Geez, she was driving me crazy. Her hair and her skin smelled so sweet, her lips were so soft and strong. I was helpless. I couldn't pull away from her and I couldn't stop. She knew it and giggled.

"Big strong Marine," she teased. "Does the Tonga woman have you in her power? Hm?"

"Yes."

"Are you weak and trapped?"

"It feels that away."

"Do you want to get away? Do you want me to release you from my spell?"

"No. Never."

"Never? Are you sure?"

"Never. I'm so happy and excited with you. I don't want to be anywhere else with anyone else. Ever."

She sighed and laid her head on my chest. "Then it must be love. And now I'm very happy too. I don't wish to be anywhere else either. I want to be with you as long as I possibly can. I don't want the war to take you away from me again."

———

SHE LOVED TO SWIM. Especially as we got into August, which was the beginning of spring. Mornings and afternoons and evenings were good. But so was the black of night. She was my mermaid. Always emerging where and when I least expected her, always laughing at the look of surprise on my face, always wanting to kiss me with our heads barely above water, her legs curled around me as if they were two lively eels with minds of their own.

This kind of intimacy and play with a woman was new to me. Anything to do with a woman was new to me. But I grew to enjoy Kalasia's free spirit more and more, and my shyness peeled off me in layers. Yet it was while I was diving with my mermaid in the ocean that feelings of dread hit me. Feelings so strong I scrambled out of the water, gasping, throwing a towel around my shivering body.

It wasn't sharks that did it, or any other kind of sea creature. It wasn't my feelings for Kalasia frightening me. It wasn't the water itself or my poor swimming ability. Kalasia picked up on it right away. She seemed to understand what was happening instinctively. "It's something to do with the war, my American man."

I sensed she was right, but I argued anyway. "I'm not even thinking about the war."

"Maybe not. But it is still in you whether you are thinking about it or not."

"Why does it only happen when I'm in the ocean with you?"

She shrugged. "Who knows everything? But islands are in the ocean."

I was going to tell her that was the dumbest thing she'd ever said when an image burned through my mind of sunlight on waves. I was sloshing through the waves and there was gunfire all around me. Bullets threw up geysers, and I began wading through bodies bobbing in the surf. It went on and on—bodies and waves and the zip-splash of bullets.

"Bud! Bud!"

Kalasia grabbed me by the shoulders.

I couldn't respond.

"Bud! What is it! What's wrong? Where are you?"

It was the craziest thing. I could hear and see her and feel her shaking my shoulders, but I couldn't snap out of it. The whole thing was too real. More real than she was. More real than me standing there wrapped in a beach towel in front of her. Finally, she just hugged me, tears all over her face and soaking into my chest. And when she did that, I looked up and realized the Southern Cross was blazing over our heads.

"What is it?" cried Kalasia. "What's happening to you?"

"I don't know. But you're helping me."

My mind was pretty much blank. Adrenaline was pumping through my body and my heart was racing. I thanked God I could throw my arms around her and feel how warm she was and pull her close. "Hold me tight," I whispered. "Hold me as tight as you can. I have to know you're real."

I was desperate. I felt like I was going nuts. She was afraid and gripped me so hard my backbone did the pop-pop-pop. I had no idea she was so strong. Her muscles and her strength were exactly what I needed. She crushed me against her and suddenly the sand was under my feet. Her nails were digging into my back. A sea breeze was flowing over our bodies. I felt it all. I began to come down.

"I'm back," I said into her shoulders, the broad and powerful shoulders of a swimmer.

"Are you sure?"

"Yes."

"What was it, Bud? What?"

"It was like a seizure."

"A seizure? Have you ever had those before?"

"No. I've never had any kind of epilepsy."

Her eyes were wide and afraid in the moonlight. "Then what? What is it? What happened to you?"

I shook my head, still hanging onto her for dear life. "It was like." I stumbled. "Like a premonition. A weird premonition. But no. No. I've never experienced anything like that before. I don't believe in them. It was a bizarre daydream. That's all. A really bizarre daydream."

"Oh, Bud. That was more than a daydream. You looked catatonic. And now you're trembling like a child."

"I'm just coming down off the adrenaline. I'm okay, Kalasia. Thanks to you. My beautiful, strong woman. I'm so lucky. Luck? No. I'm blessed." I kissed her hair and forehead. "You're incredible. My angel."

"I was scared, Bud. So scared."

"It's okay. Really. It won't happen again. That was one of a kind."

But it happened again. I was swimming alone. Suddenly I was

wading through salt water up to my waist, floating bodies were thumping against my legs and hips, machine gun fire was zinging past my head and ripping up the water. I kept going. Just going and going and going.

I broke out of the surf and onto the beach, gulping for air. I panicked and ran. Faster and faster. Till I tripped and fell headlong and lay there panting, digging my nails into my palms to get pain into my body. I only felt normal when I finally drew blood.

No one was around. I lay there about ten minutes till the adrenaline was gone and the panic with it. Then I sat up and took deep breaths. Inhale. Exhale. Slowly. Eventually, I got to my feet. I never told Kalasia about the second episode. I didn't tell Billy or Johnny about either of the attacks. Once Johnny muttered something about seeing an island out there waiting for us like a spider, and I almost spoke up. But I bit my tongue. The images I'd seen were too gruesome.

September and October were golden. Spring got warmer and prettier. Just like Kalasia. I said that to her. She laughed. "It's the magic. It's getting stronger. Do you like it?"

"Very much. Especially the woman making the magic happen."

She actually got shy and looked down at her bare feet. "I shall tell her. She'll be happy to hear that."

We were often at the hospital at the same time. I suppose I made sure of that. We weren't just dealing with Guadalcanal casualties. New Zealand troops had been fighting alongside MacArthur and the dogfaces on Vella Lavella in the Solomons since the middle of August, and that went on into October. Kalasia was not only a beautiful lover, an amazing friend, and a gift from God to a lonely and awkward Mennonite boy, she was a thoroughly competent and compassionate military nurse. I was proud of her. Proud of her nursing skills and proud she was my girl, my woman, my love. I told her that many times. She always met my gaze and answered me the same way. "You do all this under fire with men falling around you and do not lose your head. How proud do you think I am of you?"

I'd never understood the stories of men hiding out and not embarking with their units when the time came. Lieutenant Crandall said he expected a certain percentage would stow away in New Zealand once we were ready to move on. Scuttlebutt had us shipping out in November or December. Now I got why soldiers or Marines would find a cave and crawl in, impossible for the Shore Patrol or MPs to find. After almost a year in New Zealand, I had no desire to go back to hell in the South Pacific. Heaven was much nicer and Kalasia's kisses far sweeter than Jap Nambu machine gun fire. The temptation was there, and it was strong. I wasn't used to temptation having any sort of sway over me. But this temptation did.

"I love you so much I never want to leave you for any reason at all," I told her one night as we sat together on the beach under the Southern Cross. I shied away from swimming because of the attacks, but I loved snuggling with her on the shore and enjoying her warm and frequent kisses. "I want to stay and work beside you at the hospital."

"Shh." She kissed me lightly on the lips. "That is a beautiful thought and a worthy desire, but..."

"But?"

"It cannot be." She kissed me again, smiling at how much I liked her kisses and how eagerly the formerly shy Mennonite boy responded to them. "I would like it to be. But it is impossible, my love."

"Why is it impossible?"

"Because you have two hearts. One is with me. I know that. But the other is with your men. Soon they will go back into danger. You cannot let them go without you. You will wish to save as many of them as you can. I understand that. And I love you for it. You could never be happy by my side knowing they were in harm's way and you were doing nothing to rescue them. Once the war ends we can be together, my beautiful American man. But not till then. Till then we must hope and pray. You must come back to me, my lover. You must."

5

A WORLD OF HURT

JOHNNY STRANGE

Johnny Strange climbed into the ring and stared at the big man in the opposite corner. Lieutenant Burke had arranged a team match with a squad from the New Zealand Army, and the Kiwis came ready to fight. Most of the NZ folks treated the Marines pretty darn good, but there were some holdouts—guys who resented all the attention the Gyrenes were getting from the hometown folks and especially the up-close-and-personal they were scoring with the Wellington girls. He and Bud and Billy had gotten into a dust-up with some Kiwi's who insulted Kalasia and the word had gone out about Johnny Strange after he broke a few faces. Burke told him to be on his toes in this one, because the Kiwi's had come for blood. The big guy looked over at Johnny and grinned, moving his gloved hands in a 'come and get it' motion.

Manny Escobedo climbed up on the ring and pulled Johnny down onto the stool. He slapped Johnny's mouthpiece in and talked low in his ear.

"That's the guy they call 'The Slammer.' I guess one of the NZ army boys you put in the hospital is a pal of his. At least that's the scuttlebutt. I've never seen him fight, so I can't give you any tips.

The only thing I can say is he's here to return the favor, so he's gonna come out fast looking to blow you away. Try to stay away from him long enough for me to get a read on him."

The warning sounded, and Manny pulled the stool. "Stay awake kid, this guy looks tough."

The Kiwi stood over six feet, and every inch of him looked carved out of steel. He smirked at Johnny and motioned with his gloves again. "Come and get some, Yank."

For the first time since he'd joined the team, Johnny felt a twinge of... fear? No, not that, more like... uncertainty. Manny jumped down off the canvas. "Just stay away from him for two rounds if you can, kid."

The bell rang, and The Slammer came out fast, just like Manny said he would. He met Johnny almost before he left his corner and snapped a left hook in Johnny's ear that jerked his head back. Then The Slammer pressed in, hammering at Johnny's midsection with both hands. Johnny pushed the bigger man off and ripped his cheek with a machine-gun left and then stung him with a short right hook. The Slammer grinned and then plastered Johnny with a long right that seemed to start in Australia, and Johnny sailed across the ring and bounced off the canvas. Flat on his back.

The referee waved the Kiwi back and started the count. Johnny rolled over and got to one knee at five. He looked at Manny. He needed rest, but Manny waved him up frantically.

"Get up, kid, get up!"

Johnny struggled to his feet. The Slammer came after him with a roundhouse left that missed taking his head off by a hair and Johnny went inside, hanging on for dear life.

The big Kiwi whispered in his ear. "Hey, Pretty Boy, you're cute. Maybe when I'm done beating the crap out of you, you can be my good little girlfriend."

Johnny shoved the man away. He rifled a few more left hooks into the rock-like jaw and then The Slammer caught him with a huge right hand and he went down again. The Slammer backed off and Johnny crawled to his feet. Then The Slammer came at him like an express train, and then the bell rang. The Slammer swung anyway and knocked Johnny into a corner. The ref tried to wave him off, but he shouted at Johnny. "That's fer me mate, Pretty Boy. The one who's still in the hospital."

Johnny struggled back to his corner and collapsed on the stool.

Manny sloshed his face with water and daubed a cut that had opened over Johnny's left eye.

"Holy crap, Johnny, how are you even still alive?"

Johnny's head was swimming, and his vision was blurry. The Slammer stood up in his corner and taunted Johnny.

"Come on, Pretty Boy, come and get some lovin' from your daddy."

Then, as Johnny tried to clear his head, something strange happened. The Slammer's face seemed to melt, and then it was Harold Jenkins's face. Harold Jenkins, the scumbag scoutmaster who had tried to rape him when he was a kid. The liar that convinced Johnny's dad that Johnny was making it up. The jerk they let stay on that stinking church's board of elders. Jenkins!

It was Jenkins standing there, that sick smile on his face. The smile he smiled at Johnny when he knew no one was looking. The smile that made Johnny want to learn to kill. The smile that Johnny was going to beat off that hated face when he got home. Johnny heard the words coming out of the mouth, but it wasn't The Slammer's voice. It was Jenkins's.

"Come on, Pretty Boy, come and get some loving. Come on Pretty Boy…"

Johnny stood up. A fire started in his gut and then rose like magma pouring up the throat of a volcano. Manny tried to sit him down, to talk to him, but Johnny shook him off. Now he saw the hated face through a red mist, like fire or blood. The bell rang and Johnny went out. The Slammer grinned and moved toward

Johnny, confidence written on the thick, square face. But it was Jenkins's face, and there was hot fire and cold ice in Johnny's veins. The Slammer threw a vicious hook, but Johnny ducked it and let him have it with four blazing left jabs. BAM, BAM, BAM, BAM, like trip-hammers, like his BAR going off. The Slammer rocked back, and the smile went off his face.

"Found your jab, eh, Pretty Boy?"

He smiled again, but the Jenkins smile was missing a tooth. The big man leapt at Johnny and fired a volley of punches, but Johnny danced away and they cut air. The Slammer's hands dropped for a minute and Johnny stepped back in with a huge right hand that nearly tore the Kiwi's head off. Then came a crashing left that drove the big Kiwi into the ropes. He hung there and Johnny went to work. Left. "Don't ever call me that." Right. "Don't ever call me that." Left, right, left, right. The Kiwi sank down and Johnny hit him with a crashing right that tore his face open to the bone. The ref stepped in, but Johnny shoved him down on his butt and then smashed blow after blow into the helpless man's face.

Then Johnny felt the hands holding him, pulling him away.

"For God's sake, Johnny, stop! You're going to kill him."

Johnny struggled against the hands, turned to The Slammer. The man's face was an unrecognizable mask of blood and his handlers were trying to get him untangled from the ropes.

"Never call me that again, Jenkins, or I swear to God I will kill you!"

Manny dragged Johnny back to the corner. The whole place was quiet. Manny got Johnny over the ropes and headed toward the dressing room. Lieutenant Burke followed. They got into the locker room and sat Johnny down on a bench. Burke put his hand on Johnny's shoulder, but Johnny shrugged it away. He was ice cold inside and the red fog had vanished. Sweat ran down his face and into his eyes.

Manny handed him a wet towel. Then he put a cold wet one on Johnny's neck.

"Shake it off, kid, shake it off."

Johnny felt his breathing slow and his heart stopped pounding.

Lieutenant Burke shook his head. "What happened out there, kid? I know the guy sucker punched you, but man, oh man. What was that about?"

Johnny looked up. "I don't know, Lieutenant, I don't know. It was something he said…"

Manny chuckled. "Jeez Louise, Johnny, that was the damnedest thing I ever saw. You coulda' killed him."

Johnny sat, his head down. He couldn't see the hated face anymore, just a mask of blood where it used to be.

Is this what you want to do with your life, Johnny? Throw it away on a creep?

Something inside Johnny released. Not a lot, but he felt the wound up place inside him slip loose a notch. Just a notch.

"Let's get out of here, Manny. I need a drink."

"Sure, Johnny, sure. C'mon, kid, let's get you dressed. You want a shower first?"

"Naw, Manny, I'll get one back at camp. Right now I just want a good stiff bourbon."

Lieutenant Burke shook his head. "I think I need one to. Let's head over to the Majestic. I'm buying."

Johnny looked up. "You're not mad, Lieutenant?"

"Heck no, kid. That was an amazing comeback. Something I can tell my grandkids about. You're good with me. And the Kiwi can have some quiet time with his buddy." They laughed.

Johnny threw on his clothes and they headed out. Manny stopped Johnny at the door.

"Hey, Johnny."

"Yeah, Manny?"

"Who's Jenkins?"

"Just a guy I knew, Manny. Just a guy."

———

Dear Marjean,

We're going soon. They don't tell us where, but the word is out. I had hoped that Guadalcanal would convince the Japs to call it quits, but they're still hanging on. Billy thinks we're headed north, maybe Saipan, but nobody knows for sure.

Gosh, I miss you. I keep your picture close by me all the time. I think about you and little John Albert every day. I will do my best to stay alive so I can come home. I hope you still love me when I do. It's so strange loving you from a thousand miles away. I never got to know you and why you decided to just love me and be my girl, I will never know. I don't pray much anymore, but there are two prayers I pray— that I won't get killed and that you will always love me.

Until we meet again,

Johnny

———

My Dearest Johnny,

When you come home, you will get to know me better and you will understand that I decided something and I will never go back. I will always love you and that's that on that.

John Albert is getting to be a big boy now. He's already starting to talk a little and he'll be walking soon. I wish you could be here to see it, but I know when you get home you will be a great dad. I pray for you all the time. Sometimes I get so scared that you'll get hurt or killed. But I know you are a good Marine and that you will do your best in the battles.

I am learning how to cook. Cecelia, well she's the lady who has worked for my dad since I was little, she is teaching me. She says the way to a man's heart is through his stomach, so I want to have every *angle covered when you come home. Sometimes I think of the time we were together and I just ache to feel your arms around me again. Then I get shy and think maybe you won't like me... well, in that way. But I just keep going and, well, I trust the Lord that he will answer my prayers and you will come back to me. That's what I want, that's all I want—for you to come home to me, me and John Albert.*

Please, Johnny, be ever so careful. We need you to come home. I love you so much. I will always love you.

Yours forever,

Marjean.

6

AN ISLAND NAMED HELEN

BILLY MARTENS

The best thing about fly-fishing, Billy had always felt, was the absence of human voices.

The gurgle of a stream or river was fine. The sound of a line zinging out over the water. The struggle of a trout as it fought the fly with its tail flapping and its body twisting and leaping. Anything that was part of nature was good. The unspoken rule that fishers did not speak during the casting was understood. Mr. Williams knew it, pipe in mouth, as he worked at placing his fly right into an eddy on the opposite shore. Billy knew it too as he kept casting into a spot just below a small rapid. Twice he had brought up brown trout and released them. He wanted a third, and he wanted it to be large. He waded into the stream in the boots Mr. Williams had lent him. Rugby watched, tail moving rapidly.

He was not wearing thigh-high waders. None of the Williams's waders had fit and he hadn't felt like purchasing a pair for a few outings. Besides, he wanted sensation. He wanted to feel the cold burn of the waters. Its push and pull and power. Death would soon be all around again. He craved more life.

At the end of the day, the two men trudged a mile back to the truck, Rugby cheerfully leading the way along the forest path. "You know, now that the invasion of Italy is underway, they'll be sending the New Zealand troops back into the fray," Mr. Williams said, almost awkwardly.

Billy nodded. "I thought that might be the case. Your boys will be going in."

"Yes. Yes, they will. I hope you'll remember them in your prayers, Billy. Tim and Robbie. You'd get along well with them. They'd have been with us today. Their rods are hanging up in the den."

"Of course, I'll pray for them, Mr. Williams."

"Thank you. Thank you, lad. It goes without saying the whole family will be praying for you daily. When you get a chance to write, you have our address."

"I do. I promise to stay in touch."

"All that amphibious training you've been doing lately, do you think it will help?"

"I don't know. The Alligators work fine in the water and on land when it's a combat exercise. Real combat is different. Nothing works perfectly when you get to the real fighting."

"I'm sure. But you Marines will do us proud wherever you're going. Even if it's a rougher go than Guadalcanal."

Billy shook his head. "I can't imagine anything being rougher than the Canal."

"It was a fine day when you lads in the 2nd Division received that Presidential Unit Citation. You earned it. Mrs. Williams has a good picture of that one. And you're in it, front and center."

Billy smiled. "You treat me like one of your own."

"You are one of our own."

Billy was desperate to hold New Zealand's mountains and streams close in the few days left to him. He borrowed one of the Williams's horses and spent a day riding, the spring peaks of October still white and strong, Rugby trotting beside him and Bunko. He hiked peaks he had not touched and trails overgrown with weeds and bush that had not seen humans for many months, Rugby was as happy as him to be unfettered and free. They swam together even when locals warned of sharks. The saltwater stung his nose and eyes and he wanted that, he wanted the sting and bite of nature, he wanted his skin and heart to feel everything, wanted it all to be sharp and fresh and new. It was the only thing that gave him peace. The unknown island in the ocean always brooded there in his mind, and he ignored it as much as possible. *Let me live, oh Lord, let me live.*

BILLY BOARDED ON OCTOBER 31, one of the last ones. Johnny had gone on ahead with others from King Company 2/2, 2nd Division/2nd Regiment. "I want to finish the job," he told Billy. "Maybe this island will do that." Then he'd grinned. "If not, I'm happy to take the fight to Tokyo and kick Tojo's ass. And I'm just the Marine to do it."

"Yeah," Billy had replied. "You definitely are."

"How do you like our new duds?" asked Johnny.

They'd been issued jungle dungarees or combat fatigues in brown and green spotted camouflage. Even their helmet covers and rain ponchos had the brown and green spotted camo.

Billy shrugged. "Spectacular."

He had said goodbye the night before at the Williams's homestead. There had been tears from Mrs. Williams and a drooping tail and the big sad eyes a dog can generate from Rugby. They always understood a leave-taking. Mrs. Williams had plied Billy with gifts of roast lamb, mint jelly, and fresh oatmeal cookies. He promised to eat all of it on the long cruise to the island that had fashioned a web in the middle of his mind. Despite telling them not to come down to the harbor, he saw the family standing in a crowd of New Zealanders. They were keeping their distance, but they were obvious to his eye. He waved and the five of them waved back. Rugby was on a leash. Billy indicated they could let the big dog come to him. He knew Rugby wouldn't trouble anyone else. The big Huntaway barreled into him and Billy stepped out of the queue to kneel and hug the dog.

"I'll miss you," he said, burying his face into the dog's fur. "God, how I'll miss you and your family."

He stood in time to see Bud's goodbye to Kalasia as Rugby galloped back to Mr. Williams's whistle. Billy smiled. Bud was a good guy. He deserved love. The kind only a woman could give. Not that he knew what that was like. But it looked right on Bud. He never thought he'd see the day. The beautiful and statuesque Tongan woman, who turned heads wherever she went, adored Bud. And it was pretty clear Bud worshipped the ground she walked on. The pair of them kept hugging each other, unwilling to end the moment. War had brought them together. War was breaking them apart.

They weren't alone. Hundreds of Marines were kissing their New Zealand beauties goodbye. He'd heard there had been a lot of marriages. Even that a baby was on the way for some couples. Billy had no idea how a man could fall in love, marry, start a family and then head off into a combat zone where his chances of being killed or badly wounded were one in three, and in some situations, two in three. All he could do was pray for them. *God, they won't all come back. That doesn't happen. But I pray more come back than don't. That's all.*

It took the transports long enough to reach the rendezvous point, the sun pouring heat over them. A whole fleet was waiting. "All the big guns," Johnny said approvingly, as he cleaned his BAR for the hundredth time in a scrap of shade on the main deck. "The only problem is they won't leave enough Japs alive for me. Those Navy guns will rip the real estate apart. Still. I'll find a few Nips hiding in their holes. Thirty or forty or fifty. That will be enough."

The ships moved on together in one large spread-out cluster.

Seventeen carriers, a dozen battleships, eight heavy cruisers, four light cruisers and sixty-six destroyers. Billy shared his lamb with Bud and Johnny and other members of X-Ray platoon and Achilles squad. It wouldn't keep long in heat and humidity that made sweat roll off their faces in big drops day and night. In time, stogie in one hand, Lieutenant Crandall, their platoon commander, gave them the skinny, displaying maps and charts and aerial photographs.

The island's code name was Helen. It was small. Only two miles long and eight hundred yards at its widest point. To Billy it looked like a triangle. It was part of the Tarawa Atoll in the Gilbert Islands. The real name of the small island was Betio. It was lousy with Japs, Crandall warned. Then he seemed to backtrack. "Our flyboys, God bless 'em, have been bombing and strafing the crap out of the place. They say there's no activity. Either the Nips have left or most of them are with their ancestors. I tell ya, there won't be any *sushi* left alive once the battleships show up at the party. The sixteen-inch guns on the *Maryland* and *Colorado* will slice and dice whatever our planes haven't thrashed and bashed. The brass figure a day or less to swarm over the island and grab the airfield. Then we can all go back to New Zealand. Whaddya' say to that, Marines?"

The men laughed and cheered. Most of them.

Helen. It made Billy think of their poem about Ulysses. Paris had swept Helen away from the Greeks and taken her to Troy as his lover. Helen of Troy. So, Ulysses and the Greeks had come for her and started a long war. Bud had quoted some famous lines about Helen from an old play called *Doctor Faustus* by a guy named Chris Marlowe. Billy remembered the words. *Was this the face that launched a thousand ships and burnt the topless towers of Ilium? Sweet Helen, make me immortal with a kiss.* Well, maybe the Canal had been the one big definitive battle, and that was it. Helen would blow them a kiss of welcome. The few Japs alive would surrender or be cheerfully gunned down by Johnny

Strange, and they would go back to New Zealand for a spell before they returned to the States.

But privately, cigar smoking like hellfire in his teeth, Crandall shared with Achilles squad, his shock troops, that he doubted it would be that easy. "I want you guys to be ready. Be sharp. Whatever Japs are alive on Betio aren't going to lay down their Nambus and Arisakas and *katanas* and go quietly to our prison camps. They'll fight like tigers. Count on it. Just remember Bloody Ridge on the Canal, okay? That's how they fight, and that's how they die. They'll want to take you with them. Stay awake. Stay alert. Don't give them the satisfaction."

Then he pulled Billy aside. "You're a corporal now. Act like one out there. Take the lead. If Zarate or Navarro go down, you're the squad leader. The men will be looking to you. For God's sake, don't let them down."

It took a couple of weeks to get there from the rendezvous point. Bud kept hovering over a three-dimensional mock up they'd done of Betio, right down to miniature palm trees. It looked flat. It looked easy. Bud stared at it, day after day. Billy thought he looked haunted. Maybe it was his grief over leaving Kalasia. Yet it seemed more than that. There was a fear in Bud. A darkness. Billy recognized it because it was in him too. The source of Bud's anguish, outside of being separated from the woman he loved, Billy couldn't guess, though it had something to do with Betio and the Tarawa Atoll. For Billy, Betio remained the deadly spider in the center of the web, and once he landed on the beach he would be in that web. The days were almost too hot and humid to bear. But inside, Billy felt like ice.

Plucking letters from his chest pocket helped. He'd received seven from his mother while they'd been stationed in New Zealand. He re-read them over and over, sometimes two or three times a week. In one letter, his siblings had scribbled their well wishes and their news. He looked at his mother's smooth handwriting on the pale sheets of paper and compared it to the wild scrawls of his brothers and sisters and smiled. He ran his fingers over the creases from his folding and unfolding. When he held the letters to his face, he swore he could smell the house and the kitchen. The wood smoke. The deerskin. Venison. The soap his mother used on her hands. The perfumes he knew came from his sisters.

No letters or well wishes had come from his father.

The night before they were set to land, Father McKean held Mass and numerous Marines showed up. Pastor Ty Jackson also held a service that Marines crammed into. Billy sat nearby and listened. Two hours before midnight, breakfast was served for the enlisted men—steak, and eggs, and fried potatoes and coffee. Billy was done in a few minutes. He made his way back to his bunk and grew drowsy watching a card game. Bakar Zarate, their squad sergeant, Jesus Navarro, their assistant squad leader, Julio Hernandez, the other BAR gunner besides Johnny, Red O'Brien, Brian "Over Easy" Mitton and Paul Stoneroad, who was one part of the two-man mortar team. They were playing, of all things, a game of bridge. Every one of them was oozing sweat from the heat and humidity of their confined space.

"What happened to Marines playing poker?" mumbled Billy, struggling to keep his eyes open.

Zarate grinned. "The Kiwis made us sophisticated."

They were woken at midnight. Now it was the officers who had their steak and eggs. Billy got his gear together. He didn't wash or shave. No one had for weeks on board the transports. At 0330 hours, the first wave began to pile into their boats. The second wave was lining up at the same time. Billy heard a few muttered prayers and Hail Marys. The landing craft bumped alongside, Alligators for the first waves, Higgins boats for the others. Marines climbed carefully down the nets. Billy was waiting his turn, a sea breeze playing over his face, the men of his squad and platoon all around him, including Johnny and Bud. He thanked God the breeze was cool, nothing like the stifling heat inside the transport.

Just after 0500 hours, he jumped as the naval bombardment began. The dark with its half-moon turned red and orange as big guns roared from battleships, cruisers and destroyers. Flashes of exploding shells lit Betio. It only stopped at dawn when aircraft came streaking in, Helldivers cutting loose with bombs that gave off wild shrieks of destruction, Grumman Hellcats furiously raking the island with fifty-caliber machine-gun bullets. Billy had no idea how any Japanese, no matter how tough, could live through what the ships and airplanes dished out. Betio was a smoking, rumbling ruin as the sun began to stretch hands of gold and bronze over the horizon, beautiful hands that did not fit the devastation. Inexplicably, a jumble of disconnected lines from the poem *Ulysses,* that Bud had quoted often enough at Guadalcanal, darted into Billy's head. *There gloom the broad, dark seas. The thunder and the sunshine. Push off, and sitting well in order smite the sounding furrows. Until I die. Until I die.*

It was November 20, 1943, a Saturday, a day he'd go fishing or hunting or hiking in Montana or New Zealand. Thanksgiving was on Thursday. He thought of his mom setting out roast elk or moose along with carrots, and turnips, and sweet potatoes and pumpkin pie. It would be nice to sit at that table again. Oh, Lord, it would be nice.

II

TARAWA

DAY 1 — D DAY

NOVEMBER 20, 1943

7

THE DARK LAND

BUD, THE CORPSMAN

I remember the morning I stood on the deck of the *Hayes* and saw the sun begin its golden climb into the heavens above Guadalcanal. I remember the glowing phosphorescent spray kicked up by the dolphins as they frolicked in the Solomon Sea. I remember the green paradise that lay before me, palm trees waving in the breeze. Palms!

That day I was Bud; green-behind-the-ears Bud from Ritzville, Washington, a dry dusty dot on the road between Seattle and Spokane. That day I hadn't lived through Billy's poem, the one he got from General Price in basic, the one about Ulysses and his long and tortured journey to get home. That day I had not been in the Cyclops' cave, or heard the siren song, or watched my buddies get blown to hell on Circe's bloody hill. That day we waited as the first wave disembarked, pissed off because we couldn't go in with them.

The island before me does not glow golden with the first rays of morning. No, it is dark, lit only by the flashes from the roaring guns of the fleet. Dark—a darkness crisscrossed by tracer shells and broken by the flash-boom of dropping bombs. Dark—and my soul is dark too—dark with thoughts of death and bones and

Kalasia. Kalasia is back there in NZ and our parting was dark, for though she let me go I could see the fear in her eyes, the knowledge that without me her life would be forever dark. And me. I never worried about it before, but now I am—puzzled by a war that would dig me out of Ritzville and send me to Tonga to meet the first woman I ever loved, only to strip me away and set me here on this ship looking into a deep dark pit and wishing that I was anywhere but in the first wave. For I have seen this island in my dreams. I've already waded ashore, sloshing through the waves with gunfire all around me. Bullets throwing up geysers as I wade through bodies bobbing in the surf—bodies and waves and the zip-splash of bullets. I know what's coming, but I don't know how I know...

First wave! Last night, a note from Colonel Amey, our Battalion Commander went the rounds.

We are very fortunate. This is the first time American troops have landed against a well-defended beach, the first time over a coral reef, the first time against any force to speak of. And the first time the Japs have had the hell kicked out of them in a hurry.

I think it's a bunch of crap. The Brass are always saying patriotic stuff and gassing the men, but how in the world do they know what's waiting for us on that dark shore. I know better than them what's waiting. The ghosts of Hotchkiss, Malena, Sharples, McKeever, and Kramer, that's what's waiting. Visions of Ulysses' men crowd my thoughts, jerked out of the boat by Scylla, roasted on a spit in the cave of Polyphemus, turned into pigs, and drowned in the wild storms that leapt from the bag of winds given by Aoleus to get them safely home. And as my eyes strain into the darkness, I hear the shades of the men we left behind on Cactus.

"Come on, Bud. We're over here. We're waiting to see you. Come join us, death isn't so bad, it's better than what you got now. No pain, no fear, no worries, no guns, no bombs, no Japs, just the silent sleep of dust."

Man, snap out of it Buddy Boy!

So down the nets we crawl into the Higgins boats. Waiting for us closer to shore are the Alligators, the amphibious craft that will take many of us in over the reef. Lieutenant Crandall huddles with us. Billy, Johnny, Sergeant Zarate, Garowski, Levy, Skillet and Stoneroad, "Big Band," the new guys, my team, my brothers.

Crandall grunts at us. "Stay awake, you sonsabitches. I don't care what the Brass said about scouring this piece-of-shit island, I know for sure that the best of the best are waiting for us—Naval Landing Force troops, the Jap Marine Corps. These little yellow bastards have fortified this entire island—cave, pits, traps. There's gonna be machine guns, automatic weapons, dual-purpose guns and some coastal guns. Keep your friggin' eyes open. We've come too far together to lose each other now. We're going in. Semper Fi!"

"Semper Fi," we shout.

The Japs fired the first shot of the battle. A red star cluster went up, and soon after that they opened up with eight-inch guns. Where they got those and how they survived the bombardment, I'll never know. This stinking Betio is only 800 yards wide. Where did they hide them? The Higgins boats bob through the waves. We see other guys transferring into Alligators, but we stay in the Higgins. Bobbing up and down. Some guys are already seasick. We sit there waiting. The guns of the big ships stop.

"What's happening, Lieutenant?" Zarate asks.

"There's supposed to be an airstrike going on now, but as usual the flyboys are late."

The Japs take advantage of the lull and start firing at the transports. I look up and the transports are steaming away, out of the lagoon through the channel. Mine sweepers are racing across parallel to the beach, clearing mines and obstructions. Then I see two destroyers moving in to support the sweeps. It's the *Ringgold* and the *Dashiell*. The *Ringgold* takes a hit, another, but it stays and fires into the beach. Then the roar of planes and the flyboys arrive, better late than never. The Jap guns quiet down and then we turn toward Betio and head across the lagoon toward Red Beach 2.

The lagoon looks like a scene from Dante's Inferno. Smoke shrouds Betio, so much smoke that we can't see nothin'. All we see are the tracer bullets whizzing out from between the splintered palm trees. Then there's a gigantic explosion on shore and something goes up with a white-hot flare, transforming to deep red as it rockets into the sky. Ammo dump! That's some bullets and bombs that won't be killing Marines. The smoke is blowing, covering the Jap positions, and bullets are flying from every direction. Next to us an Alligator takes a direct hit and vanishes—one minute it's filled with grim, determined Marines and the next it's gone, vanished, just the smoke and their spirits floating away on the breeze. I hear them again, Hotchkiss, Malena, Sharples, McKeever, and Kramer.

"Come on in, Bud, the water's fine. It's a great day to get blown to bits. See if you can find Kramer's arm when you're swimming in. See if you can find Sharples' head."

We are taking hits against the hull. Bang! Bang! Wheeeee! A machine gun slug glances off the bow and whistles away. Then the Higgins grinds to a halt. Crandall yells at the coxswain. "What's going on?"

"We are hung up on the reef, Lieutenant. I can't move. You boys have to walk from here."

Holy crap! It's a thousand yards to the beach, and the water is three to five feet deep. There is a concussion from overhead, and then everything gets lit with a weird St. Elmo's fire. Air bursts! Whoever told the Brass that this island didn't have any more Japs on it was full of it up to their eyeballs. Crandall yells and everybody bails. The Amtracs plow ahead of us, taking hit after hit from machine guns. Then some of them bogged down and stopped. Barbed wire! Crandall yells and points. There is a pier sticking out five hundred yards into the lagoon and we had been moving to the east of it. "Go there," Crandall shouts.

Machine-gun bullets were hissing into the water, inches to the left, inches to the right. I look at Billy. His face is white, but he's not afraid. Johnny's eyes are wide open and he's grinning. Jeez Louise, that guy is a case. Three guys go down to my left, new kids in their first battle. I watch Skillet ahead of me, carrying the mortar base, and then he steps into a hole in the reef and disappears. I lunge forward and grab his collar as he's going down. I jerk him out of the hole and he stumbles ahead. He smiles that crooked grin. "I owe ya, Bud."

Crandall yells again. "Make for the pier. Make for the pier!"

X-ray platoon spreads out and moves toward the pier. The water is warm and I think of swimming with Kalasia and then a dead body bumps up against me, the grinning face of a dead Gyrene staring up. I've seen that face before, in the darkness of a fit, prophetic dreams... *Kalasia! Kalasia!*

Crap! Get me outta' this water.

I watch as Garrity and Brown herd their guys toward the pier. Then Garrity's head disappears in a gout of blood and he's gone, drifting away in the warm sea to join the ghosts of Kramer and Sharples.

"C'mon over, Bud, it's better here, no Japs, no bullets..."

Shut up Kramer, get back in your grave!

I'm warm inside my pants and I realize I pissed myself. Maclean takes over Zeus and the squads of X-ray head for cover.

Billy makes the pier first and squeezes up against it. We push right up behind him. Across the reef, the tractors are taking a beating. Some are hung up in the wire, some are knocked out. Some have landed the guys and turned to go back out, only to be blown up as they run for the deep water. I look out and see more boats headed our way, the tops of our Sherman tanks just visible over the sides.

Then someone is shouting in my ear. It's a lieutenant. "Where's your platoon leader, soldier?"

I point to Crandall. The guy has a Sniper Scout patch on his shoulder. He and Crandall pow-wow in the water behind the pier. Crandall yells at Billy. "Martens, you and Strange go with Lieutenant Hawkins. They need some shooters up the pier. The rest of us will work our way up the pier and follow you."

Johnny and Billy wade after the Lieutenant. "Stay alive, Bud!" Johnny yells.

The rest of us follow Sniper and Johnny. Up ahead, I hear Billy's 1903. Bang! Bang! Bang! I know three Japs are now dead. Johnny joins in, the deep cough of the BAR beating a counterpoint to the Jap machine guns ahead of us on the beach. Our guys are moving up the pier, shooting as they go. There are nests under the pier where the Japs are hiding, but our flamethrower guys can't fire up, so the squad goes after them one at a time.

If ever there was a hell on earth, it's this God-awful place. Out in the lagoon, dead Marines are floating. I see some guys struggling onto the beach and getting under a log seawall that runs down the beach. It's the only cover. If God ever made any place to defend, it's this island. The highest point is over in the middle and it's maybe ten feet above sea level. The Japs seem to have every angle of fire covered, and there is no place to hide except behind the sea wall and along the pier. But the Japs have zeroed in, and being behind the wall is no guarantee.

We've been here an hour. It seems like a lifetime.

<hr>

SNAFU. Crandall has been in touch with Rudy, and this entire operation is totally screwed. We sent a lot of men ashore, but only two thousand made it. Landing teams are scattered all over the place. The guys are pinned down behind the seawall. I'm following the teams up the pier, but it's hard to treat the wounded in waist deep water. Some guys died out in deep water, others are out there, bobbing in the lagoon. The seawall has machine gun ports in it, and clusters of dead Marines are lying in front of each Jap machine gun that's poking its nose through.

We worked our way to the end of the pier, and I've got an aid station set up. Even under heavy fire, our guys are bringing the wounded in. Other men are pushing the wounded out to the Higgins boats in rubber rafts. The guys aren't quitting, but bullets are everywhere and death is just a heartbeat away. One guy came in shot up real bad. We worked on him and just when we got him stabilized a stray bullet comes in and kills him. What the hell!

Colonel Shoup is ashore!

From what Crandall hears on the TBY, the situation is seriously in doubt. But Shoup has ordered reinforcements.

Out in the lagoon, the second wave is coming in. Guys are wading everywhere and dying everywhere. If I ever find the dumbass that sent us in at low tide, I'll kill him myself.

I can't see Johnny or Billy anywhere. My squad is scattered. I don't know if I will be alive at the end of this day.

Jesus, help me. Keep me alive. Get me home to Kalasia, Jesus!

8

A HERO'S REWARD

JOHNNY STRANGE

Johnny lay in a little runoff ditch that angled away from the top of the pier. It was D-Day plus two hours and the scorching sun of Helen beat down on the men huddled behind blasted mounds of coral and shivered palm stumps. King Company was scattered all down the north side of Betio, across their landing zone on Red Beach 2. Captain Rudebaker made his way to the top of the pier with Colonel Shoup and let Crandall know that some troops had even gotten diverted to Red Beach 1 and were now trying to work their way down the beach to the pier.

The first wave hit the beach at 0910 and it was there that Landing Team 2/2 met the fiercest resistance on the entire island. Heavy machine gun and anti-boat fire and thick strands of barbed wire strung across the reef had stopped many of the Amtracs and disabled others. It was Red Beach 2 where the forced wading began and many 2/2 boys floated in the surf or lay dying on the beach.

Crandall pulled Johnny into the Sniper Scout platoon with Billy when they were working along the pier and Billy was up ahead in a blown out gun emplacement having a turkey shoot with some other sniper boys. The word had come down that a lot of top-rank officers had died coming in, and the assault was now in the hands of junior officers and non-coms. Colonel Shoup was the only regimental commander who had made it ashore and two of three landing teams had lost their commanders.

Crandall dropped in beside him.

"Johnny, they screwed this whole thing up. Rudy says the only group with any cohesion is over on Red Beach 3. Colonel Amey is dead. He got cut down wading in after his Amtrac stalled. The rest of us got the crap kicked out of us coming in, and squads are fighting the battle."

Crandall pulled the chewed-to-pieces cigar out of his mouth and pointed toward the pier with it.

"The seawall and the pier are the only cover on the island. These little bastards have built themselves a perfect defense network up on top of the wall. There are blockhouses, pillboxes and a shitload of machine-gun nests. And every one of them covers the surrounding ones. We have to spot them and take them out. But it's got to be done with satchel charges and flamethrowers. They are sandbagged and fortified with concrete and coconut logs. I need you to go with me to cover these guys who are going to burn them out."

Johnny grinned. "Lead the way, Lieutenant."

So Johnny followed his lieutenant into the jaws of hell. Zarate and Navarro crawled over and Sergeant Brown and Corporal MacLean and their squads came behind them. Crandall looked around. "Where are Shanks and the Hades squad?"

Brown spit a wad of tobacco and grimaced. "Saw their boat get driven east toward Red Beach 1. I think they are trying to get back here, but it's a real shitshow over there. We may not see them until this afternoon."

Fire from the Japs was heavy and continuous. Under the seawall stretched a fifty-yard long line of wounded Marines. Johnny saw Bud moving among the dead and dying, followed by two Chaplains who were praying for the most seriously injured.

Crandall huddled with his guys. "Okay, there's a big blockhouse 25 yards due south, right over the wall. Okay, here's how it works. Strange, you get down that way 10 yards and give me enfilading fire into their ports with the BAR. Garowski is your cover man. Hernandez, you move ten yards the other way and the two BARs should keep them locked down while we haul some satchels over there and stick them up their butts. Harte and Kane, you take the Zippo and fry those little toads when the roof comes off. Strange and Hernandez wait for my signal. Three shots. Got it?"

Heads nodded.

"Okay, move out."

Johnny squirmed along behind the wall. When he had gone ten yards, he pulled off his helmet and stuck it partway up over the wall. There was no shot, so he peeked over. About thirty feet away, he could see the mound of a machine gun nest that was giving covering fire to the blockhouse. Johnny peeked up again and spotted two more nests even closer. They were facing away from him down the beach, and he could see the backs of some helmets as the Japs crouched in their holes. He got his BAR into position and waited. BANG! BANG! BANG! Crandall's signal.

Johnny opened up with the BAR on the closest nest. The rounds thudded home and he could see a gout of blood as he splattered Jap brains on the walls of the hole. Twenty yards away, Hernandez was wreaking the same havoc on the other side of the blockhouse. He swung his BAR onto the second nest and let go. One of the Japs stood, and Johnny's burst tore him in half. The flying entrails must have scared his buddies because they started jerking around in the nest trying to get the guts off. They showed just enough of themselves to end up in the same greasy pile as their comrade.

Whang! Whang! Whang! Machine-gun bullets from the third nest ripped along the top of the wall inches from his position. "Garowski, grenade!"

Ricky popped a grenade off his belt, pinned it and heaved it over the wall. Perfect throw! With a roar, the nest and the men in it lifted into the air in a hellish blast of fire.

"Yeah, Ricky!" Johnny screamed. He turned his BAR on the ports of the blockhouse. The 30-06 slugs filled the slots with a hail of death. As he kept up the firing he saw Big Band break for the fortress carrying a satchel charge. He didn't dodge, he just ran straight across the intervening space, pulling the cord as he went. The machine guns inside woke up and Big Band went down, but not before he flung the satchel straight into the port.

Two clicks and then the blockhouse went up with a roar. Johnny saw pieces of meat dressed in Jap uniforms fly through the air. Two Japs came stumbling out, but Harte was there with the Zippo and a long tongue of flame licked out and caught the Japs. Johnny could hear their screams and he screamed too.

"Take that, you little bastards! Die! Die."

Crandall moved up and waved his team over. The Marines owned another twenty square yards of Helen. Johnny knelt beside Big Band.

"Hey, Big Band, how you hangin'?"

Big Band laughed and held up his canteen. It was flat as a pancake. "The little sonofabitch shot my canteen. Knocked the wind out of me, but no blood. I'm good."

"The reinforcements are coming!"

Johnny looked back over the wall. Out in the lagoon, he could see men wading through the water. With them were Alligators crawling across the reef and taking heavy fire. It was the 1st Battalion boys. He could see the tracers and the machine guns seeking them out. But they kept coming. The water was chalky white from the pulverized coral. Hundreds of men floated in the water and here and there the skeleton of burned out Amtracs littered the reef, but the Marines kept coming.

ON AND ON THEY FOUGHT. Crawling through the sand, spotting Jap emplacements, taking them out. The hellish progress was happening not in terms of yards or feet, but inches. Each blockhouse, each pillbox, every Jap machine gun nest was its own battle. Johnny lost track of the hours, but the sun was moving into the west when they came upon the biggest blockhouse yet.

Crandall pulled his men around him and surveyed the massive structure.

"This place is holding up this whole end of the island. We have to take it out. Brown, get on the TBY and call the *Ringgold*. See if we can't get some destroyer fire on that target."

Brown called in the coordinates. When he finished, he turned to the men.

"Everybody back up and take cover. Heavy fire coming this way."

In a few minutes they heard the roar of the five-inch shells coming in. They went screaming in straight into the blockhouse, shattering the concrete building in a rain of death. Johnny could see body parts flying. Crandall motioned to Harte and Kane, and the flamethrower team moved in. Jets of horrible flames spurted from the nozzle as Harte moved closer to the burned out building. There was a burst of fire from the left that took him right in the tanks. The fuel went up with a roar and Harte turned and stumbled to his knees, screaming, his entire body engulfed in flames.

"Sammy! Dear God, Sammy!"

Kane, without hesitating, pulled his pistol from his hip and shot Harte through the head. Harte collapsed in a heap as the flames consumed his body. The rest of the squad stared in shock. Johnny turned and got a bead on the machine gun that had cut Harte down and let go with the BAR. The rest of the squad followed suit and sent a stream of hell into the Jap position. Johnny ran to the nest and stood over it, firing his BAR into the still thrashing bodies of the Japs. He fired until his clip was empty and still he pulled the trigger. Then he felt a hand on his shoulder. This time he did not pull away.

"That's good, Johnny, they're dead."

It was Crandall. He gave Johnny a light push away from the dead Japs. Sammy Kane was sitting on the ground next to Harte's fried body. He had his face in his hands, weeping. Crandall went down on one knee next to him.

"It's okay, Batman. You did the right thing. He was in hell. My pistol was in my hand when you shot him. You gave him the best gift a friend can give. Now let's go. We got a lot to do before the sun goes down."

"Okay, Lieutenant, okay. Just give me a minute."

Johnny stood silently watching Batman.

"What happened?"

Johnny turned. Billy Martens stood behind him.

"Sniper! Am I glad to see you! What are you doing back?"

"Hawk got some more of his boys as reinforcements, so he sent me along. What happened here?"

"Harte got caught in a burst of machinegun fire and went up like a torch. Batman shot him."

"Gee, that's tough." Billy walked over to Batman. "You okay, Buddy?"

"Hey, Sniper..." Batman wiped his eyes with his sleeve. "Yeah, I'm good. Give me a hand up."

Billy pulled Batman to his feet. The squad stood for a minute in silence and then Crandall grunted and they moved out down the beach.

It was dusk on Betio. D Day. Johnny and Billy lay in an improvised foxhole that was dug into a perimeter that X-Ray squad had carved out of coral and sand. Both lay silent with their thoughts. Finally, Johnny spoke.

"You seen Bud?"

"Yeah, he had an aid station set up, and he was working on the guys. I saw him when I was headed back to the squad."

"What happened over there with the Sniper Scouts?"

"Well, Johnny, if we get out of this craphole alive, we'll get us a cold one and I will tell you some amazing stories."

"Sounds right, Billy, sounds right."

The sun began going down over the far western sea. In another world, it would have been a beautiful sight. But they were lost in the bowels of hell and just outside the perimeter of the hastily dug shelters, an implacable, powerful enemy waited. Johnny looked out at the approaching darkness. What would happen? Would they live and conquer, or would the Japs push them back until they joined the corpses bobbing in the warm chalky water?

Help me, Jesus!

"What?" Billy turned to Johnny.

"I didn't say anything, did I?"

"I thought you did."

"Nothing, Sniper. It was nothing."

9

───────

THE SPIDER

BILLY MARTENS

Johnny had fallen asleep. Billy let him snore into the sand. The moment the Japs on Betio launched a counterattack would be soon enough to wake him up.

He tapped a Lucky Strike out of his pack and lit it carefully with his Zippo, shielding the flame and the red tip of the cigarette from the enemy with his hand. He looked up and down the tiny beachhead they were holding onto. It was maybe seventy-five yards from the seawall they crouched behind to the water's edge. And then maybe one hundred yards from the pier off his left shoulder and all the way down to the right. Not much real estate to cling to, and the word was all the beaches were the same—short on size and short on sweet. The invasion was on the brink of collapse.

"If I were Tojo," Billy muttered to a sleeping Johnny, "I'd come at us full bore at two or three o'clock. We'd be expecting it at midnight or one, but not at two or three. It won't take much to push us into the sea or slaughter us on the shoreline. Set up a few Nambus at close range, limber up some mortars, toss in some grenades... who knows, maybe they've even got some more five-inch guns squirreled away. Maybe they're on friggin' wheels. They can roll 'em up and blast us pointblank. Hell, I sprinted farther than our beachhead in track. It's like we're hanging onto this island by our fingernails."

So, this was the spider. This is what had stuck in his head for so many weeks. Betio was some kind of arachnid and they were caught in its web of machine gun fire and pillboxes and snipers, never to be released till the fangs had sunk all the way in and paralyzed them. Dear God. Who else had such morbid images in their head?

Billy unhooked four grenades from his web belt and laid them out in a row in the sand. That way he'd be ready for the surprise attack he felt was coming before dawn. How had things gotten this bad? He hunkered down lower and blew out a stream of smoke. Because the powers that be couldn't read tidal charts. He knew low tide would uncover hundreds of dead Marines shot as they waded into shore from half a mile out. That sweet rotten stink of human decay he remembered from Guadalcanal would fill everyone's nostrils. The smell would be what pushed them over the seawall and into the spider's web of jungle for good. If they were still here by dawn and not bobbing in the surf with the other corpses.

How many Marines had families that had adopted them in New Zealand? Families that were praying for them as they floated lifeless in the sea? Praying for them as they lay shot to pieces among the coconut palms a few hundred feet beyond the seawall? How many brides or sweethearts or young wives swollen with child were praying prayers from Wellington that no longer made any difference to the dead men they were praying for? What did God do with prayers like that?

Or what did he do with all the prayers in the U.S. that had been going up for Marines since 1941, and had followed them all the way to the Canal and New Zealand and Tarawa Atoll, only to find the objects of those prayers headless and dismembered?

Born in NYC, born in Minnesota, born and raised in Nevada, died in the South Pacific. What the heck was a Texas farm boy of twenty-one doing in a grave in the South Pacific?

And those prayers were still going up. All kinds of prayers were still going up. Because they didn't know Timmy and Bob and Charlie and Thad were dead. Dead and gone. And they wouldn't know for another couple of weeks or maybe a month. All that time the prayers would still go up for dead fathers, and uncles, and brothers and husbands. Dead boyfriends. Dead sons. What good would the prayers do?

Billy took another long drag on his cigarette and shrugged in the dark, Johnny still snoring into the beach sand, and into his BAR and his right arm. The Catholics prayed for the dead. So, maybe the prayers did go somewhere and accomplish something. Who knew? Who could prove anything? His father would say it was a superstition to pray for the dead, but that was simply his opinion. His conjecture. His belief. Others had different opinions and beliefs, and they had prayed to God about it too. Who was right? Who was wrong? It was impossible to know.

That was how faith worked. It wasn't science. It wasn't lab rat experiments or field test stuff. You had to decide for yourself. It was personal. One church said one thing, another church, another thing. You had to make up your own mind which one you thought was right. There was no guarantee you would be on the money. But you had to land somewhere.

ZIP ZIP ZIP ZING ZING

What the hell?

Bullets were smacking into the sand and the seawall, but not from in front. They were coming from behind. Coming from the water. Billy pushed himself into the spider sand and the moment Johnny woke up and tried to lift his head, Billy shoved it onto the sand too. "Incoming!" he shouted. "From the sea! Not the island!"

Crandall was suddenly at Billy's elbow, unlit cigar in his teeth. "Damn Nips aren't just shooting from the frigging pier. They must've swum out to the landing craft and Alligators they knocked out. They're blasting us with our own machine guns. Billy, take Johnny and Ricky Garowski and Leon Levy and Julio Hernandez out there and slit their damn Nagasaki throats. Leave your boots and rifle and gear here. Just take your Ka-Bars. And you take this too, Billy." Crandall thrust his Thompson into Billy's hands. "If you need firepower, use it. All your crew should have Thompsons. Grab 'em from whoever has one."

"I'd like to take Stoneroad and Big Band Harrison too, Sir."

"Stoneroad!" Crandall did a loud whisper as bullets continued to zip past them. "Big Band!"

"Stoneroad!" Stoneroad responded.

"Big Band is dead, skipper. He took two slugs to the face."

Crandall cursed. "Stoneroad, go with Corporal Martens. You're swimming out to our wrecks and killing the Japs on them. Just take your Ka-Bar and borrow a Thompson. Strip everything else off."

"Everything?"

"Go in the raw if that helps you swim better. Move."

Billy got his men in a circle. "No fatigues. They'll just soak up water and slow you down. Johnny, you and Julio take that far wreck. Key in on the bursts. Garowski and Leon, go for that wreck in the middle that's firing higher than the others. Stoneroad, yours is the one right next to it. I'll take the fourth that's behind your target."

"You have the longest swim, corporal," Stoneroad replied.

Billy grinned as he peeled off. "Yeah. I smell like a skunk. I need the swim to freshen up for Tojo's counterattack."

The men laughed and shucked their combat fatigues too. Then each of them slipped into the water and disappeared, Thompsons strapped across their backs. Billy went to his wreck like an arrow. Soon he could tell it was an Alligator and was firing all its thirties and its 37mm M6. The flames from the guns were red and orange. Nothing like the pink tracers streaming at the beachhead from the pier where the Japanese were using their own machine guns and ammunition.

Billy did a front crawl smoothly and powerfully. He swam all the time in Montana, the chill of the turquoise mountain lakes scarcely bothering him. Funny that he'd done hardly any swimming in New Zealand. The hunting had preoccupied him. It felt good to use his swimming muscles again and to feel the warm water sliding over his bare skin. He counted ten minutes to get to his LVT, Landing Vehicle Tracked.

All its guns were blazing. The enemy wouldn't be thinking about someone oozing out at them from behind. The back end was lower in the water, the nose well clear. Billy slipped out and snaked towards the turret and the gunners. He wanted to use his Ka-Bar on all four and not alert the Japanese on the other wrecks. Providence handed a stroke of luck to him.

One soldier manning a thirty-caliber machine gun stepped back several feet and leaned over the side to urinate. The others ignored him, concentrating on firing long and steady bursts at the Marines on the beach. Billy got to his feet, crept up behind him, clamped one hand over his mouth and drew the Ka-Bar's blade across his throat. Then he placed the body gently on the deck and moved quietly towards the three remaining soldiers.

He felt he had a good chance of dispatching all three with his knife. He just needed to be fast-footed. But the moment he moved up behind his victims, all hell broke loose on the other wrecks. Thompsons opened up with their distinctive chatter, much different from the thirties the Japs were firing from the LVTs. A grenade went off and hurled yellow fire at the night sky, and a soldier began screaming in Japanese. This made his targets jerk their heads around.

Seeing a nude Marine was the last thing the Japanese expected. Billy swept his blade in a wide slashing arc and took out the soldier on the 37mm and another on a thirty in a spray of arterial blood. The last gunner, who wore a headband with the

Rising Sun on it, yelled out and kicked the Ka-Bar from Billy's hand. A second kick sent Billy smashing into the side of Alligator. Then the enemy was on him with Billy's own knife.

Billy realized right away he had more strength in his arms and shoulders than the Jap. He thrust the soldier up and to the right and pinned him to the deck, holding his wrists. Smacking his skull into the soldier's nose made a snapping sound Billy heard despite the gunfire all around them and the loud explosion of a second grenade. The nose broke and bled. Billy smacked the nose with his skull a second time, and the man cried out and released the Ka-Bar. Billy made a grab for it, but the tilt of the deck made the knife skitter away and into the sea.

The soldier punched Billy in the side of the head with his free hand twice, as fast as a blink, his fingers curled into a tight fist, then kneed Billy between the legs as hard as Billy had ever been hit there. He gasped in pain and thought he was going to black out. The man said something in Japanese and yanked Billy's head down to his, smacking his forehead into Billy's, and this time it was Billy who took the brunt of the hit. He could barely see through the triple pain of being punched, kneed, and head butted.

The soldier wrapped his fingers around Billy's throat and started choking him, muttering loudly, and all Billy could think was to do the same to his enemy. He had the advantage of being able to thrust with most of his bodyweight. He clenched his teeth and bore down with all he had, his fingers like claws. The soldier kicked and thrashed and released his choke on Billy. He used his hands, trying to push Billy off. But Billy wasn't going anywhere. The only thing he could think to do was choke the Japanese soldier harder and keep putting all his power and weight into his arms.

The soldier squirmed and flapped like a fish on the deck. He pawed at Billy's arms and punched his face again and again, but Billy just dug in, refusing to release the choke. Then the soldier's movements grew less and less violent, his arms drooped, his eyes rolled back white. Still, Billy pressed down and tightened his grip on the man's throat. There was a crack as the man's windpipe yielded to Billy's strength. Billy continued to exert force.

"Hey. Corporal."

Billy glanced up at a face streaming with water in the dark.

It was Bakar Zarate, the sergeant of Billy's squad.

"I'm pretty sure Tokyo Joe's joined his ancestors, Corporal Martens."

Billy stared at the sergeant. He was naked like Billy, seawater pouring off him, Thompson slung over his back, Ka-Bar dripping in his fist. Zararte grinned. "Do I look like your poster boy Marine?"

Billy laughed. "No, Sarge."

"Neither do you. Come on. Everyone's back at the beach. Mission accomplished. Except for those rats firing at us from the pier."

"Should you and I swim to the pier?"

Zarate shook his head. "We'll go after them in the morning. I'm worried about a counterattack."

Billy finally released his choke. His body was shaking. "Yeah. Me too."

"So, let's swim back and help the boys get ready."

"All my men made it home?"

Zarate grinned. "Yeah, Corporal. All your men made it home."

Billy was staring at the man he'd choked to death. "It's kinda like the Canal, Sarge. I killed a Jap with my bare hands in a foxhole there."

"I remember."

"That was hard. I thought this one would be easier."

"The third and fourth ones will. Hey, Billy?"

"Yeah, Sarge?"

"It's called war," Zarate said. "Pearl Harbor started the slugfest."

Billy reached down and tugged the soldier's Rising Sun headband free. He put it on, climbed to his feet and followed the sergeant to the back of the LVT. Stopping, he knelt by the first soldier he'd killed, spotting a knife in a wooden scabbard at his hip. He grasped the scabbard, tugging the knife free. It was shaped like a small sword. Billy estimated the blade to be about five inches long. Zarate squatted beside him.

"Different, hey, Corporal? They call it a *tanto*. The design goes back centuries. The samurai used them along with their longer swords. That's what I want. An officer's sword. A *katana*. Where's your Ka-Bar?"

"At the bottom of the sea."

"Well, then, might as well use this. It'll cut nuts as well as anything made by Camillus in New York. And won't Tokyo Joe be surprised when you pull one on him?" Zarate slapped Billy on the shoulder. "Time to swim, Marine. That attack's coming and I'm in an itch to collect some souvenirs like you."

They stood up together, took a few steps, then slipped into the black sea without making a sound.

DAY 2 — D+1

NOVEMBER 21, 1943

10

FIREFIGHT

THE CORPSMAN

"CORPSMAN! CORPSMAN!"

I'd had those crazy premonitions about bodies floating in the surf that had made my mind shut down and my blood run cold in New Zealand. Then I'd waded onto Betio through surf just like that and hadn't thought about the premonition. But now it had come back my first night at the Tarawa Atoll. I'd stayed awake a long time trying to keep wounded Marines alive. And I'd expected a Jap counterattack. But the attack never came, so I lay down by a boy from Iowa who had just breathed his last, his hand still gripping mine, and went into the dark of dreams, hoping for images of Kalasia. Instead, I got dead Marines floating in the sea and my heart began to hammer.

"CORPSMAN! DAMMIT! CORPSMAN!"

I blinked open my eyes. The first thing I saw was that the tide had gone out. The second thing was bodies strewn all over the tidal flats the ocean had covered up. The third thing was another wave of Marines wading ashore from far out, just like we'd had to do it the day before, and they were getting shot to pieces, just like we'd been shot to pieces. Only this seemed worse, much worse. Machine guns were chattering from every part of the jungle.

Bodies were falling all over the tidal flats. Fifty, a hundred, a hundred and fifty, two hundred, three. God in heaven, it was a massacre.

"CORPSMAN!"

It was Lt. Crandall's face in my face, a cigar steaming in his teeth.

"Dammit, Bud," he growled, "you sleep the sleep of the dead. Get off your ass and follow me. Our boys are getting slaughtered trying to make their way onto Betio. Colonel Shoup, the officer in charge of all us Marines on the island, he reckons we're losing the frigging battle. Not on my watch, dammit. K company is going over the wall and we're going to wipe out every sniper, machine gun nest, pillbox and bunker that is firing at our men. I'm not pussy footing around. We're gonna cut every one of those samurais to ribbons. You're our doc, our plasma genie. So, grab your stuff and move it."

Bullets were all over us, but we were charging past the seawall anyway. I stayed at the crouch and ran as fast as I could. Our guys were blazing at snipers high in coconut trees with their Tommy guns and BARs and M1 Garands. I glimpsed Earp and Greene, Superman and Superman Too, humping it with the Big Fifty, Ma Deuce. The next thing I knew they'd set it up by a thick cluster of palms and were absolutely pounding one machine gun nest after another. I didn't even know the nests were there until bits and pieces of bone, and skin, and heads and legs went spinning up into the air.

WHOOSH!

That scared the crap out of me. An enormous wave of fire roared out to my left and consumed a pillbox made of thick coconut logs. Cripes, even the sand was burning. I could feel the heat like I was standing next to a furnace. Red O'Brien was now on the M2-2 flamethrower, replacing Frank Harte, KIA, and Red was the right choice. Even though he was well aware how Frank had got it, he ignored snipers and machine gun fire and went barreling ahead into the jungle, scorching every spot where he saw Japs or gun flashes or the shape of a camouflaged bunker. Sam Kane, Batman, who had buddied up with Harte on the flamethrower, was now Red's partner, using his MI carbine to pick off any Japs that were aiming for the tanks strapped to Red's back.

I saw Red torch another pillbox I hadn't even noticed, igniting several coconut palms at the same time. A bunch of Japs tumbled out of a back exit, two of them on fire, all of them screaming, one ready to throw a grenade after arming it by smacking it against his helmet. I hadn't even noticed the CO of our company, Captain Rudebaker, but he had his Colt 1911 pistol out and he calmly emptied it into all five of them. The one Jap fell on his grenade and his body smothered the blast. Rudy raced further into the jungle, snapping a fresh magazine into his Colt as he ran, and we all ran after him. Earp and Greene humped it with the Fifty, Earp muscled enough to fire the heavy gun as he moved, spraying the trees in front of the captain, top and bottom, shredding palm fronds so they littered our shoulders like chunks of green confetti or ticker tape.

My eyes were on Johnny when he got hit. Him and Julio Hernandez were hosing down a cluster of Nambu nests with their BARs when a sniper got his number. He dropped to one knee, face twisted with pain, but still kept blazing away with his Browning, sawing one Jap officer in half and yelling: "I got him! His frigging sword's mine!"

I was on him immediately. "Let me see, Johnny."

"I'm good as gold, Bud, let me fight."

"The bullet went clean through your shoulder, so that makes you lucky."

"Damn right I'm lucky, Doc, I cram horseshoes up my rear every morning with my coffee."

"Geez, a funny Marine, how rare is that?" I'd cut away his sleeve and was cleaning the bullet hole and sprinkling it with sulfa powder. "I'll wrap it with gauze and get you to head down to the beach."

"What! For evacuation?"

"Of course. You have a severe wound and––"

"The hell with that noise, Doctor Ritzville. I don't walk out on a fight we have to win. You think I'm gonna sit on my can on that frigging beach and watch our guys get mowed down when I could be doing something about it? What have you been drinking, Mennonite Man? Patch me up and let me get on with my work."

"Johnny––"

"I swear to God I'll bop you on the nose. Now finish the wrap and turn me loose to win the war."

What a nut case. Idaho sure knew how to grow potatoes. "I'm giving you a syrette of morphine."

"No, you're not. How can I shoot straight if I'm all doped up? You got any brandy?"

"Johnny, I'm not supposed––"

"You do, don't you?" Johnny demanded.

I made a face. "Sometimes it helps my patients when I'm probing for bullets. I know it's old fashioned, but it works in a few cases."

"Don't worry. I won't tell God. Give me a swig and a cigarette and send me on my way."

"Geez, Johnny."

"Do it!" he snapped. "You saw how our guys were getting cut down on the flats. Send me back in, Ritzville. Let me save some lives."

What do you do with Johnny Strange of Bonners Ferry, Idaho, where they make them tough and weird? I gave him my brass flask, let him gulp as much as he wanted, then placed a Chesterfield between his lips and lit it with my Zippo. He grunted his thanks. Then took out the cigarette and examined it. "Huh. Chesterfields. You been holding out on me." He jumped up and slapped me on the back. "You're a pretty good shit for a Mennon-ite, ha, ha. See you in the jungle."

"CORPSMAN! CORPSMAN!"

I leaped up after Johnny and got waved over to a Marine flat on his back, growling with a whole lot of hurt. Garowski had taken a slug in his leg. This one wasn't clean. Maybe he wanted to argue with me the way Johnny Strange would. But he could hardly get a word out. I cut away his pant leg, cleaned the wound with water and dumped a bunch of sulfa powder into the hole, shot him up with morphine, and called out to my stretcher bearers to haul him down to the beach. Then I moved on.

The boys were killing Japs, but the Japs were getting their own back too. I couldn't do anything for the commander of Mike Platoon, 2nd Lt. Tim Pincher, except drape his brown and green spotted poncho over his head. That's all I could do for three of his squads' sergeants. And all I could do for two of the non-coms in Platoon X-Ray––Sergeant Shanks of Hades squad and Corporal Lee of Titan. I didn't feel it. I couldn't afford to feel it. I pushed on into the thick green and the gunfire and the huge gouts of flame spewed by Red O'Brien. The boys were calling him The Dragon.

My body snatchers, my stretcher bearers, were so busy they were a blur. I was able to patch up Lieutenant Hawken, the CO of Fox Platoon, along with our riflemen, Leon Levy of San Francisco and Brian "Over Easy" Mitton, our Salt Lake City boy. Corporal Garcia of Hades platoon I saved with a bottle of plasma rigged to a Garand thrust bayonet first into the jungle floor. I always carried four bottles into the field, wrapped snuggly in a spare set of fatigues. I premixed the dried plasma they issued me in water before I went out. There wasn't any time to do that during combat.

I saved a kid from Michigan with a bottle and another from Rhode Island. I had dried plasma in my pack and carried extra canteens of water in case I needed to reconstitute more. I tucked empty glass bottles in with my gear too. Plasma had no red blood cells so I could give it to anyone regardless of their blood type. That was the magic. It increased the blood levels again after all the fluid loss from wounds. This brought the BP or blood pressure back to normal and staved off shock and death. Prayer was good. Prayer with plasma was better.

Three Marines came humping up with a new M1 81mm mortar for our mortar men, Tom "Skillet" Baker and Paul Stoneroad. They'd lost theirs in the drink the first day. Those three boys were sweating oceans. I found out later the tube itself was bad enough at forty-four and a half pounds, but the base plate was forty-five pounds and the mount a whopping forty-six and a half. Lord have mercy. That on top of all their other equipment. They'd had to hump a sack of mortar shells, too.

Skillet and Stoneroad had used a 60mm on Guadalcanal and to bust up a few blockhouses on Betio, but the 81mm, which they'd trained with in New Zealand, was a different beast. We'd yet to see it in action. They set it up right away and cut loose on a pillbox that was giving us grief; it was buried so deep into the dirt. Skillet actually cackled, I swear to God he did, when Stoneroad showed him the first shell or bomb. "It's the M45 Heavy HE! It has the burst radius of a 105mm howitzer! Sweet heaven, come to earth!"

They fired right away and missed. Cussing like a pair of sailors down on their luck, Stoneroad tubed it again, Skillet adjusted the angle, and they fired a second time, both of them clapping their hands over their ears. That puppy hit the pillbox dead center, and the ground heaved and burst and vomited chunks of men and guns into the air. Everyone cheered. There must have been six machine guns and fifteen bodies in the wreckage. That's how you go from caring about human life in peace time to not giving a damn about an enemy's life when it's war.

Crandall immediately assigned Corporal Navarro to hump the tube and the ammo, while Skillet took the base plate and Stoneroad the mount. I hefted Navarro's bag of tricks before he slung it onto his back using both straps––oh please, Momma Moon! The thing weighed a ton and a half! The Marine who'd run it up from the beachhead, a big muscular boy from the Alaska Territory named Crown, nodded, unsmiling. "Each one of those mortar bombs weighs fifteen frigging pounds. Your corporal has a two-hundred-pound sack."

Rudebaker overheard that. He glanced at slender Navarro, bent under the ammo on his back, and a forty-four-pound tube in his hands along with his Thompson. Then Rudebaker stared at Crown. "What unit are you with, son?"

"I'm attached to Colonel Shoup's HQ, Sir."

"Well, now you're attached to K Company and X-Ray Platoon, Achilles Squad. You'll work with Skillet and Stoneroad and Corporal Navarro on the 81mm mortar. You're the ammo bearer. Corporal Navarro, give the man the bag."

"But, Sir––" Crown protested.

"We're fighting to save Marines' lives. They still getting shredded wading in?"

"Yes, Sir. It's the devil's business."

"So, it's our business to out-devil the devil. Where you from, Marine?"

"Skagway, Alaska Territory, Sir. I volunteered."

"Me too, private. Let's go win this war."

Crown suddenly grinned. "Yes, Sir. I'm all in, Sir."

There was a loud burst of machine gun fire to our right. I heard the *WHOOSH* and smelled the reek of the flamethrower. Then there was the unmistakable hammer of the Fifty. The chatter of Thompsons and the crack of the Garands. Someone yelled: "Where's Bud?" I darted past the mortar crew and Captain Rudebaker, grateful I still had another bottle of plasma ready to go in my kit.

11

HELL'S KITCHEN

JOHNNY STRANGE

Johnny's shoulder was sore, really sore, in fact it burned like fire, but the wound had closed when the bullet went through and the sulfa was keeping it clean.

Good thing they didn't shoot me through my right shoulder, I wouldn't be able to handle my BAR.

It was D-Day +1 on Tarawa. X-ray had been killing Japs all morning. Johnny had seen nothing like it. The Japs sowed every square foot of this stinking hellhole with machine-gun nests, pillboxes and bunkers. The little toads were everywhere—under rocks, in camouflaged pits, and tied up in trees. By the end of D-Day, the Marines had pushed their perimeter only one tenth of a square mile into the hell of Betio. But there was no thought of retreat. X-ray waited through the long night, a night broken only by their swim out to the wrecked Amtracs on the reef to take care of some annoying little yellow pests. But they spent the rest of the night trembling in whatever holes they could dig themselves into. Just before sunset, the 1/10 pack howitzers came ashore on Red Beach 2. The sections came in Amtracs, rubber boats and LCVPs. Some sections got dumped in the water at the end of the pier and artillerymen carried them in through the water, taking fire all the way.

Johnny had waited all night with the rest of the guys for the for-sure counterattack that would drive them back into the blood-stained water of Tarawa lagoon. But it never came. And so, when the sun came up, the Japs had missed their big chance, and the Marines went to work.

As the morning sun rose, Johnny and the rest of X-Ray watched while 1/8 came in six hours late and bumped up against the reef. They begin the deadly wade to the beach. The machine guns started zipping in and tearing them up. That's when Crandall rounded them up and sent them to the south and west, trying to quiet the anti-boat fire, but they could not quiet it. And that's when Johnny got shot.

They were pushing toward the airfield. The communications were still screwed. They were in deep doo-doo. Bullets were coming from everywhere. Johnny was blazing away with the BAR. Julio was backing him up. They were taking out a bunch of Nambu nests when he heard a ZIP and felt the blow high on his left shoulder. It felt like it did when the big KIWI punched him. Bud was on him like white on an egg, trying to get him to put down his BAR and report to the beach. But Johnny wasn't buying. Bud cut away his sleeve.

"The bullet went clean through, Johnny. No bones broken."

"Good. Then stick a cork in it and get me going, Bud."

Johnny gritted his teeth and bummed a fag. Bud surprised him with a Chesterfield. "You been holding out on me, Mennonite Boy!"

The dreaded "CORPSMAN!" cry. Bud finished up, protesting all the way. Johnny slapped the Corpsman on the back. "See you in the jungle."

Johnny put the lit cigarette between his lips, ran over to the Jap officer he had mowed down and collected the man's sword. He looked around, saw a hole below a shattered palm trunk and stuck the sword in it. Then he hightailed it through a once-beautiful palm grove and caught up with Crandall. He was with Sniper and the rest of the squad. "Rudy just heard from Shoup. The situation here is still uncertain. Colonel Jordan is in charge of 2/2. He got over to the South shore and found a bunch of our boys in some abandoned gun emplacements over there. They are holding out, but they need reinforcements bad. We have to clean out this neighborhood and push our perimeter to the airfield."

Crandall motioned the platoon over and pulled out a piece of paper. It was a rough map with Xs marked on it. "Zarate and I went out last night, snuck around and plotted these nests. We have pushed the perimeter enough today that we can get to them. Every guy that tries to make it onto this beach is getting blasted by machine guns and rifles from right over there." He pointed to a swatch of piled rocks, coconut logs, and coral embankments. "Skillet put the M1 right here. What's the range on this puppy?"

Skillet grinned. "Thirty-two hundred yards, Lieutenant. We can shoot clear over this damned island, end to end."

Crandall handed Stoneroad the map. "Good! I want you boys to take down these nests one by one. I want the rest of the squad up front spotting. Sniper, I want you watching for snipers; Strange and Hernandez, you follow O'Brien and hose these little turds when they come out of their holes. Superman, get Ma Deuce forward and get a crossfire going. This area is going to be Hell's Kitchen and we are the chefs. I want these Japs roasting in hell before an hour has passed. We need to clear everything all the way to the airfield. Let's go!"

So Johnny went back to work. Skillet and Stoneroad started up —sending a rain of death down on the enemy positions. O'Brien was up ahead with the Zippo. Bang! Bang! Sniper's 1903 was blazing. Johnny saw a Jap up in a tree swing down like a pendulum, hanging at the end of a rope. His face had a very surprised look. Skillet's M1 shells took apart a big log construction, and like ants stirred by a stick, the Japs came boiling out. The heavy cough of his BAR underpinned the chatter of Thompsons, and the Japs went down like tenpins.

"Ducks on the pond, Julio, Ducks on the pond!"

Behind him Johnny heard the roar of engines. Turning to look, he saw an amazing sight. Jeeps were rolling down the pier.

"Jeeps, Julio, Jeeps!"

But Julio didn't answer. Johnny looked over. Julio was lying on his back, a peaceful expression on his face, his leg red with blood. Johnny ran over. "Julio, damn it, Julio. CORPSMAN!"

Bud came flying up.

"Fix him, Bud, fix him."

Julio grinned at Johnny. "I guess I zigged when I shoulda' zagged." He laughed and coughed.

Bud pulled plasma out of his kit. "Shut up, Julio. Don't make it worse." He turned to Johnny. "Swap Julio's BAR and his ammo for one of these guys' M1s. You're gonna need the BAR."

Johnny looked around. A rifleman he didn't know was crouching by a tree. Johnny yelled for him to come over. "What's your name and outfit, Gyrene?"

"Bobby McGuire. I'm a 2/8 guy. We got pushed over here yesterday comin' in and I haven't been able to get back to my outfit."

"Ever fired a BAR?"

"Yeah, some in basic. Great piece of equipment."

Johnny handed him Julio's BAR and the ammo belts. "Well, pal, now you're a BAR man in X-ray squad."

Bud grabbed McGuire's M1 and stuck it in the sand. He rigged up a bag of plasma and hooked Julio up. Then he started patching him up. He looked up at Johnny. "I don't know, Johnny, looks bad."

Julio grinned again. "Hey, Bud, don't worry about me. I'm a

tough New Mexico Spic. I eat live tarantulas with my Pabst, and even the badass Apaches don't come around when I'm in town. Patch me up and send me offshore. I'll be on the ship waiting when you boys finish up here. Kill me some more Japs."

Johnny gave Julio a little slap in the face. "Okay, buddy, I'll take your word. And you better damn well be alive the next time I see you."

"Hey, Strange! I thought you'd be back in the states knocking the crap out of Joe Louis by now."

Johnny turned around. Colonel "Red Mike" Edson stood there grinning. He had a western revolver slung in a cartridge belt around his waist. That "come and kill me if you think you can" look was in his eyes.

"Afternoon, Sir. When did you come ashore?"

"An hour ago. What's the skinny?"

"Better with you here, Sir. I'd say things are looking up."

"Yeah, well, you boys are putting up a hell of a fight. Shoup has got things in hand, we got light tanks ashore on Beach Green and 1/6 is with them. I think the tide has turned."

Julio looked up from the ground and nodded. "You done, Bud? I'm feeling a little woozy."

Bud slapped on the last of the bandage and yelled for some stretcher-bearers. "Get this man to the beach on the double."

Julio left on the double, and Johnny grabbed McGuire. "Stay with me and watch what I do. You'll get used to Betty quick and then it gets fun." He nodded to the Colonel. "Good to see you, Sir. Watch your ass."

The Colonel smiled and waved them off and they scooted down past the last blown Jap fire pit and caught up with Crandall and the outfit.

"What's up, Lieutenant?"

"I think we are getting to these bastards, Strange. Look."

There was a dead Jap lying in front of him and he toed him over with his boot. The haft of a sword was sticking out of the

Jap's belly. "This chickenshit bailed on the Emperor. We're finding a lot of them like this. They must know something we don't."

"Edson's ashore, Sir, and he says we got tanks and fresh men ashore. That and the pack howitzers are making a difference."

There was a rumbling through the trees and an M4 Sherman Tank came grinding up. It had the name "Colorado" painted on the side. The top was burnt black and there were some major dents in the armor, but she was running. The driver popped his head out.

"Need any help, boys? I go where the Marines go."

Johnny nodded. "Sure, but how did you get so black?"

The driver laughed. "Jap threw a gasoline bomb on the turret. I was lit up like the 4th of July. But we hustled the old girl back to the beach, went for a swim and put the fire out."

Johnny laughed. "Any more where this one came from?"

"Well, only about five of us made the beach and each of us is fighting their own war. We found out we need to have infantry around us, or the Japs can get up close and take us out."

Johnny jerked his head toward the airfield. "Wanna go hunt some Japs?"

The driver stuck out a thumbs up. "Lead on, Gyrene."

THAT NIGHT WAS NOT SO FEARSOME as the first night. The pack howitzers had built themselves an emplacement and were systematically clearing the beachhead of Jap gun emplacements. They found more and more Japs that were dead by their own hand in the pits and hideouts that pockmarked the center of the island. The 1/8 was ashore on Beach Red 2 and 1/6 had come ashore on Beach Green along with more tanks and artillery. The brass fully committed 2nd Div to the invasion of Tarawa. Now the Japs were in a pocket on the wide west end of the island and they had seen some on the east end wading across to Bairiki, the next island in the chain.

X-Ray squad followed the tank for the rest of the afternoon and pointed out the Jap emplacements as they went. What the 75mm gun on the tank didn't kill, O'Brien fried with the Zippo or the squad sawed up with the BARs, Thompsons and M1s.

Stories about individual acts of bravery and sacrifice were circulating on the line. They heard about the young rifleman from Texas who picked off six snipers and then walked nonchalantly back through massive Jap fire and sneered back over his shoulder, "Shoot me down, you son-of-a-bitch." There was the Oklahoma sergeant who walked between tanks, guiding them from one pillbox to another and shrugging, "They asked for an intelligent Marine. I ain't so smart, but I went anyway." They heard about Lieutenant Hawkins, "Hawk," the leader of the Sniper Scout platoon, who spent the night of D-Day marking out Jap emplacements and then attacking them during the day, crawling boldly forward on a position fortified by five machine guns, firing point blank into the portholes and then finishing the Japs off with grenades before being mortally wounded.

Johnny crawled into his foxhole as the sun was going down. Before he nodded off, he looked out at the bodies of Marines lying dead on the sand of Betio.

Remember these guys, Johnny. Stay alive so you can tell John Albert. He has to know that we don't have to solve our quarrels this way...

Johnny looked over at Billy, asleep in his hole. He chuckled.

"I'm glad Billy didn't hear that," he laughed under his breath. "People wouldn't think I'm so nuts anymore."

1 2

THE TIPPING POINT

BILLY MARTENS

"*C*ripes! Another sniper!"

"Just keep going," panted Billy. "This one can't shoot for shit."

"You said that about the last one, Corporal!"

"And we're still here, aren't we?"

Billy continued to jog through a jungle shredded by naval guns, Nambus, mortars, 75mm Marine pack howitzers, Sherman and Stuart tanks, 30.06 rounds from the Garands and the short, rough, wicked bursts from fifty-caliber machine guns. And the 7.7mm Jap sniper bullets from Arisaka 99s that sliced apart coconut fronds and palm trunks and kicked up jungle dirt when they missed Marines. A dozen empty canteens banged against Billy's body. His brown and green spotted combat fatigues were black with sweat. Five other Marines ran with him, oozing just as much sweat, canteens slung over their shoulders, all but one aping Billy's disdain for sniper fire and not even bothering to duck.

Before he saw the beachhead, Billy smelled it. But it wasn't the tang of saltwater and clean air. It was the ugly, sweet stench of humans rotting. It had been obvious when they lit out over the seawall that morning. Now, in the late afternoon, it was much worse. Billy couldn't beat off the nausea as the reek filled his nostrils. He had to stop and puke up a can of C rations. The sight of the beef hash made him upchuck again. The smell of charred flesh a flamethrower left behind had been bad enough. His nose was full of it. His fatigues were putrid with the stink of gas fumes, greasy smoke, burnt hair and skin. But the thick odor of dead Marines in the sun for two days proved too much.

Grunts were wading in from their LVTs and taking fire. Bodies were still bobbing in the surf, only now they were bloated and doubled in size. The bodies in the sand at the shoreline were just the same. He stared at one sergeant who was face up, his eyes blobs of jelly that bulged out of his sockets and drooled over his cheeks. He noticed the tanks offloading from boats onto the pier, more Shermans, quick to roll over the sand and grind their way into the jungle. "Thank God for them," muttered Crown at Billy's elbow. "The more bunkers and pillboxes they poke their snouts into the better."

Billy looked up from the swollen corpses just as a string of Willys followed the tanks off the pier. All of them were towing 75mm pack howitzers. He was still feeling queasy, but he tried to crack a joke. "If that many jeeps are here, the battle's over." No one laughed. They were all staring at the bloated bodies that had mesmerized him. He was about to say something else when there were two loud blasts he wasn't expecting. The blasts snapped his head around. A couple of Shermans had positioned themselves to fire out to sea. Their shots bracketed a wrecked Alligator the Japs had been firing from the night before. Their next shots blew the LVT to pieces. Then the two tanks began blazing at another wreck, their 75mm cannons belching smoke and flame and heat.

"The HQ's over here," said Crown, heading off to the left. A sniper's bullet spit sand over his boondockers. He snorted. "And I just polished them for dress parade." This time the men did laugh. And just kept walking as if the brass had declared the area secured and all the snipers killed or captured.

The HQ was makeshift. One part was out in the open under a poncho rigged like an awning to keep off the blazing sun. The other part was a dugout. Colonel Shoup was under the poncho awning surrounded by Marines and war correspondents who were as dirty and grimy and sweaty as Billy and the men with him. One of the colonel's staff officers looked up from a map of Betio when Crown suddenly appeared at the command bunker. "Where the hell have you been, Skagway?"

"Fighting the damn war, Major Shark, Sir." Crown saluted. "I kinda got hooked up with K Company, 2nd Battalion, 2nd Marines, when I dropped off their mortar bombs. These guys with me are from the K's different platoons––X-Ray, Mike, Victor and Fox. We've been kicking butt, sir. I was pretty sure you wouldn't mind me doing that."

"No need to salute!" snapped Shark, returning the salute. "Where are you situated?"

"We're close to the airfield, Sir."

"The airfield! You'd have to have cut through a lot of jungle to get to the airfield, Skagway."

"Yes, Sir. We did that. And we took out every sniper, machine gun nest, pillbox and bunker we could find on the way."

"The hell you say."

"I was going to give the colonel some numbers," Crown explained, "but I lost count. Some of those buggers were dug in pretty deep, Sir. We threw everything at 'em. Flamethrower, Ma Deuce, grenades, the 81mm mortar. Sometimes that did the trick. But we had a Sherman tag along for a while, the Colorado, and later on there was another named Lucky Strike, and we thanked our lucky stars for those puppies, I tell you. They peeled quite a few onions for us, Sir. But a lot of it we had to do on our own without any support. So, we just did whatever we needed to do."

"How many pillboxes?" Shark wanted to know. "How many machine-gun nests?"

"Dozens, sir. It wasn't just K Company. The Second was everywhere, doing all the damage they could with all their companies. We knew the boys were getting shot up wading in from the reef. We did everything we could to knock the Japs out of the picture."

"I'll tell you something, Skagway. And it's no military secret. We might lose the farm, along with the feed, the livestock and every hired hand. The machine gun fire and the blasts from Tojo's big guns have been wiping out our reinforcements. It's a crapshoot whether we'll be able to hang onto this frigging island. But, by god, Jap fire is growing less and less. Our men aren't getting mowed down like they were a few hours ago. What's happening to all the Nip Nambus and pillboxes? The Navy will say it's their sixteen-inch shells. The Hellcats will say it's their strafing and bombing runs. I'll give the devils their due. But I'm listening to you and I know damn well it's the grunts who are stopping the slaughter. You boondockers are digging out those Jap gun emplacements toenail by toenail. What the hell are you doing here telling me all this? Is every hot damn Jap dead, and you got oceans of free time on your hands, Marine?"

"No, Sir. We're here for supplies. We need mortar bombs, belts of fifty cal and thirty cal, 30.06 cartridges, grenades, a fresh flamethrower tank, dried plasma, morphine, sulfa powder, water. We need it all, Sir."

"And you six mean to lug all that back on your own?"

"Have to, Sir. We couldn't spare any more men. The boys are in a hell of a fight, sir."

"Well, dammit, why didn't you tell me that five minutes ago instead of standing there jawing about the damn salmon run in friggin' Alaska?" Shark jumped up and slapped on his helmet. "This is the frigging tipping point, Marine. The hot damn frigging tipping point. And the battle needs to tip our way. I'm going to get you a couple of Willys to carry all the gear you need to win this fight, and I'm sending more armor up there too. Stop gold-bricking, Skagway. Get the hell back into it while we've got their yellow backs against the wall and they don't have a pot to piss in."

Crown grinned and saluted. "Aye, aye, Skipper!"

"And stop that saluting, dammit!"

Nothing much had amused Billy since he'd left New Zealand. If he survived the Tarawa Atoll, he sometimes wondered if anything would amuse him again. Major Shark, however, brought a smile to his face. Shark shouted and cussed and commanded and in less than half an hour one jeep was loaded with all the supplies with Billy at the wheel. A second jeep was crammed with the other five Marines, Crown at the wheel with Shark beside him. Two Stuart tanks, "hot off the damn press", led the way into the jungle. And they were the first to be hit.

A shell ripped apart the second Stuart in line. The jeep full of Marines was right behind it and Crown had to swerve off the track and bounce off a tree to avoid the blast. Billy was back of Crown's jeep. The concussion from the exploding tank knocked off Billy's M1 helmet, and the heat wave singed his hair and eyebrows. He was wearing the Rising Sun headband he'd taken off the Jap on the Alligator, and it took a scorching too. The report of the big Jap gun, which came immediately after the tank blew up, was loud. So loud Billy knew it was no mortar or field gun.

A few moments later, the lead tank sprang into the air and burst into blue and orange flames. Again, Billy's mind took in the crash of the Jap gun while he remained frozen in his jeep. He'd heard it before. When they'd taken out a blockhouse. It was the sound of a 140mm coastal defense gun. Then he thought: *The guys in both tanks are frying.* On top of that, it came to him: *We're all going to fry.* And he was out of the jeep and running hard.

He jerked the fresh flame thrower out of the back and took it with him, tugging the straps over his shoulders as he raced past the first jeep, its occupants all out and flat on the jungle floor. Predictably, Shark had the presence of mind to cuss: "Hot damn,

Marine, you're running right into their fire!" The Jap gun roared a third time, for which Billy whispered a prayer of thanks. The bright yellow flash showed him where the camouflaged blockhouse was. He also prayed their shot would miss. A quick glance back showed him the shell had landed about a hundred feet behind his jeep, but it hadn't knocked the Willys over. Their supplies remained intact. There would be no fourth shot from the 140mm naval gun.

Later, it was Shark who wondered out loud what the Jap gunners thought when they saw a Marine coming right at them, yelling his head off as he triggered a flamethrower, a Rising Sun *hachimaki* wrapped around the top of his head. A Japanese Imperial army *tanto* in its wooden scabbard, slapping off his thigh. Screaming *BANZAI* as a sheet of flame spewed from his hands right into the coastal gun and its crew. Hearing about it, Red O'Brien spat tobacco and called it "dumbass beginner's luck." But he didn't call luck what happened next.

Over two dozen soldiers poured out of the back of the blockhouse, shooting at the burning tanks, shooting at the two Willys jeeps, shooting at the Marines pushing themselves into the dirt, shooting at the wild *gaijin* who was still hollering *BANZAI*. He swept them with flame again and again. Not a shot touched him. Not a bullet grazed his skin. Several kicked up dirt around the Marines' heads, several thunked into the sides of the jeeps, many more cracked and splintered the coconut palms around the men. But Billy never felt the sting of one shot, even though Crown counted over a hundred bullet holes in the tree trunks, in the jeeps, and in the earth around the jeeps and the flattened Marines.

"The Japs were shooting into the flames," one man said. "It was like they were shooting into the sun. Shooting blind. That's the only explanation."

"The only explanation," growled Shark, "is sheer guts."

The blockhouse was burning. The jungle was burning. The

Japanese were burning. The stink of charred flesh and burnt hair filled Billy's nostrils. Some of it was his own. His eyebrows and eyelashes were gone. His face was seared. His hair was torched. His hands were black.

He said nothing after it was over. Just stood silently with the wand of the flamethrower white-knuckled in his fingers. It was still dribbling gobs of fire onto the ground. Smoke drifted up from his combat fatigues and his body.

"This is one hell of a thing, Marine," said Shark, the first man brave enough to approach Billy. "One hell of a thing. Why do you wear that Japanese headband, son? Is it some kind of religious belief you have? Is it for honor? Are you telling the Japs that you're just as much a warrior as they are? That you have just as much courage?"

Billy didn't lift his head, just continued to watch everything burn.

"It keeps the friggin' sweat out of my eyes," he said.

DAY 3—D-DAY + 2

NOVEMBER 22, 1943

13

THE DRAGON'S TEETH

BUD, THE CORPSMAN

I only had an hour of sleep last night. You'd think I would sleep the sleep of the dead, but my mind was awake and I dreamed... dreamed that I was Ulysses, back home on Ithaca, surveying my kingdom, doling out rewards and punishments, the Trojan war and all my travels behind me. My wife lay beside me, but she was not a fair-skinned princess of the Greek Isles, she was a bronze beauty with long dark hair who had never aged, her small skirt tied about her waist, her long legs strong, powerful, and her proud breasts bare to a tropical sun.

But her loveliness was not enough and in my dream I arose and took ship, for I could not rest from travel. I wanted to drain the cask of life to the lees, whatever the lees are. I am everyman who has traveled the seas; I have defeated the Cyclops; I have sailed my ship through the deadly straits, past Charybdis and the snapping jaws of Scylla.

I have seen the delight of battle on men's faces. I have heard the clash of sword on shield and felt the splintering of a spear in my hand. I thought the world was calling me, the places I have not been sang my name, and I have watched my men snatched from the deck in the jaws of the beast. I have sailed to the land of the dead and I am part of all that I have met, and it hurts, because I'm just a kid from Ritzville and I've seen more death and hell than any one man should ever see.

In a perfect world, I would never have left our little house on Jackson Street. I might be a television repairman, just to please my dad. On a day like this we'd be down by the big crossroads hunting pheasant in a burned-off wheat field lying alongside the stretch where 395 comes up through the flat dryness of the Inland Empire and marries I90. The cars stream by, bringing folks from Pendleton, Walla Walla, La Grande, Baker City, Seattle, Wenatchee, Spokane… The cars have kids in the backseat with snotty noses pressed against the window glass, the tiny world they left behind when they drove out-of-town past The Last Chance Café is now sliding away to distant horizons… as the wind furls the sails and the many-oared ship slips past the quay and points its bow toward the hell-hole islands of the central Pacific.

And then I am not Ulysses, but I am a suitor, trying to steal the heart of fair Penelope and the long- dead Ulysses comes among us, disguised as a beggar, and his hands bend the great bow of the long-gone king and the arrows sink into the hearts of the thieves that would steal his kingdom, and Telemachus is with him, but it's John Albert, and Ulysses spares me, and Ulysses is Johnny Strange and the scepter in his hand is not a scepter but a Browning Automatic Rifle and the isle is not fair Ithaca, but an island called Helen set like a crouching beast in the heart of a blood-red sea.

And then Ulysses hands the scepter to his son and now it is a Samurai sword and Penelope is Marjean, her lovely face smiling, for her king has returned… Telemachus orders me to kneel before him and the sword goes up and then I feel the bite of steel on my neck and I am seeking, seeking in the darkness for it is never too late to seek a newer world and I want to leave this place of death and return to the Happy Isles, to Tonga, to my own Pene-

lope who waits for her long-journeyed king on a white sand
beach, with the porpoises playing in the deep blue Solomon Sea
and then I'm on the *Hayes* off Cactus and the ghosts of Hotchkiss,
Malena, Sharples, McKeever, and Kramer are calling to me,
"Come on, Bud. We're over here. We're waiting to see you. Come
join us, death isn't so bad, it's better than what you got now. No
pain no fear, no worries, no guns, no bombs, no Japs, just the
silent sleep of dust. And see if you can find Kramer's arm on the
way in..."

"BUD!"

Sweet Jesus, what?

"Corpsman! Wake up, we're going in."

And I'm with Billy and Johnny in the land of the living and
Hotchkiss, Malena, Sharples, McKeever, and Kramer are bones,
the bones I will carry my whole life, and now there are new
bones—Pincher, Garrity, Shanks, "Big Band," and Harte, but
Harte isn't bones, he's ashes, just burnt ashes in the fire-pit of
Hell's Kitchen, and Sweet Jesus, how will I ever sleep again with
these bones and ashes, bones and ashes...

"Bud, dammit, wake up..."

I'm awake, but I can't shake the dream. Fire, death, screams...
Cassandra stands on the walls of Troy and begs the king of the
city to ignore the huge wooden horse. But the men of Troy throw
open the gates. "It's an offering to our gods. The Greeks have
fled." They roll it in. Inside the horse, Ulysses and the Greeks
wait, faces set like stone. Out of sight of the city, Agamemnon and
the fleet await the signal. Ulysses and his men clamber down
ropes from the belly of the horse.

'CORPSMAN!'

I run to the sound, the cry that means another man down.

For two days the Japs sowed death out in the lagoon. The
bullets from this place, the place the living call "the pocket,"
poured like angry wasps across the quiet waters, and men died in
rows. The burned out LVTs and the dead men bobbing in the

surf are silent witness to death dealt from this place. They killed us as we came ashore, as we lay in the burning tropical sun behind the seawall, as we made our way down the pier. They killed us in the night, running into our foxholes and stabbing us. They shot us from trees, from under rocks and from behind logs.

But they did not know they were sowing the Dragon's Teeth. For out of the death they dealt rose a mighty army, infused with the spirits of dead warriors. Now, here on Beach Red 1 and 2, the warriors that sprang from those teeth press forward. They open the gates of Troy and the waiting army pours in. Behind them, an army of the dead urge on the living. Malena, Sharples, McKeever, and Kramer—Pincher, Garrity, Shanks, "Big Band," and Harte. "Kill them Johnny, kill them Billy. Make them pay for every man who will never go home, make them pay for the bones rotting in the mud of Cactus, make them pay for the dead entombed in the waters of Pearl."

"CORPSMAN! CORPSMAN!"

Billy and Johnny press ahead of me. Crandall, Brown, Zarate, McGuire, Crown, Navarro, Skillet, Stoneroad, O'Brien—Fire, death, screams... If only the Japanese had listened to Cassandra, if only they had not opened the gates and let this mighty army into their kingdom. But now we are here, the soldiers of the Dragon's Teeth, and the spirits of the men we loved and fought beside are with us, and we come to return the death they gave us. They send out their Hectors, but we have Achilles—and we remember.

"CORPSMAN!" Again the cry!

But we are not afraid. We are not singing the Marine Hymn. We are singing the death song, and we are dealing death. BANG! BANG! Every time I hear Billy's 1903, I know another Jap has died. Death! Death! The deep cough of the BARS beats rhythm to the song. Death! Death! The chatter of Crandall's Thompson. Death! Death! O'Brien pulls the trigger, and the Zippo belches—Death! Death!

I feel a burning and I look down at my arm. There is a tear in

my sleeve and I'm bleeding. The little jerks tried to kill me! I'm
out here trying to keep men alive and the bastards are trying to
kill me. And a rage comes up in me and I no longer care about
the living. I want to see them dead, all of them. Stretched out in
rows with arms and legs blown off and faces gone. I look for a
gun, anything to kill them with.

"CORPSMAN! CORPSMAN!"

"Hey, Bud, you're bleeding!"

"I'm okay. Give me a gun!"

Someone hands me a gun and I kill. I see Japs running from
cover and I shoot them. I see them go down and a fierce joy rises
in me. The city of Troy is burning and I kill, kill, kill. I hear
Cassandra on the wall.

"Don't let them in, it's a trick."

But I am going in. I climb down from the horse. Ulysses
stands with me and he is grinning and then his skin falls away
and he is death, death on a pale horse and I ride the red horse of
war, and my sword sings in my hand and the people run screaming, for death has come among them at last and the city of Troy is
burning. The army of The Dragon's Teeth comes behind me—
Malena, Sharples, McKeever, and Kramer—Pincher, Garrity,
Shanks, "Big Band," and Harte. But now they are shouting at me,
their pale faces sad in death. "Kill them, Bud. Kill them."

And I remember my promise when I left Ritzville, and I stood
before that tough old sergeant in Spokane and looked him in
the eye.

"I'll do anything you want. I'll drive trucks, I'll load ships, I'll
cook, I'll... I'll be a medic. But I won't kill. No, Sir, I won't kill."

And now I am killing, killing. "Vengeance is mine," saith the
Lord. And I am his strong right hand and I am killing for the
Lord, and the Japs are screaming from the wall, "Don't let them
in, it's a trick," but we are inside the city and we are killing them
and then someone is standing before me and I know who it is.

It's Jesus...

He looks at me with eyes that contain the universe and he shakes his head.

"Bud, what are you doing?"

"I'm killing, Lord, killing your enemies. I'm killing for you, for your name's sake."

And his eyes grow sad, sad with the eons of sin and death that his great enemy sent upon this world and he says, "If your enemy smite you upon the cheek, do not smite him, but turn the other cheek. If your enemy is hungry, feed him; if he is thirsty, give him something to drink. In doing this you will heap burning coals of fire upon his head."

"But, Lord! I am heaping fire upon his head. I'm killing him."

"Life, Bud, not death."

"But Lord..."

"BUD, WAKE UP!

It's Johnny, and he's shaking me awake, and I try to clear the cobwebs from my aching head. Billy hands me a metal cup, and it's got something hot and brown in it and it's coffee, oh thank you, God, it's coffee.

"Get up, Bud, we gotta go. The Japs have made a stand in their headquarters. We got them surrounded—we are going to need you. This one is going to be a nightmare."

14

SAN JUAN HILL

JOHNNY STRANGE

"Holy Jesus, Mary and Joseph!" Brown spit a wad of tobacco, as he, Johnny and the rest of the squad lay prone behind a tangle of fallen palms and peered over the top of the logs. About fifty yards away stood an enormous structure.

Crandall clenched a cigar in his teeth. "The blasted Japs knew what they were doing when they built that. It's reinforced concrete, and the walls must be five feet thick. And they've banked sand all around it to protect the walls. We've sent rifles, tanks, and even 75mm self-propelled guns against it. We had the Hellcats bomb it twice, and there it stands. Crap! We have to get up on top."

It was D-Day + 2 on Betio. The hot tropical sun that was burning the faces of the Marines was also baking the hundreds of dead bodies scattered everywhere. With no time for burial details, the bodies were cooking in the tropical furnace. Men who had died on D-Day were now swollen beyond recognition, and the stink was inescapable. It soaked into Johnny's uniform and adhered to his body. Japs who had committed Hari-Kari now lay in distorted positions, their guts exploding out of their bodies like huge grotesque worms.

Johnny stared at the huge pillbox. With the banked sides, it reminded him of something. "Looks like we got our own San Juan Hill to charge up, Lieutenant."

"Yeah, Strange, but that's not the worst of it. Look over there."

Johnny's eyes followed the pointing finger. The afternoon sun glinted off the steel walls of a pillbox behind the bombproof. To the left was a coco-log emplacement. They were mutually supporting.

"Those positions have kept 2/8 and what's left of 3/8 pinned on the beach between the main pier and that little pier down the beach. We have to destroy them to get our guys moving again."

Brown grunted. "We got these and then there's 'The Pocket' over there between Beach Red 1 and 2. They've got Major Hays working on that one, but I think we'll have to go help him after we take this slimebag out."

There was movement behind them. Johnny looked around. A platoon from 1/10, the Weapons Company, was moving up to join them. Behind them a Sherman came rumbling through the debris accompanied by another platoon of mortar men.

Johnny grinned over at Billy. "Hey, it's Lieutenant Largey in *Colorado*. Now we're talking about a butt-kicking, Sniper."

Billy, quiet and grim as he always was in battle, gave Johnny the thumbs up. A Lieutenant scrambled up next to Crandall.

"I'm Alex Bonnyman. I brought my demolition guys to help you take that mother out."

Crandall grinned through his cigar. "Glad to have you, Lieutenant. What's the plan?"

Bonnyman looked over at the bombproof. "I want you to edge your guys up as close as you can and get a crossfire going into those ports. That will give me time to get my boys up on top. We can drop our charges down the ventilation shaft and flush them out. I need two hot shots to get up on that hill with me."

"Strange, Sniper, you're attached to demo for the next hour. Follow this guy wherever he goes."

"Sir, yes, Sir!"

Johnny grabbed Billy by the arm. "Stay close, Menno boy, and let's clean this puppy out. Watch your butt."

Billy finally grinned. "I don't have much of a butt left after they starved us on Cactus."

Bonnyman nodded. "Let's go, Marines."

Inch by inch, the Marines edged forward, rifles cracking, the BAR hammering away. A Jap appeared on top of the bombproof. CRACK! One shot from Sniper and the Jap tumbled down the hill, his face a mask of blood.

Bonnyman grinned. "That's good shootin', Marine."

Meanwhile, the mortar boys were shoving rounds at the other two emplacements. Stoneroad and skillet dropped one home and watched it arc over toward the big coco log emplacement. Right down the pipe! WHOOOMP!! A gigantic explosion shook the ground.

The Marines ducked and covered while debris rained down around them.

"Ammo dump!"

Johnny heard *Colorado* cranking to the left. Largey got in position and sent several shells crashing home. The last one took the roof off and four or five Japs ran out. The surrounding Gyrenes shot them to rag dolls.

Johnny and Billy followed Bonnyman to the mouth of the position and killed many of the defenders, but the Japs forced the team to withdraw to replenish its supply of ammunition and grenades. Bonnyman huddled the men.

"Okay, Strange and Sniper, I want you right beside me, putting bullets into every opening you can see. We are going back and blowing this baby."

Johnny and Billy kept close as they pushed the attack. Slowly, inch-by-inch and then yard-by-yard, they pressed up to the walls of the huge bunker.

"Follow me, boys," Bonnyman yelled as he began clambering

up the side of the structure, dragging a bag of satchel charges. Up, up, up and then, they were on the top. Bonnyman and his men began knocking the tops off the ventilation pipes. Then the grenades and the satchel charges went plummeting down into the darkness. BOOM! BOOOOM! Explosions rocked the fortress and like a wasp nest stirred with a stick, the back doors opened and over one hundred Japs came rushing out. They started up the sand sides.

"Over here, men!" Bonnyman stood on the forward edge of the roof, Johnny and Billy right beside him, firing into the mass of men.

Bonnyman turned. "More charges, bring me more…"

Shots rang out and Lieutenant Bonnyman dropped. The rest of the men rushed to the edge and flung grenades and satchels down into the mass of Japanese soldiers below. On and on they fought, men dropping on the roof, but more men dying below.

BANG! BANG! BANG! Shot after shot rang out from Billy's 1903. The 30 caliber slugs from Johnny's BAR ripped bodies apart. At last the Japs broke and ran back down, joining the hysterical Japanese erupting from the bunker's east and south exits, but more Marines were waiting, and they cut loose with rifles, machine guns, grenades and 37mm canister fire from the regimental artillery. Not one Jap survived the hellish crossfire.

Then it was quiet.

"CORPSMAN! CORPSMAN!"

Johnny saw Bud climbing up the hill. He swung over the side. Johnny was kneeling by the Lieutenant's side. Bud ran to Lieutenant Bonnyman's side and felt for a pulse, but Bonnyman was dead. He looked up and shook his head. Billy came and knelt down beside them.

"Gee, that's tough, Johnny. He was a real Marine."

"Come on, Sniper, Bud, let's get him off San Juan Hill so the demo boys can blow this dungheap up."

Together they lifted Bonnyman's body and carried it down the hill. At the bottom, the men of the demo squad and X-Ray platoon came to attention as they carried the body by.

"Present... Haaarmmms!" rang out, and every Marine lifted a slow salute.

THE WAY to the airfield was now clear and the 2/2 and 1/2 boys still on the beach began moving across the island toward the airfield. The rest of 2/8 and 3/8, the boys who had run into the murderous fire on the reef on D-Day crawled up out of their positions and pushed the perimeter toward the center of the Island and the airstrip. By the end of the day the Seabees were already driving their bulldozers onto the strip, still swept by Jap rifle fire, and leveling out the shell holes and miniature coral mountains.

At dusk, Crandall called his boys together and briefed them. "2/8 and 3/8 are across the Island to the south shore. Their fire is merging with 1/6, which is pushing its way up the south shore. It looks like we are almost done here. We still got the pocket between Red 1 and Red 2 to handle, but those Japs aren't going anywhere tonight, we got them boxed good, and I think the plan is to finish them tomorrow. One thing, though—scuttlebutt has it that the Japs are changing their tactics and coming out to fight. So I want everyone on the ball tonight. Buddy up and one guy awake at all times. We might get a banzai."

Johnny bolted a round home in the BAR. "I'm for that, Lieutenant. I haven't seen but a few hundred live Japs since we got here. There's a lot of them turning to dirt in their holes though."

Billy nodded and patted his 1903. "We are trying to make that happen to as many of them as we can."

Johnny saw Bud sitting a way off, with his head down. He walked over and sat down.

"Hey, Menno boy, whaddaya' know?"

Bud looked up, and he looked beat. "Lemme look at that shoulder, Johnny."

Johnny had forgotten all about the shoulder and as Bud pulled off his shirt, he realized that it was still sore, but it had not yet put him out of action. Bud looked him over.

"Geez Johnny, that wound would have put a lot of guys outta action, but good. Yours has sealed up, no bleeding and no swelling. Does it hurt?"

"Yeah, it's a little stiff, but I'm still functioning."

Bud glanced at Johnny's right shoulder. There was a small, lightning bolt-shaped scar in almost exactly the opposite place. "That's where you took the Jap bayonet for me on Cactus. You got a matching pair now."

Johnny grinned. "Yeah, well, that's enough for me, Bud. I got enough to show John Albert, and plenty of stories to tell."

Bud finished redoing the bandage and gave Johnny his shirt. "Just keep sulfa on it and keep it clean."

"Hey, Menno boy, you look pretty beat. You getting any sleep?"

"Not really. I had weird dreams last night, and I woke up tired when you boys dragged me over to the battle of the bunker."

"San Juan Hill? Yeah, that was something. I will remember that Lieutenant Bonnyman for the rest of my life. What did you dream about?"

"Nah, you don't want to hear it."

"Sure, break out one of those Chesterfields and tell me all about it."

"Okay, Johnny, but by the time we get off this piece of crap island you're going to owe me a carton."

"So, what's the dream about?"

Bud looked down. I dreamed I was Ulysses…"

"Not that junk again?"

"Come on, Strange, you said you wanted to hear the dream."

"Okay, okay. Sorry."

"Well, I was Ulysses, and I was inside the Trojan horse, you know the one the Greeks left outside Troy as a peace offering and then they sailed away. But they didn't actually sail away, and the Greeks were hiding inside the horse. But the stupid Trojans dragged the horse inside, even though one of the Trojan women who was a prophetess stood on the wall yelling at them to leave it alone and get back inside."

Johnny knit his brows. "You're right. That is weird."

"That's not the worst part. I was with Ulysses killing Trojans and they turned into Japs and one of the little scumbags shot me. I mean, I'm trying to keep people alive and he shoots me. It pissed me off, and I grabbed a gun and started killing."

Johnny looked at Bud.

"Yeah, yeah, I know Johnny—shocking to hear ol' Menno Bud talk about killing. But I was. I was shooting those little frogs like there was no tomorrow and then one of them turned around and it was Jesus."

"Jesus? That is weird."

"Well, he called me out for killing and reminded me I'm supposed to love my enemies."

Johnny saw that Bud was troubled. "Ha, ha, Bud. Love your enemies in Ritzville maybe, but not out here. You can put that 'love your enemies' junk where the sun don't shine."

Bud just shook his head. "I don't know, Johnny. If it's right in Ritzville, shouldn't it be right everywhere?"

Johnny stopped. For a moment the faces of Marjean and Jon Albert swam into his vision.

Do I want my boy to go through this—ever?

He shook his head. "You know, Bud, that's a good question, a good friggin' question. I don't know the answer and I don't think I ever will. And until they run these little yellow snakes to ground and stomp them flat, I think we can just put that one on hold."

15

TEN THOUSAND YEARS!

BILLY MARTENS

Corporal Billy Martens's head was in a fog.

As night rushed in––as it did so quickly in the South Pacific, nothing like the long sunlit evenings of Montana's spring and summer––he tried to flick his Zippo lighter. But his fingers would not do it, and his brain couldn't tell them how. After eight or nine tries, Billy gave up with a curse and left the cigarette in his mouth, unlit. He glanced around in the dusk. He scarcely knew where his squad was in the shell-shattered jungle. He saw Johnny, who was half-asleep. Billy wished he could sleep. All told, he figured he'd caught about ten hours from D-Day on Saturday morning to now, nightfall on Monday.

At least on Guadalcanal there'd been breaks from battle to battle. Tarawa was constant warfare with no end in sight. Day after frigging day. *Give up and die already,* he growled at the Japs. *There's nothing left to defend, but blown pillboxes, shell holes and the stumps of coconut trees. And your pals' scorched bodies rotting on the sand.*

He saw the burning bodies again. He'd aimed the flamethrower at the Japs running from their blockhouse. He'd turned every one of them into sticks of charcoal. Had that only been yesterday? Was yesterday Sunday? He fished for his Zippo again and flicked it, cupping his hand around the tiny flame so a sniper could not see it. The jungle, what was left of it, was still lousy with Nip snipers. Light out, he kept his hand curled around the glowing tip of his Camel as he smoked.

Billy thought about the blue and green flames licking the dead soldiers. He'd wondered out loud about the colors. Sergeant Zarate had told him it was the gases and chemicals in the human flesh. Just like certain trees burned with bright colors when they released substances locked in the wood and bark. Billy inhaled on his cigarette and remembered all the campfires in the Rockies with their different flames—red, green, purple, blue, yellow, orange, white. He'd probably associate corpses on fire with logs and branches on fire for the rest of his life. He shrugged and exhaled smoke from his nostrils. He felt nothing for the men he'd swept with death. They were just things that caught fire and threw up smoke and sparks.

"Okay, let's go, we're moving out." Zarate tapped Billy on the back. "Stub the cigarette, Corporal, and shake a leg."

"What?" Billy stared at Sergeant Zarate. "Now?"

"Now is a good time. K Company is reinforcing."

"Reinforcing who?"

"I'll send you a postcard." Zarate hurried into the torn-up jungle. "Get the boys to hustle."

Billy was slow to respond. Reinforce who for what? Did the brass really think the Japs were up to something? How many were left alive? A hundred? A hundred and fifty? He kept smoking.

"You coming to the party, Billy?" It was Johnny. Toting his BAR on his shoulder. "It's not far."

"Nothing's far on this godforsaken island."

"What's with you tonight?"

"Nothing that isn't up with me every night. I'm tired of the whole damn fight."

"Can't last much longer. There's nowhere for those buggers to go on this postage stamp except into the sea."

"Or straight at us." Wearily, Billy climbed to his feet. "Let's go kill something."

"You're lit."

"And I'm going to stay lit. So, if you don't want a Nip marksman to miss my cigarette and put a slug in your heart, take care how close you stand to me."

Johnny half-laughed. "Our good Mennonite boy."

"That's me."

"See, Menno Simons, here's the thing. You droop around like this and you wind up asking God, your soul and the whole damn universe questions about life and death and the price of corn in Nebraska. You've been made weak by war and fate. Remember that poem Bud is carting around? *Made weak by time and fate* is how it goes, if I remember right. I scribbled a few lines down and keep 'em in my pocket. Who'd believe it? Anyway, you go into your moods, Billy Boy, and kinda disappear inside your head. A recruit couldn't be blamed for thinking you're the last Marine he'd want as his non-com or to have his back in a firefight."

Johnny stuffed some Red Man in his mouth, something Billy had never seen him use before. "The truth, of course, is something else again. We heard about Banzai Billy. How you torched those Japs when you were with Major Shark and Crown, bringing up ammo and resupply. You crisped them. Came out of your stupor and gave 'em hell. Scuttlebutt has Shark putting you up for the Silver friggin' Star. If I didn't know better, I'd say, *Billy Martens? The preacher's son? He did that? Not a chance.* Because you crawled back into your hole and acted like you were the most docile creature on Helen. But I know better. You may feel weak and weary now. But you won't stay that way. Not when lives are at stake. Not my good Mennonite boy. No, sir. Bud saves Marines. So do you. Hell, maybe I do too, but it's not my intent. I just wanna pop the snake-eyed bastards. You kill 'em to keep the rest of us breathing. There's a difference. So, you know, our poem applies to you. The last lines."

Billy waited, unsure where Johnny was going with all this. It wasn't like him to ramble, and it gave Billy a bad feeling that a shitstorm was going to come down that night. Johnny spat a stream of tobacco juice. Then he cleared his throat as if he were going to deliver some kind of oration.

"Made weak by time and fate," he said, *"but strong in will to strive, to seek, to find, and not to yield."*

"What?" responded Billy.

"It's you, Billy Boy. You may be tired and sick of the whole damn war. But your will remains strong. You'll keep fighting, striving, seeking. Finding whatever it is you find each time you go into battle. And you won't yield. You'll never yield. I know it. God knows it. You know it too, even if you deny it." Johnny spat again. "Bud calls you Vulcan now behind your back since you lit those Nips up."

"All of your talk tonight is driving me crazy. Who or what the heck is Vulcan?"

"The Roman god of fire." More spit. "I expect we'll see Vulcan again tonight."

Billy shook off a shiver. "You won't see anything tonight, Johnny. The Nips are more worn out than I am. I saw at least twenty today that were blown to bits. They'd triggered their Arisaka 99s with their toes and shot their heads off. That's what they'll all do. Toe their triggers and end the war *hari-kari* style and make the Emperor proud. No Roman god of fire for you tonight, my friend. I was hoping I'd actually get six hours of sleep."

They came at four in the morning.

Billy had stayed awake till two. Then he'd drifted off. When he felt himself slipping, he enjoyed the sensation and let himself go. It was platoon commander Crandall's shout that jolted him awake ––"Flares! Gimme those friggin' flares!" ––and a frantic voice crackling over the platoon radio: "There's too many of them! We're overrun! Repeat! The enemy is overrunning our position!"

Billy stared into the blackness. Hundreds of yards ahead he saw the flash of light like the flash of a lightning storm. The ripping sound of rapid machine gun fire and the crash of mortars was the thunder. Flares popped green over shattered coconut palms. Hundreds of bodies were hurtling at them, waving swords and flags. They screamed.

"BANZAI! BANZAI!"

Johnny's BAR thumped. Then the Big Fifty, Ma Deuce, erupted, flame streaking from the muzzle, its huge tracers stitching the Japanese attackers. Tom Baker, Skillet, opened up with the 81mm mortar he called Pretty Boy. Paul Stoneroad feeding the tube with mortar bombs, Jesus Navarro and Sammy Crown squatting beside them, their Thompsons raking the Japanese attackers. Billy watched the enemy fall under the hail of bullets and disintegrate in the red fire of mortar explosions.

It made no difference. The other Japanese ran over the twisted and torn bodies and roared into the Marine lines, shooting and cutting and strangling, wrapping their hands around Marine throats and choking them to death as they shouted battle cries. Billy didn't get off more than a dozen rounds from his Thompson before an officer crashed into him, shrieking and swinging his samurai sword. Billy narrowly missed being disemboweled. The officer swung his sword again, his raging face freakish green in the light of the flares.

Billy's train of thought stopped. He just reacted. Seizing the officer's outstretched hand with the sword in it, he cracked the elbow backwards over his knee and snapped the arm in two. The man howled in pain. Billy plunged his Ka-Bar straight into the open mouth. Two more of the enemy jumped him. He wrestled with them, his helmet flying off, his *hachimaki* headband now obvious, and finally cracked their heads together with as much force as he could bring to bear, dazing both. He dispatched them with his Ka-Bar, swiftly slitting their throats. He severed arteries. Blood spurted into his eyes.

Wiping the back of his hand across his face, he yanked the sword from the officer's death grip, straightened, and swung it just in time to decapitate another hard-charging officer wielding the same curved sword. He kicked the man's head away as if it were a soccer ball. Then he waded into the swarm of Japanese attackers, screaming his own *BANZAI,* slashing open stomachs, slicing off arms, removing heads with single blows.

Three times, he swiped off two heads at once. He crossed swords with an officer, the metal of their blades clanging sharply above the grunts and screams of hand-to-hand combat going on all around them. Marines and Japanese were destroying one another. Billy destroyed too, getting under the officer's guard and sawing him in half with two strikes. A soldier kicked the sword out of Billy's fist, did a roundhouse and knocked Billy flat on his back, then pounced. He kneed Billy viciously between the legs and tightened his enormous hands about Billy's throat, bearing down with his body weight, thrusting huge thumbs into Billy's flesh, grinning with a kind of savage joy at besting his American enemy.

"I drink Maline blood," the soldier grunted through clenched teeth. "I drink it like sake. Soon I drink yours. You die, Maline. I kill you very good."

Billy tried to pry the man's meaty hands from his throat, but the soldier shook his head and pressed down harder. Small lights swirled in a black soup in Billy Martens's brain. A part of him remembered his knife. He groped for it and found it in its scabbard on his web belt. It was slick with blood. He could barely grasp it.

The soldier's threats in Japanese and English helped Billy remain conscious. He was listening to them. In order to do anything with the Ka-Bar, he was forced to grip it by the blade.

The razor edge sliced into his fingers and palm. He yelled in pain, a pain that broke through the blackness of the Japanese soldier's choke hold, and rammed the knife through his enemy's ear and into his brain. The soldier collapsed on top of Billy.

Billy lay under the corpse for a moment, catching his breath. He listened to the crack of Garands and Arisakas, the death rattle of Nambus and Tommy Earp's Fifty, the blast of grenades, the crunch of bones and necks breaking, the choking gasps of men being strangled. Then he shoved the body off him, found a Thompson with its stock chopped up from sword blows, and blazed away at close quarters, cutting several of the enemy in two. Once it ran empty, he threw it down and scooped up another, emptying it point blank into men's stomachs and faces.

He grasped a sword again, longer than the other *katanas* he'd used, immediately impaling an officer with a quick upward thrust. He felt nothing as he tugged the blade free of the man's flesh and bones, slicing the blade in a swift arc at another's head. It made no sense he should remember what banzai meant at the moment he made a fresh kill, but it popped into his mind just the same.

It was a greeting.

Ten thousand years of long life!

DAY 4 — D-DAY+3

NOVEMBER 23, 1943

16

SLAUGHTERHOUSE

THE CORPSMAN

The Japs kept coming and coming.

I couldn't get to most of our casualties. They were tangled under the feet of the men who were fighting. Marines hacked at Japanese with knives, bayonets, and gunstocks, shot them point blank in the face, rammed Thompson barrels into stomachs and fired entire magazines into their guts until intestines spewed out in shreds. The Japs beheaded with swords, seized Marines and ignited grenades that blew them both apart, stomped their boots into necks until bones and cartilage snapped, choked boys from Mississippi and Iowa and Texas to death with their bare hands.

I thought of ancient battlefield descriptions. Walking on corpses for two miles and never touching the ground. Blood to the stirrups. Body parts strewn to the four winds. Eyes. Tongues. Fingers. Feet. Kneecaps. Necks. Faces gone. Legs gone. Toenails gone. Ravens ready to descend and feast.

Naval shells from destroyers descended on the Jap formations. They had their distinctive howl. We were calling in fire from 75mm pack howitzers too. The air was filthy with dust and dirt, with bits of skin and the spray of blood. I spotted Sergeant

Brown of Titan squad sprawled at the edge of the melee, but closer to the swarms of Japs. I was sick and tired of not being able to do more. I grabbed my satchel and ran towards him.

No one paid any attention to me. They were busy massacring each other. Two dead Marines, chests shot away, and one dead Jap officer lay beside Brown. The Jap reeked of sáke. Stabbing, and the snapping of backs and the crushing of skulls went on less than a hundred feet away. Brown was barely conscious. His wound was a slash to the lower stomach. I hated any kind of stomach wound.

He whispered for water. He begged for water. I couldn't give him water. Not with his belly cut open. I unscrewed my canteen, splashed a thick piece of gauze and put it partway into his mouth to suck on. Then I cleaned and wrapped his cut, one eye on the butchering going on a stone's throw away. I'd already decided I'd use Brown's Colt 45 if they attacked me. I pulled it from his holster and tucked it into my web belt.

The pacifist letting them murder his patients wasn't going to happen in this war or any war I was in, conscience and theology be damned. It was one thing to talk about not using violence when the house was safe and warm. It was even one thing to crawl out and treat the wounded under normal battlefield conditions, however intense, or care for casualties after the fighting had moved on. It was something else to save a wounded man with a banzai slaughter going on off your right shoulder, the bloodlust up in the combatants, and every Marine being fair game for the Imperial Japanese Army.

I was surrounded by Japs now. They'd pushed our guys back. I was alone. I'd made up my mind I would defend my casualty with any means at my disposable. Praying that wouldn't mean my teeth, and my fists and an ugly level of savagery if Brown's pistol and Ka-Bar failed. But I would do it. Damn it to hell, I would do it. I wasn't going to lose Brown to a Jap bayonet or point-blank gunshot.

His bleeding had stopped. It was hard to tell how much he'd lost. Most had soaked into the jungle crud. I was going to throw him over my shoulders and make a run for it. Hoping that wouldn't make things worse. Hoping my legs would hold up. Hoping we wouldn't catch a Nambu burst or a Type 97 grenade or get cut down by our own troops. Who the hell even knew I was out here? They were too busy battling to stay alive to keep an eye open for their corpsman.

Maybe the Japs would have seen me and come after me. The Japs were pretty intent on breaking our line and were surging over the Marines to my right. But maybe one or two of them would have split off and come for my blood and for Brown's head. It was that kind of killing spree. I never had the chance to find out.

"BUD! GET THE HELL OUT OF THERE!"

It was Lt. Crandall screaming at the top of his lungs.

"GET AWAY FROM THE FRIGGING JAPS! WHAT ARE YOU DOING? THEY'RE DROPPING ARTILLERY ON YOU!"

My sweet God in heaven. The whole scramble of Japs wasn't more than seventy-five yards from our lines. Artillery? They were calling down artillery that close to our own men?

"RUN! RUN, GODDAMIT!" Crandall pumped his fist up and down. "GO! GO!"

I took off, Brown over one shoulder. Every yard was my life and Brown's. Bullets nicked the ground ahead of me. I heard the whistling at the same time as the first shell hit. The ground flew apart at my back. The shock wave made me stagger. But I kept running. There was another blast and another. Not big enough for naval guns. It was our 75mm pack howitzers. Rounds showered the Japs like hail. I was hammered with rock and stone and God knows what else. The jungle floor shook and heaved.

I fell. I got up. I fell a second time as the 75mm guns tore the banzai apart. The force from the blasts struck me like a typhoon. I struggled to my feet, clutching Brown to my back. Maybe I wouldn't make it. Maybe it was too much. I'd always thought I could handle anything. Ever since I was a teen. But this? Maybe not this.

The roar of the explosions made my head burst. Blood squirted from my nostrils. I could feel it running out of my ears. I dropped to both knees. The boy from Ritzville, Washington, who'd dreamed of seeing Orcas from his own boat one day, had nothing left to give. The 75mm shells fell and fell, and they did not stop.

Suddenly Marines were all over me. Zarate peeled Brown off my back with Crandall's help and Johnny had my left shoulder, Billy my right. They lifted me off the ground and lugged me the last twenty-five yards. "What the hell's gotten into you, Doc?" Johnny demanded. "You bucking for a posthumous Medal of Honor?"

The howitzers ripped the holy hell out of the Japs for another five minutes. When they were done, the banzai was done. The whole brawl hadn't lasted more than an hour. Scorched corpses lay in heaps for hundreds of yards. I was told later they counted out four hundred Nips or more. Zarate said it was a little less than four, but not by much. I spent a moment gazing at the smoke and dust and death.

I thought about Civil War Sherman, who we'd named our tanks after. *You might as well appeal against a thunderstorm as against these terrible hardships of war. War is cruelty. There is no use trying to reform it. The crueler it is, the sooner it will be over. War is hell.*

Stonewall Jackson came to mind too. Though we hadn't named anything after him, his cavalry commander, Jeb Stuart, got the nod for our light tank. *War means fighting. The business of the soldier is to fight. Armies are to find the enemy and strike him, to invade his country, and do him all possible damage in the shortest possible time. This will involve great destruction of life and property while it lasts. But such a war will of necessity be of brief continuance, and so would be an economy of life and property in the end.*

And there was his other thought. *My religious beliefs teach me to feel as safe in battle as in bed. God has fixed the time of my death. I do not concern myself with that, but to be always ready whenever it may overtake me. That is the way all men should live and all men would be equally brave.*

As for me, Bud the Bookworm, who was always reading everything military from the past—*The Iliad, The Odyssey,* William Tecumseh Sherman, Julius Caesar, *The History of the Rise and Fall of the Roman Empire* by Gibbon, *The Art of War* by Sun Tzu—I didn't know what I thought anymore about war and pacifism and faith and killing. I hated the destruction. I hated the body count. I hated seeing people maimed for life by bullets and bombs and shrapnel.

But suppose you let the enemy take over and rule you like a Hitler or Mussolini or a Tojo? Suppose you're a Jew and the Nazis are in charge? Or an Ethiopian facing Italian tanks with spears? A Spaniard getting massacred by Franco's fascists? Or torched by Nazi planes dropping incendiaries on your hometown of Guernica? Suppose Tojo shows up in China and Manchuria and says, "Rape. Murder. Pillage. Enslave." What do you do then? Go to church and pray and that's all? While people are being slaughtered by those who have no conscience and no mercy and no soul?

I joined the other corpsmen and helped get plasma going into all the wounded Marines. Including Brown. Once I was certain he'd stabilized, I got him and a bunch of others evacuated out to the ships and the surgeons. They patched him up. He made it. God alone knows why. Both of us should've been blown to bits.

Too many grunts were worried about me. Chewing an unlit cigar, Crandall passed me a chunk of his busted pocket mirror. Okay, yeah, I was butt ugly. Dried-up black blood in my ears and down both sides of my face. More of the same in my nostrils and goop that had run into my mouth. All kinds of cuts and abrasions and bruises that were purple or green or yellow, depending on how fresh they were or how much they'd healed. I soaked a rag and wiped my face clear.

Except for my beard. I was proud of my Tarawa beard. It was bigger and better and much darker than anyone else's in the platoon. But for Superman's. Tommy Earp on the Fifty. He looked like a gorilla. And liked it that way. Bumming cigars from Crandall, promising to pay him back in Japs killed, he decided he'd keep the look until the end of the war.

"The Nips can't grow beards worth a damn, so I'll terrify the *mochi* out of them," he laughed in his growly grunty way. "Maybe I'll be the new USMC poster boy. Get to go on USO tours with Meg Myles, and Jean Rogers and Betty Brosmer. Oh Dear God, Betty! 38-18-26! Marine Corps Heaven!"

Johnny stared at him, pale-eyed and smoking a Camel. "So, is that the pinup you keep folded in your pocket? The doll you BS everyone into thinking is your girl waiting for your victorious return?"

Earp flared. "What if it is? Dreaming of her keeps me alive and keeps me sane."

"Did you tell her that?"

"Damn right I did, Strange. Look closely, cupcake, and eat your heart out."

When Earp brought out his pinup, and unfolded it, beautiful penmanship covered the bottom left corner of the shot, and momma moon, the shot was stunning. The entire platoon crowded around to get an eyeful, Marines elbowing one another out of the way to improve their view. *To my Superman, Tommy Earp, big beautiful Marine! Thank you for fighting for your country and for me and keeping me safe! Love and kisses, big boy! Betty* (with an enormous heart she'd drawn in)

Triumphantly, Earp tucked the pinup back into the breast pocket of his fatigues. He gloated at the hang dog expressions most of us wore. All the guys wanted a knockout like that telling us we were big beautiful Marines. Of course, I had a knockout like that telling me I was a big beautiful Marine. But Earp flapping his pinup around just made missing her worse than it already was. I wanted her in my arms. It hurt like shrapnel biting deep into the skin.

Enjoying his moment in the sun, and our pain and suffering, Earp lit up the Cuban he'd begged off Crandall after the banzai, when he'd used his Fifty like the flail the Grim Reaper always toted around with him. To rub in the pinup that much more, he took a long, lazy draw on his stogie, still smirking, and blew a thick stream of smoke into our faces: "I sent Betty B the pic of me in my dress blues back at graduation in California. That's what got the hotcake drooling. You boys are shit out of luck. I'm her Marine, not any of you slobs, ha ha."

Well, yeah, but he was a slob too, Betty Brosmer or no Betty Brosmer. We all were. Beards, dirt, dried blood and four days of caked sweat. Johnny was a mess of scabs and scars and slashes, and his beard grew in ugly. Really. Even he admitted it. Of course, Johnny, being Johnny, didn't give a hoot how his beard grew in or how he looked. That had nothing to do with mowing down Japs with what he referred to as his Lucky BAR.

And Billy? He really was Banzai Billy now. The moniker was his for life. Or until the end of the war. Billy was nothing less than a Marine Samurai. He had his Rising Sun headband. And the long *katana* in its scabbard or *saya* he'd strapped to the pack on his back. He showed us how he could draw it out and use it in one swift move. Crandall and Rudebaker, King Company CO, allowed it was a weapon, not a souvenir, and let Billy keep using it in combat. Billy swore it was the most effective tool for hand-to-hand fighting, and no one disagreed. Johnny told me Billy had got into his Blood Mood during the banzai brawl and had seen him behead or gut at least a dozen Japs with different *katanas* he'd grabbed. This, the largest, which Zarate said was called an *odachi,* great sword, or *nodachi,* field sword, had a blade three feet long. Johnny had watched Billy skewer an officer with it.

Plus, Billy had put his Jap knife, his *tanto,* with its wooden *saya,* back on his web belt because he'd lost his Ka-Bar in some Nip's ribcage. Dressed like he was, leaving his helmet off so the enemy would see his *hachimaki* and be startled long enough for him to deal a death blow at close quarters, he looked more like a renegade from one of our Raider battalions. Especially with his evil beard. Though no beard looked as evil as mine. Except maybe Tommy Earp's. Though whether Betty Boop would like him that way over the clean-shaven Marine in the pic he'd mailed her, we may never know?

I didn't get to hang around the battlefield long and help with the casualties. At 0800, they ordered our company to provide support in a final "clear the jungle" operation. We moved out, all ammo'd up and C-rationed full. The sun was already too bright and too hot, and my head was too tight. I thought I'd seen enough slaughter on Guadalcanal. Now, after the butcher shop of a Jap banzai, I'd seen a long way past more than enough. I wanted an end to the bloodshed of Betio.

Since we'd landed on Saturday, four days before, there'd been a pocket of Jap resistance dug in between Red Beach 1 and Red Beach 2. It had never been dealt with. There'd been too much other fighting to do. Maybe we thought the Japs would just surrender when the rest of the island fell around them. It hadn't happened yet, but that didn't mean it wouldn't happen once they saw they were being encircled. It was my prayer as we tightened the noose. K Company moved in from the east, where we'd originally landed, between Red 2 and Red 3, and I kept looking for a white flag without a big, red, round sun on it.

But I should have saved my prayers.

The Japanese don't surrender.

17

JOHNNY IN THE POCKET—0700 D-DAY+3

JOHNNY STRANGE

Johnny checked his clips and felt for the grenades hanging in the pouch on his belt. He worked the BAR's action and snapped in a twenty-round clip. McGuire sat beside him, aping his motions.

"How long you been a BAR man, Johnny?"

"Since the day I hit the beach on Cactus. That's when I really started to appreciate this baby. Before that, it was just a gun." He lifted his BAR and studied it, looking for dirt or sand anywhere on it. He pulled a rag from his pocket and wiped a bit of debris from the sights.

"Yeah, somethin' about these BARs that give you genuine power, Bobby. I never met a Jap yet who could keep comin' when one of these mothers cut loose on them."

He looked over at McGuire, who had pulled a rag from his pocket and was wiping an imaginary bit of debris from his sight.

The kid wants to stay alive. He's smart.

"That's Julio's BAR. He's my friend and a great Marine. I hope he makes it. Don't go shaming him by throwing that down and running when the shit hits the fan."

McGuire shook his head and lifted his chin. "I ain't run yet, have I?"

"No, so far you done good. But over there..." Johnny pointed in the general direction of Red Beach 1... "over there is 'The Pocket.' The last of those rat bastards left alive on this island are there. From what I hear, they're the best the Japs have, and they are just waiting for us to dig them out."

Crandall came by, crouching low, with Zarate right behind him. "Okay, we're going with 1/8. Lock and load. The estimate is that there are about five hundred of the Banzai boys right in The Pocket. They are dug in good. But they are in for a surprise. We got some help coming." He checked his watch. "The show should start any minute."

Just then Johnny heard the roar of incoming planes. Looking up, he saw wave after wave of carrier fighters and bombers. The lead plane swooped down and cut loose with his 50 caliber, raking the ground in front of them. The rest of the planes followed right in at the tops of the shattered palms strafing The Pocket with withering fire. Johnny saw McGuire, pale-faced and crouching down as the merciless attack continued. He laughed.

"Keep a tight butt, kid, or you'll crap your pants. Here comes 1/10."

Colonel Rixey's pack howitzers had moved up and now they let loose with a thunderous barrage, bouncing shells up and down Helen's tail for fifteen minutes. Then there was a moment of silence.

SALVO! It was the Navy's turn and shells came rocketing in from the lagoon and from out on the open sea. Fifteen minutes of burning, roasting hell unleashed on the bastards who had cut 3/8 to ribbons on D-Day and 1/8 on D+1.

Johnny was screaming. "Kill them, kill them." Mountainous explosions rocked the island. They shredded trees that had survived the first three days of battle to toothpicks. The last scream of an incoming shell died away and there was a moment of awful silence.

From across the sand came the cry, "LET'S GO, MARINES!" 1/8 and the pickups from 2/2 moved forward. Beside them the engineers with flamethrowers and the two surviving Shermans on the island moved forward, light tanks and men with Bangalores following.

"Stick with me, kid," Johnny yelled at McGuire. "Just do what I do and you might live through this."

Fifty yards, 100 yards, 150 yards, little resistance. From isolated strong points—pillboxes, deep trenches, dugouts—the Japs fired back at the inexorable tide. A company-wide line started moving across the island. It was 200 yards before they hit the first real trouble. A series of supporting bomb-proofs faced them, and from the gun ports came the familiar cry, "Maline, you die!"

But the commanders didn't flinch. "Strange, get your BARs on that dugout, NOW!"

Johnny and his shadow pushed forward. There was a huge bunker ahead of them. Then the Japs inside broke from their cover. There was a narrow exit channel at the building's rear, and at least seventy-five Japs came boiling out. Hearing a familiar rumble, Johnny turned to see the *Colorado* moving up beside him. Johnny banged on the side and Lieutenant Largey stuck his head out.

Johnny pointed at the bunker and yelled. "Get 'em Lieutenant, they're getting away." Largey swung around, brought his .75 down and fired point blank at the packed exit.

McGuire watched wide-eyed as the bowling ball shot flattened the mass of Japs. "Holy crap, Johnny, will you look at that?"

Johnny heard Crandall yell. "Strange, get inside and check the place out."

He and McGuire moved to the entrance. "Cover me, Bobby, I'm going in." Johnny fired a burst through the door and scrambled inside. There was only a little light from the portholes and it took Johnny a minute to get adjusted to the light. He looked to the right and then to the left...

WHAM! Something hit him hard from behind and his BAR went skittering across the floor, followed by Johnny. Quick as a cat, he was on his feet. Out of the darkness came the biggest Jap he had ever seen. Dirt and blood covered the man, and he had a shit-eating grin on his face. "Want to pray with me, Maline?" The Jap grinned and kicked the door shut in McGuire's face.

Johnny looked at the Jap. The big man had no weapon in his hand, but he didn't need one. Somebody had been feeding this gorilla because the muscles rippled beneath his torn tunic and his legs looked like tree trunks coming out of his shorts. Johnny looked for his BAR. It was against the wall across the room. The Jap moved in like a panther and swept Johnny's feet. Johnny hit the deck and rolled to the side as the monster Jap leaped with both feet to finish him. Johnny was off the floor and on his feet.

"Wanna 'pray?' Sure shithead, I'll 'pray' with you."

Johnny closed in and hooked a left into the Jap's mouth that tore it to bloody shreds against his crooked teeth. He sent the payoff punch to the chin after it, but the Jap ducked it and took it over the eye instead, showering them both with blood. Johnny threw another left, but the Jap grabbed his hand, dropped to one knee and threw Johnny over his shoulder. He landed on his back and the wind went out of him, but the Jap hesitated just long enough to let Johnny roll away. Johnny could hear McGuire pounding on the door.

"Johnny! Johnny!"

The Jap closed in again, but Johnny let him have it with three machine-gun jabs that rocked the monster back. But the Jap just grinned and went for the leg sweep again. Then, in the dark of the bunker, Johnny heard Manny Escobedo's voice. "It's like this, kid. Every fighter has his own way of winning. If you know how he scraps, you can use it against him."

This guy knows Karate, but he doesn't know boxing. I gotta keep on my feet and don't let him get his hands on me. Stay away from him.

The brute closed in, but Johnny danced away. The big man tried to grab Johnny's arm to throw him, but Johnny slipped it and let the big man have it in the wind with two lightning blows. LEFT! RIGHT! The big Jap grunted and stepped back.

...Bastard doesn't like that!

The Jap came at him again, grinning through bloody teeth, and again Johnny let him have it in the wind. The big man's hands dropped and Johnny saw his chance. He let him have the left and then an enormous right that came all the way from New Zealand and took the Jap right on the point of his chin. The man stumbled back and went down. Johnny was on him like a tiger. LEFT! RIGHT! LEFT! RIGHT! He smashed his fists into the prostrate Jap's face and it turned to bloody mash. The Jap thrashed a few times, a spasmodic jerk, and then he was still. Johnny kept smashing. Everything that he had held inside since 1941 came rushing to the surface. The last conversation he had with his dad filled his brain like a throbbing machine.

"I'm joining the Marines, Dad. I'm going away to war. I've packed my bag and I'm outta' here. Tomorrow I'm getting on the bus down to the Recruiting Station in Idaho Falls and signing up. And you know what, Dad? I want them to teach me to kill. I want them to make me love it. And when they finish with me I hope they send me to the worst battles where there are thousands of Japs because when I get there I will shoot and stab and blow up every Jap I see. And when I've killed enough, and cut enough and blown enough Japs up and I'm hard inside, and unfeeling, I will come back to Bonners Ferry and find Harold Jenkins and beat him and cut him and stab him until he's just a rotting piece of meat. So help me God."

Faces from his dreams filled his mind as he battered the big Jap beneath him. LEFT! RIGHT! JENKINS! LEFT! RIGHT! BENNETT! BLOODY RIDGE! AOLA BAY! BUD IN THE HUT!

SNIPER! KREMER! BIG BAND! SHANKS! CACTUS! DIE YOU BASTARD, DIE!

The door crashed open and McGuire was beside him, BAR at the ready. Johnny looked up, his face a mask of blood. He could see the horror in McGuire's eyes. He looked down at the Jap. The man's face had disappeared—as if Johnny had shot it off with a mortar. The bones of the nose disappeared into the monster Jap's brain. Gray matter mixed with blood and fluid oozed out of what was left.

"Johnny! Geezzus, Johnny!" McGuire laid a hand on Johnny's shoulder, but Johnny jerked away.

"DON'T TOUCH ME OR I'LL KILL YOU!"

"Okay, Johnny, okay." McGuire stepped back. Johnny looked at him and then something broke inside him as he stared at the dead Jap beneath him. A feeling like he was gonna puke jerked his guts and then he was sobbing—sobs racking his body and great groaning sounds breaking from his lips.

This is what it is. This is what I wanted. This is why I came...

McGuire's voice was softer. "It's okay, Johnny. It's okay. C'mon, buddy, we got to blow this place. Gotta get out. Let me help you."

Johnny took a deep breath and nodded. McGuire helped him to his feet. "Get my BAR, will you, Bobby?"

McGuire looked around, saw the BAR and hooked it over his shoulder. Then he put his arm around Johnny and led him toward the door. They walked out into the sun. Crandall, Zarate, Billy and Bud were standing there. They stared at Johnny.

"Shit oh dear, Strange." Crandall had a look of awe on his face.

"What the hell, Johnny, what the hell?" Billy came and stood beside him.

Bud nodded. "You okay, Johnny? What the hell happened in there?"

Johnny shook his head. "I found what I came here for, Bud, that's what happened. I found what I came here for."

18

THANKSGIVING DAY

BILLY MARTENS

Thursday, November 25, was Thanksgiving.

Billy smoked a Chesterfield and thought about roast elk in huckleberry sauce, bighorn sheep grilled with lemon slices and mint leaves, baked moose and blackberries, rose pips and wild mushroom stuffing. He even thought about barbecued Canada goose while the others jawed about turkeys raised in pens for slaughter. He contributed nothing to the conversation. Johnny rightly figured he'd gone back into his Montana cave again.

The squad, what was left of it, lay sprawled by the airfield. Bakar Zarate, Johnny Strange, Billy Martens, Tom "Skillet" Baker, Paul Stoneroad, and Jesus Navarro were all that remained of the original group that had landed together on Guadalcanal in 1942. Bud was another, embedded with the squad, even though he served all of K Company. Red O'Brien, a reinforcement on the Canal, was still with them. Sam "Batman" Kane, Tommy "Super-man" Earp and Sid "Superman Too" Greene, had all been attached to the squad on Guadalcanal, and they'd made it through. That was it. The only others were Tarawa replacements.

Sammy Crown, who they'd filched from headquarters, and Bobby McGuire, who took over the BAR from Julio Hernandez, wounded in action and recovering on one of the ships.

They were at the airfield because everywhere else on the island smelled worse. Especially the beachhead, where bloated corpses still bobbed in the water or were sinking into the sand. There was one plane on the field. An F6F Grumman Hellcat. It had landed the day before. The Seabees were bulldozing and grading and grooming the airstrip for heavy bombers.

There were still Japanese bodies scattered around the edges of the strip. Billy could see one about fifty yards away. The man's right hand was gone, and his chest. He'd done the *seppuku* thing, ritual suicide, holding onto a grenade until it detonated. That wasn't the first suicide Billy had seen where a grenade had been used. Their company CO, Captain Rudebaker, briefed his platoons that only one Jap officer had surrendered, along with sixteen soldiers. That was it. Out of a force reckoned at over thirty-five hundred troops. You died by naval fire or ground artillery, you died by Marine bullets and knives and flamethrowers, or you died by your own hand or your comrade's hand. There were no crocodiles here like there had been on Guadalcanal.

The grunts called it Hawkins' Airfield. After a Marine Lieutenant killed taking out pillboxes on the second day of fighting. Scuttlebutt had Hawkins getting the Medal of Honor. Billy watched a bulldozer while he spooned up his C-rations. They'd lucked on tins of M-units labelled *Meat and Spaghetti in Tomato Sauce*. Bud had scored cans for the entire company, the crates being mislabeled as medical supplies. Each man in the squad had three or four tins. They were cooking them over a small fire Jesus Navarro had lit using dried out coconut logs. The sweet smoke of the burning wood was heaven to Billy and the others. It masked the stench of rotting corpses that enveloped Betio like a cloud and had penetrated into their fatigues and under their fingernails and into their skin.

They all figured it was a pretty good Thanksgiving meal. No one ever got spaghetti in red sauce. Maybe the Navy boys and the flyers on the carriers enjoyed steak, and eggs, and gravy and beans. But Navy never sat down to spaghetti and meatballs. The squad felt like kings. The entire company did.

Bud had come up with B-units too. He never told anyone how he got his hands on them. These were the candy tins. Everyone got crackers and sugar tablets. Small cans inside the big can might give you instant coffee, a powdered lemon drink shot with vitamin C, or soup bouillon, also powdered. Then you'd get candy-coated peanuts, or candy-coated raisins, or *Charms* hard candy, or vanilla caramels or *Brach's* chocolate. All of this was way better than the D-ration chocolate bars that tasted like crap and were so hard you needed a round from a pack howitzer to break them up. A lot of horse trading went on once the squad opened their B-unit rations and found out what they had inside.

Billy craved soup and crackers. He wanted those items more than instant coffee or *Charms*. Zarate was happy to offer up his bouillon for Billy's coffee. Jesus wanted the chocolate. Sammy Crown wanted *Charms* and the lemon drink. Skillet had to have peanuts. Red O'Brien was into raisins and vanilla caramels. So was Sid Greene. They were forced to outbid one another to win caramels and raisins from Sam "Batman" Kane and Bobby McGuire. Tommy "Superman" Earp fought with Crown over *Charms* and with Zarate over coffee. Bud traded anything for M-tins of *Meat Stew with Beans* and *Meat Stew with Vegetables*. This went on for eight or nine minutes. Finally, everyone settled down, satisfied with their loot. Batman Kane grumbled that no one would give him spaghetti for his peanuts.

Everyone got chewing gum. If you smoked, you got cigarettes. You had a choice between *Craven A, Philip Morris, Player's* or *Wings*. Billy went for a brand he'd never smoked before—*Philip Morris*. Johnny decided on *Player's*. Skillet, *Wings*, Stoneroad, *Craven A*, Red O'Brien, *Player's*. Superman complained so much about not having a stogie that Bud went looking for Lt. Crandall and begged five cigars off him. Superman ate all the spaghetti he could hold, topped it off with several packages of *Charms,* then leaned back and lingered a full hour over his first Thanksgiving cigar, a Havana.

Others brewed coffee. Billy heated broth. The mood grew so relaxed––except for the ones who ate too much, too fast and got the runs––that Bud relented and tugged two bottles of medicinal brandy from his pack. He would not have any further use for it on Betio, so he encouraged the men to pass the bottles around. Johnny declared he was so touched by Bud's sacrifice for the common good he surrendered six bottles of sake he'd stashed away. He kept one for himself and let the others go. However, Billy noticed he only passed one bottle of brandy on and kept the other at his side. Which didn't matter. Everybody got buzzed enough without it.

Billy slept like a stone for over two hours by his watch. The only ones awake when he sat up at four in the afternoon were Bud and Johnny. The others were curled up around him. Both Johnny and Bud were smoking. Billy wasn't sure if he'd seen Bud take a cigarette before. They had tossed empty sake and brandy bottles and tin cans into the fire pit. They were all burnt black. Smoke was still curling up from the ashes.

"Got a headache?" asked Johnny.

"No," Billy responded. He did, but he had no intention of admitting that to Johnny Strange.

"The grave detail woke you up," Johnny informed him. "Not us."

Billy glanced to his left. About a hundred yards away, Marines were piling Jap corpses in a heap, far from the tree line. "They're going to light them up," Johnny said. "The Japs do a lot of cremation anyway." A jeep zipped past with dead Marines in the back. They went about two hundred yards and stopped where the

Seabees had scooped out a pit. Two Marines carried out the dead one at a time and lay them gently in the earth. Billy could see there were already other bodies laid out.

"A mass grave?" Billy asked out loud. "For our own?"

Johnny flipped his cigarette butt into the ashes. "They're doing it with care and respect. Whole squads and platoons were wiped out. A lot of their buddies aren't alive to dig them personal graves. We have to get the bodies underground or turn them into sparks or we're going to get disease. Those boys there will salute when the dozer comes to push earth over the grave. Before we leave this death trap, the brass will make sure there are a few ceremonies to honor the fallen. It's the best the Corps can do, Billy. You can smell the rot just like everyone else. I'll bet you they'll give us new uniforms on the troop transports and throw these into the sea."

"For the sake of argument," Billy replied, "the ships have laundry facilities. They can wash them."

Johnny shook his head and used his Zippo to get a fresh *Player's* going. "There are some things you can't wash out, Billy."

The jeep went back and forth a few more times. Then the Marines waved a dozer over. As it covered the grave, Billy got to his feet. Bud and Johnny hesitated a moment, then joined him, both a little unsteady. Billy tugged off his Rising Sun headband and stuffed it in a pocket. Then he saluted. Johnny and Bud saluted with him. The three of them held it for about three minutes until the dozer had finished. They held it while the Marines on grave detail came to attention and offered their salutes to the fallen.

The bulldozer rumbled back to the airstrip. The Marines got into their jeep and drove off. Bud and Johnny took their cue from Billy. Rugged and raw, bearded and scarred from blade cuts, grenade fragments, rough blasts and the near misses of Nambu and Arisaka 7.7x58mm bullets. They held their salutes another minute till all was quiet. Even the heavy equipment smoothing out the landing strip had paused, Billy saw, for a smoke break. He waited just that little bit more. Then dropped his salute slowly, so slowly. The others did the same.

Bud began to pray. "We've come from across the ocean. Lord God, we've come across many oceans and many seas. Not for money, and not for fame, and not for glory. There isn't money in this, few will remember who we were, and one day our deeds, however noble, or sacrificial, or patriotic, will go the way of dust and die with our generation and the generation that follows. I know it's an imperfect way to do it, with guns and knives and bombs, but still, Lord, we're trying to set our nation free. And not just our nation. Many nations. We're trying to set a world free. I'm sorry there's so much blood. Sorry there's so much death. Sorry so many we cared for have fallen. Sorry we hated so much and killed so many who opposed us. We just don't know any other way in a world so cruel and violent. We don't know any other way to stop the tyrants and murderers and invaders and destroyers. We only know how to meet blow for blow until we defeat the killers of mankind. If we just sit by, the innocent and helpless die. Millions are enslaved. Millions are tortured and executed. Millions are cut adrift from life and limb. If war is bad, bondage and mass slaughter of the unarmed and helpless is worse. Better the heroic fight, however savage, that finally brings the break of day, over the greater evil that brings an unending night. They think we will not fight. The despots and dictators and tormentors and persecutors think we are too weak to fight. That democracies and republics will not make a stand. But we will fight. We will die. We will give our lives. And we will win. Remember us, Lord. Remember the fallen and remember the living. Remember why we fight. Remember why we took up the sword. Remember our names. Remember us with mercy. Remember us with love. Remember us with honor. In Christ's strong name. Amen."

Johnny would never talk about the salute by the airfield on

Tarawa Atoll. He would never talk about Bud's prayer. He would never talk about the tears that cut through the grime on his face and slipped down his throat and across his neck and the skin over his heart. But Billy saw them when he opened his eyes at Bud's "amen." Johnny's eyes, dark with pain, met his. But they never talked about that either.

19

CHARON'S BARGE

THE CORPSMAN

I stand alone on the gloomy, barren shore, spear in hand—I read that somewhere and it fits my mood. But I don't have a spear, just a bagful of morphine syrettes. The garbage of war litters the beach—burned out Amtracs, packs, helmets, rifles, tanks that couldn't get over the seawall, and bodies—rotting bodies already sinking into the sand, merging once more with the dirt they sprang from. Out in the lagoon the transports wait, swaying to the Betio tango, locked in a slow-motion dance with the strange armless, legless, faceless human debris bobbing on the gentle waves, the awful flotsam and jetsam of war.

I watch the dance. Inside I'm cold, detached. It's only bodies —I've seen plenty. But outside my face is wet because I'm crying. Lieutenant Pincher, dead; Sergeant Garrity dead; Sergeant Shanks, dead; Corporal Lee, dead; Captain America, dead; "Big Band", dead—lips that once ripped out smokin' Harry James riffs shot away by a Nambu. Most of them are in the graveyard. It's larger now and barricaded by coconut logs to keep careless feet from disturbing the shades that rest there. But not Harte, he's not there; he's a pile of dirty ashes that's scattered all over the island by now. Not Shanks, at least not all of him because his head disappeared when a 50 caliber slug caught him in the face on D-Day.

There are heads and arms and legs and guts all over this tiny little piece of coral dirt. And forget about the Japs. The Seabees just dug pits, got a bulldozer, pushed the bloated dead Japs into the hole, dumped gasoline on them and lit them up. One guy laughed as the funeral pyre sent blackened pieces lifting into the hot, stinking air. "Hey, these bastards love cremation, so we're just helpin' them on their way to whatever heaven they think they're going to."

Dead people floating on the air like dying leaves in a Ritzville September.

I remember when we left Cactus, Billy and Johnny and I stood on the beach and cussed that god-forsaken toilet and laughed. But I'm not cussing or laughing today. We fought through all those months on Cactus and lived. Billy and Johnny and me got to New Zealand, and we were alive and we left New Zealand alive, in one piece. And the guys who didn't die on Cactus were with us. We came all the way to this little hump of coral, alive, and still fighting. Then Thantos bestirred himself, and came on a stinking wind as we waded through a hail of death and clambered onto this God-forsaken island, walking like marionettes across a reef that didn't have enough stinking water to cover it. And then we died. We died by the thousands.

Okay, some of us lived, but I don't know if we are the lucky ones. Ahead of me looms the blown up Jap headquarters and from the vast yawning hole in the side of that terrible bunker, I hear the voices of the dead, strange wailings and faint cries... The crowd of formless shades on the dark shores is larger now. The voices are strident. They gather around me. Kremer and Hotchkiss, Malena, Sharples, and McKeever, now Pincher and Garrity and Shanks and Hot Lips are there on the shore... Plucking hands, thin bodyless voices...

"Corpsman, Corpsman... come find me, I'm lost, I can't find my way..."

What are these pale ghosts to warriors that have slain Polyphemus, have climbed Circe's bloody hill, have stood before the gates of Troy and watched it burn to ashes? But I'm done. I can't face the dead anymore—anything but that.

An unfamiliar voice joins the chorus. "If you would see thy fair Kalasia once more, Ulysses, and see fair Ithaca shining in the dawn, you must seek the dead Tiresias in the land of the dead. There you will find what you seek."

Oh crap. Isn't this the land of the dead? The shades press around me.

Lieutenant Pincher comes. "Why did they choose this place, Bud? Why did we come so far just so the Japs could kill me? I had a wife, a kid..."

"I don't know, Lieutenant. Maybe it's the quickest way to Japan."

Garrity grins at me. "Who assigned this hell-hole to the 2nd Div, Bud? Why did they choose us? I wanted to live, and now I'm dead."

"The Brass, Sarge, you know, the Brass. Somebody had to do it, Sarge, somebody had to do the job and we drew the short straw."

Garrity spits and it's not tobacco, it's a bloody wad from lungs that an exploding grenade ripped to shreds. "Right, Bud, the Brass. Those lard-asses sit in their offices and send us into hell, and they don't give a damn. If you get back home, Bud you find them and tell them we didn't want to die, we didn't want to die..."

His voice trails into a horrible gurgle and then like smoke he is gone... The ghosts call and cry out. The howling of the formless... the inarticulate find utterance in the ether. The waves of weird and hopeless voices rise, fall, undulate, now loud and shrill, now sobbing into silence. Little eager whispers filled my ear...

"Bud?"

A hand touches my shoulder, but I pull away.

"Bud? Bud?"

I look up and it's Billy. Johnny is beside him. I reach out and touch him. He's real, solid, alive.

"Bud, are you okay, pal?"

"So many died, Billy, so many died. And what for? Did they have to die? Why, God, why?"

And now I'm crying, great sobs shake my soul, and I wonder if I will ever see the goodness of the Lord in the land of the living again…

THE 2,000-MILE TRIP to Hawaii is the epilogue to a horror story. It's like getting a letter that ripped you a new one and then ended with, "P.S. I'm not done with you yet." By D-Day+3 on Tarawa the stench of the dead bodies was so strong that guys would just vomit, walk along and just lean over and vomit, like it was a normal activity. The smell clung to our skin, our clothes, the sand, the trees, and it hung in the air, cooking in the blistering sun, a blanket of death. When we left Betio, it followed us. It fills the ship and sticks to the bulkheads. It's in the bunks and the sea breeze never pushes it away. They didn't have any clean uniforms for us, so we ride all that way in clothes that have blood and gore and pieces of our friends and dead Japs still clinging to the cloth. They disinfect the ships, but it just adds an awful new angle to the horrible stench of death. We all lost our gear in the shuffle, so we have nothing.

Every day they drop more Marines into the sea. Guys who were still alive when they evacuated them to the ships, but died from their wounds. Where did they get all the flags? Every day more flags wrapped around dead bodies, slipping into the sea. Charon's barge leaves a trail of death, like breadcrumbs marking our way back to Helen—as if we would ever want to find our way back to that God-forsaken lump of coral again.

This is the way, walk ye in it. Follow the breadcrumbs. The bodies of your friends will show you the way back to hell.

The sea birds circle, crying, but they can't feast on the flesh because they weigh the bodies down. Where did they get all the weights? Did they know this many were going to die? So much death.

———

AND THEN WE get to Hawaii. We nose into Pearl Harbor and for hours they unload the wounded, sending them to the hospitals. I see Julio on a stretcher, pale and drawn, and the blanket over him showed the outline of only one leg as they carry him toward the gangplank. I walk beside him. His hair is plastered to his head.

"Hey, Bud!" Lips cracked and his brown skin whiter than mine.

"Jeez, Julio, what happened?"

"Awww shit, Bud. The Jap machine gun opened me up good, tore the meat and the tendons and shattered the bone halfway up my thigh. They just couldn't sew it back up again, so they took it off. All the king's horses, right?" He grins, but his eyes are sad.

"That's the shits, Julio, I'm sorry."

"Don't have to be sorry, Bud. I'm a tough spic, I'll get by. I'll miss chasing those damn Apaches outta town though." He grins again, and a little piece of Julio shines through.

"I'll miss you, Gyrene. But you'll be going stateside."

"Yeah, stateside. Wonder what work the farmers around my town will have for a one-legged spic. Oh well, God knows."

"Yeah, God knows, Julio. Semper Fi, buddy. See you when I see you."

"Semper Fi, Bud. See you when I see you..."

And then he's gone down the gangplank and I think about that leg, just another breadcrumb marking the way back to Betio.

ONCE THE WOUNDED ARE OFF, the transport makes its way back out of the harbor and heads 200 miles south to Hawaii. We hoped that we would settle into a nice big camp with palm trees and *wahines* dancing the hula... you know, those slack-key guitars making that whiny Hawaiian music. No such frigging luck. They load us up in trucks and we go sixty-five miles over the worst road I was ever on. Up, up, winding up the side of two big black volcanoes until we hit this saddle right between them.

Hilo had been warm, but this place is as cold as Snoqualmie Pass in November. No palm trees, no *wahines,* just rangeland, barren, dry, cold as a witch's tit. Icy fog and mist, wind that cuts. When we climb out of the trucks, we find the camp area staked out with flags and sticks, but no friggin' camp. They have stacked the platforms for the tents in long rows, and the tents are still rolled up. No blankets, no fires, just barren land. And here we stand, with our tongues hanging out, shelter-less, raggedy-ass Marines—orphans, strangers in a strange land.

Johnny shuffles alongside me, Billy right behind him. "What in hell is this?" says Johnny. I look at him, and he looks at Billy, and then Billy starts laughing, laughing his ass off. And there we are—the three Menno boys, me laughing so hard I almost crap myself.

Three weeks of misery. In the day, we work in the chill rain and mist. By night we freeze under whatever shelter we can throw together. No blankets, no sleeping bags. When our regimental officers try to scrounge some blankets out of the Army warehouse, the little prick that runs the place politely declines our request. Fortunately, we had General Richardson over in Honolulu and our boys made a stink. Well, when he heard about it, he flew over personally and ripped that jerk a new one wide enough to drive the Colorado through. We got those blankets quick, I'll tell you. The camp rises and then the Seabee's roll into town. After that, things happen quick. When General Smith and his staff get back from Betio, the camp is almost done. Christmas this year will not be a good one, but we will survive. We survived Tarawa, and in honor of that little piss-hole of an island, we name the camp after her.

Camp Tarawa.

III

HAWAII

20

CHRISTMAS CARDS

Johnny Strange

Marjean Langston stood at the window of her father's house on School Street in Sandpoint, Idaho. It was the day before Christmas, 1943. Behind her she heard John Albert giggling as he tried to escape from his grandfather, a wild bear crawling after his grandson.

Marjean looked over at her son who was working his way down the couch, wobbling as he went, while her dad closed in on his hands and knees, emitting low growls as the little boy shrieked with glee.

He's been walking for three months. I wish Johnny could come home and see him.

Finally, her dad caught the boy, grabbed him up and squeezed him tight. Johnny was laughing and struggling, but Grandpa held him tight.

"Rowrr, I got you now, John Albert. I'll take you back to my cave and eat you up."

"No, Gippa; no gippa," the little boy clung to Dr. Langston, giggling.

"Okay then, John Albert, how about we go in the kitchen and get some bear food we can both eat?"

The little boy nodded and off they went.

Marjean's heart was full and empty at the same time. Her dad had fallen in love with little Johnny from the moment of birth, and she was so relieved that the little boy had a strong male figure around the house. But he needed his real dad, he needed Johnny at home. She often sat with her son and a picture of Johnny in his uniform.

"Daddy," she would say, pointing at the picture. "Dada," John Albert would say, pointing at the picture, but Marjean knew he had not made the connection. Only when a flesh and blood Johnny Strange walked through the door, would her life and her son's be complete.

Outside, the wet Idaho snow drifted down. It had been a harsh winter, and the streets were feet deep in drifts, unless the snowplows were out. The gray sky matched her mood.

What will happen to us, Lord? Will we ever be a family?

She watched as the mailman trudged down the street, bundled up in his blue winter mail carrier uniform. He went up to the next-door neighbor's porch and dropped some mail in the slot. She had been waiting for a letter from Johnny for weeks. His last letter had come from Wellington, New Zealand. It had been newsy, but distant. That was just before Halloween, and she had not heard since. She had not received a telegram either, but she was not Johnny's wife, so she doubted she would ever get one. But if something had happened...

... His friends would let me know...

Bob, the mailman, was approaching the porch. He looked up and saw Marjean standing in the window and smiled. He held up a letter! Marjean's heart leaped as she rushed to the door and flung it open.

"Hi, Marjean! I think you've been waiting for this." He handed her the letter and she glanced it over.

Marjean Langston, 2235 School Road, Sandpoint, ID.

She saw Johnny's name above the return address.

Hawaii, he's in Hawaii...

"Oh, thank you, Bob, thank you."

"Just doing my job, Marjean." But he nodded.

"Would you like a cup of coffee, Bob? I have a letter to send, and now that I have this, I can address it. You might as well come in and warm up, while I do."

Bob grinned. "Coffee sounds like heaven right now. It's colder than... well..." he grinned again... "well, it's cold."

Bob stomped his boots off on the mat and stepped inside.

"Cecelia, Cecelia!"

"Yes, Miss Marjean?" The Langston's maid, Cecelia, popped her head out of the kitchen door.

"Don't we have some hot coffee on the stove?"

"Sure do, Miss Marjean."

"Would you get Bob a cup while I run upstairs?"

"Sugar and cream, Mr. Bob?"

"You know how I like it, Cecelia." The postman set his bag down and stood, slapping his arms against his chest.

Marjean ran up the stairs. She went into her room and set the letter down next to the one she had waiting. She pulled out the last page and wrote a postscript under her signature.

P.S. I got your letter on Christmas Eve. Merry Christmas, Johnny, I love you.

The envelope had Johnny's name on it, but no address. She took up the pencil and copied the address on her letter. She put the letter in and licked the envelope. Then she set Johnny's letter against the mirror.

I'll read it when I can be alone.

She went back downstairs. "He's in Hawaii, Bob. He's safe."

Bob nodded. "I saw that. Our boys had a big scrap out on a

little island called Tarawa. They lost a lot of men. The stupid congressmen say that they lost too many, that the Marine commanders sacrificed them for an island they didn't need. Some of them are calling for investigations and lots of people are up in arms."

Marjean shook her head. "Yes, I've been reading about it in the papers." She didn't tell Bob how her heart had gone cold every time she read another story; how she was terrified that Johnny was hurt or even… "You'd think if the Marines could stand the dying, we civilians could stand to read about it."

Bob shook his head. "Civilians don't know nothing. I was in the Meuse–Argonne offensive. Our boys died by the thousands. The Germans killed or wounded over one million men at the Somme. A few thousand died on Tarawa, but most of them were Japanese, so I sure don't know what all the fuss is about. There's a story going around that the Marines made a 'reckless' assault and that the Marine Corps was too careless of its men. I don't believe that."

Cecelia brought a basket of hot doughnuts from the kitchen. "Just made these for Christmas, Mr. Bob, would you like one?"

The postman smiled and took one. "Will you marry me, Cecelia?"

The maid blushed beet red through her dark skin. "Oh, Mr. Bob."

Dr. Langston came down the stairs. "I put Johnny down for a nap. The bear wore him out." He saw the postman and stuck out his hand. "Hi, Bob."

Bob stuck the doughnut in his mouth and shook the doctor's hand. Everybody laughed.

"I read that Admiral Nimitz said we have knocked down the door to the Japanese homeland. The Japs have had it their way for a long time, but now we have a spear aimed right at their heart. My bet is that we move on the Marianas next, Saipan or

Tinian. And to heck with the naysayers. Our boys are doing the job they went for and I don't hear them complaining."

Bob finished his doughnut and gulped the last of the coffee. "Well, folks, I gotta get going. I have a lot of mail to deliver and some last-minute shopping to do. Oh, I almost forgot these." He handed Dr. Langston a handful of gaily colored envelopes.

"More Christmas cards from patients and friends. I'll put these on the mantle."

Marjean watched Bob as he walked back down the sidewalk and turned toward the next house. "I got a letter, Dad. From Johnny."

Dr. Langston leaned over and gave his lovely daughter a kiss. "Well, you better go read it. John Albert is asleep and I'm heading out to the kitchen to make sure nobody snuck any stinky cheese into those doughnuts."

Cecelia scowled. "Oh, Dr. Langston, I wouldn't put..." Then she saw the grin on his face. "Oh, you!"

They went into the kitchen and Marjean headed upstairs. She went into the room and shut the door behind her. She leaned against it, her heart pounding as she stared at the letter leaning up against the mirror.

What if he doesn't love me any more, what if he got wounded, what if, what if...

A verse popped into her thoughts.

Be anxious for nothing, but in all things, with thanksgiving, make known your needs and the peace of God which passeth all understanding will guard your heart and mind in Christ Jesus.

I am anxious, Lord. Would you help me? I need Johnny. And if I can't have him home, I need to know that he still loves me...

She walked to the dresser and picked up the letter, her heart in her throat. She sank down on the bed and opened it, her fingers trembling.

. . .

Dear Marjean,

I'm alive and I didn't get hurt, well not bad. I got a Jap bullet through my shoulder, but it was way up high and just went through. Bud patched me up. Now I have a scar to match the one I got on Cactus. (That's what we called Guadalcanal.) Billy's okay and Bud's okay. The three Menno Musketeers made it through again.

We are in Hawaii. I'm sorry it took so long to write. We came back from our last fight at the end of November. When we got here, they trucked us up the mountain and dropped us off in the middle of nowhere. We had to build our camp before we could take some R&R. But now we're settled in, and I had time to write. I hope this gets to you before Christmas.

Thank you so much for the picture of little John Albert. I got it before we left New Zealand. My gosh, he's getting big. And walking and talking, too. I wish I could be there to see it. But I promise you this, Marjean. I will be there for our next baby and our next one after that. And that's what I wanted to say.

When I was out on Helen, the island we fought on, I had to come face to face with some things that have been bothering me for a long time. I can't talk about it in the letter, but I'm hoping that when I get home, I can tell you about my life and some bad things that happened to me, when we are face to face.

I have a lot of hate in me, and I used that hate to keep me going. That hate made me into Johnny Strange, Jap killer, Tojo's Terror. Killing Japs kept me going. It made me feel like a man, because there were some things that made me feel not so much like one. I know that sounds confusing, but one day, I'll tell you.

Well anyway, out on Helen, I had to kill a man with my bare hands. I know that sounds awful, but when you are in a battle fighting for your life, you do whatever it takes to live. Because I want to live. I want to live so much. Every letter I get from you tells me how much you love me. At first I didn't believe it could be real, but then I see your picture and I see the love in your eyes and I know it's for me. And when I killed that man it was like all the hate that had been twisting me up *inside kind of unwound a little and suddenly there was room for some love. I never wanted to love anybody because I knew nobody loved me. But when I looked down at that guy, I realized that I had been going about this all wrong.*

Bud said it to me one time, and I think I'm getting it. He said hate gives me a reason to live. But it's stretching me so thin one day I'll just disappear. Then he asked me to think about something. Something new. He reminded me you and little Johnny are waiting for me and I have a long journey to get there, filled with a bunch of danger and lots of Japs—Japs who want to keep me from ever getting home. And those Japs don't want to just kill me, Marjean; they want to kill you, and little Johnny and everybody who doesn't kiss the ass of their emperor. Bud said we're here to do one thing—kill Japs. He said in a perfect world Jesus would have it otherwise, but it's not a perfect world and I have to make sure I get home. The way home for me is over and through the bodies of the Japs. But I shouldn't think about the bad things that happened when I'm killing them, that's death. He said I should think about you and John, that's life and that's what will make me a real man in the long run. Kill the Japs, kill them good, but do it to keep my family safe.

And I think I understand. It's you and little Johnny who make me real, who give me something to live for, not killing. And so I just have to ask you. Please never stop loving me. You are my rock, you're what I'm anchoring my soul and my life too. I will live, Marjean. I will live to come home. And one day you'll see me coming, and then our life will start. If I was a good writer, I could put down all the ways I love you, but I'm just me, Johnny Strange, and I'm better for knowing and loving you. I'll come home to you. I love you.

Johnny

MARJEAN LOOKED down at the letter and tears dropped from her eyes.

I know what happened to you, Johnny, and I understand. And I pray every day that you will come home to me. I love you so much...
Merry Christmas, Johnny Strange.

21

SILVER STAR

BILLY MARTENS

"Well done, Marine."

"Thank you, Sir."

"You gave the Japs hell."

"Aye, aye, skipper."

Billy thought back to sweeping Jap bunker rats with fuel as they fled their burning blockhouse. The roar from the flamethrower sounded like a powerful wind in his ears. The stink of the gas was in his nostrils along with the reek of burnt hair and skin on fire. The screams he refused to allow to the surface. But he saw the huge sheet of orange flame that spewed from the wand in his hand. He was death. He was Vulcan.

The Silver Star was pinned over his heart. Just as it had been pinned over his grandfather's heart twenty-six years before. Tarawa for Billy, Chateau-Thierry for his grandfather. He'd read about the battle that took place in France in 1918.

The Germans had broken through the lines of the French Sixth Army and reached the Marne River, less than fifty miles from Paris. Heavy machine gun fire from the Marines had kept the Germans at bay and covered the French retreat. A couple of days later the French troops and the Marines had counterattacked behind the explosive curtain of a creeping barrage. It had taken a fellow Marine on a visit to Montana to tell Billy what his grandfather had done to win the Silver Star –– wipe out two machine-gun nests single-handed and drag four wounded Marines to safety, including a high-ranking officer.

The Purple Heart had come four months later at Blanc Mont Ridge, when American forces had driven the German Army from Champagne. By then, only weeks before the end of the war, Billy's grandfather had been assigned to the Sixth Machine Gun Battalion, 4th Brigade, 2nd Division of the United States Marines. The 2nd Division! A sniper had almost taken the young Marine's head off. But here was the grandson today, sporting a Silver Star, and part of the same division in the same Marine Corps. Billy felt like it was all too real to be real. He saw Johnny staring at the Purple Heart they'd pinned on Johnny's chest. No jokes, no snide remarks, no contempt. The medal meant something to Johnny, too.

Billy fell out with the others. He unpinned the Silver Star and turned it over in his hand. *For gallantry in action. William T. Martens.* He took his grandfather's out of his pocket. *For gallantry in action. David J. Martens.* Billy smiled and shook his head. God did strange things with families and war and history sometimes. Some very strange things.

He jerked his head up when he saw Johnny take off at a run. Johnny Strange never ran for anyone or any orders unless he was in combat. He watched Johnny stop in front of an elderly Hawaiian gentleman in a pale blue suit and dark tie. The man had been standing with invited guests from nearby Waimea and Hilo. Johnny actually gave him a short, quick bow, Japanese style. Billy couldn't believe what he was seeing. The two men spoke intensely for a few minutes. Then Johnny glanced around, spotted Billy, and waved him over. Johnny was pretty excited.

"Billy, this is Mr. Kimura," Johnny gushed. "He used to live in the States and his son Mas and I were great friends. They moved to Hawaii, and I wrote them a few times. Now Mas is with the 100th Infantry Battalion. They've been fighting in Italy. Japanese-American kids from Hawaii, Billy. Fighting for America and laying a licking on the Nazis."

Billy took the man's hand and bowed slightly too, though he didn't know why. "It's a pleasure to meet you, Sir, though I have to confess I don't know much about the 100th. They were at Monte Cassino, weren't they?"

The man nodded and smiled. "Yes."

"I was telling him," Johnny said, "that they never let us off the base, or I'd have driven to Hilo to visit him and his wife."

"I received the invitation to attend the medal ceremony," Mr. Kimura told them. "I saw John's name listed as one of the recipients. Of course, it was necessary I be here. We are proud of everything you Marines have done in the South Pacific. Japan has no time to attack us again because they are too busy with you."

"Do you know where Mas is now, Sir?" asked Johnny.

"I know where he was. In Salerno, last fall. Then the 100th began fighting at the Benedictine monastery in January. Monte Cassino. Casualties were high. But my son wrote after they were finally pulled off the line, so we knew he had survived. They began calling them The Purple Heart Battalion at Cassino. Their motto is "Go for Broke". Our boys were sent to Anzio in March. That is where they are fighting now."

Billy smiled. "That's really their motto, sir?"

"Yes. They have a bone in their teeth. Something to prove. So many of our people are interned in America. We will show the United States who we truly are. There is another Nisei unit now. The 442nd. It left Hampton Roads a week ago on the first of May. I expect they are headed for Italy. Where else would they go? Most of them are Hawaiian, just like the 100th. Many volunteered for the 442nd from here. But we were never interned. Not so many volunteered from the mainland of the United States. The mainland Nisei are furious about being caged like animals along with their families. Are Italian-Americans or German-Americans interned? But the 100th have already proven Japanese-Americans will fight for their country. For Hawaii and for America. And die."

Their conversation was interrupted.

"Excuse me, Corporal Martens," a private said, saluting. "Your CO wants to see you."

"Captain Rudebaker? What for?"

"I don't know, Corporal. He's waiting in that tent over there." The private turned to Johnny. "He wants to see you as well. You are Private Strange, aren't you?"

"Last time I looked at my dog tags." Johnny turned and apologized to Mr. Kimura. "I'm sorry, Sir. I would love to talk with you some more."

"Go and do your duty. I will be here another hour. Perhaps you will be free before I return to Hilo."

"It was a pleasure meeting you, Mr. Kimura," said Billy.

Mr. Kimura bowed his head. "You earned the Silver Star at Tarawa. The pleasure is mine. No. The honor."

RUDEBAKER WAS SITTING BACK behind a beaten-up desk smoking a cigar. "A Cuban from Lt. Crandall." He returned their salutes, blew out a stream of smoke and told them to stand easy. No one else was in the tent. He exhaled another white cloud, his sharp blue eyes continuing to examine the two young Marines. "Congratulations on your medals. What I have to say doesn't leave here. Understood? Any breach and you'll find yourselves in the brig until we ship out for Island X. Now, tell me, what are your thoughts about Island X?"

Johnny shrugged. "There are a couple of dog-eared maps of the South Pacific going the rounds, Sir. I probably won't get the names right, but some say a place called, umm…, Iwo Jima?"

"Why Iwo Jima?"

"Well, scuttlebutt has that it's a volcanic island. And Big Island here is full of volcanoes. Including the two right by our base. Like Buster Brown, you make us run up and down every morning with full pack, Sir."

Rudebaker smiled. "Hmm. Any other guesses?"

Billy spoke up. "The cane fields, Sir."

"What about the cane fields, Corporal?"

"That says jungle to me. Fields, not volcanic cones. You make us do war games in those cane fields all the time."

"So?" prodded Rudebaker.

"So, from what we can pick up from the locals, some of whom have been on a lot of the islands between here and Japan, I'm thinking Palau. Or Guam. Saipan. Maybe you'll jump high and take us to Okinawa or Amami-o-Jima or Sakishima."

Rudekbaker puffed. "Want some advice, Marine? Don't think too much."

"Aye aye, skipper," Billy responded.

"You'll find out soon enough. Sooner than you want. But I didn't bring you here to play Name My Island. I'll make it short and sweet because I know you both have a rodeo to get to. Private Strange, we're going in with Windtalkers this trip. I'm assigning you to work with them. Two Navajo boys from the Southwest. Their communication skills will be critical to our mission. Absolutely critical. You will help them do their job. You will keep them alive."

"You mean I'm going to be some sort of glorified babysitter, Sir?"

"Belay that, Marine. You'll still be with Company K and your own platoon and, believe me, you won't be hanging back. You'll be in the thick of it. You'll save lives if you protect the Windtalkers. The Japs won't understand their language. It's too complex. They'll listen in on our communications, but they'll still be in left field. They will try to capture one and torture the words out of them. The Navajo can't be captured, private. And they can't be killed. I'm giving you this assignment because you know how to fight, no holds barred. So, I need you to fight for the two Navajo Marines that will be embedded with our men. By fighting for them, you'll be fighting for the entire division. Understood?"

"Yes, Sir."

"Understood, Private Strange?"

"Aye aye, skipper!"

"Don't let me down. You'll meet the Windtalkers in a couple of days and go through some training with them." Rudebaker set down his cigar on the edge of the desk. Several black burn marks from other cigars and cigarettes were obvious. He spent a moment looking at Billy. "A Silver Star, Corporal."

"Yes, Sir."

"Just like your grandfather."

"Yes, Sir."

Rudebaker drummed his fingers on the desktop. "I'm not going to name the tribe, Corporal Martens. Not yet. But we have been in contact with a small resistance movement on one of the islands the Japs occupy. It's our target island. They'll be crucial to our mission, like the Navajo are. They know every foot of Island X, they know where the enemy's strongholds are, and they'll guide us where we need to go. They hate the Japs. They're perfect allies. Except."

Billy waited. "Except, Sir?"

"They're a rough-and-ready bunch, Corporal. They've been cutting Jap throats and breaking Jap necks for years. With their bare hands. I'm not kidding. Their men are exceptionally strong and exceptionally ruthless. So are their women. In fact, the leader of these guerillas is a woman. Six-foot-forever and incredibly formidable by all reports. The Japanese call her *Yamata-no-orochi.* Or just *Orochi. Orochi* is old Japanese for *great snake.* The *Yamata* part refers to an ancient legend about an enormous serpent, huge beyond imagining, that had eight tails and eight heads, ruby red eyes, and a stomach dripping with human blood. Trees grew on its back, cypress and pine, and it was so big it covered eight valleys and eight hills."

Rudebaker stopped. Billy and Johnny waited.

"There's your lesson in Nip culture for the day," Rudebaker suddenly continued. "That's how much the Japanese fear her. They believe she entwines herself around her victim's bodies and slowly and savagely crushes them to death. Like a python or boa. And that she enjoys meting out this kind of death, using no weapons but her own strength and guile. She has let soldiers escape just so they can spread panic by describing how she killed other soldiers and officers. Apparently, she specializes in officers. The Japs have put out rewards for her capture or death. Hoping to tempt the islanders. But no one will turn her in."

"What am I supposed to do with her, Captain?" asked Billy. "Lasso her?"

"We need her men. And her women. You will be embedded with their force. So will Private Strange and the Windtalkers. And the guerillas will be embedded with Platoon X-Ray and show K Company where to strike. You will work directly with the woman, Corporal. Code name Serpent. Not much of a code name. The Japs will figure out who that is right away. But we want them to. We want them to be afraid."

"Umm, when do I meet this... Serpent, Sir?"

"Sooner than you think, corporal. We plucked her off Island X by sub almost two months back. Pearl has been pumping her for intel and getting her to draw maps. She'll be going back in when we hit the beaches. There's just the one hitch."

"What's that, sir?" asked Billy.

"She has to approve of you. She studied in the States when she was younger and thinks American men are soft. Her plan was to wrestle you and find out how tough you were. We managed to spare you that possible humiliation. She will be at the rodeo this afternoon. You won't recognize her. She'll look like a man. But if you do well on the steers, I imagine she'll give you the thumbs up.

If not, we'll have to find someone else to work with her. This isn't so odd, is it, Corporal? You must have some rough-and-ready Montana cowgirls in your neck of the woods, am I right? An Annie Oakley or a Big Nose Kate?"

"Yes, Sir, we have gals who can outride and out shoot a good many cowboys. They put up hay faster and rope better. And at the state fair, they can more than hold their own in the wrestling ring or taking on broncs at the rodeo."

"Think of Serpent that way and I'm sure you'll make out fine."

The two Marines left the tent, shaking their heads.

"Holy crap," muttered Johnny, "holy crap."

Billy drew a steer called Volcano in Hawaiian, another whose name translated to Firestorm, and a third that was not a steer, but a bull, whose name was American — Crazy. Billy was sure he'd lose his seat on Crazy, but he hung on and the Marines cheered and whistled at his victory. He stood in the dust and looked up at the faces and knew one of them was Serpent. But all the faces looked the same.

That evening Rudebaker found Billy and offered him a Havana.

"You made the grade, cowboy," he said.

SHORELINES

THE CORPSMAN

*M*y love,

You can't imagine the joy I experienced when I finally received a letter from you.

Of course, I knew where you'd been. We all knew. We saw the terrible pictures of the bodies floating in the surf. I wanted to be brave. I told myself I would not cry. But no, I wept for days. The photographs of Tarawa broke my heart. I knew I would have to wait weeks and weeks before I would know if you were alive or dead.

It was very hard, my love. So very hard. If only I could say I had faith you were still with us. But I didn't know what to think. Instead of thinking too much, I worked harder and did double shifts. When I wished to pray, I went to the shore. The beach reminded me of you. Of us. I prayed, looking out over the ocean. It seemed to me to have no end. I knew the waters I touched with my fingers would soon reach you at your island and touch you there. You see? Even when I knew not a thing about your fate, I believed you were alive.

Your letter turned my night into day, as they say. Now you can make my joy complete by telling me that Tarawa was your last battle. That others will pick up the work now. That two islands were enough.

Yes? Can you tell me that? Please, please, tell me that if you can tell me anything.

You see my lips pressed against this paper. Your favorite shade of lipstick. Oh, ha ha, my American guy, I know lots of things about you that you don't know I know. I know what your favorite perfume is as well.

My love for you is a great burning inside.

Please be done with this war and come back to me.

Your forever girl,

Kalasia

My Kalasia,

I've been writing every week, but not sending them. I was waiting for yours. Thank God, it came today.

I love thinking about you on the New Zealand shoreline looking towards my island here.

Without saying too much, because I don't want the censors to cut my letter to ribbons, I have a seacoast too, but I'm not on it. I wish I were. But sometimes I can see it. I have a skyline instead. That's my shoreline to you.

Tarawa was a rough time. We were on the Canal for six months and we only fought on Tarawa four days, but it felt to me like Tarawa was a whole lot longer. I never slept. I can't remember grabbing much more than an hour here, an hour there, maybe three hours in total on any given day. There were so many casualties. But you know all that.

I'd like nothing better than to return to New Zealand. I'd like nothing better than to be where you are. But I'll never be done until the war is done. I can't leave the boys high and dry. I just can't. Sure, there are lots of other corpsmen. Maybe enough to take care of the islands to come, maybe not. But I have to be here, no matter what other corpsmen are available. I have to be with my platoon and my regiment. I have to take care of them. It's my responsibility.

The war can't last forever, Kalasia. But it's still with us.

So, our love will just have to outlast it.
Bud

MY LOVE

I have this picture of you looking out over the world.

You're in the sky and I'm on the sea.

So, fly to me, Mr. American Guy. I'm not that far, am I?

I keep myself busy. I read a lot. I read your Robinson Crusoe again. Though parts of the book are not to my liking anymore.

So, I've known you for two years now. But it feels like two hundred because so much has happened and we've gone through so much.

I pray for the Japanese to surrender.

I can only see this war with them getting worse and worse as you draw closer to Tokyo. But I pray anyway. Because who knows?

I love you, my Marine man. Come back to me.

You've done enough.

Kalasia

MY BEAUTIFUL BEAUTY,

Every letter from you is a gift from God.

I want to make you happy. But I can't tell you the things that I know will make you the happiest woman in New Zealand. For anyone in this war, it is the same. Most of us are in it till the end unless we get the million dollar wound. But I'm like the guy in our company who has three Purple Hearts. He could have shipped out to San Francisco or San Diego after Tarawa. Nope. He isn't going to let his buddies down. So, I've taped him up, and stitched him up, and glued him together, and him and his M1 Garand are still with us.

He is me. Or I am him. I have no interest in going back to the United States or going back to New Zealand if my buddies are still out there fighting the enemy. As much as I love you, I could never be at peace knowing I was with you while none of the other guys could be with their wives or girls. You'd hate having me around because I'd be so restless and irritable, always grabbing for the next newspaper, always hovering around the radio for another news flash. Even if I was working at the military hospital and saving lives, I'd be thinking about my platoon and how I wasn't there to save any of them. I'd be miserable and make you miserable too. I either come to you when the war is finished or I come to you in a pine box.

Bud

MY LOVE,

Please, please don't talk about pine boxes. Okay, my lovely Marine man? Honestly, I can't think about that, I refuse to think about that. Never again. Please.

I still want you to come back to me soon. War or no war. I love that you care about your men. But I want you to care about me too. They have lots of corpsmen who can see to their needs. There is only one corpsman who can see to mine.

Only one.

Love,

Kalasia

MY BEAUTY,

Perhaps a story from the Bible will help you understand.

You know Uriah the Hittite? A brave soldier in the army of King David? He was married to Bathsheba. So, you'll recall David slept with her. Committed adultery. She became pregnant with his child. David was desperate to make it look like it was Uriah's child. So, he gave Uriah a temporary leave from his combat duties and sent him home to be with Bathsheba. But Uriah would not do this. He told David his men were at war and camped in open country. How could he return home when they couldn't? Sit back and eat, and drink and make love to his wife?

David kept trying. He made Uriah have a meal with him and got the good soldier drunk. Still, Uriah had enough strength and honor not to return to his house. He slept at the entrance to David's palace in Jerusalem with David's servants. So, David sent Uriah back to the front with sealed orders for his commanding officer. David told Uriah's CO to put Uriah where the fighting was the most vicious. Then have the troops pull back and leave him exposed and make him a target. Uriah was on his own and easily overwhelmed by an enemy attack. An enemy banzai.

They cut him down, Kalasia. His own general betrayed him. His own king, his own president, betrayed him. But what I'm trying to say in talking about all this is that I'm Uriah. I can't go back to New Zealand and back to my girl when my men can't do the same. Don't you think they'd love to be under their own roofs again? Eating a good home-cooked meal, sleeping in their own beds, kissing their wives, or girlfriends, or their fiancee? Looking forward to Sunday church and a good football game in the afternoon?

Instead, they're going to be sleeping in the jungle with danger all around. Getting bayoneted, knifed, blown up and shot. "Corpsman!" they'll yell. "Corpsman!" They'll scream my name. "Bud! Where's Bud? I'm hit!" But Bud won't come. Because Bud is lying on a beach with his woman and eating a ham and cheese sandwich that he's washing down with lemonade. My wounded are dying of thirst and leaking blood into the sand, and I'm safe with my woman on a warm sunny beach in New Zealand.

I can't do that, Kalasia. I can't. I have to be with my boys until they're home safe. That's all there is to it.

You're going to have to understand.

I'm Uriah.

Love,

Your Marine

My love,

Please don't be angry with me. I'm just acting the way any woman would act.

I want you safe and sound and in my arms again.

I don't want your body bobbing in the surf at the edge of some sandy beach far away.

I don't want you buried in some mass grave on some island I've never heard of.

I want you here with me. I want you here with me for a hundred years.

Anyone in love would want that.

Just come back to me. Come back to me as soon as you can.

Please, my love.

Please.

I love you

KALASIA,

I'm not angry. Just not a very good letter writer. I come across crankier than I am.

I was hoping the censor would eliminate my stupidity. It's just that I love these guys.

I'd never say to their faces, Hey, I love you! They'd beat me up! Ha ha!

But I love them. Not the same way I love you. A love for a woman is a different thing. Just as the love of a mother for her son or a son for his mother is a different thing.

But what I feel for the boys is still love. We're brothers. Those who are still here after Guadalcanal and Tarawa are family now. We've been through hellfire and come out the other side. Not unscathed. The boys with peach fuzz on their cheeks at Tonga are long gone. I'm not sure where they all went. But the boy that was me said adios at Bloody Ridge on the Canal. I never saw him again. The guy I was left with was not a boy. And his hands were covered in blood.

Not blood he took from somebody else. That kind of thing was for the fighting Marines to deal with. But the blood was all over him just the same. He thought he could save everyone. Well, he couldn't even save half. That's the guy who took over from the kid who grew up during Prohibition reading about Al Capone, and Eliot Ness and a Chicago bursting with Tommy gun fire. Now he's got Tommy gun fire all around him, but it's no adventure the way it looked like it was in the '30s. This guy that took over from the kid is a man I have to say I don't know.

His heart is hard. It wasn't in 1941. But it's granite now.

I can glance at a wounded Marine, see it's no use, squeeze his shoulder or pat his back, and move onto the next without batting an eye. On the Canal, I might have shed a tear early on. But by the time that fight was over, my eyes were dry. Tarawa? Tarawa was Dante's Inferno. I only knew pain and loss on that shithole island. I never had enough gauze. Never enough syrettes of morphine. Never enough plasma. Never enough time. I swear to God I wouldn't have minded if the Japs had taken me out. But I lived just to watch others die.

I've got to make it up to the boys. Got to go with them to the next island. In my gut, I know it will be bad. Worse than Tarawa or Guadalcanal. All the more reason I need to be there. I want to save more of them this time. Send more of them home alive. Do a better job.

You have to let me do this, Kalasia. You have to love me and let me do this. You have to pray for me. For us. I need your strength. Without that strength, I fall. I know that. I can't do anything unless you believe in me.

Bud

THE RED ROAD

JOHNNY STRANGE

Johnny Strange looked at the two men in front of him. One was fairly tall for an Indian, about 5'7". He looked young, but strong. The other was older, short, his face already lined and burnt dark. Neither of them smiled at Johnny, but stood with impassive faces. They almost looked Japanese to Johnny, but different. High cheekbones, deep black eyes, powerful faces, lithe bodies. Johnny stepped forward with his hand out.

"Hi, fellas, I'm Johnny Strange. The Brass assigned me to show you the ropes and get you acclimatized to King Company."

Neither of the two men put their hands out to shake Johnny's. Johnny stared at them and lowered his hand. "What's the matter with you guys?"

The younger one scowled. "No like'um white man. Maybe we scalp'um." He put his hand on the hilt of his KA-Bar. The older man nodded. He pointed a stick he was holding in his hand at Johnny. "Me count'um coup first. Then you scalp'um."

Johnny stepped back and put his fists up. "Oh yeah? Well, you bastards don't look much different from the Japs I've been killing for two years. You want my scalp? You'll have to take it, but I wouldn't want to be in your shoes in about five minutes."

The two men looked at Johnny and then at each other, and then they both burst out laughing. The young guy put out his hand. "Damn, Strange, don't get your skivvies in a knot. We always spring our 'crazy Indian' bit on the white boys. Most of them crap their pants. You seem cut from sterner stuff. I'm George Atsa, and this is Fred Niyol." The two men laughed again and Johnny grinned.

"Yeah, good one. I'll just remember to keep you guys in front of me at all times in case you revert." He stuck his hand out and the two men shook it.

"C'mon fellas, let's go get some chow and you can fill me in."

The two men waited for Johnny, but he grinned. "Nope, after you. Like I said..."

The two Navajos grinned and went out the door, with Johnny right behind.

"So what's with this Wind-talker stuff, fellas?"

"Officially, they designate us Code talkers, Johnny. There are about five hundred of us in the Marines and the Army. We transmit coded messages by speaking in the Navajo tongue. The Japs don't have the faintest idea what we are saying and they don't have the brains to figure out that America has real Americans doing the talking."

"Real Americans?"

Fred grinned. "Well, we were there first."

Johnny shook his head. "Belay that shit, Fred. After surviving Cactus and Helen and two Purple Hearts, I think I paid my dues."

Both the Navajos nodded.

"They say your code talking is critical to the war effort."

George nodded. "Yeah, we had some of our boys on Tarawa

and they helped. If it hadn't been for the communications snafus and the crummy radios they gave us, our guys might have won that fight all by themselves."

"Yeah, well, we'll see what happens when we get into the next shitstorm. You boys may be tough, but you haven't met a little slant-eyed prick whose only goal in life is to die for the Emperor and take as many 'malines' with him as he can."

Fred spoke up. "I think you will find that we make the grade, Johnny."

"I hope so, fellas. I have my orders—to stick with you like stink on shit. You don't go anywhere without Johnny Strange and his BAR taggin' along. I can't let you get killed, and I can't let you get captured. That means if you don't pull your weight, I might have to shoot you."

George grinned again. Johnny already liked him.

"Not before I scalp you first, white boy."

Fred looked at Johnny for a long time. "Well, George, if Johnny is going to be our babysitter, I guess we will have to make him a tribal member so we won't have to tell the folks back home that we were nurse-maided by a white man."

George looked at Fred and then over at Johnny. "Yeah, that's the ticket. If Johnny-boy here can cut the mustard, we'll induct him into the tribe."

They both stood up. "Be at that big rock out behind the latrines at dawn."

"What if I don't show?"

"Then I guess we'll put in for a transfer. No sissy white boys in the Wind Talkers."

They turned to go. Fred turned back. "Wear your skivvies and a tee. No shoes. Oh, and no beer or meat before."

THE SUN WAS JUST SENDING its first rays over Mauna Kea when

Johnny showed up at the designated spot. George and Fred were waiting. They were both in what looked like loincloths and bare-chested. Each had small leather bags on lanyards around their necks. They nodded at Johnny but didn't speak. Fred motioned for Johnny to follow. After they had walked for a few minutes, they came to a dome built of dirt and sticks. It was about five feet high. There was a small entrance with a tarp over it. A fire burned in front of the dome. Beside it were three buckets of water and a pile of smooth stones. Several of the stones were in the fire.

"Tell him what's happening, George, while I prepare."

Fred turned away and faced the morning sun. He chanted in a low melodious voice. Johnny couldn't understand the words. He looked around.

"What's happening, George?"

George answered. "Niyol is a shaman, a medicine man of our tribe. Our tribe has great respect for him. It is my honor to travel this road with him, to fight for our country. Out here he is Fred Niyol but back home in the Four Corners he is just Niyol, the Wind. I am Atsa, which means Eagle. He is preparing us for the sweat lodge ritual."

"Yeah, I know what that is. My friend, Mas Kimura, was very big on steam baths. I did a couple with him."

"Well, this is more than a steam bath, Johnny. Ceremonies of the sweat lodge include rites of preparation, prayer, and purifica-tion. The 'sweat' is an important spiritual tradition for us and is something that defines our identity as a people and a tribe. It brings about personal and tribal healing. It is said that those who undergo the sweat lodge ceremony together become relatives. That's why we invited you."

"What's he saying, George... Atsa?" Johnny whispered.

"I will repeat it for you, so you know what's up."

George closed his eyes and whispered.

"Grandfather, Mysterious One,

We search for you along this great red road you have set
us on.

Sky Father Tunkashila, we thank you for this world.

We thank you for our own existence.

We ask only for your blessing, and for your instruction.

Grandfather, sacred one, put our feet on the holy path that
leads to you,

and give us the strength and the will to lead ourselves and our
children

past the darkness, we have entered.

Teach us to heal ourselves, to heal each other, and to heal
the world.

Let us begin this very day, this very hour,

the great healing to come.

Let us walk the Red Road in peace."

Johnny nodded. "That's a good prayer, George, a good prayer."

"Yeah, when Fred got here, he had a vision. The Wind told
him we would meet a 'strange' one. So he built this sweat lodge in
preparation. Then The Wind sent you to us. So we will go into
the lodge to seek purification, healing, and protection for the
time ahead."

"The wind told him?"

"Yeah, Johnny. There's a lot that goes on in this world that we
don't understand. We say that going into the sweat lodge is like
entering the womb of the Earth Grandmother, and the heated
stones are her body, the fountain of life. After the ceremony,
when we come out, it is like being—"

"Born again," Johnny whispered.

"Yes, born again." George looked up. Fred had turned, and he
nodded.

"Let's go, it's time."

Fred pulled aside the tarp and Johnny went in. Inside it was
hot, scalding hot, and dark.

There was a hole in the ground. Fred and George came in

with several more stones from the fire on a plank between them. They tipped the board and let the stones roll off into the hole. George went back and fetched one of the water buckets. Fred opened his leather bag and pulled out some herbs, which he passed to Johnny.

"Sage, sweet grass and copal. I brought it from Arizona. Watch me and burn them when I do. I have a lighter."

George came back in and he had a small drum. He closed the tarp, and they were in the dark. Johnny felt a little uncomfortable, but George began a soft rhythmic beat on the drum accompanied by a low chant. Johnny felt his breathing slow and his body relax. And then he realized why.

The drum is keeping time with my heartbeat.

A flare of light in the darkness and Fred was holding the sage in the flame. He nodded and Johnny held his above the lighter. A sweet savor filled the air. They did the same with the other herbs. Then Fred took a ladle of water and poured it on the stones. Intense steam filled the room. Johnny sat breathing it in. It was hot, but he could take it. They sat for a long time, with no sound except the soft beat of the drum and the slow chant. At last, Fred spoke.

"The sweat lodge is a way of prayer to connect with the earth and sky around us and to uplift the spirit. The Wind told me you would come to us, that you were a 'strange one.' It is not just your name, but there is a dark place in your heart. The Wind showed it to me."

Johnny felt a twist inside him. The dark place was there, for sure. Since he left home, the dark place had become his identity. It was a place of death and pain, and it made Johnny who he was.

"The dark place is not who you are, Johnny."

The soft voice hit him like a punch in the gut.

"What!"

"The dark place is not who you are. It is the block that keeps you from becoming who you really are."

The drum stopped, and George opened the flap. "That is the end of the first door, Johnny. We will go out and salute one of the four directions. Then we will come back for three more doors. You up for it?"

Johnny took a deep breath. Fred's words had shaken him. But he knew the words were the truth. "Lead on, George. I can take it."

The three men faced one direction, and Fred prayed in Navajo. Then they went back inside. In later years, Johnny didn't remember the exact details of what happened in the lodge. But he remembered Fred's voice, telling him things about himself that nobody could have known. And as he burned the herbs and listened to the drum and the songs, he felt like a great weight was lifting off him. Later he would remember that, despite the intense heat and the darkness, it was like being washed clean in a cool mountain stream; the sun sparkling on the water and diamond flashes burning away the darkness and the rot of that time in his boyhood. And for the first time in years, Johnny Strange felt clean.

And when they stepped out for the last time, Fred picked up his Ka-Bar and took Johnny's hand and George's. He made a slight cut in all their palms and then they put their hands together and the blood from each cut mingled.

Fred nodded. George smiled. "Now you are our brother. We walk the Red Road together. We will be your tribe and your friends. You will watch over us. We will not forsake one another, even in the darkness."

Johnny nodded. "Semper Fi, guys. Semper Fi."

24

ISLAND X

BILLY MARTENS

Billy Martens watched the Marines leave Pearl Harbor without him.

A fleet of over five hundred ships had carried away most of the 4th Marine Division on May 25, a Thursday. It took the 27th Infantry Division along with them.

On Monday the 29th, the faster transports of Attack Group One set to sea with the rest of the 4th Division. The next day it was Attack Group Two's turn. They steamed out of Pearl carrying the 2nd Marine Division. Billy's division with Billy's men. His buddies.

He was watching from the deck of a destroyer. But the destroyer was attached to Attack Group Two. So, this time, ten minutes after the task force had cleared the harbor and were well underway, Billy's destroyer followed, swift as one of his hunting arrows.

The proud sailors had nicknamed their fighting ship *Sub Killer*. They had seven officials, but swore up and down, as only a salty sailor could, they had deep-sixed three more they hadn't been given credit for. Billy moved from the foredeck to the stern so he could watch the creamy wake. It reminded him of white water back home. And home was over two years gone. The frothing seas the ship's screws churned up was as close as he was going to get to Montana for a long, long time. It didn't matter. It wasn't like he had a girl back home waiting on him like Johnny did.

Mennonite boys were raised not knowing a lot of things. He thought about it, watching the wake and watching Hawaii vanish in the blue distance. They didn't teach them about war, about girls, about dancing, or about sex. They weren't allowed to go to the movies or play cards. They considered church, the Bible, hymn sings, ranch chores, spring and fall roundups, and hunting for meat for the table sufficient. Yet any moment now someone would escort him to a hush-hush meeting with a woman born and raised in the South Pacific who, by all accounts, was a brutal Amazon warrior, someone who destroyed Jap soldiers with her bare hands and, for all he knew, bare feet and bare legs. "She'll eat you alive," Johnny had joked. "You'll never make it to Island X. They just needed to toss someone into the ring she could practice her skills on." She probably would eat him alive. What did he know about talking to a woman like that? What did he know about talking to any woman?

The guys said he had done okay at the USO show the week before, but Billy knew he'd messed up. Out of that vast crowd of Marines, they'd singled him out, called him up on stage, and got him slow dancing with the most beautiful woman he'd ever seen, Carole Landis, an actress and a stunning blonde. Marines were hollering and whistling, the band was playing a song he'd never heard before. She was smiling, and soft, and pretty, and perfumed, and he was tripping over her tiny feet. She'd been kind.

"Don't worry about it, Marine," she'd whispered as they moved around the stage. "Just follow me. You've done enough for your country. Now let me do something for you."

"I'm sorry," Billy had mumbled. "I'm so clumsy. I must embarrass you."

"You're not embarrassing me at all. I love dancing with a genuine hero."

"I'm no hero, Miss Landis."

"Carole. What's your name, Marine?"

"Billy."

She leaned her head on his shoulder and Billy thought he'd die. Nothing in his life had felt as wonderful as this, even if he had two left feet. It was like getting drunk, but it was a lot better than getting drunk. She not only looked good and smelled good, she felt good in his arms. So warm and such a perfect fit.

"I want you to remember me, Billy," she said as the dance wound down. "And I want you to write me. Here." She slipped a small piece of paper into the breast pocket of his uniform. "I don't do this for everyone. But that will work a lot better than my fan mail address. Okay? I'm serious. I know you have another battle coming up. You're going to survive, trust me. When you do, and it's over, I want you to write me. Please. I'm with show people all the time. I just want to know a regular guy. A hero. My hero, who's fighting to save us all."

Carole kissed him on the cheek, and the Marines erupted with a roar. She laughed and patted the red lipstick mark. "Don't let them razz you too much, Billy. You did fine. Good luck with the next island. Don't forget to write me. I mean it. I'll be watching for that letter. You wouldn't want to disappoint me, would you?"

Crandall was the first one to get in front of Billy. "Good Lord, Mennonite Man. Is this a "God opens the heavens" moment or something? What the hell was that?"

"I don't know, skipper."

"Well, dammit, its gotta be God. Or else you were born with Montana horseshoes up your butt. Which is it?"

"Both."

Crandall laughed and thumped him on the back and shoved a Havana between his lips. "Damn right. You are the luckiest

Marine in the South Pacific right now. Stick close to me when we go in on Island X. If your luck rubs off on me, I'll still be alive seventy-five years from now and smoking Cuban cigars on Maui."

Billy's squad leader, Sergeant Bakar Zarate, gave him a punch on the shoulder. "What the hell, Billy? I thought you'd be KIA up there. How can you dance with a woman like that and not die?"

"I think I am dead, Sarge."

"Yeah, I think you might be."

Red O'Brien leaned in close to examine Billy's cheek. "I'll be damned. I think you took a bullet. Corpsman! Hey, corpsman!"

Bud came over, grinning and pushing his way through swarms of Marines. "What is it? Did Billy's heart stop?"

"Damn. You're right. It should have. Why is he still on his feet, Bud?"

"He's a medical miracle. What else can I say? Any other Marine, we'd be digging a hole at the side of the stage there."

"But he took a bullet, Bud," O'Brien insisted. "Look."

Bud leaned in close like O'Brien. "You're right. You'd think it might be lipstick, but no. We're a combat unit." He turned Billy's face to the side. "No exit wound. It's still in him."

"You mean in his heart?"

Bud shrugged. "Where else?"

"Geez, knock it off, you yard birds," Billy laughed.

Tommy Earp, Superman, showed up. "Can't you operate, Bud?"

"Nah. It's too close to everything vital."

"Won't it kill him, eventually?" Earp asked, lighting a Camel with his Zippo.

"Not if he learns to live with it."

Earp passed Billy his pack of cigarettes, and Billy took one. Earp lit it for him. "You gonna live with it, cowboy?"

"I'll never wash my cheek again."

Earp nodded. "Easy to get away with that, with the kind of

war we're fighting. Lots of dirt. Clean your face and the muck always finds its way back. We'll wash after Japan surrenders."

"Earp," Billy replied, drawing on his cigarette, "I'll never wash off Carole Landis. Ever. She stays there till you put a helmet on my rifle and sink the bayonet into the ground."

Sammy Crown, the tall, hefty Alaskan, put his arm around Billy's shoulders. "Here's a bigger thing. Did you get her phone number?"

"Better. I got her house address in L.A."

"In your dreams."

"Yep. In my ever-loving dreams."

"A Marine with dreams. A rare bird." Crown looked towards the stage. "Hey, she's gonna sing. Let's shut up."

Carole had signed her address and written *My Hero* underneath. Obviously, she'd had it ready before he joined her onstage. She intended to give it to whichever Marine lucked out and wound up in her arms for three or four minutes. Realizing that, he came close to ripping the note up and throwing it away. But the piece of paper had her perfume on it. And she had kissed him on the cheek. And something he would never tell a soul, that was his first actual kiss. His mother, grandmother, sisters and aunts didn't count. He wasn't going to throw that kiss away. Billy Martens wanted that memory until a day came if and when a woman he loved made the memory unnecessary.

The gossip was Carole Landis put in a good word with the brass and got Billy bumped to Platoon Sergeant. As Lieutenant Crandall spelled it out to him, the guerillas on Island X were pissed the Corps had assigned a lowly corporal to work with them and demanded three stripes above a rocker and got it. Billy would work hand-in-glove with Crandall, with Johnny and the Navajo Windtalkers, and with the guerillas. Zarate was bumped to Gunnery Sergeant and would be glued tight to K Company's CO, Captain Rudebaker, helping him run the show. Oh, and Johnny Strange? It was Corporal Strange now, two chevrons on the sleeve, because the powers that be had determined working with the Navajo required a non-commissioned officer.

"It's not as if they handed the chevrons to you two jokers on a platter," said Crandall. "You earned them on Tarawa. Hell, you earned them on the Canal. They're long overdue. So, haul ass on Island X and show us we were right to promote a pair of damn pacifist Mennonites, okay?" Crandall had laughed. "Lordy, Lordy, what in hell's name has happened to the Corps?"

That was the official explanation. The unofficial was what held with the Marines. Carole Landis made the generals jump. That's why it was suddenly Corporal Strange and Sergeant Martens. That's why Billy wasn't shipping out on the same troop transports as the rest of the division. That's why they'd stuck him on a destroyer with no other Marines around. He was going to rendezvous with Carole Landis and have a sweet trip to Island X, eating steak and eggs and enjoying her company, while the rest of the 2nd Division got crammed into troopships like sardines and ate beans. Scuttlebutt had Billy Martens not even going ashore, at Carole Landis's request.

Garowski and Levy had come to him, all stitched up and fixed tight after being shot up on Tarawa. They were worried the scuttlebutt was true.

"Billy, we need you to go in with us," Levy had pleaded. "You fight like hell. No one is going to feel good heading into the surf and into Jap gunfire unless you have our backs."

Billy was surprised. "What? Where is this coming from?"

"You won the Silver Star," Garowski jumped in. "We all know what you did to that Jap pillbox on Tarawa. How you took out machine-gun nests on Guadalcanal. That you track and kill snipers like a hunter. You're tough, Billy. I mean, Sergeant Martens. You care what the hell happens to us. We don't need you watching the show from the deck of a destroyer with a pretty girl by your side. We need you on the beach."

"What makes you think I'll be sitting on the deck watching you land?" demanded Billy. "I'll be right beside you, Ricky."

"That's not what the scuttlebutt is. There's a woman waiting for you on that destroyer and we figure it has to be Carole Landis."

"Dammit, Ricky, it's not Carole Landis."

"Then who is it?" asked Levy.

"I can't tell you that, Leon."

"Why not?"

"Because I can't. It might compromise the mission."

"What mission?"

"Leon! Ricky!" Billy had exploded. "I am going to rejoin the division before the landings. I will be right beside you when our LVTs go in. If it makes you any happier, Carole will be right there with us in Marine green, camo helmet and clutching an M1 Garand with a big bayonet. No makeup. Tough as shit. The Japs will run like hell when they hear her scream for their blood. Satisfied?"

Levy and Garowski stared at him. Then burst out laughing.

"That's the craziest thing I ever heard," said Garowski.

Billy clapped him on the shoulder. "Rest easy, Marine. I'm going in with my platoon. Promise. So, spread the word."

Garowski grinned. "We sure will, Sarge."

Sarge. It made Billy feel strangely good. Solid. In one piece. It also made him feel old. Was he old? He was going to turn twenty-one. How old was twenty-one? He felt like he was forty or fifty. If forty and fifty felt tired to the bone.

"Sergeant Martens?"

Billy looked up from the blue ocean swells, saw the naval officer, and saluted. The officer returned the salute.

"Please accompany me, Sergeant."

The officer took him to a wardroom that was spotless and empty, except for a Marine colonel, a vice admiral and a tall woman in Marine shirt and pants. His eyes remained on her as he sat down with the officer on the other side of the table. She was the most unpleasant looking woman Billy had ever seen. Her fatigues were many sizes too large and rendered her shapeless. Her hair was dyed a bright yellow that was too yellow and too bright. Her teeth were painted black. Any makeup on her brown face seemed determined to ensure she looked far more ferocious than she appeared at first glance. He met her gaze. Hers was as steady as an M1 carbine's steel sights.

The contempt for Billy oozed like venom from eyes black as a patch of deep jungle. The kind that blocked out all sunlight. He refused to flinch. This made her lips curl in a smirk that said, "Oh, is the weak little American going to fight back? You won't take me long to finish, believe me." It reminded Billy of the stare-off between boxers before a match. He had seen Johnny Strange face down many opponents in exactly this fashion. Then watched him go on to pummel them into oblivion. Billy wasn't about to let her pummel a tough Montana boy. Or wrap her arms and legs around him like a snake and snap his back or crush out his life. Or let her fingers tighten like steel cables around his throat. Her smile said otherwise.

The Marine colonel took the floor. Inexplicably, he asked to see Billy's Silver Star and the one that had been awarded to his grandfather. Billy brought them out of his pocket. The colonel examined them. Then he passed the medals to the vice admiral, who glanced them over before handing both to the woman. She turned them over and bit into each one. Then she laid them on the table with the stars facing up.

"Pretty trinkets," she mocked in a deep voice that made Billy think of jet black coffee. "What did you do? Nice guy talk-talk some Japs into surrendering?"

Her English was perfect with a trace of the New England bite.

"Yale?" asked Billy.

Her eyes were hooded like a serpent's and revealed nothing. "Did you do the nice guy talk-talk or not?"

"I used a flamethrower."

"Ah. You let fire do your killing for you. I told them I wanted a Marine Raider. Someone who only needs their hands and legs to destroy the enemy. But I got you."

The colonel and vice admiral did not intervene, so Billy asked if he could smoke. The colonel nodded. Billy lit up a Camel and stared at the woman. Then he said, "There was plenty of hand-to-hand on Tarawa. I killed with *katanas* and Ka-Bars and Tommy guns. I beheaded. I cut men in half with bullets and Jap blades. Blades they'd honed like razors. Lots of times there wasn't any opportunity to use swords or guns. So, I employed muscle. My good American muscle. I choked, strangled, gouged, tore open, bent and broke many an enlisted man and officer. I ripped out hearts and lungs and intestines. Killing doesn't bother me, Serpent. Neither do rivers of blood. If you prove false to our mission on Island X, I'll dispatch you in fifteen seconds using just one hand. And you'll be dead forever."

"That will do, Sergeant!" snapped the colonel. "We're all on the same side here."

"If you say so, Sir."

"Serpent's intel has been invaluable to us. She's killed more Japs than you have."

"If you say so, sir."

"You're going into Island X together. She knows every square inch of the island. It's her home. She'll help you tear the guts out of the Jap army, pillbox by pillbox, machine gun nest by machine gun nest."

"Soldier by soldier, officer by officer," Billy added, never taking his eyes off her face with its perpetual sneer.

"That's right, Sergeant." The vice admiral finally spoke up. "We expect your complete cooperation. She has the same rank as you in our eyes. This island is critical, Sergeant Martens. It's no exaggeration to say its capture would put the Empire of Japan on its deathbed. Permanently. We'd have them by the throat."

"With our bare hands?" prodded Billy.

The admiral actually smiled. "Yes." He glanced at Serpent, who remained locked in her contempt for Billy. "Midway in '42 stopped the Jap advance. But the capture of Island X will be the genuine turning point, Sergeant. It will be Tokyo's defeat. If we gain this island, I'd say the war will be over in a year, perhaps less. Island X is the biggest test for the big guns of the United States Navy and the guts and grit of the United States Marines. Show our allies here what we're made of, Sergeant Martens. Show them they did right to fight beside us."

Serpent made a gesture with her hand. "May I, Sergeant?"

Billy flipped his pack of Camels over to her. "Anything for one of our allies, Sergeant."

She put a cigarette in her mouth and stared at him.

He slid his USMC Zippo across the table.

She lit up and continued with her boxer stare-down through the streams of white smoke.

"My women and men will be waiting for us once we land," she said. "The youngest is a sixteen-year-old girl as tough as a shark. The oldest a seventy-seven-year-old woman as formidable as naval gunfire. Don't underestimate any of them."

"I won't," Billy promised. "Don't underestimate Achilles Squad or Platoon X-Ray or K Company or the 2nd Marine Division either, or the Corps. We'll get the job done. With our guns. Or our Ka-Bars. Or our bare hands."

She deliberately blew smoke at him. "We'll see, Sergeant."

"We will for sure see, Sergeant. Tokyo Rose says Island X is Saipan."

"Do you believe everything that Nip bitch says, Sergeant? I hear the Marines are in love with her and listen to every broadcast she makes."

Billy smiled and took his time responding. He was happy to see this annoyed her. "She plays American big band songs for us, Sergeant. The Marines appreciate that. Even from a foe."

The rest were maps and coordinates and intel. At first, the colonel and vice admiral still called it Island X. Sergeant Martens and his platoon would follow Serpent's lead. They attached Corporal Strange and his Navajo Windtalkers to Martens's command. K Company and the 2nd Division would follow Martens and Serpent up the west side of the island. The army would be on their right flank, the 27th Infantry Division. The 4th Marine Division would be on the army's right flank, taking the east side of the island. The colonel finally shrugged, glanced at his watch, the face of which was under his wrist, military style, and pulled a map out of his leather satchel that had SAIPAN printed across its top. This map clearly showed place names. Mount Nafutan, Mount Kagman, Hashigoru, Laulau, Tanapag, Mount Tapotchau. He tapped a spot on the west coast.

"Garapan, the largest population center on Saipan. They call it the 'Tokyo of the South Seas.' You have to take it, Sergeant Martens. The 2nd Division has to secure it as swiftly as possible. I have my concerns."

"What concerns, Colonel?"

"It will require street fighting. House to house, like Italy, like Stalingrad. Not like the jungles of Guadalcanal and Tarawa."

"My men will handle it, Colonel."

The colonel glanced at Serpent and back at Billy. "I'm sure of that. But civilian casualties are always high with this type of combat, Sergeant. Too high. But unavoidable. It's not just Garapan. There are sugar cane plantations, farms, villages, all over the island. Your approach to Garapan will take you past many of them. There are over twenty-five thousand Japanese civilians on Saipan. Korean laborers, thousands of Chamorran islanders. It's inevitable that they will get caught up in the fighting and take casualties. But the fewer the better."

"Aye, aye, Sir, we'll do our best. Perhaps Serpent will be able to encourage her people to evacuate their homes before the battles start."

She refused to look at Billy. Instead, she made a point of crushing out her still-burning cigarette into the back of her hand. She didn't wince. "My people only want to be free. To be as free as the gulls that swoop over the sea. First it was the bastard Spanish in 1668, who removed us to Guam while they turned our land over to hogs and cattle to feed the crews of their unholy galleons. Then Carolinians from the Satawal Atoll were permitted to settle on Saipan in 1815 and steal our land and our rights. After that, it was the Germans in 1899, who did nothing to free us, but left us to the cruelty of the Spaniards. Finally, it was the devils from Japan who conquered Saipan in 1914 and were awarded complete control by the monsters you called the League of Nations. They thought they had the right to cut us up and sell us away, as if we never existed. Tokyo brought in Japanese settlers and said the land was theirs to develop as they wished. They pushed us to the side. Now there are tens of thousands of Japanese and not even four thousand Chamorros and Carolinians to oppose them." She fished a second cigarette from Billy's pack and lit it. "We want the Marines to liberate us. Not kill us, while they are fighting the enemy. We want our island back. It's been three hundred years. We want freedom. Help us get that."

IT TOOK JUST two weeks to reach Saipan. Billy never saw the woman again until the early hours of the 15th of June. Only the Marine colonel and vice admiral met with him daily to go over details. By June 15, it was D plus nine in Normandy. Monte Cassino had surrendered on May 17 and this led to the big push out of Anzio. Mas Kimura and the 100th Infantry Battalion had destroyed the last German troops blocking the approach to Rome. This cleared the way for the Eternal City's liberation on

June 4. But the 100th was not granted the honor of being part of the victory parade.

An LVT nudged up to *Sub Killer* and Serpent scrambled down the cargo net like a fast spider. Billy took his time. He had a full pack, she didn't. He dropped in among grinning faces and took a lot of slaps on the back. Johnny Strange, Corporal Johnny Strange, Bonners Ferry, Idaho, was smoking a Lucky Strike, two tough-looking Navajo crammed in beside him, George Atsa and Fred Niyol. The 81mm mortar team was stuck together in a tight knot to one side, all of them giving Billy the thumbs up: Tom "Skillet" Baker of Caspar, Wyoming holding onto the mortar's base plate, Paul Stoneroad of Santa Fe with the mount, Corporal Jesus Navarro––senior corporal to Johnny Strange and assistant squad leader for Achilles, a hard hombre from Rodeo, New Mexico––held the tube, while Sammy Crown, the big Alaskan from Skagway, was carting a load of mortar bombs.

Billy spotted the new man they'd picked up on Betio to replace Julio Hernandez. Julio had lost a leg, pulled through, and was back home in Las Cruces, New Mexico. Young Bobby McGuire, who they called Bobby Mac, was from Sebastopol, California, where he'd been a champion running back in high school. He stood clutching his BAR, looking at Billy, then looking away, unsure. Red O'Brien, The Dragon, Caldwell, Idaho, flamethrower pack heavy on his back, offered Bobby a cigarette and started talking to the kid Billy figured was eighteen, maybe only seventeen. The boy had seen combat on Tarawa Atoll. He wasn't green, but he'd never done a landing under fire. This would be his first. Sam Kane, Batman, from Chicago, Red's partner, joined them, chewing a cigar which meant Lt. Crandall was near.

Crandall, commander of Platoon X-Ray, was at the back of the LVT as it churned and lurched towards the beaches on the west side of Saipan, biting on the end of his ubiquitous Havana. K Company's CO, Captain "Rudy" Rudebaker, from Denver, standing right next to Crandall, had one in his teeth too, except it was lit. Gunnery Sergeant Bakar Zarate, Mesquite, Nevada, was talking to them, an unlit cigar between the fingers of each hand. Billy wondered what the Gunnery sergeant was going to do with two of them once he hit the beach. The thought had no sooner entered his head before Zarate turned around and handed the cigars off to Tommy Earp, Superman, NYC, who triggered the Big Fifty, which was at his feet, and his partner, Sid Greene, Superman Too, Sioux Falls, South Dakota, who carried the fifty-caliber ammo and the mount. The machine gun team grinned their thanks and, like Rudebaker, quickly put their Zippos to the Havanas.

Bud was by himself. Lost in himself, more like. His dark eyes met Billy's. He nodded once and looked down. Billy figured he was brooding over Kalasia in New Zealand, not his home in Ritzville, Washington, a pain Billy was spared unless he riveted onto Carole Landis which he had no intention of doing. She had melted away in his mind like ice cream in the sun.

"Hey, Sarge." It was Leon Levy, the San Francisco boy. "She sure doesn't look like Carole Landis."

"Or any woman I've ever seen, anywhere," added Ricky Garowski, Seattle, M1 Garand in his fists, knuckles white as the LVT pitched and yawed in the ocean swells.

Billy glanced to the front where Serpent stood tall, straight, proud, silent and alone. Now that the dawn light was stronger, he could see her face more clearly. Besides the scraggly yellow hair and black teeth, it was painted with all kinds of dark lines and stark patterns and angry colors. She still wore the same oversized combat fatigues. It was like she was from another world or another century. For a moment, gazing at her sharp profile, Billy thought he glimpsed a powerful yet feminine beauty. But then whatever he'd seen was gone, and the harsh lines and severity were back.

She refused to look at anyone. The location in which she had positioned herself in the LVT meant she would be first down the ramp and into the wild fury of Japanese fire. She carried no firearm. Not even a knife. Billy got the sense she felt hindered by the shirt and pants and would rather peel them off and attack the Japanese stark naked, howling her battle cry.

"Damn," hissed Garowski, "she scares me more than the Japs do."

"I guess that's the effect she wants," replied Billy.

A wave smashed over the side and made him duck, soaking everyone, and generating yells and curses from the Marines.

Serpent didn't even flinch.

"See?" said Levy. "It's like she's made of stone."

Billy put a cigarette between lips dripping with saltwater. "Let her be. She has a lot on her mind. She wants to set Saipan and her Chamorro people free. And we're going to do our damnedest to help."

Hearing this, she turned her head and looked at him. The look cut Billy in half. But also, for the first time, it brought a shaft of light and open sky with it.

25

HOW MUCH MORE...

BUD—THE CORPSMAN

I got a bad feeling about this.

Cloudy moonlight speckles the sides of the silent blacked-out fleet as we move through the waters off the northern tip of Saipan. It is midnight and I am on the deck. I haven't slept very well since we left Pearl. The island rises dark and hidden off the port side of the transport. It's different from Cactus or Helen. Not as big as Guadalcanal, but not an atoll like Tarawa. There's a big high mountain right smack in the middle and beaches all along the eastern coast. That's where we are going ashore.

Everything about this trip feels fractured, out of whack. And there's a big question rooting around in the back of my brain— how long can we keep doing this before we all get it? I mean get it, not a shot through the fleshy part of the arm or a stab in the shoulder that puts you in and out of the hospital, but get it— dead, done, rotting in the sand like the thousands who died at Tarawa, or turning into mud or alligator shit like some of our buddies on Guadalcanal.

Things didn't start out well on this trip. Before we left Pearl, there was a big SNAFU. We came down from Camp Tarawa and were on the ships in the main harbor waiting to sail. Pearl splits into two enormous bays and over in the West Loch they parked a bunch of LSTs. The ordinance boys packed them to the gunnels with ammo, gas, mortar rounds. They had those LSTs lined up beam to beam along the Tare piers. And then they jammed the decks with Marines, a lot of our 2nd Div boys, for the long haul to Island X. They had turned the boats into floating bombs, and then they packed our guys right on top of them. What the hell were they thinking?

Some guys were loading ammo on a boat, and they dropped a mortar round and it went off. At least that's what I heard. There was scuttlebutt that a Jap mini-sub might have snuck in and fired a torpedo, but who the hell knows. Whatever caused it, that row of boats went up like the fourth of July. I heard it from clear over on my ship. Then I get the call that they need all the medical help they can get, so I get off the boat and head over in a truck. When we got there, the place was an inferno. Sailors and Marines were jumping into the water as the flames and explosions jumped from boat to boat. Oil and gas poured into the harbor and got set on fire.

That's why I haven't slept well. I keep hearing the screams of the men floating in that sea of burning oil; I keep hearing the roar of gasoline drums and stores of ammo exploding as the fire leaps from ship to ship along the crowded mooring. When it was over, six of those big LSTs were toast, burned to the waterline. There were dead and dying guys lined up on the docks and dozens still floating out in the water. 2nd Div lost ninety-five men. A lot of them were fresh meat replacements, but there were a lot of guys I knew from all the way back to Cactus.

I mean, what a bunch of shit. These guys make it all the way through Cactus and Helen and then get burned to death in Pearl harbor because some fools used LSTs as ammo boats. So that's how the trip started. Not a happy augury, as Ulysses might say.

And Billy's gone. They made him a sergeant and stuck him on special duty with this gal who looks like one of the three witches from MacBeth. I mean, this gal is scary—six feet tall, with bright yellow hair and black teeth. I just glimpsed her when Billy was going aboard a destroyer. I guess she's a Chamorro, so it doesn't take but one eye and half a brain to figure we're going to the Marianas, Saipan, maybe, Guam.

I am proved right about three days out when Rudy calls all the King Company platoon leaders together and gives them the skinny. Saipan it is.

And Johnny? He got stuck with two Navajo code talkers. I guess they make a difference in the war effort, but they aren't friendly and besides that I don't like Indians much. Call me narrow-minded, but my only experience with the Noble Red Man was with the braves that used to drive down from the Colville reservation heading for the Pendleton Roundup. They always stopped in Ritzville to tank up, and I mean tank up. I remember some real brouhahas on hot summer nights, when they decided to re-stage Custer's Last Stand. Anyway, I didn't much care for them. Fred and George, Johnny's new compadres, are okay, I guess, but they keep to themselves and include Johnny in a lot of their pow-wows, so Strange is not around much.

So Billy's gone, and Johnny's AWOL on the reservation, and I'm the one Menno boy worried about this next dogfight. It's not like me. Something's weighing on me and I can't seem to get it off my chest.

"Bud?"

I jump and turn. It's Zarate. What's he doing out here? I haven't seen him since he got his triple chevrons.

"Hey, Gunny, whaddaya know?"

"What are you doing lurking around out here, Bud? I looked in your rack, but it was as empty as Tojo's brains."

"Awww, I'm just feeling a little skittish, Sarge. Billy and Johnny aren't around, and I don't know any of these new kids. Seems like the old gang is busted up."

"Not like you to be down, Bud. But if you think we busted the team, you got another think coming. Get your butt in gear and follow me."

So I fall in behind Zarate, and we head for the Officer's quarters. There's a wardroom below decks and he shoves me in. Well, what the hell? King Company brass—Rudy, all the platoon leaders, Corporal Navarro and newly minted Corporal Johnny Strange with his two scalp hunters. Crandall grins at me, the ubiquitous Havana in his mouth chewed almost in half. Johnny pulls out a chair.

"Sit down, Philo," he says with a big grin on his face." He never calls me Philo unless something is up.

I look around the room. Rudy pipes up. "Now that we got our team assembled, let me give you the rundown. Tomorrow at 0843, 2/6 and 2/8 are going ashore with the assault teams. Except for one Rifle Company, 2/2 is being held in reserve."

I hear groans around the room.

"Belay the noise and let me finish," Rudy smiles. "We are in reserve because they selected us for another mission, something that fits a veteran team of shit-kickers like King Company. Working with a Chamorro resistance group lead by a fighter we know as Serpent, King Company will go ashore north of the main assault. 2/2 will stage what looks like a second landing north of Tanapag Harbor, but it is a diversion and we fed that information to the Japs so they won't respond. That means they will know it's a fake, not pay attention and concentrate their defense on the beaches south of Garapan. That will let us get King ashore and into the hills behind Garapan. There we will spot enemy pillboxes, artillery emplacements and mortars. We will destroy what we can and call in Naval and Army artillery on the rest."

He looked over at Johnny Strange and his two impassive companions. "Corporal Strange, you and your two code talkers will be critical to this mission. We'll see if the Japs can figure out what the hell these guys are talking about."

Everybody cracks a smile, even Johnny's two red brothers. But I'm still feeling out of the loop until Rudy looks over at me.

"Bud, you're the best corpsman I've ever seen. If you were a combat Marine, you'd have a chest full of medals. And you still might get some."

"Not a Purple Heart, I hope, Captain."

Rudy grins. "Not on my watch, Bud. And while we are at it, I have something for you. Please stand."

I stand up and to my surprise I am blushing. Rudy nods to the rest of the guys and they all stand and come to attention. He picks up a small leather case and pulls out two badges. One is a Marine Force emblem surrounded by two leaves. I've seen that one before. The other is a badge with an eagle, a red cross, and two chevrons.

"This comes directly from Red Mike. In view of your meritorious and gallant service on Guadalcanal and Tarawa, I hereby designate you a Fleet Marine Force Enlisted Warfare Specialist, and promoted to the rank of Pharmacist's Mate Second Class, by order of Brigadier General Merritt A. Edson. Congratulations, Corporal."

Rudy hands me the badges. The room explodes with applause. I look at the men standing around me. When I met most of them, except for the Captain, Lieutenant Crandall and Sergeant Zarate, these guys were wet-behind-the-ears kids from Idaho, Alaska, Washington, New Mexico and everywhere across our country. When I got to Camp Elliott, I was just a big dumb Hambo from nowheresville, U.S.A. And then we went to war and everything changed. I watched these guys become men. Maybe that's why I got a bad feeling. I've lost a lot of good friends in this frigging war, and I don't want to lose any more. I mean, how many times can a man get in a landing craft and head ashore in the face of concentrated enemy fire and not take a fifty caliber right in the teeth? How many times can he push through the jungle with Japs behind every rock and hidden in every tree and not get his head blown off or his guts shot out?

I have my ghosts. From Eddie Kramer, the first guy who died looking up at me with his arm blown off on Cactus, to the hundreds of guys lying on the beach under the seawall on Betio, screaming because the morphine wasn't strong enough to dull the pain of having both their legs blown off. I still get that freeze in my soul every time one of my men dies. And I'm looking at the men around me and I know what's bugging me. I don't want any of these men to die, and some are going to die, anyway. And that's the shits.

Rudy breaks into my mental wool-gathering. "Sit down, everyone. I've saved the most important part of our mission to the last." He reaches down and picks up a face-down picture off the table. It's a blurry photo of a Jap Officer—high-ranking by the look of his collar and cap.

"This is General Yoshitsugo Saito, commander of the Imperial Japanese Army 43rd Division, the crack Jap troops Tojo deployed to Saipan. If Saito was at full strength, we would be in a shitload of trouble. Fortunately for us, he suffered heavy casualties from sub attacks when he was transporting his troops here." He pulled out another picture. It was a scary-looking guy in full dress uniform. "This is Admiral Chuichi Nagumo. He is also on Saipan and is Saito's right-hand man. Their headquarters are somewhere in the hills behind Garapan. Tonight the Chamorro fighter known as Serpent is coming aboard with Sgt. Martens. We will embed her and her team with us, and they will hopefully lead us to Saito. We will have a short briefing before we embark at 0400. Questions?"

There was silence. I lifted my hand.

"Pharmacist's Mate Parmalee?"

"Sir, would you mind if I prayed for the team?"

"Not at all, Bud. I think we are going to need as much help as we can get."

When I pray, I try to make it to the point. I figure God has enough incoming he doesn't want to wade through all the pontifications, so he's happy when somebody makes it short and sweet. So that's what I do.

"Lord, you know these men, you know their lives, you know their hearts. I'm asking that you would set your angels as guardians around us and help us all to leave this battle alive and in one piece. Amen."

But I still got a bad feeling about this.

IV

SAIPAN

DAY 1 — D-DAY

JUNE 15, 1944

26

ONCE MORE INTO THE BREACH, DEAR FRIENDS—0400 D-DAY SAIPAN

JOHNNY STRANGE

The sea pounded against the sides of the huge LST, but the transport ship moved smoothly, cutting through the waves. Above Mt. Tapotchau, the moon was sliding down into the indigo pre-dawn. Behind them to the south, the massed artillery of the vast landing fleet was pounding Saipan into rubble. Dozens of LSTs were forming a three-mile long point of departure beyond the reef. It was going down! The hammer was about to strike the unprepared Japanese army on Saipan. King Company was going in again! Before dawn, X-Ray platoon packed into four alligators at the front of the ship.

Johnny Strange waited in the Amtrac parked inside the LST. With him were Bud, Fred and George, Crandall with his cigar, Zarate, and the rest of X-ray. Fred and George sat next to him, quiet, impassive. Johnny chuckled.

George looked at him. "What's so funny, Kemosabe?"

Johnny shook his head. "You know, for Redmen, you two look kinda pale."

The two code-talkers looked back at him and then they chuckled too. Fred nodded. "I must tell my sister I had to become a paleface before I could fight in this man's Marine Corps."

Billy Martens had come aboard the night before, and now he sat next to the nastiest-looking woman Johnny had ever seen with yellow hair and black teeth, Wilma Shottmeir back in Bonner's Ferry, was coyote ugly and fat, but she was Marilyn Monroe compared to this gal. This gal looked like she was a forged steel gargoyle. And when she stared at you with those black eyes, it made your skin crawl. There were other members of her team scattered throughout the alligators. They were equally repellant.

Johnny took a deep breath and thought about Marjean—her corn-silk hair, her beautiful face, her little wolf teeth.

Thank you, Lord.

Johnny jerked in surprise.

Whoa! Where did that come from?

The LST moved steadily toward the shore. Rudy had briefed the Platoon leaders and noncoms after chow at 0200. "We're going in over the reef at the north end of Tanapag Harbor. They won't be expecting us, so we'll get over quick. Down and dirty. In fast and off the beach."

The woman called Serpent stood next to Rudy. Her voice was pitched low, broken and cold, like crushed ice mixed with diesel oil.

"Saito had his headquarters in a schoolhouse on the south side of Charan Kanoa, but when the fleet started bombarding he moved. My people on the island say he is in a cave south of Mt. Tapotchau. We will have to hunt him down."

She pointed to the map. "When we hit the beach, there are machine guns and pillboxes here, here, here, here and here. The Japs didn't have time to finish their fortifications, so many of these are only half completed. My people have already cleared the way through the Jap beach defenses..." she pointed again... "Right here. Follow my lead and I'll get you into the hills with minimum contact."

Johnny watched Serpent as she moved. She looked like a coiled spring ready to explode. He noticed Billy was staring at her. It was hard to tell she was a woman. Her shapeless black tunic hid everything between her neck and her knees.

She looks like she can do what she says! She's wrapped tighter than I am.

Bud slipped in next to him.

"Hey, Strange, whaddaya know?"

"Looks like a great big vaudeville show over here, Bud." Johnny nodded at Fred and George.

"These are my two code-talkers, George Atsa, and Fred Niyol. I'm babysitting them through the rest of the war. You know, burp me, feed me, change me."

George grinned. "Like hell, white man. We'll be taking Jap scalps and hanging them on our lodge pole by sundown today."

"This is Bud, guys. We've been together since boot camp." Johnny nudged Bud. "Don't let their 'crazy injun' talk fool you. These boys would rather drive around Phoenix in a DeSoto than ride a horse into the sunset."

Bud was interested. "So, what's up with this code-talking? Haven't the Japs figured out that you're just using your own language?"

Fred scratched his neck. "Yeah, that's Type Two Code. Many Code Talkers use their everyday tribal languages to convey messages. A message such as, 'Send more ammunition to the front,' will just go over the radio. However, the Navajos, Comanches, Hopis, and Meskwakis use special codes based on their languages. These are Type One Codes."

Bud nodded. "How does that work?"

George broke in. "To develop our Type One Code, the original twenty-nine Navajo Code Talkers first came up with a Navajo word for each letter of the English alphabet. Since we had to memorize all the words, we used things familiar to us, such as kinds of animals."

"Yeah, we talk about these things all the time, animals, sea creatures, birds, eagles, hawks, and all those domestic animals,"

Fred said. "We're thinking, why don't we use those names of different animals—from A to Z. So A, we took a red ant that we live with all the time. B we took a bear, Yogi the Bear, C a cat, D a dog, E an elk, F a fox, G a goat, and so on down the line."

"So, how does it all work?"

George said something. "Moasi ne-ahs-jah lha-ch-eh dzeh gah dzeh moasi dzeh tkin a-keh-di-glini dzeh lha-cha-eh."

"What did you say?" Bud asked.

"Code received. Simple, but the Japs are going crazy trying to figure it out."

Johnny shook his head. "It's all Greek to me. Hey, Bud, congratulations on the promotion. No one deserved it more than you."

"Thanks, Johnny," but Bud didn't look happy.

Johnny put his hand on Bud's shoulder. "Something eating you, Bud? You've been mooning around the boat since we loaded at Pearl. You missing Kalasia?"

Bud nodded. "Yeah, that, and… well, we didn't get off to a good start with that big kerfuffle over in West Loch." He knit his brows. "I been thinking, Johnny, a lot—about what we will do after the war. I know you're going home to Marjean, but what will you do?"

Johnny shrugged. I guess I'll go see my buddy, Danny Carrabello, and see if he'll give me a job in his garage."

"Yeah, that sounds right. I remember how you gave Butterworth one in the chops when you fixed the General's jeep after the Crucible. I thought the little bastard would crap himself, he was so mad."

Johnny chuckled. "Yeah, that *was* a high point, wasn't it Bud? But what about you?"

Bud looked down at the deck.

"C'mon, Bud, what?"

"Well, don't laugh, Johnny, okay?"

"Hey, Bud, shoot. I'm your pal, remember?"

Bud swallowed. "Well, I was thinking maybe I'd get the G.I. Bill and go back to school."

"Yeah? What would you study?"

Bud looked over at Johnny. "I want to be a doctor, Johnny."

"Wow, Bud!!!" Johnny stared at his friend.

"Yeah, ambitious for a hayseed from Nowheresville. Right?"

Johnny grabbed his friend's hand. "I think it's a great idea, Bud. Like Rudy said, you're one of the best Corpsmen in this man's Marine Corps. You'll make an exceptional doctor."

"Thanks, Johnny. That means a lot." He paused for a long moment...

"Johnny, I want to ask you a favor. And that's what's buggin' me."

"What's that, Doc?"

"Keep your head down in this next fight, okay. I've had an unpleasant feeling about this entire operation, and I think it's because I'm done with watching my buddies die. I don't think I could take losing you or Billy..." Bud glanced around. "Or any of these guys, but I got this gut feeling... well, skip it. We've come a long way together, all of us. So just do me a favor and don't do anything stupid, okay?"

"You got it, Bud. I'll be slicker than snot on a doorknob. The Japs will never see me until I'm putting this baby up their rear." Johnny patted his BAR. The two code-talkers grinned.

Johnny heard Crandall bark. "Get ready for landing, we're going in."

Bud shook his head. "Okay, Johnny, see ya when I see ya." He still didn't look happy.

THE SKY WAS INKY, and the LST moved up onto the reef. The ramp came down and the big transport disgorged King Company like a baby barfing. Alligators churned up over the reef and headed straight for the beach. In the distance they could hear the boom and roar of the massed artillery from TF 68.

"Spruance is giving those Japs hell, Johnny," Bud whispered.

"Yeah and let's hope all the Japs are looking down there and not up here."

Then there was a soft crunch as they rolled up on the beach and the 2/2 Marines piled out. They spread out and headed for the tree line. Billy and Serpent moved ahead into the shadows. There was a shriek and then several quick bursts from a Thompson. Johnny came up to the trees and found Billy standing with Serpent. Sprawled out on the sand was a dead Jap—Serpent was standing over him. She had sliced him open from his nuts to his Adam's apple, and he had a very surprised look on his face. The Serpent held up her knife, licked the blood off it, and then spit on the dead Jap. Beyond them were four more very dead Japs. It looked like they had been sitting under the trees drinking Sake, because there was a bottle next to them. Billy patted his Thompson.

Serpent gave a low whistle, and several men and women in black materialized out of the trees. The rest of the Company moved out and Johnny could hear the alligators leaving the beach and heading back to the transport. Serpent signaled, and Rude-baker got his men moving into the trees. Down the beach Johnny could see some machine-gun nests with black shapes sprawled in among the silent weapons. Serpent's team had done their job. The show had begun.

***

KING COMPANY MOVED through the hills behind Garapan until they reached a point where they set up a perimeter and hunkered down. One hundred men, trained to kill and toughened by action in the Guadalcanal jungle and the bloody beaches of Helen. As the day lifted, they could see gigantic clouds of smoke and hear the explosions from down the island. From their vantage point they could see a chain of artillery positions set among the hills overlooking the landing beaches. The guns were keeping up a constant barrage, and the Japs had sighted them to put their payloads right on the beach.

Crandall shook his head. "Boy, somebody screwed the pooch when they didn't take these Jap guns out. They are murdering our boys."

Zarate nodded. "2/6 and 2/8 are getting creamed. It's like Guernica. The bastards are blasting the beaches."

Rudy came down the line. "We're lucky. The Japs don't know we are here yet, so we will take out as many of these positions as we can, before Tojo's boys figure out they have some guests who crashed the wedding."

Serpent slipped into the group and Johnny noticed that she had moved silently.

"We have the first artillery emplacement spotted. Here are the coordinates." She handed a piece of paper to Rudy.

Rudy gave it to George, who looked at it and then tore it into small bits. "Nothing written after this, okay." Serpent nodded.

Rudy slapped Fred on the back. "Okay boys, fire up that radio and call these coordinates in. It's time to give the Japs back some hot lead."

George got the radio live and called in and then handed the mic to Fred. He spoke a stream of words. The radio popped, and then another stream came back. Fred smiled and looked up at Rudy. "Message received, stand by for fireworks."

The emplacement they were watching was about a mile away, hidden in some trees. They heard the roar of incoming shells. The whole grove exploded in a hell-storm of fire. A cheer went up.

"Belay that," Rudy shouted. "Rig for silent running." He motioned to his platoon leaders and had a quiet conference.

Crandall came over to X-ray platoon. "Okay boys, we have to

prepare, move it quick. The Japs may not understand Navajo code talking, but they sure as hell can figure out we got some spotters behind the lines, so I imagine they'll come looking soon enough." He patted Fred on the back. "Good work, Private. You may help us put together Tojo's last stand."

George grinned. "It won't be the first time, Lieutenant."

THE SERPENT STRIKES

BILLY MARTENS

*B*illy was asleep in the jungle dark.

To him, there was nothing darker than the jungle at night, especially the equatorial jungle. A Montana winter's night didn't come close.

On Guadalcanal, in the Solomons, they'd been below the equator.

On Tarawa, just barely above the line, yet the Gilbert Islands, Bud had explained, were still considered equatorial.

He'd argued that the Marianas, where Saipan was located, although much farther north than the Solomons or Gilberts, was still inside the equatorial belt.

"So, when night comes, Billy, it will come almost as fast and complete as it did on the Canal and Tarawa. And it will be just as dark. As dark as a coal mine sunk deep into the earth."

Billy wasn't dreaming about coal mines or equators. He was being stalked by a panther that blended so perfectly with the jungle night Billy could only see its eyes. They burned with an eerie blue light. Its fangs gleamed like white fire. Billy raised his rifle to shoot. But the only thing in his hands was a pair of dry socks. He'd been about to pull them onto his feet when the panther appeared. Now he was without a weapon. He looked at his hands. That's all he had to fight with.

"Wake up, Marine," a voice whispered in his ear. "It's time to hunt."

Billy shot up, reaching for his new Ka-Bar. He was shoved back to the ground, pinned, and the knife swatted out of his hand. He knew he was dealing with a Jap infiltrator and tried to wrestle free. The Jap kept him pinned with one arm while with the other smacked a powerful fist into his face and rang his bell. Then the fist became a claw and squeezed his throat with so much muscle Billy began to pass out. He tried to keep fighting, but the Jap had overpowered him. He was finished.

Suddenly, the hand left his throat. Billy gasped for air. The Jap chuckled in the dark. "My soft Marine sergeant, I could kill you with one hand. How will you ever free my island from the enemy when even a little woman can defeat you?"

Serpent. Damn. Billy felt humiliated, but refused to show it. "I was asleep. And you're not little."

"I know you were asleep." She continued to whisper. "All I needed to do was clasp one small hand over your mouth and nose. I'd have suffocated you in moments. Or I could have coiled myself around you like the serpent you and the Japanese say I am. That would have been more satisfying. I'd have broken your back in seconds and all the bones in your body too. As you can see, I'm far stronger than you, my so very soft American sergeant. I fear you won't last long on the island of Saipan. Still, we need to work together. So, strip, Marine, and let's be on our way."

"Strip?"

"Like me. Clothes and uniforms slow a warrior down and make too much noise in the jungle, brushing up against every-thing. The enemy says you Americans are not only soft, but that you are no good at night fighting. We already know you are soft, don't we? They may be right that you have no stomach for hand-to-hand combat at night either. We'll find out. Strip. I won't have you endanger my life by running through the jungle like an ox."

"What about the others?" demanded Billy.

She laughed darkly. "What others? This is just you and me. Prove yourself, Sergeant. You didn't want to wrestle me in Hawaii. I can understand how your loss would have damaged your sense of manhood irreparably. And in front of your men? Imagine the humiliation. So, now you can wrestle the Japanese instead. But one thing is certain. If you do not show me you can kill with your bare hands, my guerillas will not be here with your platoon tomorrow morning. We cannot fight beside men who do not have the physical strength to defeat the foe. Now strip. No knife. No rifle. Oh, don't worry, Marine. You don't have anything I haven't seen before. And ignored. Men mean nothing to me. I said, no knife. You must show me what you can do when you only have your body as a weapon."

Billy unbuttoned his shirt. "I've fought the Nips hand-to-hand before. And in the dark."

"Good. Then it will be easy for you."

He shed everything, feeling awkward. Her face was expressionless. She was not that obvious in the dark, and he realized she had smeared mud all over her skin. He got an impression of broad shoulders, muscular arms and legs, height, and power. She exuded a kind of menace, as if she were a jungle beast. He turned his back to her as he tugged off his boxers. She laughed.

"How pitiful men are. Do I intimidate you, Sergeant?"

"No."

"Do I frighten you?"

"No."

"Liar. All men fear me. I am more than they are and therefore I make them less. I've never been bested by one in wrestling or boxing. Only using my hands and legs, I've killed over two hundred Japanese men since I was fifteen. You should be frightened of me. I could snuff out your life with only a few seconds of effort."

Suddenly, her hands were all over Billy's naked chest and stomach and legs. She was applying mud. He drew back, but she seized him by the arm and yanked him closer. He could see her smirk. They both knew that in unarmed combat she could crush him in moments. He stopped struggling and let her have his way and make him black from head to foot. Then she broke into a run.

It took everything he had to keep up with her. The slap of tree branches and jungle vines against his naked skin cut and scraped his flesh. She whispered as she ran, scarcely panting: "There is a large pillbox. It has a naval gun. At dawn, they will blast your LVTs and the beaches again. They have sentries around the perimeter of the pillbox. Some are dug in. There are twelve of them. We will kill all twelve. Then your men can come up and use their grenades and flamethrowers to destroy the gun. Or we can destroy it for them."

Billy's breath was ragged. "Just the two of us? Twelve sentries?"

"Having trouble breathing, Marine?" She smirked. "Don't worry, little man. I'm worth eight or ten of you. If you can kill just one soldier, we'll make out all right. If you can't, well, I'll kill your soldier and mine and we'll still make out all right. Ha ha. I don't need you, Sergeant. I brought you along simply to test you. No more talking. Hand signals only. I trust you can manage hand signals."

Billy was gasping by the time they reached their objective. The only reason he knew they had reached the pillbox, after running through the pitch-dark jungle for ten minutes, was watching Serpent jump into a pit he'd never noticed and wrapping her well-muscled arms around two Japanese heads. She squeezed ferociously and with short, sharp, savage jerks, snapped their necks. Billy watched the men sag like empty sacks. It had taken her maybe twenty seconds and there hadn't been a sound from her or her victims.

Serpent looked at him and pointed into the dark, but sprang in the opposite direction. An officer had appeared and was about to blow a whistle. Billy swore she made him swallow it, leaping on him, covering his mouth with one hand, snapping back his head with the force of her thrust, trapping him between both legs, and bringing them together like a vice till Billy saw blood spurt from the officer's nose and heard the popping of his ribs and backbone. A look that combined a furious killing rage with a wild, savage joy held Billy spellbound. She was like a demon or a wild jungle cat. But he had business to attend to.

Serpent had spotted two soldiers sharing a hole with a Nambu machine gun a hundred feet away. That's what she had pointed at. She killed the officer so swiftly Billy knew she'd spare a moment to watch and see if he got himself shot or eliminated his target. Damn, how did she get into his head so much? He needed to be cold and hard and empty of thought. The Japs swung the Nambu on him, but he was already on top of them, kicking and punching and butting with his head. He broke one's nose with a strong left, the other's face with a head butt, then stomped down on the taller soldier's windpipe as he fell, breaking it. Desperately, he twisted his fingers around the throat of the second soldier, more concerned about Serpent's reaction to his fighting skills than whether his foe had a knife he might ram into Billy's gut. In a fast minute, Billy had strangled his enemy. He heard a laugh behind him.

"Slow and awkward, Sergeant, but you obtained your objective. It feels good, doesn't it?" Panting from his kills, Billy looked up into a perfectly beautiful and perfectly wicked smile, black teeth in the black night. Transfixed by the strange attractiveness of her macabre grin, he didn't notice at first that she had another Japanese officer under one of her arms, granite bicep bulging into his throat, scarcely making any effort at all to trap him there, while he wriggled and gasped, unable to cry out or speak. She looked to be enjoying both his helpless struggle and Billy's sudden fascination with her rough femininity. Then, without breaking off her eye contact with Billy, and, he suspected, gloating at having each man in her power in different ways, she tightened her choke on the officer's neck, her muscles veining, and jerked his head upward with a vicious tug. The sound was like the snapping of dry bamboo. She let the officer drop, not even looking, still staring at Billy.

"Do you like how swiftly I can kill the enemy? Without blinking or feeling remorse? The only feelings I have are satisfaction that I've won and a certain amount of pleasure in the power I possess to end life." She jumped. "Hurry, before the six on the other side of the pillbox try to contact these sorry excuses for men."

They darted into the black, his lungs and legs burning. She suddenly motioned him to crawl, and he dropped to the jungle floor. He still couldn't see the pillbox the sentries were guarding. But he saw her wrestling with three men. As with all her other attacks, there was no sound from her or them. She worked with a silky, powerful precision, as if she were a leopard. His eyes were well adjusted to the night, and he could see her feline muscles rolling and rippling under her mud-dark skin. She dealt swiftly and silently with one, cracking his Adam's apple with a fierce elbow blow. Dealt with another by trapping his head between her knees and giving it a sudden twist to the right, breaking his neck, while fighting off a third soldier who attempted to bayonet her.

Very quickly the tables were turned on that soldier and she was on top, gouging out his eyes with her nails, smothering his screams with one hand, finishing him by crashing her fist into his throat repeatedly, her eyes lit by a wildfire that both terrified and dazzled Billy. She was a cougar in the Montana forest, beautifully, powerfully, and efficiently bringing down and slaying her prey. Her sleek, smooth, muscled body was in perfect condition, her claws and fangs sharp and merciless, her hunger absolute. She pretty much broke the soldier in half. Then she led Billy noiselessly towards their final victims two hundred feet away.

The Japs were peering into the dark, apparently having heard nothing, yet still suspicious, sensing the presence of an enemy. Billy got ahead of Serpent. He hurtled through the blackness and launched himself onto two soldiers, pinning them under his body weight. He wrapped an arm around each soldier's neck, a skill Serpent was fond of employing, and squeezed with all his might, cutting off their shouts. A third soldier sprang onto his back, growling in Japanese. He did not stay long. Billy felt him get pried off. The soldier gave a cry that was a mixture of gasping and gurgling. Billy glanced back and saw Serpent, who looked to be a foot taller than the Jap, standing behind her enemy with her arms twisted around his neck.

His struggles were useless against her strength. He kicked wildly, flailed his arms, tried to smack his head and helmet back into her face. She smiled grimly and avoided his blows, her muscles tightening around his neck, choking him to death while Billy did the same to his two. She finished the job first and came to tower over Billy, watching him bear down, seeing the soldiers strike at him with their fists and feet, the blows growing weaker until they stopped altogether and their tongues rolled out of their mouths.

"You must get faster," Serpent hissed as Billy climbed off the two bodies. "But at least you have some muscles and you are not a coward. Now, quickly, gather up all the grenades you can. My fighters will be here soon."

"Your fighters?"

"Yes. My guerillas. I've changed my mind. I'm not waiting for your platoon to reach us in the morning. My fighters are going to take out this pillbox on their own. We will show you Marines what we can accomplish without your help."

She smiled her black-toothed smile that mixed beauty with

evil, the serpent's smile that allured and hypnotized its victims. The smile that fascinated him. He could see she knew it and liked it. It was another hold she had over him besides being stronger and faster. Her eyes laughed at his predicament.

"My poor little Marine sergeant," she whispered. "Have I made you that helpless against my charms and spells so quickly? How delightful. I will put your enthrallment with me to good use in combat. Now, gather all the grenades you can find."

"Why?"

"I'm a sergeant as much as you're a sergeant. And I lead the resistance your commanding officers desperately need to conquer this island. I matter more than you do. Obey me, Sergeant Martens. I give the orders. I won't take orders from you."

Billy glared defiance at her. "No."

She glared defiance back. "No? Is that what I heard?"

"I'm not taking orders from you, snake woman. I'm the Marine here. You'll take them from me. Understood?"

She punched him in the stomach, and he doubled over in pain. Then she brought her knee up into his jaw with a crack. He staggered. Her large, thick fist slammed into the top of his head. He crashed to the ground, dazed. She kicked him and pushed him flat with her foot. She ground it into his throat. He grunted and fought to wrench it from his neck. He might as well have tried to shift a steel pillar. She smiled with all her black teeth and pressed down harder. Billy clawed at her leg helplessly.

"You will obey my orders," she said. "I am your commanding officer on Saipan. No one else. Is that understood?"

Billy squirmed under the pressure of her foot on his windpipe and could not speak.

"Understood, Sergeant? Nod your head. You can still do that."

Billy fought a little longer, pawing at her leg, a long leg knotted with muscle. Then he gave in. He jerked his head up and down. She released her foot from his throat. Then reached down, clutched him by the hair of his head, and hauled him to his feet.

Billy cursed, swaying and lurching and desperately gulping air. She had humiliated him once again. Damn.

"You're no woman," he spat.

She laughed. "And you're no man. I'm more of a man than you are. And more of a platoon sergeant. I will give the orders. You will obey them. Have you grasped that concept yet?"

"Yes."

Her long, strong fingers were still knotted tightly in his hair. She gave his head a savage shake. "What did you say? Snap it out or else."

"Yes, Sergeant!"

"Good boy. Now, collect the grenades and bring them to me. If you wish to cover yourself before my fighters get here, see if you can find clean garments from among the dead. It's up to you. They won't care one way or the other. But a timid American like you from your timid culture would. Am I right?"

Feeling a mixture of rage and shame, Billy made his way from Jap body to Jap body. For a few minutes, he had felt like a tough warrior from a Marine Raider battalion. Serpent had quickly taken that away and made him feel small, smaller than he'd ever felt in his life. It was like they'd been to a branding of newborns in Montana and she'd hauled him down into the dirt and castrated him along with the other bull calves. Grinning and making it look easy while the other cowhands gathered around to watch and jeer. He hated the feeling and swore he would get to the point where she respected him and treated him like an equal. It made him furious that she had so much influence over him, but she did. He was determined to prove himself to her or die trying.

He found thirty-one Jap grenades. The kind they armed by smacking the tops against their helmets or into the ground. He also found a pair of shorts in a pack––clean, comfortable and the right waist size, along with a leather belt. Serpent made no comment when he returned except to tell him to keep three grenades for himself. He cinched his belt tighter and stuffed them into his pockets. She ignored him. Her women and men were emerging from the darkness.

Most of them wore dark tops and pants that reminded him of pajamas. They carried American weapons, Thompsons, but he saw a few M1 carbines as well, and several Colt 1911s strapped to women's hips next to Ka-Bar knives. Billy was surprised that Serpent took a minute to introduce each of them, considering how much contempt she felt for him. But he supposed it had more to do with honoring them than being respectful to a lowly man she had stripped of his manhood.

Their faces were black with mud, so Billy was sure he could never put names to faces in the daylight. He tried to concentrate and retain what Serpent told him. Even in the dark, and despite the thick mud, Billy could see how handsome, slender and well-built the women fighters were, just like Serpent. Tasina, sixteen. Kamia, twenty-two. Latasi, twenty-nine. Sirena, thirty-five. Amista, eighteen, the only one who smiled at him, her teeth white as moonlight.

Billy was surprised that a stout fighter, with a figure like a bull, was a woman of seventy-seven, not a man. She looked as grim as a death head. Hudana picked up on the doubtful look on his face when Serpent announced her age. She smiled with teeth as black as her leader's. "I have killed ninety Japanese. All younger than me. It was my pleasure. I will kill more. Watch, Mr. American."

There were four men. All slim, all as strong as the women, all unsmiling. Chataga, twenty-one. Gamomo, forty. Husto, sixty-six. Poyo, seventeen. They only nodded their heads at him and he nodded back. Hoping that Serpent would not crow at how she had physically overpowered him several times that night, Billy said nothing. He was worried she would contrive matches and pit him against each of her fighters, women and men, then laugh as each defeated him, one after the other. Including sixteen-year-old Tasina, who came off as if she were twenty-five, as cocky and muscular as Serpent. And the skinny seventeen-year-old Poyo, who exuded as much self-confidence as any Marine that Billy had ever met. Hudana, he knew, would relish the opportunity to go against him in unarmed combat. He had no illusions about what the outcome of that contest would be.

But Serpent was intent on proving the prowess of her fighting force to the United States Marines. Hudana told her K Company would arrive at the pillbox in an hour, led by another of the Chamorran women, Mira. Serpent turned to Billy with a sneer curling her lips——"Mira is only fifteen, but she is more than you." Then she spoke to the others rapidly in their own language. The translation she offered Billy was spoken just as quickly. "We know where the air vents are. We know where their hidden entrance and exit is. You will see that the opening for the naval gun is obvious. The sentries who would stop us are dead. We hope the ones manning the naval gun will come out and check on them so we can force our way in. If not, the other openings will suffice."

Billy followed her and the others. Even when he was on top of it, he scarcely noticed the enemy fortification. It was bound in coconut tree trunks, circled in concrete, and stacked with green bamboo layered between vast amounts of sand. It reminded him of blockhouses on Tarawa. Serpent led him to the dark opening for the naval gun. She warned him that at the first flicker of movement Nambus trained on the opening would fire immediately. The Chamorro had tried to take out pillboxes before and had lost too many fighters. She was determined to succeed this time. She wanted the Marines to find a smoking wreck when they arrived. She craved their awe and their respect.

When her attack happened, it happened quickly. A patrol emerged from the hidden exit. Billy could see the four Jap soldiers and an officer from where he was crouching. Tasina, Hudana, Chataga and Poyo were lurking nearby, hoping and praying there would be an inspection of the pillbox and the sentries. Hudana killed two men quickly, bearing them to the ground under her weight and easily choking them to death, one massive hand squeezing each throat. Tasina garroted another from behind, looping a strip of leather around the soldier's neck, planting her knee in his back, and pulling backwards with all her strength, which Billy could see was considerable. Poyo slapped his hand over the officer's mouth and thrust a Ka-Bar into his heart five or six times. Chataga merely karate chopped his target on the Adam's apple, a swift, vicious, accurate blow, and watched the soldier drop.

All four guerillas charged into the pillbox, guns firing. The other Chamorro quickly joined them. But Serpent planted a large hand on Billy's chest. "You will not. It is for us to do. It will be our victory."

"Serpent ––"

"If any of the enemy gets past us, you may slay them. But let one live."

"Why?"

"I want him to tell his army that Chamorro women and men destroyed their pillbox here. Not Marines. Chamorro islanders. I want him to sow fear."

Then she rushed through the entrance without a firearm, her hands curled like claws.

The firing went on for about forty-five seconds. Two Japs scrambled from the exit and Billy pounced on one, letting the other escape into the darkness. They wrestled among the thick stands of bamboo, constantly slamming into the tall canes. Well aware of what Serpent would say if one of her fighters had to intervene to save his ass, Billy was far more brutal than he'd been on Tarawa. He bit off an ear, bit off the nose, then smashed the soldier's skull to jelly with a rock while choking him out with the other hand. Panting loudly, he stared down at the bloody pulp of a face and felt nothing.

"Wow, American man, I'm impressed."

Billy looked up at Tasina, who was smirking at him, one hand holding a Tommy gun, its barrel curling with white smoke, the other hand holding an apple she had bitten into.

"I'm impressed too."

It was the young woman with the white smile and long, lanky figure, Amista. She was chewing an apple too, her M1 carbine slung over her shoulder, a sword shining with blood in her fist. Her face was spattered in blood. She grinned.

"Chamorra told us you were not a good fighter," Amista said in an English with an attractive accent. "Clearly, you learn fast. I look forward to seeing what you do to your next foe."

Tasina chewed her apple, still smirking at him. "Me too, American man."

Billy kept staring at Amista as she ate her apple and gripped the *katana*. She gazed back and laughed prettily, as if they were at a party or a dance. "The officer did not want the apple in his pocket or the sword in his hand. So I relieved him of both. He did not seem to mind being killed by his own blade, Mr. American man. It was as if he welcomed it. This made my task so much easier and pleasant." She was still smiling when she said, "The bastards all deserve to be gutted like pigs. I was happy to give him a *hari-kari* experience and watch his entrails spill into his hands. The Japanese tortured my mother, father, and older sister to death."

"I'm sorry," Billy mumbled, mesmerized by the sight of two beautiful Chamorro warrior women standing so proudly and defiantly in front of him. "I hope you have other family."

"I do." She kissed Tasina's cheek. "This is my little sister."

"Your little sister?"

"Yes. Isn't she perfect?"

Billy didn't know what to say. "You're both perfect."

Amista's smile grew. "Why, thank you, sir."

"How is it you two speak American so well?" Billy asked.

Amista shrugged. "Our leader has taught us. For years

Chamorra taught us to read it and write it and speak it. As if we were university students at her Yale. We knew Americans would come after Pearl Harbor. We knew nothing about Marines. We just knew Americans would come." She extended her apple to him. "I would like to share the rest of it with you, Mr. American man. Okay?"

Billy hesitated, then took the apple from her and bit into it. He could taste her lips and mouth where she'd already chewed. It sent a fast tingle through his body. She nodded.

"Good, hey?" she laughed.

2 8

THE CHAMORRO

THE CORPSMAN

We came up on Billy and the Chamorro at dawn and I swear to God, he was not the Billy we'd landed with on Saipan . He looked like he was from a frigging Marine Raider battalion. Heck, he looked like a frigging Chamorro native. Which was not a bad thing. This teen Mari was leading us through the jungle, and all the guys thought she was stunning. She made me think of my gal from Tonga. Sure, Kalasia was taller and browner and had bigger bones, but they both seemed to have a lot in common. The pride, the dignity, the beauty, the warmth, and the courage.

So, there's Billy with Serpent and her fighting force, most of whom were women. Behind them was a pillbox billowing with dark smoke. They were beautiful, proud, powerful women that made every Marine's heart flip. They dressed in black tops and pants like pajamas and carried all kinds of weapons––Thompsons, 1911s, M1 carbines, Ka-Bars, Jap grenades, *katanas*, wicked looking take-your-head-in-one-swipe machetes. One man had a Nambu machine gun he held like a rifle. Their faces and hands were caked in dried mud and spattered with blood. Billy didn't look any different, except he was naked to the waist and sporting a pair of Jap Army shorts. I was going to say he was taller, but Serpent was as tall as he was, and two other girls who looked to be sisters were only a few inches shorter. He looked like he belonged with the Chamorro and not with us.

Captain Rudebaker stood surveying the burning pillbox and the Jap bodies littered around it, hands on his hips, talking to Serpent. I examined each corpse. Not one of them had a bullet hole. Broken heads, broken necks, broken arms, caved-in chests, gouged out eyes. But no bullet holes or knife wounds. They'd all been killed in unarmed combat. Billy told me the bodies burning inside had been shot or knifed. Or sliced by *katanas*.

I looked at a few wounds of the Chamorro. One of the men was Husto, who said he was sixty-six, but looked more like fifty. He asked for a cigarette and smoked it happily while I dressed the path a bullet had made scorching across his forearm. A young woman named Kamia had been slashed on the leg. I dealt with that, sprinkling it with sulfa powder and wrapping it in gauze. I asked her if she was in pain and she shook her head. Had it been a sword? She nodded, asked for a cigarette, smoked it for a few moments, and finally spoke. Her English was impeccable. Including the slang.

"Yes, for sure. He had his little *katana*." Her pretty lips curled in derision. "A few blows and I took it from him. This was not a difficult task. Then I plunged it into his bowels until he had no bowels." She blew out a stream of smoke from her nostrils. "I felt like Superman."

"You felt like Superman?"

Suddenly she grinned, which transformed her face. Her dark eyes flashed with beauty and strength. "Yeah, for sure. I was stronger than him and faster than him. He could not stop me. I was the man of steel." She blew out more smoke, always using her nostrils. "Now I have his steel. And I will use it on others. This is a wonderful thing. I like it." She smiled into my eyes. "It is ironic."

Someone had bitten through Billy's left earlobe, but he swore it wasn't one of the Chamorro. "I had a fight with a Jap. This Chamorro bunch only uses weapons as a last resort. They prefer to kill quickly and quietly with their hands and legs. I had to show them a Marine could do what they do. I saw Serpent in action. It was like a Batman comic book. She's a frigging whirlwind in combat. POW. SOK. WHAM."

I cleaned and taped the bite. He'd already had shots for tetanus. "Just like you."

"With guns and swords, maybe, Bud. I have a long way to go to fight like Serpent. Or to defeat her in a match, to tell you the truth. She's strong as a horse and fast as a rattler. She's kicked my ass two or three times. Has muscles of iron. And loves to taunt her victims."

"Sounds like she has a thing for you, Billy."

"Ha. The only thing she has a thing for is proving herself superior to all men and rubbing their noses in it."

"I'm pretty confident you'll turn the tables on her. I'm also pretty confident that's what she wants."

"Yeah? So, since when did you become the Corps' expert on the ways and wiles of women?"

"Since Tonga," I told Billy. That was the truth, too. "I love Kalasia, Billy. I love her for who she is inside. You know that. But also know I never could run from her eyes or her hair or her figure. She was too much for this American boy. Still is." I patted Billy on the shoulder. "Is Serpent too much for you?"

"Oh, yeah."

"But you like her."

Billy lit a cigarette. "I don't know."

"Oh, for sure, Marine, you know. I'll bet a sawbuck you like her physical strength, you like the fight in her, you like the way she can defeat the enemy with her bare hands. You like the fact she can overpower you. You probably like the way she looks too."

"Are you kidding, Bud? Black teeth? Frizzy ugly yellow hair?"

"Have you seen her smile?" I asked him.

"Oh, sure, I've seen her evil little smile," he replied.

"And?"

"And nothing."

"Was that all there was to it? Just some kind of evil, bewitching smile?"

Billy shook his head. "Damn. She knows how to get into my brain. She smiles, and she looks wicked. But she also looks good in some weird way. I get pulled in. Shit, Bud, I find her fascinating. Why the heck should I find her fascinating?"

I smiled. I got it. "Because you've never met a woman like her before. And you like everything about her. Even the stuff you think you're not supposed to like."

"I don't. I don't like the weird stuff."

"Yeah, you do."

"I don't like the black teeth."

"The Chamorro think it's attractive. Plus, it scares the crap out of the Japs. I heard they do it because animals have white teeth and they want to be different from the animals."

"Different from the animals? She makes me think of a jungle cat the way she moves. She's a leopard. A panther. A tiger. Do you know she fought the entire night naked? One of her girls brought her the outfit she's wearing, and she only put it on because she knew you guys were coming."

"And you love it," I insisted. "You love her power. You love the leopard and the panther. You love the strong, deadly woman she is."

"I don't, Bud, for crap's sake."

"You do," I pushed. "You don't just love the power she has over the enemy. They're putty in her hands. You love the power she has over you. You're putty too. She can twist you and shape you anyway she likes. And you like her to have that kind of power. No one else ever has."

"You're nuts."

"Face it, Billy Boy. A strong woman attracts you, the stronger the better. Other guys would run from her muscles and her might. At how easily and happily she can kill the enemy. They'd be afraid of her. Geez. Six-foot of raw female power just burning to lay a beating on someone. They saw her lick blood off the knife she used to gut a Jap. Serpent is a she-devil to them. But not to you. You like the way she is. You like what she can do to you. You like the way she makes you feel."

"What are you?" snapped Billy. "The pope, the chaplain, and Mother Mary all rolled up with Sigmund Freud? You want me to lie down and tell you about my dreams?"

"I already know your dreams. I'll bet you've dreamed about her already. Haven't you? It may not have been a carbon copy of Serpent, but you knew damn well it was her. You saw that rough Chamorro beauty in dream language. Am I right?"

"Shut up, Bud! Just shut the hell up!" Billy threw down his cigarette. "Go be a shrink in someone else's head. Get out of mine." He stomped off. Then he stopped and glared back at me. "And she's not a beauty, okay? Knock it off about that. She has black teeth and ugly hair, and she's dripping in blood. She's no Lana Turner. She's no Rita Hayworth. She's not the woman I danced with at the USO show in Hawaii. So, give it a rest."

"But you see past the teeth and hair and blood, Billy. I know you do. You see the shining light way back of it all."

"Oh, for Pete's sake, will you shut it? A shining light back of it all? So, now you've got us in a Marine Corps version of *Going My Way* and you're Bing Crosby the frigging singing priest?"

The movie had come out in May and a bunch of us had managed to beg, borrow, and steal passes to get off base and see it. Maybe I would make a good Bing Crosby. Bing or Bud, Billy couldn't get away from me. Impressed with how the Chamorro had taken out the pillbox with no casualties, Rudy ordered Achilles Squad to attach themselves to the islanders and move out well ahead of X-Ray Platoon and K Company. Johnny and the

Navajo joined the advance team. So did I. Rudy expected a lot of brawls to ensue, armed and unarmed. He was right.

OUR APPROACH up the left flank of Saipan, an assault that took us away from the coast and into the interior, was honeycombed with machine-gun nests, pillboxes, blockhouses and spider's nests—snipers. The Chamorro preferred night fighting, but we had to push through during the daylight hours because we had to keep pace with the 27th Army Division on our right flank and the 4th Marine Division on their right flank. Serpent hated losing the advantage of darkness and stealth. One of her men, Gamomo, was sawed in half by two hidden Nambus firing together, something she swore could never have happened at night. Losing Chataga, hit by a sniper in broad daylight, made her curse the Corps and the IJA, the Imperial Japanese Army. Once darkness fell and we bunkered down, she took her fighters and Billy into the jungle to avenge the deaths.

He never told me what happened. I had to put some stitches into him and a few of the others. Tasina had cut notches in the stock of her M1 carbine. So had Kamia, who could have stolen my heart if I weren't already in love with my Tonga gal, Kalasia. It's almost as if she knew. She saw me glance at the fresh white cuts into the wood, seven of them. She smiled, smoking a Player's I'd given her. "It was easy, Bud," she said, keeping her dark eyes fixed on mine. "Don't worry. I can handle the Japs and the jungle. But thank you for caring about me. I like it."

Our 81mm mortar, Pretty Boy, and Big Fifty, and The Dragon and his flamethrower worked it by day. The Navajo called in artillery and air strikes on massive blockhouses that bristled with roaring naval guns, barking Jap mortars, and crackling Nambus, all reinforced by dozens of tree snipers. Serpent and Billy and her guerillas worked by night, slipping into the bamboo stands and coconut groves after the swift equatorial sunset. Always returning muddied up and bloodied up. The women proud and disdainful of Marines who would not fight at night if they could help it. Smoking cigarettes before grabbing some sleep at dawn. Making sure the Marines saw the fresh notches they'd cut into the stocks of their carbines and Thompsons.

Typically, the Chamorro never came to me for help unless they had a severe wound. Kamia kept showing up after every night assault. Even a slight cut warranted my attention. I never said a thing about it, just went along with her game, whatever it was.

"You keep putting notches into your carbine and you won't have any stock left to shoot with," I teased her.

Always her sweet smile. You'd think we'd been talking about a hymn she liked in church. "You know I don't need a gun to kill with, Bud. My hands are sufficient."

"I do know that, Kamia."

"Does that trouble you?"

"No."

She prodded me playfully with her bare foot, the skin on it as tough as iron. "Are you sure?"

"I like knowing you can defend yourself."

"It matters?"

"Of course, it matters. What happens to all our combatants matters to me."

"Some more than others?" She prodded me with her foot again. "I fight naked, you know."

"Uh ... Billy told me about that, yeah."

"It's so much easier to run and wrestle. But it terrifies the Japanese men. They don't know what to do with me."

"I'll bet," I responded, finishing up with her third and final cut.

She blew a stream of white smoke from her nostrils and grinned, shoving me back on my can with a powerful thrust from her foot. She laughed, her black eyes flashing with sunlight. "Would you?"

I prayed about this. The *"lead me not into temptation"* kind of prayer. It's pointless to say I wasn't attracted to her. I adored Kalasia, but Kamia definitely tested me. I told her about my Kalasia and she congratulated me on loving an island woman, but it didn't stop her from amusing herself with me. I couldn't send her to anyone else for medical aid and I refused to be nasty to her, a brave young woman. So, I just had to tough it out and pray.

I prayed for Billy too, but in a different way. I wanted him to be tempted, and I wanted Chamorra to be tempted too. Maybe not to go all the way, but I wanted them to fall for each other, and fall hard. I didn't know what that would look like, but I knew if Billy was ever going to love a woman she needed to be Montana strong and much more than he could handle. That was the only way he'd stay interested. He had to latch onto a mustang.

After all, Billy was a wild concoction himself. Cowboy, mountain man, Mennonite, hunter. Raised to be a conscientious objector, but born with warrior in his blood. God had placed him in a pacifist family, but gifted him for combat. Who understood such complexities and complications? Yet Stonewall Jackson had been raised Presbyterian and fought like hell. Lee had been Episcopalian and had fought like double hell. Lincoln had been blessed with a Quaker general who fought as hard as Lee or Jackson. So, who could understand it?

Blessed be the Lord, my strength, which teacheth my hands to war and my fingers to fight. My goodness, and my fortress, my high tower, and my deliverer, my shield, and he in whom I trust.

I just knew Billy would never be happy with a sweet, peaceful, cut-the-crusts-off-the-sandwich-bread, Sunday-go-to-meeting, I-only-wear-dresses, regular American housewife. Chamorra was his best bet. I simply needed them both to realize they were meant for each other. And I needed Chamorra to realize it more than Billy because, so far as Billy was concerned, it was clear to me she had already got inside his head and heart. I wanted him to get inside hers.

But I didn't know if Billy was impressing Chamorra by how he dealt with Japs on their midnight excursions. I only knew one thing. If God so arranged things that Chamorra saw the big, brave, gunslinging cowboy Billy could be, once he jumped on his stallion and rode into the Wild West, she'd be hooked for life. So, I prayed. Funny thing about prayer. You can wait for months, or years, or a lifetime for an answer. Other times, God's right there. Like, on a Sunday morning, June 18, 1944.

We got caught in an ambush, despite all our precautions and our Chamorro scouts. The Nips hit us with Nambus, and mortars, and grenades, and snipers, and had us in a crossfire that was knocking us out. Bobby Mac went down from a burst of machine gun fire that ripped his left leg off below the knee. I gave him a syrette of morphine, wrapped a tourniquet around his thigh as tightly as I dared, and yelled for my body snatchers to get him back to the field hospital a half-mile back. I didn't think he'd make it. But he was only the first of many.

Tommy Earp took a slug to the shoulder that had him bleeding out like a frigging river. Sid Greene, Superman Too, had to take over manning the Fifty. Sam Kane, Red O'Brien's backup on the flamethrower, was blown to pieces by a mortar bomb that landed right in his lap. Hades Squad, right behind us and led by Sergeant Schott and Corporal Rosenbaum, were decimated by point blank fire from one of the big coastal guns.

The Japs liked to camouflage them and use the 20cm/12 short everywhere. They zeroed in this one to drop its shells right behind the advance force, which was us, Achilles. Hades had our backs. A few fast rounds were all it took to wipe out the entire Hades Squad of twelve men. I scrambled back to look for survivors, but there wasn't a single man left alive. Heads, arms, legs, and torsos without limbs were all I could find in the smoking, torn-up earth.

The Navajo were calling in an air strike. Johnny frantically hosed down Jap machine-gun nests with his BAR to keep his code talkers alive while bullets ripped up the air all around them. Two Chamorro women were trapped ahead of us. The fighter named Latasi sprinted up to help them and was shredded by streams of Nambu fire coming from four different directions. Chamorra, Serpent, howled in rage and pain as she watched Latasi's body disintegrate in front of our eyes. She was helpless to save Latasi. And helpless to save the two who were still trapped and pinned down––Tasina, the sixteen-year-old, and her sister Amista. I knew Billy liked them. For all I knew, he liked them more than Chamorra. But, like them or not, prayer or no prayer, I wasn't prepared for what happened next. Maybe God wasn't either.

We knew the planes were on their way from the carrier. We also knew the girls were close enough to the blockhouse to get killed by the bomb drop. We kept our heads down and prayed for the best as a storm of gunfire raged over us and around us. Even Chamorra knew there was nothing else we could do. The only person who didn't seem to know it was Billy. Crazy Billy.

No one had spotted him snaking away through the jungle. No one had even given Billy a thought. We were worried about Tasina and Amista and our own asses. Suddenly, the crazy fool was right behind the Jap machine-gun nests, roaring out of the bamboo and coconut palms with a Thomson blasting away in each hand and two more slung over his back, Sergeant Comic Book Marine. He cut four nests to ribbons in seconds, his Tarawa headband, the *hachimaki,* with its rising sun streaming from his head. Then he turned on the Japs in pits with their mortars and rifles, and on all the grenade throwers, slaughtering them, shoving a barrel into one *katana*-swinging officer's gut and emptying his magazine, slicing the Nip in half.

"What the hell, Billy?" Johnny yelled, peppering the Japs trying to escape the berserk US Marine with his BAR. "You think you're frigging John Wayne in the frigging *Fighting Seabees*?"

I glanced at Chamorra. She was aghast, her black teeth clenched, her wild eyes wilder than they'd ever been, her hands curled into tight fists. "My god, oh, dear god, what the hell is this? How could I not see this? Who is this devil?"

Billy dropped two empty Thompsons and ripped the second pair off his back and ran towards the sisters, machine gunning snipers out of the trees, screaming something we could not hear. The naval gun tried to depress enough to blast him, but all it could do was fire rounds over his head and way behind Achilles. We all heard the whine of incoming aircraft at the same time. Crap, how I prayed. Get out of there, Billy! Get the girls and get out of there!

One of them was wounded and couldn't walk. Billy scooped her up as if she were a kitten and ran with her under one arm, still firing up into the trees with the Thompson in his free hand. The other sister sprinted beside him. Then we saw her fall. Hit. The entire squad groaned out loud at the same time. But I knew damn well Billy would never leave her behind, and the rest of us knew it too. He threw away his Thompson, bent, picked her up, and came running towards us, Jap bullets kicking up dirt around his boots, holding onto both Tamisa and Amista with all the strength he had left.

I jumped to my feet. "You crazy fool! You crazy fool, Billy! Run! Run! INCOMING!"

The aircraft were on top of us.

They were diving. I could hear them diving. I heard the scream of wings. So did everyone else.

Suddenly, Marines were on their knees, exposing themselves to get off better shots at the treetops, blasting away, covering Billy's run, and the Chamorro were kneeling and standing and firing with them. The first bomb struck in a boil of black smoke and bright orange light. The force of the blast flattened Billy, but he got up and kept coming. The Marines and Chamorro refused to take cover and kept firing. A second bomb fell. A third. We watched the naval gun, uprooted, sail into the air and flip once, along with dozens of palm fronds and stalks of green bamboo. The blast wave was massive. Billy went down and did not get back up.

The Navy fliers dropped ten bombs. They shattered the blockhouse. It burned like a Roman candle, smoke pouring into the jungle and the sky. The last explosion had scarcely died away before I heard Billy yelling, "Corpsman! Corpsman!" I jumped up and ran for him and the girls like the devil, heedless of snipers. I didn't expect the squad and Chamorro to run with me, guns blasting at the coconut trees. But they did.

I dropped next to Billy and the sisters. There was blood everywhere. Johnny hefted Billy up under one arm and began lugging him back to our position. "Banzai Billy," he growled, "god help us."

Sammy Crown carried Amista back, and Garowski lifted Tasina in his arms.

"Hey," Garowski joked, "I thought you'd be light."

Despite her pain, she gave him her best smile. "I'm not, American man. Lots of muscle."

I set everything to rights in a few minutes with gauze and sulfa powder. Once I got the bleeding stopped, I knew the sisters would be okay. It had looked messy out in the field, but none of the three had lost so much blood they were in danger. To be honest, though, Billy took longer than a few minutes to set to rights. I had to pick steel out of his back for an hour.

I lie. You didn't need a medical degree to remove the shrapnel in his back. Just a steady hand and a strong stomach, which Amista had in spades. She asked if she could do it. I said yes. If you'd seen the shine in her eyes like I saw it as she bent over Billy, you'd have known what hero worship looked like. You'd also have realized if Billy had wanted a Chamorro bride, Amista would have said yes before he got the words out of his mouth.

They shot Tasina through the arm, and they clipped Amista on the shoulder. No harm done, really. Not on those two. They were tough as Sherman tanks. They'd be fighting again in a day. I turned to other casualties and left Amista to worship Billy, pick out the shards of steel, sponge up the blood, and tell him what an amazing man he was. While her younger sister, Tasina, made every attempt to usurp her, tipping her canteen to Billy's mouth, spoon feeding him a traditional pudding she'd made and carried in her pack, and rubbing his shoulders while Amista glared at her.

Now you might have thought this episode would have Chamorra at Billy's feet too. It didn't happen that way. While Tasina and Amista swooned over their brave Marine, Chamorra maintained her distance and, if anything, treated Billy with more disdain and contempt than she had before.

What the hell? That was the one part of my prayer that didn't work out very well.

29

YOU CAN'T GO HOME AGAIN

JOHNNY STRANGE

The wheels of the 1940 Chevy Coupe crunched against the curb as Johnny slowed to a stop in front of the enormous house on School Road in Sandpoint. It was late August, and though it was morning, the Idaho day was already warming. Johnny rolled the car window down and in the silence he could hear some songbirds trying to make the morning coolness last. Down the hill, at the end of the road, visible through the trees, the Pend Oreille River flowed by, deep and still and inviting. Dark, fresh, Idaho river water, not the briny sea he had sailed coming home. Not the dark, breaking waves of Guadalcanal grinding the gravel into sand and the bones into mud, or the blood-filled lagoon of Helen with its bobbing bodies like small buoys—buoys that marked the departure point of another Marine from this war and this life.

His heart was pounding. He had come so far, and now he wanted to start the motor and drive away. He put his foot on the starter switch...

"Don't do it, Strange."

Crandall? What are you doing here?

"Don't do what, Lieutenant?"

"Don't run, Strange. This is what you've been fighting for. If you run, you die. You might as well die right here."

You're right, Lieutenant. I might as well die right here.

Johnny pushed down on the handle and swung the car door open. He got out and stood, straight and tall in the morning sun, the dress uniform crisp against the rising heat, the double chevrons plain on the shoulder. On his chest were the campaign ribbons and the Purple Heart and the division citation. Johnny Strange took a deep breath. He looked at his kit in the back seat and then left it there.

I may not be staying long.

Another breath, deep, resigned.

Get it over with, Strange, and then you can get on with your life.

He willed his feet to take the first step, and then he was striding up the walk and standing at the door.

Ulysses, the Wanderer, home to Ithaca...

His white-gloved hand reached out, pulled back, found the doorbell button. He pressed it. From inside he heard the chiming of the bells, deep, musical, what he expected from the house of a wealthy man.

He waited for a minute, almost turned and walked away. Then he heard the steps coming down the hall. A woman's steps.

Marjean!

The door opened and an older black woman stood looking at him, a question in her eyes. Then dawning recognition.

"Mr. Johnny?"

He nodded. His hands opened and closed and he willed them back to his sides.

"Oh my, Miss Marjean thought you were coming tonight."

"I caught an early flight into Spokane. And took a bus. And got my car..." He stopped, stood silent.

The woman turned. Her voice was rich and melodious. She called out. "Miss Marjean, Miss Marjean."

From somewhere in the house, a voice. That voice. Clear, like a mountain stream, like bells and ice.

"What is it, Cecelia?"

"Someone to see you, Miss Marjean." The woman smiled and motioned for Johnny to come in. He stepped inside, stood in the hall, waiting...

Someone came to the top of the stairs. He looked up. A woman. She had on a simple housedress. Cornsilk hair, green eyes, little wolf teeth. She stopped, stared down. "Oh, my God. Johnny? But I'm not ready. I have a dress, I... I..."

They stood staring at each other. He the Marine, she the fawn poised for flight. He took a step toward the bottom of the stairs. He didn't want them to; he wanted to be strong, let her tell him to go away, but his arms lifted. Then she was flying down the stairs, running to him, plunging into his arms. He felt the steel of her clasping hands around his back, felt her breasts pressed into him. "Johnny, oh my God, Johnny!!"

His arms slowly went around her. Then he was crushing her to him. Life, she was life, and he had returned from hell and the grave and she was welcoming him home and the days between them fled like snow on a sun-warmed field. She was lifting her face and tears streamed down. "Johnny, oh my God, Johnny."

He bent to her, and she pulled his face down and then he was kissing her and all the passion and heat and love that lay dormant in him for all those months and years rose and it was like he couldn't breathe, and he felt so alive, or like he was dying or....

He pulled away. "Marjean, I... I'm back, I..."

"Johnny! Johnny!"

A hand shook him...

"Johnny, wake up, man."

He opened his eyes.

Bud? What the hell?

"You okay, Johnny? You were groaning. You sounded like you were dying."

He closed his eyes, opened them, sat up. "I'm okay, Bud. I must have been dreaming. I was home, Bud, home with Marjean."

Bud smiled, the sad smile that Johnny knew well. The sad smile that came with trying to save men with no guts, or legs blown off, or an arm gone and only a bloody stump remaining because they pulled the damn igniter too soon. The smile he first saw when Eddie Kramer died and Bud looked up and shook his head.

"Sorry, Johnny. Didn't mean to interrupt. Go back to sleep. It's a couple hours to dawn."

"Where's Billy?"

"He's out with Serpent. They spotted a big gun emplacement at the head of the ridge down the valley and the Chamorros went to take it out. He won't say it, but I think he's really taken by Serpent."

"The Chamorro? Billy?"

Bud grinned, and this time there was life in it. "Yeah, I think there's more to Serpent than meets the eye." Bud moved away and Johnny lay back. He closed his eyes...

<hr>

THE HOTEL WAS in a rundown part of Spokane. Weeds grew in the cracks that marred the concrete sidewalk in front. The sign said "HOTEL ELITE," and under that "Rooms, 25¢ a night." The narrow stairwell ran up between a pawnshop and a small grocery store. Johnny started up. He was in civilian clothes, jeans, a pullover sweater, dark coat. He felt his KA-BAR against his hip, under the jacket. At the top was a Dutch window looking into a reception area. There were overflowing ashtrays on the counter, and the stench of cigarette butts rose to his nostrils. An old man sat in a chair behind the glass, listening to the radio, a half-empty bottle of Coke on a stand next to his chair. The old man glanced up, saw Johnny standing there.

"Yeah, whaddaya want?"

"Jenkins, Harold Jenkins. Does he live here?"

"I don't know no Jenkins, mister. Take off."

The ten-dollar bill felt crisp in his fingers as he pulled it from his pocket. He slid it across the counter. The old man's eyes widened.

"Jenkins, Harold Jenkins. Maybe this will help you remember."

The old man got to his feet and shuffled to the window, his down-at-the-heel slippers making a strange scratching on the bare wood floor. "You a cop?"

"Nope, just an old friend."

"Well, I might have a monthly name of Jenkins, let me think…"

Another ten. The old man's tongue licked an errant bit of spit from his lips.

"Yeah, now I remember. Down the hall, room eight." The clawed hand scooped up the money. "Sure you ain't a cop?"

Johnny walked down the hall until he came to room eight. He stood at the door, his heart pounding. Then he pushed the door open and walked in.

A man sat on an iron bed against the wall. He was naked except for his underwear. A toilet stood in the opposite corner in a stall, and the room stank of urine and feces. A half-drunk bottle of booze on the nightstand beside the bed. A single bare bulb on a wire from the ceiling. The man looked up. He was unshaven, his lank hair plastered against his skull. His eyes looked out of sunken sockets, and he was missing some teeth.

"Who are you?"

"Don't you know me, Jenkins?"

The man's eyes opened. Then Johnny saw the fear. It seemed to come from somewhere deep inside, and as it came, the blood disappeared from the man's face. "Johnny? Johnny Strange?"

"Yeah, Jenkins, Johnny Strange."

Jenkins shrank back against the wall. "Whaddaya want?"

Johnny didn't know how it got there, but the KA-BAR was in his hand. The light from the overhead bulb glinted off the burnished steel. "What do you think I want, Jenkins?"

Johnny could see sweat pop out on Jenkins' brow. "Are you gonna kill me, Johnny?"

"Yeah, Jenkins, I'm gonna kill you. Slow, long, painful. I will make you pay for every hour, every minute, every second that you stole from me."

Jenkins raised his hands. "Please Johnny, I meant nothing by it. I couldn't help myself."

"You lying piece of shit, you hurt me, you scarred me. And not only me... there were others, little kids. You're a scumbag."

"You're right Johnny, you're right, I'm that and a lot more. Look, my dad did the same thing to me and it messed me up. I know it's not an excuse, but..."

He put his face in his hands. Johnny could hardly hear him. "I wanted to be a normal guy, I wanted to have a wife and kids, but there was always that feeling inside me." He looked up, eager, excusing. "Maybe I wanted to get back at my dad for what he did to me."

"You said you were a Christian, Jenkins. You said you believed in a God who could work miracles. I heard you preach about it. Why didn't you ask your God to help you? Why didn't you talk to somebody?"

"I asked God, Johnny, I begged him to fix me. You don't know how many times I begged him."

"Yeah, after you raped another kid, you begged him. I know you, your kind. Men and women just like you filled the pews of our church. You go to God and ask for forgiveness and then you go right back to your sin." He looked at the blade and then at the man on the cot. "You're a filthy pig. You deserve to die."

Johnny stepped forward. Jenkins reached down and suddenly there was a snub-nosed revolver in his hand, a hand that was shaking.

Johnny laughed. "You think I'm afraid of that pea-shooter. I've got machine-gun bullet holes through me, Jenkins. I've faced down Nambus and mortars. I've killed men with my bare hands. I've been stabbed with bayonets. You're a miserable little piss-ant compared to what I've been through. Go ahead and shoot. I'll have your guts on the floor before you can get the second shot off."

The hand with the gun dropped back down on the bed. Jenkins turned away from the blade. A pause, a whisper. "Do what you came to do, then."

Johnny stepped in front of the man, the KA-BAR pressed against Jenkins' throat. A thin trickle of blood started down. The man looked up, and there were tears pouring down his face. "I'm sorry, Johnny, I'm so sorry."

Johnny willed his hand to plunge the knife into Jenkins throat, but it wouldn't move.

Is this what your life is about, Johnny? Is this all there is?

Johnny jerked, like electricity had gone through him. "What?"

Jenkins' eyes had a question. Johnny willed his hand again, he wanted it to push the knife slowly into Jenkins' neck, wanted to hear the man choke on his own blood, feel him writhe on the end of the knife like so many Japs had writhed as he killed them, but again... nothing.

This is not your job, Johnny, it's mine.

Johnny looked down at the knife.

What the hell? I came all this way...

Johnny Strange!

And suddenly, like someone had pulled a plug, the hate drained out of him. He looked down at the wretched face.

"You're right, it's not my job."

"What?" Jenkins watched as the hand holding the knife fell to Johnny's side. Johnny stepped back. "I'm not going to kill you Jenkins, you're already dead." He turned to walk away.

"Johnny?" Johnny looked back.

"Thank you, Pretty Boy." That simpering voice, the vulgar grin, the devil looking out of Jenkins' eyes.

"You bastard." Johnny started toward him, but the gun went up quicker... into Jenkins' mouth and the hand jerked. BANG! Blood and brains flew against the wall, and the sound shattered the small room. Jenkins slumped against the wall, the back of his head gone. Footsteps running down the hall. The old man. "What the hell..." He stared at Jenkins. "You better get out of here, kid, before I call the cops..."

Johnny felt something welling up in him, rage, fear, hate, bile, vomit...

"Johnny! Holy Mary, Johnny, wake up. We gotta go. The Japs are coming for us..."

30

THE SUGAR CANE WAR

BILLY MARTENS

Johnny Strange stopped dead and held up a hand, clutching his BAR in the other. Garowski, who had taken over the second BAR from Bobby Mac, stopped right behind him. They were at the edge of a clearing. The June heat and light hammered the jungle around them and the long sweep of green grass that spread out before them. And the fields of neatly planted sugar cane that stretched for acres.

The rest of the squad, platoon, and company were in single file behind the two men who were taking point.

Johnny waved a fly away from his face. It returned instantly. He ignored it.

"Not a soul," muttered Johnny. "Where is everyone?"

"Maybe in their houses there?" suggested Garowski. There were rows of homes nearby. He swiped thick drops of sweat from his forehead and added, "Or that bunker?"

"Well, they'd better not be in that bunker. The boys'll be tossing explosives into it, along with cans of diesel fuel. Then O'Brien adds the dragon."

"I know, Corporal. But Zeus Squad fried a bunch of civilians in a bunker yesterday by mistake. Rudy will go ape if we do that again."

"I'm aware of that, Garowski. But how the hell are we supposed to know which bunkers have hidden Nambus and naval guns and which have civilians? It's only been a week and scuttlebutt already has us losing more men than we lost in the whole frigging fight on Tarawa."

"Another platoon got in shit for taking out Korean laborers thinking they were Japs."

"Ok, Garowski, I get the picture."

"Just saying, Corporal."

"Yeah, yeah, just saying. What the hell are we supposed to do? Go out there holding a bunch of coconuts with straws in 'em for the kids? Or throwing hand grenades and cutting up Japs with our BARs and Ma Deuce?" He looked back at the men behind them. "Take ten, guys. Pass the word."

"Thanks, Corporal," replied Fred Niyol, one of the Navajo code talkers.

Garwoski slumped back against a coconut tree and took off his helmet. Sweat and the helmet's weight flattened his hair. "Anyway, isn't Sergeant Martens supposed to be sending back word? Or Corporal Navarro? I thought the two of them and the Chamorro were our scouts?"

"They are our scouts. I don't know where they are. Hey, Garwoski. Take a run back to Rudy. Tell him what's up. Ask him what he wants us to do."

"Me? A runner? In this heat?"

"Yeah, you, Garwoski. Quit goldbricking and haul ass."

Niyol grinned. "It's not the heat, Garwoski. It's the humidity. I can't stand the humidity."

"I can't stand the jungle," complained Garowski. "I wish I was back on a park bench in Seattle."

"Get moving!" snapped Johnny. "Shit, Garwoski, remember Pearl Harbor, will ya?"

Garowski hadn't been gone half a minute before Amista suddenly slipped up behind Johnny. He jumped. "Geez, girl, stop this warrior woman shit. If you'd had a knife, and we'd been at war, my head would be tied to your belt by my hair."

"I don't need a knife." Amista didn't smile. Her dark hair framed her pretty face and eyes with long, sweaty strands. There were lines of dried mud on her face like tiger stripes. She was in her black pajamas and gripping a Thompson. "They sent me to tell you not to do anything to the bunker. It's full of children and their mothers."

"What the hell?"

"Where else do you expect them to go, Corporal? Your bullets would slice right through the thin walls of their houses."

"So, who's in the houses?"

"No one."

"No one?" Johnny repeated.

"They're booby trapped," Amista told him.

"Crap."

"The enemy is in the cane fields. They are using farmers as shields. Japanese farmers."

"Great. Exceptional. Where are the other men?"

"They shot some for resisting. Others are in the bunker with their families."

"So, these aren't your people?"

She stared at him. "No! Not like the Chamorro you burned up yesterday."

Johnny had nothing to say. He lit a cigarette and offered her one. She shook her head. He smoked a moment.

"Some things don't add up. Why'd the Japs let you place people in the bunker?"

"We saw the enemy force coming to set an ambush for your men. So, we arrived at the farm ahead of them. We coaxed the women and children to take shelter."

"Why would Japanese farmers want to hide from Japanese troops?"

"They aren't hiding from Japanese troops, Corporal. They're hiding from you. They're hiding from the bullets. The people know there will be a battle. That's how we convinced them to use the bunker. The Japanese soldiers realize the women and children are there. They aren't going to bother them."

Johnny narrowed his eyes, smoke curling up from his cigarette. "Yeah? Then it still doesn't add up. If the Japs want their people safe, why are they using some of the men as shields?"

Amista narrowed her own eyes. "It is an honor to die for the Emperor."

Johnny thought about this. "How many Japs are in the sugar cane?"

"Hundreds. As much as a thousand. Perhaps more."

"And what's in that cane with them?"

"They've set up machine-gun nests. They have their Type 89 Grenade Dischargers, what you call knee mortars. But they do not prop the base plate against their knees or thighs, Corporal. It would break the bones."

"Thanks for the lesson, professor. How the hell are we going to get down there and engage them? They'll cut us to ribbons before we reach the sugar cane. There must be two hundred yards of open grass we have to get over."

"I'm going to guide you, Corporal."

"You? Guide us? How old are you?"

Amista stood straighter. "Eighteen. Mira guided you and she was only fifteen."

"Yeah?" Johnny snorted. "So, that's it? Just eighteen?"

"Sergeant Martens is only three years older than me. You can't be much older yourself."

"Yeah, well, honey, I'm a Marine, they have trained me to kill Japs in combat."

"I've been killing Japanese soldiers long before Pearl Harbor,

Corporal. Only Chamorra and my sister Tasina have killed more."

Johnny nodded and ground out his cigarette under his boot. "Yeah, Billy's told me the Batman stories. I suppose you'll say you killed all those men with your bare hands?"

"Or legs. It is not difficult for me to kill a man. Nor is it unpleasant. I enjoy ending the lives of our enemies. I will guide you safely into the cane, Corporal. After that, take care of yourselves." He was going to interrupt, but she held up her hand. "Send several companies around to the far side of the cane fields. Send them through the jungle. When they are ready, attack from this end at the same time they begin the assault at their end. Keep the Big Fifty right here to kill the Japanese who try to escape the vise and run out into the open."

"The vise? Who are you? General Douglas frigging MacArthur?"

"I was told to tell you this."

"By who?"

"Sergeant Martens."

"Billy." Johnny shook another cigarette out of his pack of Chesterfields, but didn't put his Zippo to it. "Why isn't Chamorra coming back and explaining all this to me? Why'd they send you?"

"Because." Amista hesitated. "Because, Corporal."

"What is it?" Johnny demanded.

He thought she blushed under her tan skin.

"The sergeant and myself... we are together much of the time. He explained everything to me and told me to relate it to you. I understand it better than Chamorra does."

"Where are Billy and Corporal Navarro? Where is Chamorra?"

"In the sugar cane. They will strike the Japanese when you do."

"Okay. I'm going to have to let my CO know what's up."

Amista's voice took on more authority. She surprised Johnny. "We must act quickly. Or they will discover your sergeant and corporal as well as our guerillas."

"All right. I'll see if our Navajo can make radio contact."

"Corporal."

"What?"

"You can't use flamethrowers in this fight. You'll burn us all alive once the cane ignites."

Johnny nodded. "Got it. I can see why Billy likes you. It's not just your beauty, it's your brains and your strength. He does like you, doesn't he?"

She did not lower her eyes. But he saw the blush again under her skin.

He smiled. "Dumb Montana cowboy is smarter than I thought. Yo! Niyol! Atsa! Get me the K Company CO! Get me Rudebaker!"

"Yes, Sir, Corporal!"

"Don't call me sir, Atsa! You want a sniper to hear and shoot me?" Johnny spotted Bud and went over to him. "We're going into the sugar cane. You ready?"

"I've got my dried plasma, water to mix it with, morphine, sulfa powder, and miles of gauze, if that's what you mean. It's going to be a mess fighting in those canes."

"Yeah. When isn't it a mess fighting on these shitty islands? So, tell me something. What's up with Billy? I thought you said he had it bad for Chamorra."

"He does."

"So, what's with this Amista thing?"

"Well, you can see how beautiful she is. No yellow hair or black teeth. And she's every bit as strong and courageous as Chamorra."

"Okay, but —"

Bud clapped a hand on Johnny's shoulder. "I've been praying about it, but I'm not God. Maybe Amista is better for him than

Chamorra. If you've been watching, Chamorra wants nothing to do with Billy, even after his heroics a few days ago. If anything, she's treating him with more disdain and more contempt. Challenged him to a fight the other day and swore she'd kick his ass in front of the men. Mocked him out. She is pushing him farther away. Amista is drawing him closer and closer. He really likes her."

"Yeah, well, that's easy to do."

"Corp!" shouted Atsa. "Got the CO!"

"Time to go," Johnny said to Bud. "We can figure out Billy's love life later."

They got the go ahead and were on the move in fifteen minutes, following Amista's tall, lithe figure, making their own path, snaking through the dense jungle. She had tied her hair into a tight braid, which every Marine stared at. It took forty-five minutes before she brought them to their jump off point. She pointed through the jungle growth with the barrel of her Thompson.

"The cane fields are two hundred feet from here," said Amista. "I'm sure the Japanese are watching the jungle and have mortars and Nambus ready. You'll just have to move as fast as you can. Like you did when you landed on the beaches. I will take four companies around to the other side of the sugar cane. When you hear us open fire, attack. It will take about fifty minutes for me to get the companies to where I need them to be."

"Thank you," Johnny said. He pressed two packs of Camels into her hands. She slipped them into a pocket in her pants. "Good luck."

Amista smiled. "I relish fighting, Corporal. I like its dangers and I like to win. It's all I've known since I was thirteen. It does not frighten me. But it frightens the men I kill. I enjoy their eyes. I see surprise and fear and pain when I engage them. Then I see they like my beauty and like my strength. By the time they are dying, the fright and pain and surprise are completely gone from their eyes. Only their admiration for me is left. I find it fascinating. You'd imagine the fear of death would take over, but it never does. Their eyes shine for my womanhood and my power. It's very curious."

Johnny nodded. "And you like it." It wasn't a question.

Amista put a cigarette between her lips, and Johnny lit it for her. She blew a stream of thick white smoke from her nostrils.

"Yes," she breathed. Her smile was warm and full. "I like it. I'm a warrior, Johnny." She used his name for the first time. "I'm not an American housewife. Or your Saturday night girlfriend sipping a Pepsi and nibbling a cheeseburger. I don't neck with my steady in the back seat of a Chevy. I have better things to do with my hands." She laughed and placed her lit cigarette between Johnny's surprised lips. "Good luck to you, Corporal. You'll need it more than I will. I'm in my element now, like a shark in the shallows. Fighting in the sugar cane will be what you call close quarters combat, yes? Well, the prospect thrills me."

The gunfire we were waiting for exploded at the far end of the cane field about forty minutes after Amista vanished. Johnny had the squad gung-ho and charging out of the jungle in less than sixty seconds. The crazy thing was the first person Johnny saw after he led them in the sprint across the grass, through blistering Jap machine gun fire and tracers, and crashing into the thick stalks of sugar cane, was Amista. She was basically tearing a guy's head off from behind, her young muscles obvious as the sleeves of her top rode up to her shoulders. And she wasn't silent like Billy always said the Chamorro were during night kills. She was shouting something in her language as she destroyed the man, finishing him with a foot stomp that crushed his throat. Johnny doubted there was any of the romance or admiration of her womanhood she'd suggested would be in his eyes as she slaughtered him.

He just had time for, "What the hell are you doing here?"

Amista did not respond. Fighting had exploded all around

them among the ten-foot-high sugar canes. She seized a Jap by his hair and smashed his face into her knee three times, shattering his nose and skull.

"We met my Chamorro fighters on our march," she panted as she swiftly made the soldier her next victim. "Jesus and Billy were with them. Jesus volunteered to lead the Marines the rest of the way to the far side of the cane fields. So, I remained with Billy and my guerillas. Once we heard the gunfire, we plunged into the sugar cane. Only a hundred feet from here."

"Our Jesus?"

Amista grunted as she threw her enemy over her knee, bent him, and broke his back with a loud crack. She let him fall like rags, flashing a dark smile at Johnny. "Your Jesus. Not the one from heaven."

Japs swarmed around them in the canes. They quickly surrounded Amista and her sister Tasina, and the woman Johnny knew that Bud liked named Kamia, and the older woman Hudana, who was built like an ox. It only took a glance from Johnny to see the enemy was not doing well with any of the fierce female Chamorro warriors. Jap necks were being snapped, backs broken, and arms and legs cracked over female knees with a swift ease. It made him think of the ferocious stories of the legendary man-killing Amazon female warriors he'd read about in secret when he was a teen. He couldn't get enough of the war stories, which he found both repelling and compelling. He always returned to them. Now he was seeing their battle stories spring to life in front of his eyes and exerting the same force on his mind.

Sirena, the most muscular of the Chamorro fighters at thirty-five, her hair shaved to the scalp, was grappling with an officer, both of them shouting at each other. Johnny guessed, while he plunged his Ka-Bar into a Jap stomach with a battle cry of his own, that the officer must have outweighed Sirena by eighty pounds and had at least six inches in height on her. It made no difference to Sirena. In the whirl of twisting bodies, slashing *katanas*, punching fists, and spurting blood, she quickly outmaneuvered the big Jap, got her arms around his neck, and twisted it till it broke, yelling in her language. She saw Johnny's shocked look. "Don't worry, Marine. Lucky for you, I am on your side."

There was a rifle blast by Johnny's ear. A Jap had shot one of the Chamorro women in the guts. She cried out and fell, eyes white. Before Johnny had a chance to react, Amista screamed like a demon and leaped on the Jap, wrapping her legs around his chest and butting his face with her skull, cracking open his nose. While he shrieked in pain and threw his hands to his face, she locked her ankles behind his back and squeezed his rib cage, letting out a war whoop as he snapped his head back in agony. In English, Johnny heard her growl, "Die in pain for killing our Haani. Die in pain and go to hell, dismayed that woman in all her power, a power mightier than your own, has defeated the Empire of Japan."

Johnny was suddenly locked in a struggle with an officer who had hurled himself against him and encircled Johnny's throat with large, thick hands, strangling him. The officer smiled as brutally as anyone else taking satisfaction in conquering their foe that hot, sweaty afternoon in June. He muttered in Japanese and forced Johnny to the ground between the tall green stalks of cane, driving his thumbs into Johnny's flesh with a grunt of satisfaction and certain victory. He did not get any farther than that. The Navajo code talkers fired their M1 Garands at the officer at point blank range five or six times. When Johnny sat up, pushing one very dead Jap off him, his mind still swirling from the choke hold, he saw Billy.

His friend was swinging his *katana* from Tarawa, combat pants on, but no shirt. It sheared sugar cane stalks along with Japanese necks. His body and face were a sheet of blood, and Johnny could make out wounds that had sliced open his friend's skin. He noticed that Amista watched Billy for a moment, but did not approach. She saw that the blood rage was upon him, he guessed, and that he didn't need any help from her. Instead, she pounced on a soldier who was trying to fire a Nambu at a cluster of Marines, wrestled him to the earth, and applied a choke hold. He kicked and flailed and tried to swat away her hands. Johnny watched her demolish him as if he were reading a story from his Amazon books.

It may be a rough ending, Tokyo Joe, but you'd do the same to her if you had the upper hand. Enjoy your death under her dark beauty and her expert hands. Most of us don't get that. Just a bullet with no face and no charm.

Johnny saw several Marines go down and saw one beheaded. Then watched two more Chamorro women and a man get shot. He didn't know their names. He jumped to his feet and cut loose with his BAR, bringing down three Japs. Then it was too difficult to shoot without shooting someone he didn't want to hit. Nearby, Garowski was smashing a Jap's head in with the butt of his BAR. Leon Levy was swinging his Garand like a club. Red O'Brien had latched onto a machete and was doing nasty work with it. Johnny joined them, slashing with his BAR like a scythe to chop down the enemy, one after another.

Billy finally spotted Johnny, cracking Jap skulls like a madman. Billy shook his head. Close quarters combat always unleashed the beast. No mercy was asked, and none given. A Jap lifted his pistol and pointed it at Billy, and Billy didn't even blink. He was in some kind of weird place and didn't even rush the man or swing his *katana* at him. But while he stood there, rigid, young Mira leaped at the Japanese soldier.

Mira turned out to be as ruthless a warrior as the other Chamorro the Japanese had enslaved for so many years. Billy did not know her entire story, but he knew she had lost family to the cruelties of the Japanese Army. She gave a yell and jumped up, striking the Jap's head in mid-air with what Billy knew was a front snap kick. He heard the crack as the Jap's neck broke under the power of her young muscles. Billy found it ironic. She was using karate on the very people who had invented karate in the first place, and she was defeating them with it.

The Marines and Chamorro were carrying the fight forward through the sugar canes. Billy joined the battle again, *katana* in one hand, a Colt 1911 he'd scooped off a headless Marine in the other. He shot several of the enemy in the face from inches away, the blood and bone and skin peppering his face and naked chest. For a moment, he was face to face with Chamorra. She leered at him with her black teeth. He moved past her and blasted off the back of a Jap officer's skull.

He saw Red O'Brien spearing a Jap through the mouth with a sharp shaft of sugar cane. Paul Stoneroad was rolling over and over with two Jap soldiers until Billy beheaded one and Sirena smashed the other's skull with a powerful kick. He came upon Hudana, the tough seventy-seven-year-old, crushing the head of a man trapped between her huge legs. Behind her, Kamia, the woman who liked Bud, was throttling a Nip by forcing his Arisaka rifle across his throat and thrusting down with all her strength until his tongue rolled out and his eyes went white.

There was Skillet, firing his 81mm mortar, Pretty Boy, into a cluster of Japanese that Billy could barely see, maybe two hundred feet ahead among the tall green sugar canes. The mortar bomb shredded dozens of canes and dozens of bodies. "They were massing for a banzai, Sarge," Skillet grunted. Billy thrust his sword through a man's chest and suddenly faced off against a giant; a tall, muscular, and bearded Japanese who was wielding an axe, killing Marines left and right as he swung. He came after Billy and Skillet. Billy raised his sword to fend off the blow and the gigantic man laughed, swiping with his axe and shattering the blade. Then he aimed a stroke at Billy's head.

Suddenly the Jap didn't have a head. A grenade blast behind him ripped it right off his neck. The body remained standing upright, not even swaying, axe still gripped in its hands. Then it fell forward into Billy. He grimaced, shoved the corpse away and kept going.

The momentum of the attack through the cane fields propelled Billy forward over Jap machine-gun nests, discarded mortars and Nip bodies tangled and twisted among the green canes. He saw Amista peeling herself off a high-ranking officer she had slain, wiping a hand across her mouth as she looked down at the body, ripping off his insignia and pocketing it. She spotted Billy and joined him as the Marines surged ahead, Thompsons chattering, knives stabbing, M1 Garands cranking out big, heavy, bone-splitting 30.06 bullets. Grenades burst and shards of cane showered heads and backs.

Suddenly, Marines were hollering cease fire and Billy saw Jesus Navarro and hundreds of Marines rushing forward to link up with them among the tall green canes. But if the Marines were finished, the Chamorro weren't. Sirena garroted a colonel, a *Riku-gun-Taisa*, she had found hiding in the canes nearby, pretending to be dead. She saw Billy watching her and ignored him, carrying on with her work. The colonel gasped and kicked and clawed grooves into the earth with his fingers. The moment she ended him, Sirena stood up, a strip of wire dangling from her fingers, and faced Billy defiantly.

"They have tortured and killed our mothers and fathers, raped our daughters, murdered our brothers. Drowned our children in the sea. If I could make death even worse for them, I would do it. Suppose you had not come? They would have continued to butcher us and enslave us for another thousand years. Now we can be free if we fight hard enough. So, we will fight hard enough. If we leave none of them alive at the end, I will praise God. It is better than they deserve. I would rather see them tormented for a whole eternity. Always screaming. Do I sound terrible to you?"

"Christianity believes in a hell where sinners are punished like that," Billy told her.

"Yes? Then tell me how I may become a Christian."

"Not all Christians buy into that, though."

Her black eyes blazed. "Believe me, I will. And I shall make the Christian God follow through on it."

BILLY FOUND Bud at his aid station a few hours later. It was set up by the houses which had been disarmed of their bombs and trip-wires. There were hundreds of wounded, but with extra corpsmen from the division they had all been taken care of. They headed many of the casualties out to the hospital ships. Billy offered Bud one of the cigars Lt. Crandall had been handing out, as always. They walked towards the cane fields and then sat on their helmets, smoking.

"Back home, if they saw us fight like this," Billy said, looking tired, "they would call us murderers or sadists. Or worse."

"Some might."

"But how else can you fight that kind of fight, Bud? If you aren't brutal their brutality kills you."

"Civilians would never understand unless they had to be in it. Most wars have been fought this way, when you think about it. Sure, there were catapults and archers and pots of boiling oil. But they did the greater part of the fighting face to face with swords and knives and battle axes and hatchets. It was very personal. You saw your enemy's eyes. Often enough, you killed him with your own hands. The Amazons fought this way too, if those legends are true. It's just like Ulysses and the Greeks battling Hector and the Trojans, Billy. The poem by Tennyson we're always quoting sounds grand. But they didn't just use their weapons, they used their hands to choke and break and kill. Not much has changed when it comes to close quarters combat in 1944."

"I don't know why I ... why I sometimes feel good when I'm ... killing someone with my own two hands," Billy moaned. "Isn't that wrong? I don't mean wrong for a Mennonite or a Christian. I know they'd condemn it. I mean, wrong for a human being."

"I think a lot of it is relief, Billy. They were going to kill you. But now you're killing them. They've lost. You've won. Every second you destroy them is bringing you closer to your own survival. It's a good feeling when you know they're going to die and you're going to live."

"What about the Chamorro women? And men? The guerillas? They relish the combat. They want to go on killing Japs day after day."

Bud puffed slowly on his Havana. "I think it's more complicated for the women. Women have hardly ever had power over men. They've always been controlled and dominated. Now, here in combat, they turn the tables. When they defeat a Jap using their own physical strength, suddenly women aren't weaker. Instead, they're superior to the men they overpower and kill."

"I guess it's like finally beating up a bully who's been harassing you for years."

"Exactly. This is sweet revenge on the Empire of Japan. These Chamorro women and men have been under the Jap heel a long time. They've seen family and friends and lovers tortured and killed. Finally, they can fight back and punish the soldiers who have occupied their island and brutalized their loved ones. No wonder they enjoy giving the Japs their comeuppance."

Bud returned to the casualties. Billy still felt ill at ease with himself and the sugar cane war. He stood smoking his cigar. An arm snaked through his and a head leaned against his shoulder.

"Hey, big tough Marine man," Amista teased. "Have some time for an island girl?"

"Hey, you smell great."

"Yes. I washed in a stream near here. For you." She was licking a piece of sugar cane. "Want some?"

Billy smiled. He still felt awkward touching a woman. But he put his arm around her. She was wearing something like a tight yellow dress that hugged her body and left both her shoulders bare. "I like it."

"My dress or my scent or me? Or maybe the sugar cane?"

"The first three."

"Good." She dropped the sugar cane on the grass. "I'm happy. Now, I want to show you something."

"What's that?"

Amista tugged on his hand. "Come on."

She led him back into the canes. Into a high patch that was unbent and untrampled. No one had fought in this spot. She was almost as tall as him, so their eyes were at the same height. Sunlight and green spread over her wet, dark hair and freshly washed face. Her midnight eyes took in the light and the green too. She laced her long, powerful arms around his neck and leaned into him.

Billy thought he was going crazy. His heart was pounding and his head whirling. The heat of her body, its softness, its firmness, her smooth skin, her pretty muscles, it was too much. He thought he was going to pass out. He had no idea what to do with his hands.

"What ... what ... did you want to show me?" Billy managed to get out.

She smiled. "This." She gently brought his face to hers. "My hero. You saved my life a few days ago. I've never properly thanked you."

"Amista, you don't have to——"

She interrupted him. "I do."

Her lips were incredible. Soft and firm and warm like her strong, slender body. She moved her perfect mouth over his rough one. Her kiss hit him hard. It was sharp and hot and full of strength. His brain exploded. He thought he was going to fall. He felt her arms go around his body and grip him tightly. "Don't worry, my sweet, strong American man, I can hold you up," she cooed. "It's easy for a big girl like me."

His entire body trembled, and his knees buckled. The well-honed muscles in her arms came into good use. Her hold on him tightened even more. She chuckled happily. "My sweet American man, I really do have to keep you on your feet. What is this island girl doing to you? Whatever it is, it appears she's winning."

She stroked his face. "Let's not stop, Billy." Amista had never used his name before. "Let's never stop. The war can go away for a few hours." She pulled him down to the ground, a summer breeze stirring the sugar cane above their heads. "Kiss me for a thousand years. Two thousand. We have all the time we need, don't we?"

31

THE NATURE OF THE ENEMY

THE CORPSMAN

*J*esus, Mary and Joseph! What is with these people? After the fight in the cane fields, X-Ray surrounded a bunch of Japs and told them to surrender. We trapped them in a ditch, and our guys were all around. They had no way out and they knew it. We could hear them jabbering away, and then a bunch of grenades went off. When we investigated, we found the fools had blown themselves up rather than surrender. There were heads and guts all over the place. What the hell?

Speaking of heads and guts, this place is already stinking. There are dead guys, Americans and Japs, all over the place. I remember Betio stank like this. Once the tropical sun gets on the bodies, they go quick. The Japs are yellow at first and then they turn green and in about a day they turn black and split open like an overdone hot dog on a too-hot grill. We are trying to get our wounded and dead off the field, and at first the Japs tried too, but we've been pushing them hard and as they move back, they started leaving their dead. It's a mess.

And flies? One of our guys who got sent back to the hospital ship for a day with a flesh wound said he was standing on the deck drinking some Joe and a swabbie came by and grabbed his cup.

"Whaddya do that for?" Our guy says.

The swabbie points to the cup. "There are flies in the cup."

Our guy grins. "Yeah, but only three."

Word has it that the hospital ships are filling up fast. That's bad news, but better than trying to treat the guys on the beaches, what with that curtain of steel dropping on them. The first day, June 15, was rough, we heard. The Japs had the beaches zeroed in with their long-range guns. There was no place to hide on those beaches. Now it's the end of the week and our boys have moved inland and pivoted toward the north end of the Island.

And so on we go. We've been north of the major action, trying to get rid of some artillery that's been pounding 2nd and 4th Div to pieces down south. On Betio, it was machine guns and rifle fire. Now most of our dead are from mortar and artillery shrapnel. So we are trying to find the guns. The Japs have them well hidden, but these Chamorros grew up here and they know every nook and cranny of the island so we're just moving along picking off Japs as we go. We have to be careful though, because there are a lot of Japs between us and the guys moving up from the beaches.

These Chamorro women are something else. As soft as my Kalasia is, that's as hard as these women are. Oh yeah, a few of them are beautiful and sexy, but when you watch them in action, it's frightening. Hate fills them and I think it's because these stupid Japs do not understand how to conquer a country. They come in, rape the women, kill the men and put the children into slavery. The Chamorros hate their guts and when they kill a Jap they make sure the Jap knows who their killer is. I mean war is war, and it's hell, but when you add in a personal vendetta and red-hot hate, it gets sickening.

I thought Billy was going for the one the Chamorros call Serpent but there's another young one, Amista, that's got her eye on the lad. Billy won't know what hit him if one of these gals gets her hooks in to him. Billy's tough, but as far as women go, he's Baby Billy. So if he falls, might as well wrap him up and send him home, stick a fork in him, he's done.

So anyway, I've been thinking about these Japs and the way they don't care about life. To me, next to knowing God, life is the most precious thing we have. I think we got put here to fulfill a destiny and we shouldn't just throw our life away. Oh, I know my buddies are getting killed all around me and that doesn't sit too well with me. But I can tell you this, I've looked down at enough guys with their guts ripped out, or their face blown off, or legs and arms gone and I can tell you this—there isn't one Marine I've served with who doesn't fight for every minute of life with the same intensity that he fights the enemy. And that's the deal. What I know is that death is the great enemy. God didn't design us to die. How do I know that? I'm a medic. I've treated wounds that should have been the end of some guy, and two weeks later they are back on the line. The human body is an incredible machine, a gift from God. It repairs itself like magic and to throw it away like these Jap guys do is just beyond me.

I think it is a total misunderstanding of who God is. I been checking it out and what I found out is that all Japanese soldiers hold the Shinto belief that death in battle is transformation into godhood, what they call "kami." The secret of the early success of the Japanese soldier in the Pacific War was that he loved death more than his enemy loves life. In the beginning of the war, when they were going up against the Americans in the Philippines, the British in Malaya and Burma, and the Dutch in the East Indies, the Japanese were always outnumbered and out-gunned, but they still won. Even when the tide of battle turned against them after Midway and Guadalcanal, the Japanese continued to force heavy losses on us at Tarawa and now here. That's because they just don't give a crap. Our guys think about getting home to their wives and girlfriends, but these Japs couldn't care less.

In Shinto, worship of Japan is synonymous with worship of

the gods. No Japanese soldier will miss out on the chance to join the pantheon by giving his life. At the other extreme, he would never disgrace his nation and emperor by surrendering or running away. That would keep him from becoming a god. And you know what I say? Bullshit.

These poor bastards have got their heads so far up their rear end they can lick their tonsils. There is one God. Sure we know him as a trinity, Father, Son and Holy Spirit, but that's the way we know him and the various revelations of his character. And here's the terrible news for poor little Japs that think they will join up with the gods and live forever as a master of the universe, it ain't gonna happen. God is God and we are his creation. Sure, he's got a place for us to be with him when we die, but he shares his power with no one. I guess I'll sleep on that one.

———

TODAY IT HAPPENED. I got shot. No, I didn't get all torn up, in fact it's more like a nick. It's where I got it that makes my face turn red. We were in a firefight up around some caves in the cliffs east of Garapan. The Japs have these hills filled with machine-gun nests and mortar pits. They get in there and we have to blow them out or burn them out. A machine-gun pinned us down, and the boys were working around to put the Zippo on it when I heard the cry, "Corpsman!" I turn around and just as I do, I feel something tug at my pants. I thought nothing about it until after we clear the cave. Johnny walks by and grins. "Your butt's bleeding, Bud."

Sure enough, I feel my butt and my hand comes away red. I look around and Strange and his Arapahos are grinning at me. Johnny spreads his hands and shakes his head. "Don't ask me to fix it. I ain't going near your rear end."

George gets a solemn look on his face. "I don't think you'll find anyone to fix that, Corpsman—not in this man's Marines."

Well, shit, I need a patch on my ass and these fools are

playing games. I look over at Billy. He shakes his head. "Not me, pal. I'm your friend, but this is asking too much of a red-blooded guy."

"So what? You jerks are gonna let me bleed to death?"

Just then Hudana walked by. The old gal grinned at me. "You need someone fix your ass?"

Well, I'm blushing red as I hand her a compress. She doesn't say a word, just jerks my pants down around my knees and shoves me down on my face. There I am, butt-naked for everyone to see. Hudana puts on the compress and fastens it down. Then she slaps me on my unwounded cheek. "When you need your diaper change, you come see Mama Hudana."

Every guy in the squad is roaring. I think I would have rather gotten shot up good and sent back to the hospital ship, rather than this. Just as I'm pulling my pants up, Crandall walks by. "That's a cheap way to get a woman to touch your butt, Corpsman."

Now I'm done for. I don't think I'll ever live this down.

ONE THING the Big Brass worried about during our invasion of Saipan was the Jap fleet. Word was that they were coming to destroy Admiral Spruance and the American fleet, paving the way for 30,000 more Jap soldiers to land. If that happened, we were dead meat. So we were all worried about it. Then on June 21, Rudy came and told us the big news. The Japs sent their carrier force after us, but Spruance got word they were coming and sent out ships to stand between us and the Jap fleet. The Japs had one of their tough guys in charge, Admiral Ozawa. On June 19 they got into a big dustup. Problem for the Japs was that all their expert pilots got killed at Midway and Coral Sea. And our guys had already destroyed a lot of planes stationed on Tinian, Guam, and northern Saipan. So when they went up against us, our pilots were far superior. They had brand new pilots that had never faced combat, and we had battle-hardened aces. At the end of the first day, the Japs lost 300 planes against 29 of ours. Boy, when Rudy told us that, the entire company danced a jig. That, coupled with the fact that our subs and planes found Ozama's fleet and sunk several carriers and other ships, decimated Japan's ability to keep on fighting. By the end of the battle, the Japs were high-tailing it. That left us to do our business unhindered, and the battle for Saipan moved into high gear. One of Spruance's pilots got shot up and had to land at Aslito airfield. He said the dogfight was like shooting turkeys. So from then on everyone called that battle "The Great Marianas Turkey Shoot."

By now we had 50,000 troops ashore and we were kicking Jap butts all over the island. What we forgot about was the nature of our enemy. The Jap soldier is a dedicated and well-trained fighting man. That coupled with what I've been talking about, his complete disregard for death, makes him tough to beat. What we could see after we crushed their fleet was that the Japs didn't have a chance at winning this war. But you know what? Nobody told the Japs. And a few days later we found out just how desperate the Japs could be.

THE LADY AND THE TIGER

JOHNNY STRANGE

"This has turned into a shit-fest!"

It was the day after the fight in the cane field. Rudy Rudebaker slammed his helmet down and leaned against a Devil's-claw tree. The squad leaders and non-coms gathered around.

"What's up, Captain?" Lieutenant Crandall cradled his Thompson as he chewed on the last of his Havanas.

"Well, the Dogfaces of the 27th Infantry Division are making a friggin' mess of things. They assigned the 105th to clean out the Nafutan Peninsula by day two. Now we are into week two and they are still screwing around. And then, when the 2nd and the 4th got off the beaches and made the swing north, the 106th and the 165th got all tangled up in themselves during a march to take over the center portion of the line and delayed the whole attack 'Howlin' Mad' had planned. I'm telling you, General Smith is pissed."

Rudy went on. "The 4th Div and the 2nd Div Marines are getting infiltration and enfilading fire on their flanks because there is a big hole in the middle of the line where the Army is supposed to be. It took them all week to move up the valley to

Mount Tapotchau; 2nd captured the mountain but the whole thing is limping along. Sad. The Doggies did an outstanding job on Cactus, but they sure are acting like pussies out here."

Rudy pulled out a map. "Okay, here's the deal. On D-day the 2nd came ashore here above Charan Kanoa. The 4th hit the beach south of them. The 27th didn't come ashore until D+1 and didn't even get into the front lines until June 17. The 4th did their job, cut across the bottom of the island, captured Aslito airfield on D+3 and then turned north."

Crandall pointed to the bottom of the map. It showed a peninsula jutting out into the Philippine Sea. "That's Nafutan. There are a lot of artillery emplacements there, buried in the caves. The naval bombardment couldn't dig them out. So they sent the GIs over there to handle it. But they've been taking their time. It seems the army has a different way of going about things."

Zarate scowled. "Yeah, if they take some ground and then come under fire, they politely give it back. And every time a sniper takes a shot at them, they just hunker down and scream for artillery."

Johnny Strange listened to the conversation, but his mind was somewhere else. The two dreams still haunted him. He couldn't shake them, and he wondered what was going on. Marjean and Jenkins—so different and so real. He could still feel Marjean's body pressed against his, her lips soft and warm. He wanted to remember the love he felt; the love pouring out of a beautiful woman who belonged to him, body and soul. He tried to stay focused on Marjean, but Jenkins kept crowding in—the leering face, the sick grin that Jenkins used to give him when no one was looking—the grin on his face when he killed himself in the dream. Johnny had awakened knowing that no matter what Jenkins said or promised, he would always go on raping little boys.

Is it always going to be like this, Lord? Am I always going to deal with hating Jenkins? Somebody has to stop him, Lord!

Johnny chuckled.

Boy, that's good. I am losing it. Now I'm talking to God, just like Bud.

"Something funny, Strange?"

"No, Sir." Rudy was speaking again and Johnny tried to focus in.

"So here's our part in this." Rudy pointed to a town on the map. "The main body of 2nd Div is advancing up the West side of the Island. They've had some tough fighting around Mt. Tapotchau and now they have captured the mountain, they got orders to clear the Japs out of Garapan. They are getting ferocious resistance. They need help, so I have orders to rejoin the 2nd and help clear the city."

"May I say something, Captain?" Rudy turned in surprise. Chamorra was standing a few feet away.

"What is it, Sergeant?"

She moved into the group. The woman always amazed Johnny.

It's no wonder they call her Serpent—she moves like a snake. Fast, quiet. She's deadly, a viper.

When Serpent hunted Japs she stripped down, either to a simple loincloth or sometimes she went naked. Johnny had seen the Chamorro women in action and they were not ashamed of their bodies.

Billy was the one who worked with Serpent the most. They seemed to have some kind of competition going, like a love-hate thing. But Billy, aside from wondering what made the girl so bitter, was unstinting in his praise. "Yeah, except for that fright mask of a face, she's got the goods, Johnny. I never saw a naked girl before, so being around these Chamorros is... well, it's hard."

Johnny grinned. "Yeah, I'll bet it's hard."

It was the first time Johnny had ever seen Billy blush. "I didn't mean like that, Johnny."

When she was around the marines during the day, Serpent

wore a shapeless black smock that reached to her knees, so Johnny didn't watch her much. Besides, the black teeth and the yellow hair dispelled any hint of femininity.

Before she could speak, a message came in on the radio. Fred listened as the code came over the radio, gave the return code that he had received the message, and then shook his head.

"What's up, Private Niyol?"

"The shit has hit the fan back at headquarters, Captain. 'Howlin Mad' has relieved General Smith of command of the 27th."

"Whoa!" said Zarate. "I hope that's just latrine rumors."

"No, Sergeant, it's straight from headquarters. 'Howlin Mad' got so angry at the 27th's lack of progress that he sacked General Smith right out at the front lines. They got a new guy, Jarman, who's replacing all the command officers with his own guys."

Rudy shook his head. "That will not sit well with the top doggies back in Hawaii. Not a good time for inter-service squabbles."

Crandall moved the cigar from one side of his mouth to another. "What's your take on it, Captain."

"Personally, and this does not leave this meeting, I think 'Howlin Mad' Smith is a complete asshole. Yes, he developed the amphibious landing theories and yes, he's a skillful administrator, but he's a bully and a loudmouth who will never admit he's wrong in a thousand years. Don't bet on this blowing over. The 27th's General Smith is a likeable guy, but he's always been tentative and when the army boys got into Death Valley, I'm sure they just didn't have the same balls that marines do. But sacking him in front of the entire army is a fool's errand. Very unfortunate."

Rudy shook his head. "Well, we got our own worries, we'll let the Brass hats sort this one out." He nodded to Serpent. "You were saying, Sergeant?"

She put her finger on a hill on the map that was slightly north of the mountain.

"General Saito is hiding somewhere near this hill. We know it as Hill 500. He is the supreme Japanese commander of all troops on Saipan. It is said that Admiral Nagumo is with him. If we can find them and kill them, we can break the whole Japanese command chain on this Island."

Johnny looked at Serpent. She had a strange, eager look on her face, like a crocodile that's about to catch a swimming deer.

Rudy nodded at her "Go on."

"I want to take X-Ray squad with my Chamorros and find Saito."

Johnny looked at her face and he could see something take Serpent over. Her face hardened into a mask and her hands curled and uncurled.

She's got a lot of hate! Like me.

Rudy shook his head. "I'm sorry, Sergeant. We have our orders. The 4th has swung right onto the Kagman Peninsula and is mopping that area up. The 105th and the 106th are moving up the island on the east side of the mountain and 2nd Div is swinging left and inching toward Garapan. The 2nd needs all hands on deck to clear out the city. I'm afraid your mission will have to wait. You Chamorros know Garapan, we don't. We need you there."

"But Captain, this is the man who has brutalized my people, murdered, raped and tortured. With him gone, the Japanese army will fall apart."

"I'm sorry, Sergeant. I've got my orders."

Serpent looked at Captain Rudebaker for a long moment. Her black teeth bared—almost a snarl.

Johnny felt a chill pass over him as he watched the woman's eyes.

Boy, I bet Rudy doesn't know how close he is to dying right now. That's a big hate.

Serpent brought herself back and saluted. "Yes, Sir." She turned and walked away.

JOHNNY SAT WITH CHATAGA, one of the Chamorro men. He handed Chataga a Lucky Strike, and the two sat smoking in silence. Johnny spoke. "What's the deal with Serpent and this Saito guy?"

Chataga took a long draw. "Saito came in April to Saipan with the IJA 43rd Division. Before he came, the Japs treated us like slaves, but we could deal with that. When Saito came, things changed. He was a pig. He started passing Chamorro women around to his officers, and he shot a couple of husbands who objected. The second week he was here, a Chamorro tried to kill him. He missed Saito but killed three of Saito's staff. Saito rounded up as many Chamorros as he could and lined them up in front of his headquarters. He told the Chamorros that he would kill thirty of them for every Japanese soldier that the assassin killed in the attack. One family he rounded up was Serpent's family—her father, mother, two sisters and her older brother. Serpent was away in Hawaii training and was not with them. Saito picked ninety Chamorros and one of them was Serpent's father. He was a schoolteacher, so beloved among us. He was a quiet man, but he was not afraid. Saito had the prisoners kneel before him, and then his aide beheaded them one by one. When they came to Serpent's father, he would not kneel to Saito. Saito screamed at him, but he would not bow. Saito asked for Serpent's family to be brought to him. While the soldiers held her father, Saito had his men tear the clothes off her mother and sisters, and twenty or thirty soldiers took turns raping them. Then he ordered Serpent's father to bow. He would not, so they shot his wife and Chamorra's sisters. Then he brought the son forward."

"He looked at Serpent's father and spoke to him. 'This is your son, your heritage. If you do not bow, I will kill him.' Serpent's brother, Anghet, told his father not to bow. Saito became enraged, pulled his sword and beheaded Anghet."

Johnny shook his head.

I knew I recognized that hate.

Chataga went on. "Anghet was my best friend. We grew up together. I was in the group they did not kill. They let us go and I escaped into the hills. That is why I fight the Japs—to avenge my friend. After Anghet died, we watched as Saito took Serpent's father, stripped him naked and put him in a cage hung up on a pole in front of his headquarters. It took her father ten days to die. When Serpent returned, she already knew what happened to her family, and she was different. Before she left to learn to be a soldier, she was more of a patriot than a killer. After she came home, I did not recognize her. She is a different person. She is a glorious leader, but I am sad for the young, kind woman that left us. She did not return."

"Jeez, Chataga, that's tough." Johnny sat for a moment, thinking about what Chataga had said. Bud came and sat down beside the two men.

"What's up, Johnny?"

Johnny shook his head. "Damn it, Bud, how do you do that?"

"Do what?"

"Don't play innocent, Philo. You know what. Get inside my friggin' head."

"Well, what's up then?"

"Chataga here was telling me Serpent's story. What happened to her is awful. I watched her face when she was talking about Saito. She's got the same hate that I do, but she's got a lot more reason. They murdered her brother, raped her sisters and mother and then killed them, and tortured her dad to death." Johnny took a deep breath. "I didn't get raped, Bud. Jenkins tried, but I got away. After it happened, I just felt bad—scared, angry and humiliated. I think what made me the maddest was my dad knowing what Jenkins tried to do to me and sweeping it under the rug, just so his stinking little church wouldn't get an evil reputation."

Johnny paused and then shook his head.

"You know what, Bud?" Johnny looked away and his voice got quiet. "I need to grow up. When I see Serpent's hate and hold my stuff against it, it's a joke. Mine is more like righteous indignation. When I go home, I think if I take this hate back with me, it will kill everything I have with Marjean. With her, I have love, hope, everything good. You told me a long time ago that I need to stop killing for hate and kill for love, for my girl, to keep her safe and to keep these Japs away from her. I heard what you said back on Cactus, Bud, but I didn't get it. Now I do. When I look at Serpent I can see me, all twisted up, hard, unfeeling. I can't give that to Marjean. She deserves better."

Johnny wiped his eyes with his sleeve.

"I need help, Bud. I need to change. My story is nothing compared to Serpent's and yet I've spent too long twisted up like a knot. I had these weird dreams the other night... Well, the one about Marjean wasn't weird... and I think... well, I think those dreams might have been telling me something, Bud. Like Marjean is life and... and Jenkins is death."

Bud put his hand on Johnny's shoulder and for the first time in a long time the man-to-man contact didn't freak Johnny out. "It's like an old story about a lady and a tiger, Johnny. You have a choice. You can open one door and a lady comes out, or you can open the other and a tiger comes out. And the tiger will kill you. It's up to you."

Bud shook a smoke out of Johnny's pack and lit up. He was quiet for a long time. Then he looked at Johnny, hard.

"You're right, Johnny, you need help, but not from me."

"What are you saying, Bud?"

"I think it's time you got reconnected with the guy who's kept you alive through Cactus, Helen, and now this. You're gonna live, Johnny, through all of this, and you're going home. But you need

Him watching over you. Because this entire war is a crapshoot and we all could be dead tomorrow, I would get back in touch today."

Johnny looked at Bud for a long time. "Maybe you're right, Bud. Maybe you're right."

Bud grinned. "You know I am, Johnny. I got an inside track."

33

DELIGHT OF BATTLE

BILLY MARTENS

"Are you afraid of me?" Amista asked.

"No," Billy replied.

"Do you think I'm a terrible person?"

"No, I don't. You mustn't harbor those kinds of thoughts in your head."

"But I've taken life. I've taken many lives. And I feel no remorse."

"You're a soldier. No less than any Marine or any of the dogfaces on our right flank. Fight or be a slave forever. And fighting means killing. If you don't kill them, they kill you. The math is simple, Amista."

"But I delight in it. I like to fight. I savor my wins. As if I were savoring a stick of ripe sugar cane."

"Who likes to lose? If you lose the battle, you lose your life. What a relief, what happiness, when you survive, and your enemy is defeated and lying at your feet. Remember the poem I've been telling you about? *Ulysses*? The great war long, long ago between the Greeks and Trojans?"

"*I've drunk delight of battle with my peers, far on the ringing plains of windy Troy*. I remember. He delighted in the fight too, didn't he?"

"He did. And Bud, our doctor, tells me most of it was hand-to-hand fighting, . Close quarters combat, eye to eye, swords and spears and knives, yes. But also, bare hands. It was about gouging eyes, biting off ears, and choking to death with strong fingers and even stronger legs. It was vicious kicks that broke bones and skulls and windpipes. Exactly like your kind of fighting, Amista. It's the savagery of the female leopard and the female tiger, defending their own, that puts terror and weakness in your enemy's heart and limbs."

"I am a beast of prey, am I? Better be careful, my tiny little sergeant."

"I'm very careful."

"I like to ... what did you call it the other day? When you were reading to me from that holy book you carry in your pocket?"

"Rejoice over your enemy."

"Yes."

"Do not gloat over me, my enemy, for though I have fallen, I will rise again. My enemies will collapse and fall, but I rise and stand firm. Though a righteous warrior falls seven times, they will get up, but the wicked will stumble into ruin. Then they returned, every warrior of Judah and Jerusalem, with Jehoshaphat at the front, going back to Jerusalem with joy, for the Lord had made them rejoice over their enemies. The Lord is my strength and my song, he has given me victory. The Lord has given me revenge on my enemies, the Ammonites. For you, Amista, it's the Japanese."

"Ohhh. That is all very good. Thank you, my American man. Thank you, Billy."

The two of them were about fifty yards from Marine lines, resting in each other's arms in the jungle night. It was four in the morning. She reached up and unbuttoned his top so she could lay her head against his warm skin and listen to the beating of his heart, something she loved to do. One hand idly played with the hairs on his chest and traced patterns of swirling lines and circles.

"Do you desire me, Sergeant?" she asked.

Billy stroked her smooth black hair. "You ask so many questions you know the answers to."

"A woman likes to ask them just the same. Even warrior women. Do you find me exciting?"

"Very exciting."

"Different from your American women?"

"Very different."

"And you don't mind the difference?"

"I like the difference."

"You're not afraid of the leopard?" Amista asked him. "My strength and my feline ferocity ... it does not repel you?"

"Do I look like a man who is repelled?"

She slid her hand over his stomach. "I like your strength too. I like that you always want to fight not only for my island, but for me."

"I tried to do that tonight. You were too fast for me."

She laughed softly and pinched his skin. "And for them. I have never taken on three men before. It did not go well for those soldiers."

"They seemed confident, at first."

"Of course. Safety in numbers. Cowards. One had me by the throat. From behind."

Billy nodded, twisting his fingers in her long strands of hair. "That's when I saw what was happening. I ran to you."

"My sweetheart. That is how your American girls say it, yes? But I flipped him over my head and locked my legs around his neck and crushed his windpipe quickly. Kicked out with my feet and brought the other two down before they could use their bayonets. Got one's head between my ankles, the other's in a chokehold under my arm. It worked perfectly to squeeze with all my might with my entire body. How swiftly I broke them."

"Very swiftly. They were dead when I reached you. And I did not take over fifteen seconds from where I was standing."

"How easily I killed them does not trouble you?"

"It would trouble me if you did not know how to defend yourself."

"It does not upset you I delighted in my kill? That I exulted in it? That I rejoiced over my enemies?"

"No. I believe God gave you the victory. I'm not kidding. I pray for you every day. My cougar."

"What is that?"

"The powerful panthers we have in Montana. We call them cougars. Or mountain lions. They are two hundred pounds of muscle and stealth and ferocity."

"Ah, I like that. So, am I your cougar, sergeant?"

"You are."

"I revel in the hunt and kill. Especially when the odds are against me and I still defeat my foe. I enjoy their shock and dismay when they realize I have overpowered them."

"Bud, our corpsman, told me the body releases adrenaline in a do or die situation. This gives a person more strength and more speed. And once you use your body and your muscles strenuously, he says it releases even more good stuff into the bloodstream. This good stuff gives you a tremendous sense of exhilaration and euphoria. It cuts pain. You feel powerful. Like you can do anything and achieve anything. You are roused, energized, galvanized. Bud's words."

Amista laughed. "Oh, American man. Too many words for me."

"It's like a drug. As if Bud shot you full of morphine. You're exploding with strength. You're Superman. And you love it. You can do anything. Defeat anyone."

"Mmmm. I like that. I enjoy thinking of myself as Superman. Bending steel bars and lifting Japanese tanks over my head and crushing a dozen Japanese soldiers at a time. Ha."

"I don't want you to feel you're some kind of ogre for rejoicing over your enemy. You need to win. And the drugs the body pumps into your system make you feel good about fighting and winning. That's how God built you, built all of us. Except not everyone's a warrior like you. But let me tell you a story about another woman who was. Her name was Jael. So, an enemy of Israel, General Sisera, whose king was Jabin, is defeated in battle by the Jewish army and he escapes to Jael's tent seeking shelter and a hiding place."

"Why her tent?" Amista asked.

"She was the wife of Heber the Kenite who was on peaceful terms with the general's King Jabin."

"Okay, sergeant."

"Jael knows who he is. She welcomes him into her tent––"Come in, my lord, come in with me. Don't fear me." He comes in and drops and she puts a blanket over him. He's thirsty, so she gets him a skin of cool milk. He falls asleep. To quote the holy book, *Jael, Heber's wife, put her hand to the nail, and her right hand to the workmen's hammer, and with the hammer, she smote Sisera, she smote off his head, when she had pierced and stricken him through his temples.*"

"What?" Amista sat up and faced Billy. "That's treachery. I can kill in the heat of battle, but I don't think I could kill like that."

"Not even the Japanese general who has been tormenting your island and murdering your people? Not even Saito Yoshitsugu?"

Her face took on sharp lines, falling into a strong frown. "I don't know. Maybe him."

"The Jewish general, Barak, comes galloping up, looking for Sisera, and Jael comes out of the tent to meet him. She says, "Come, and I will show you the man you are looking for." So, Barak follows her back into the tent and there's Sisera, stone dead. He sees the tent peg Jael has driven through his head. She tells him she slew the enemy general with a few quick, powerful blows of the hammer. Jael smiles as Barak looks at her in surprise. She enjoys his shock and discomfort. There's still blood and bits of bone and brain on her hands and on her face and robe. She hasn't bothered to wash any of it off. She doesn't want to. She likes it there. She wants Barak to see it. Wants him to know for sure she was the one who dealt the death blow. She, a woman, a powerful woman. No doubt she smirks as his eyes go from the blood and gore and the slaughtered general and back to her. She is exultant, euphoric, happy with what she has done, proud of herself. The man is dead at her feet. She has defeated him. The holy book says, *Blessed above women shall Jael the wife of Heber the Kenite be, blessed shall she be above women in the tent. He asked for water, and she gave him milk in a lordly dish.*"

Billy paused.

"And?" demanded Amista. "Go on!"

"You already know. She pounds the tent stake through his skull. It says, *Between her feet, he sank, he lay down. He collapsed. He fell. He died at her feet.*"

"Oh, it is so powerful! I feel even stronger now about fighting for my island and my people. I feel stronger about rejoicing over my enemies when I strike them down."

"Something else. A woman named Deborah was leading Israel. It was Deborah who ordered her general, Barak, to attack their enemy, Sisera, and his army. But Barak was afraid to fight, and he said no: "Not unless you come with me and hold my hand." She says, "All right, I'll come with you and hold your hand. But the honor of killing Sisera will go to a woman." And it did. God set it up so Jael would kill Sisera and get all the credit. He made sure the warrior spirit was in her, the spirit to fight and to kill. And it was. So, my Chamorro beauty, you're in good company when you fight the Empire of Japan and glory in your victories. Just like Jael gloried in hers, and made sure everyone knew she had triumphed over her enemy just using her own two hands."

Amista quickly kissed him. "Ohhh, you make me feel so free and strong. I have a secret to share with you, Billy, my big tough American man. We Chamorro are not, umm, considered a people that chase after things. We take our time. It gets done when it gets done, you know? The settlers who were brought here from Japan differ from us. They want to do business, make money, build large farms. That is why our fighters have surprised the Japanese soldiers. Suddenly we are laying traps for them and outfighting them. They no longer have us under their power. We have them under ours. It's confusing for them. I will tell you something else."

"What's that?"

"I like to fight and have the victory. All of us Chamorro fighters do. But we don't just fight to fight. We want our freedom and once we gain it, we want to live in peace. You want to live in peace too, don't you, Billy? You don't want to be a marine all your life and go from war to war, do you?"

Billy leaned his head against her and she wrapped her arms around him, kissing the top of his head. "There are some men like that. Every country has those who make a career out of being in the military. They spend their lives in uniform. That doesn't make them warriors, though. A warrior can be a civilian who goes out to fight when he or she is needed. My country was like that in the beginning. Long ago, regular people had to be the fighters. Farmers, fishermen, carpenters, businessmen, they had to leave their homes and shops and fishing nets and fight."

"That is like us," Amista replied. "I wanted to be on the water and dive for things I could sell, like sponge or pearls. My sister wanted to be someone who learns and performs our traditional dances. Chamorra wanted to be a teacher. Sirena hoped to learn to fly. But now we have to fight." She rocked him gently. "So, let us sleep for a few hours. Then rise as the sun rises from the sea and continue the battle to free my island. One day we won't need to fight anymore and then I can hold you in my arms all day and all night. Would you like that?"

Billy smiled, his eyes closed. "I would like that more than anything else on earth."

———

THE WAR MADE BILLY afraid now. Afraid of losing her.

A cluster of 140mm Jap guns pinned King Company down that morning until the Navajo used code to call down fire from pack howitzers. One Jap shell took off the heads of two Chamorro next to Amista. Another shell burst near Billy and sent his helmet flying. He never found it. He never heard again for half an hour either. Everyone else knew when the shells from the howitzers were coming in. He only saw them hit and destroy the 140mm cannons, hurling them into the air.

Bullets erupted at Amista's feet as the platoon ran forward to take out a pillbox. Several of her friends fell, all women. Billy wanted to tackle her and pin her down beneath him. He almost did when he saw a stream of tracers skim past her shoulder. But he knew in his gut she'd be furious with him. Amista did not want a man being her nursemaid. She wanted a man that respected her courage and strength and was a partner, not a knight in shining armor galloping up to save her. Amista didn't want saving. She didn't need it. She just wanted a man to fight at her side.

She scrambled on top of the pillbox, found an air vent, and dropped two Japanese grenades into it, arming them by slapping them against her thigh. She had no sooner done this than a Jap came out of a camouflaged exit and fired at her with his rifle. He was a good shot and just about hit her. Billy saw the chips fly from the bamboo roof. Amista coolly put three bullets in the Jap's head with her M1 carbine. Explosions within the pillbox sent black smoke spewing from the air vent. More soldiers broke from the exit. She shot them all.

At night, after a quick raid, she led Billy into the jungle, trusting her sixth sense to warn her if any Japs were nearby. But the Japs in their sector were terrified of the Chamorro night fighters. They had stopped thinking the dark was a safe place for them to move around in and hunt Marines. If they came out of their caves and other hiding places, they moved with caution, wary of what lurked behind trees and bushes. That did not save them. Just after sunset Billy and Amista had killed five who were crouched behind a thick cluster of bamboo, hoping to ambush Marines and Chamorro. Their deaths had been swift and silent. They had used no weapons.

Billy forgot all about war and death once her lips brushed over his when they were alone. But this time Amista could not sustain her passion. Billy had his first experience of the chill that comes into a man when a woman appears to be no longer interested in him. He didn't know what to do when she pulled away and leaned against a coconut tree with her eyes closed. He didn't speak. But she murmured softly, and her voice was like a night breeze slipping through the coconut fronds high over their heads.

"We lost so many of my people today. We have lost Chamorrans on other days. many over the years before you and the Marines landed, . But the two getting killed right next to me by the 140mm guns, then four more at the pillbox. I knew them all so very well. It was too much. I have not been with a man before and I feel I should talk to you, but what do I say? What are the words? We have been loving each other and when we have spoken of war, you have wanted me to feel secure about killing men so that my island could be free. To not feel bad because I am happy to kill these men. Truthfully, I do not feel out of sorts because I rejoice over my enemy. And you must understand I do not feel out of sorts because of anything you have done. I am feeling dead inside because so many of my friends are gone. We should not have been fighting out in the open after the sun was up. That is not what we do. We fight by night. The darkness covers us. But now we have decided to fight beside the Marines during the daylight hours. Because of that, we lose many of us. If this keeps up, few of us will be alive to see Saipan gain her independence. Yet why should you be the only ones to battle the enemy when the sky is bright? Why shouldn't we bear the same danger? It is our island you fight for, after all, not your own. Why should we hide in the shadows? Oh, Billy, now I do not feel like rejoicing over my enemy when they die at my feet. I am weeping because my friends die at mine."

Unsure how to respond, Billy moved next to her and put his arm around her. Amista nestled against him. They slept. At dawn, the two of them moved out with the rest of the platoon, driving north. She joined her sister and the other Chamorro, ready to fire with her M1 carbine. Just like every day that had gone before, they dealt with snipers and Nambus and bunkers and pillboxes. They took casualties, killed the enemy, set bunkers on fire with diesel fuel and flamethrowers. Prayed to God they'd been right and hadn't torched bunkers where civilians were hiding. Found the headless bodies of Jap soldiers they'd trapped who had placed grenades in their mouths rather than surrender.

BY DAY AND BY NIGHT, Amista continued to slay Japanese soldiers with her bare hands. Her grief over the deaths of her friends had put pain in her blood. But she still wanted to defeat the enemy that chained her island to their will and killed her people with impunity. She might stand over their bodies for a moment in triumph. She might allow a smile of victory to flicker over her lips. She might spit in their dead faces. Yet Billy had seen Marines piss on Jap corpses in derision. Seen them cut ears and fingers off for souvenirs, take scalps, pry gold teeth out of dead mouths. Boil the skin and hair off Jap heads and send the skulls home to their mothers and girlfriends. Amista's kills, however fierce they might be, were not more brutal than any of that. And not more brutal than flamethrowers frying a man alive, fifty-caliber bullets ripping a face up at point blank range, or Ka-Bars severing throats and stabbing out eyes.

Nor were the Japanese fighting with clean hands. Many of them tortured and mutilated Marines and islanders. Bud had told Billy about Manchuria and about Nanking and how cruel the Japanese soldiers had been in China, even to pregnant women. How Jap officers had held beheading contests with each other, straining to decapitate the greatest number before having to re-sharpen their swords. He related what had happened to American prisoners in the Philippines, on Corregidor and during the Death March of Bataan. He'd told Billy what he knew about the POW camps and photographs that been smuggled out of tortured, beaten, starved and skeletal American prisoners. To say nothing of the Australians, Kiwis, Brits, and Canucks who they brutalized in the same way.

"I don't want war, Billy," Bud had said. "And I don't like it. I'm still the pacifist among the three of us Mennonites. But the Japs brought hell and damnation down on their own heads. If we kill them in hand-to-hand combat, at least they fought back. Their Chinese and American captives never did. Nor the civilians they've been slaughtering for decades. So, I do not judge you for how you slay the enemy in combat. I do not judge the islanders for fighting back against their oppressors. I do not judge Amista for rejoicing over the enemy she has broken with all the ferocity and rage she possesses within her soul. The Japanese have done far worse to her people and to the Filipinos and to the Chinese. They've done far worse to the Marines and dogfaces they capture and to the bodies of those they kill. *If my people would listen to me, how swiftly I would subdue their enemies and turn my hand against their foes.* Go forth and subdue the Japanese, Billy. Let them fall at your feet and let the world rejoice. Then we can all breathe again. And make homes for ourselves and our children in peace."

Billy related all this to Amista.

She listened, her large dark eyes fixed on his as they sat together in the night.

An hour before, the platoon had come upon Japs bayoneting three Marines to death. The enemy had them tied to coconut trees and made sure they did not strike any vital organs so the men would suffer as much as possible for as long as possible. By common assent, although unspoken, the Marines fell on the Japanese soldiers with their bare hands, just as the Chamorro guerillas fought. They tore the Japs limb from limb. One escaped. The two sisters, Amista and Kasina, ran after him, caught him, and dealt with him as ruthlessly as the Japs dealt with their captives. Except their bayonets were their fists and feet.

After chow and the swift tropical sunset, Billy and Amista had gone aside. They had just begun to talk when Lt. Crandall came by. Even in the dark, Billy could see the long, unlit cigar sticking out of his mouth. He beckoned to Billy.

"It's not like I haven't noticed," he growled. "Hell, the whole platoon notices. I haven't said anything because I don't give a shit. So long as you keep fighting and keep leading your platoon, it's eggs in my beer."

"Thank you, skipper."

"Don't thank me. Thank whatever god you believe in for finding a girl who likes your stinking, unwashed hide. It's difficult for me to comprehend. Take care of Amista, sergeant. Don't lose her to some craphead who wants to die for his Emperor and take her along. Got me?"

"Aye, aye, skipper."

"Here." Crandall handed Billy two cigars. "They're Mexican, but they're fine. Maybe she'll smoke one at breakfast."

"Thanks, skip."

"Carry on with your duties, Marine."

Crandall laughed and walked away.

Billy didn't think Amista would take the cigar, but she did, slipping it into a pocket. Then she wanted Billy to pick up where he'd left off before Crandall appeared. Billy went over all the thoughts about war and killing and cruelty that had been eating at him all day. Thoughts that had come to him unbidden. Even while the platoon blew up bunkers and hurled grenades into machine-gun nests and crawled on their bellies through the jungle like pythons.

"Is that it?" she asked when he'd finished.

"Well, except to say that when I was on Guadalcanal, and when I was in New Zealand, I'd meet Marine Raiders."

"What are they?"

"They're like you."

"They're like me?"

"They fight like you. A Marine Raider's body is a weapon. They use knives and guns too, but they use their hands, and feet, and their teeth and garroting wire as much as they use anything else. And if I can believe half the war stories Raiders told me, drunk or sober, then it's safe to say they kill as viciously and pitilessly as any combat unit in the South Pacific and Europe. Of any army. And have no qualms about it. *If it's kill or be killed, then it's better to kill and take satisfaction in a job well done,* I was told. I asked one of their officers who had defeated twelve Japs all by himself, in one fight, how he felt about it."

Billy put the Mexican cigar in his mouth.

"And?" Amista demanded.

"And?" Billy echoed.

She growled. "Oh, I hate it when you stop before finishing. I feel like putting you in a choke hold."

"He said, *I felt good, Marine.*"

Amista ran a hand through her hair. "I don't always understand all your big words and complicated sentences, sergeant, but

I think you're trying to make me feel better about guerilla warfare."

"War isn't a movie show. You can't prettify war. There's no popcorn and Pepsi and a soft seat under your ass. It's dirty and raw, and once it gets rolling, it's necessary to kill and maim the enemy to get it over with as quickly as possible. Guerillas do it dirtier than anyone else. So, they bring wars to an end sooner than anyone else."

"I'm not troubled by how viciously I fight against the bastard Japs, Billy. They're more vicious than I am. But you? Are you troubled by how I fight?"

"I've killed hard too, Amista."

"I know that."

"I've thought about my actions. I've turned them over in my mind like a spade overturns clay. I've worried about my lack of conscience when I kill. I've talked to chaplains about it, you know, holy men, priests. I've read my holy book, the Bible. Prayed. I was raised in a home where it was considered a sin to resort to violence of any kind, never mind the raw violence of war. Yet here I am. I don't have notches cut into my gun stock. But I know I've killed a lot of men. I've been as savage as anyone. In desperate moments, in times of combat, those hellish seconds of life or death, the paint gets stripped off our souls. The layers of veneer that make everyone look so good and fancy are really pretty thin. They lift differently for everyone, but eventually they lift and they're gone, and it's you. Naked. Killing so they don't kill you. Chopping off fingers and ears. Choking someone to death and feeling good when it's over because they're dead and you aren't. Civilization is gone. It's you or them, and there's nothing else. If you want to drink in the sunshine again, look up at the Southern Cross, sip coconut milk or kiss a pretty girl, or even read the Bible, make sure you're the one breathing when the fight is over. Whatever it takes."

Amista leaned forward and kissed him on the cheek. "You

know what I think, sergeant? I think you are talking to yourself. Not to me. But you wanted me along to hold your hand. Like Barak needed Deborah."

"Thank God, you're Deborah and not Jael."

"Who says I'm not Jael? But you're not Sisera. Or Saito. So, you have nothing to worry about. At least from tent pegs." She pulled Billy into her arms. "Come here, my big, brave, pretty Marine. Let's sleep." She rocked him. "Shh. *The lights begin to twinkle from the rocks.* That's how it goes, doesn't it? My memory for words is very good.

The lights begin to twinkle from the rocks. The long day wanes. The slow moon climbs. The deep moans round with many voices. Come, my friends, 'tis not too late to seek a newer world. Push off, and sitting well in order smite the sounding furrows. For my purpose holds to sail beyond the sunset, and the baths of all the western stars, until I die.

DAY 16 — GARAPAN

JULY 2, 1944

34

CASUALTIES

THE CORPSMAN

There are days you hate, but you cannot forget them. It's like one of Billy's red-hot branding irons has seared their imprint into your brain. December 7, 1941, is one of those days in my head—Bloody Ridge on Guadalcanal. The days we fought on Tarawa. Then came another, as bad as the others, July 2, 1944. The day we began our street fighting in Garapan, the capital of Saipan.

We'd been heading for Little Tokyo from day one, but it had taken us two weeks of tough slugging to get there. I knew the casualties were long past the Tarawa body count. I think some guys started feeling that their number would be up any day soon. It's a hard feeling to shake once it latches onto you. It's a doomsday sensation. The bullet with your name on it is out there in some Jap's gun that he's going to fire today or tomorrow. Once it's on its way, it will find you. It doesn't matter where you are or if you think you're safe. It will catch you. It will hit you. It will kill you.

We'd started finding the enemy in caves in the mountains on our approach. They liked to hide in those damn holes till night-fall and then pour out like spiders to give us hell. So far as our platoon and company went, the Japs fostering the idea we were afraid to fight in the dark was just what our resistance fighters counted on. Chamorra and her guerillas squashed the spiders by the hundreds throughout June and into July. The Chamorro expected no mercy and gave none to the Japs they crushed to death between their hands and legs and under their feet. Since they were infested with the enemy, we began treating the caves like we did the bunkers. Gasoline, explosives, hand grenades and flamethrowers.

But there were still too many civilian casualties. Many of them hid in the caves and the bunkers and wouldn't come out, even when Chamorra pleaded with them in Japanese or the Chamorran tongue. She complained it was because the Jap troops had convinced civilians the Americans would murder them and their children. Husto, her tough but kind sixty-six-year-old man, had volunteered to go into a deep cave when they'd heard a baby cry and coax the civilians out into the open. Jap soldiers had been in the cave too, and we heard Husto's cries that they had captured him and that they were cutting off his hands and feet. Immediately, more of the Chamorran fighters rushed into the cave to save him. This was just what the Japs wanted, of course. They shot the fighters to pieces with rifles and pistols. Then they blew themselves up.

Chamorra never sent any of her people into a cave again. If she couldn't get anyone to respond to her calls to come out, we considered the cave hostile and treated it as such. Sometimes we had a good moment. Civilians would make their way to us. That was a cause for breaking out the chocolate bars and chewing gum for the kids. Chamorra began taking her fighters to the caves at night and either ambushing soldiers when they came out or pouncing on them when they returned. If they returned. Her fighters and other Marines, not just Billy, were ready to deal with the Nips in the jungle dark. Now and then, the Chamorro fighters found civilians in the caves, and persuaded the women and children and men, Japanese or Korean or Chamorran, to leave and follow them to safety behind Marine lines.

WE KNEW the Navy had blistered Garapan with heavy bombardments from the time the Marines landed on Saipan. We'd hear the shells sizzling overhead. By the time we'd fought ourselves to the outskirts and got some binoculars on the city, it looked like the dirty gray photographs we'd seen of Stalingrad in the newspapers and newsreels. Almost everything had been leveled and, from what we could see, the streets and boulevards were choked with rubble from shattered office buildings, restaurants, temples, and houses.

It was a zoo. We knew there'd be snipers, machine-gun nests, mortars, even artillery. All dug into that frigging pile of bricks, masonry, and steel girders twisted to shreds from the heat of high explosives. It was going to be a messy business. And fighting in cities, even cities blown apart, wasn't our forte.

"Give me the damn jungle any day," growled Lt. Crandall, who was in a foul mood because his last Havana had been shot out of his mouth a few hours before we reached Garapan.

"He was aiming for your head, boss," Zarate reminded him. "So, you can thank God you still have it."

"I'd rather have my cigar," snarled Crandall.

Our company was on the move at the crack of dawn. Chamorra's Guerillas, as we began to call them, scouted through the wrecked and ruined city ahead of us. We had only been underway about ten minutes when there was an avalanche of machine gun fire and everyone hit the deck. There was the cry from Chamorra: "Corpsman!" I got up and ran. Billy was right behind me. And right behind Billy was Johnny.

Platoon Titan got behind the Nambu and used grenades to take it out. I dropped beside Poyo, the skinny seventeen-year-old boy, and Amista. Both were riddled with bullets. Blood was streaming through the fabric of their dark tops. Billy went to his knees beside Amista, his eyes wide in disbelief. She saw him. Fighting the pain, she reached for his hand and squeezed it with all her strength. Poyo was already gone, so I focused my attention on her, trying to staunch the blood flow, grabbing Leon Levy for a second pair of hands to apply pressure. But I knew I could not win. She was going into irreversible shock and the trauma to her body was too great. Billy was still gripping her hand when it went limp. And when Amista died, so did he.

Mennonite or not, Billy had always been a fighter, but he'd been a fighter who harbored second thoughts. That Billy Martens disappeared before my eyes. The one reborn on Saipan had no second thoughts. No doubts. No confusion. War was war, and you fought it hard, and you fought it without any qualms. It was not only meant to be, it had to be.

He let go of Amista's hand, placing it gently on her heart. Then he got up and turned to Johnny. "Give me your BAR."

"What? What the hell are you going to do with it?"

"What do you think I'm going to do with it? Give me all your spare mags too."

Johnny's no soft touch. But he wasn't going to argue with his friend. Not with Amista lying dead at their feet. He gave Billy his BAR and a pack heavy with extra magazines. Billy slung the pack over his back, held the BAR at his hip, barrel pointing forward, and began to march through the shattered buildings and broken streets of Garapan. We watched him go forward, mesmerized. No one moved a muscle to stop him, not even Crandall or Rudebaker. They stared like the rest of the platoon.

A sniper behind a pile of scorched bricks took a shot at him. Billy kept the BAR at his hip and swung his whole body towards the shooter. He fired three times, the big, heavy 30.06 bullets cracking through the air. The second and third shots hit the sniper and tore him open. We all saw it. Billy continued his forward march. Other shots rang out. Billy kept marching and shooting from the hip. No running. No crouching. Just a steady upright march, the BAR firing like clockwork. When one mag ran dry, he tossed it away, dug another out of the pack as he moved forward, snapped it into place, and continued firing.

"Well, crap!" Johnny looked around quickly, saw Garowski, grabbed his BAR out of his hands, snatched the belt of mag pouches off his waist, and went after Billy, BAR already snapping out shots at a Nambu that had opened up. The Nambu peppered a pile of rubble behind Billy. But Billy ignored it and kept marching, putting three rounds into a Jap who stood up to throw a grenade. The grenade exploded in the Jap's hand as he fell and killed three other soldiers crouching next to him. Johnny emptied a mag into the Nambu gunners, taking their heads off and silencing the machine gun.

That was it. The entire platoon surged forward, firing, ducking, running. After X-Ray, it was Titan and Zeus. Then the other companies, spreading out, taking cover, blasting Japs out of their nooks and crannies and spider holes. Billy kept marching and shooting from the hip, and Johnny kept pace with him. I was sure I was going to see them both go down, but that never happened. When I responded to calls for a corpsman, it was always for other Marines. It was the craziest thing I saw in the war.

I'd seen Billy go wild. We all had. Whenever that happened, he was always running and leaping and screaming and spraying bullets from a Thompson or swinging a sword and loping off heads. This zombie marching, Japs bullets zinging over his head, his face set like stone, no shouts, no yelling, no sprinting. Just a dead man walking in a straight line like a frigging Frankenstein. It made my blood run cold. It was like he wasn't human. Just a machine. Or something out of a voodoo spell.

When I finally caught up with the platoon, they were just passing a Buddhist temple that was in bits and pieces. Billy hadn't stopped. Neither had Johnny. K Company was spread out all around them, rooting Japs out of cellars and from behind tumbled down walls, hurling grenades, torching Nips with flamethrowers, shooting them in the face from six inches away. And when it was necessary, ripping the enemy apart with their bare hands.

This was Billy's grief. His terrible grief. A grief the Japs had inflicted when they killed the first woman he'd ever loved. A grief they paid a terrible price for. Billy had turned lifeless, uncaring, unfeeling. He was simply a walking rock. He killed everyone in his path. When he ran out of mags, he put up his hand and someone always ran up and gave him more. They might get shot running the ammunition to him. But not a single bullet grazed Billy.

SUGARLOAF HILL with its limestone caverns. Flametree Hill with its blood-red flowers. Observatory Hill with its fifty-foot lighthouse. The 2nd Division mauled them over. On July 3, a Monday, we pushed through what was left of the city's business district and the empty homes of the well-off, many of whom had been killed in the shelling or in the fighting between the Marines and Japanese troops. Suddenly we were at the shoreline and the sea. I was next to Billy as he washed his hands, his face, his hair, his chest, everything. A lot of the Marines in our platoon stripped down and swam and scrubbed their bodies with sand. I was there when the guerillas joined us and Chamorra walked proudly into the sea, swimming far out until she was a speck. I watched Billy watch her.

"You wouldn't think she'd cry," Billy said to me. "But she was standing behind you when you were treating Amista. She didn't bother to wipe her face clear. Like anything else she does, Chamorra doesn't care what others think."

"Did she speak with you?" I asked.

"No. We only talk when it comes to attacking the Japs. The last night Amista and I fought beside Chamorra, she liked my kill and said so. That was it."

"Was Amista ever jealous of her? Because I know you had a thing for Chamorra once."

"Probably still do. Amista knew. She didn't care. She was never jealous. "As long as we're alive, I know you will be with me," she'd say. "If one of us isn't alive, it doesn't matter anymore. If you are gone, in time I will find another man. You must do the same if I am taken from you. It is important that you carry on. Grieve, but keep fighting and find a woman to love you as much as I do. That's what I want for you." That's how strong and free and beautiful Amista was, Bud. Dear God, it feels like I was just part of a bad war movie. I can't get to the end of it and get myself out of the cinema and out of the dark."

"I'm sorry, Billy."

"I'll make the Japs sorry. That's who'll be sorry."

"The fighting's pretty much done in our sector, Billy. And tomorrow's the Fourth of July. We'll celebrate."

Billy was scrubbing his grimy combat fatigues in the saltwater. "I'll celebrate by hunting Japs, Bud. I'm going to request a transfer to the 4th Division. Word is they're still duking it out on the other side of the island."

"Think Rudy will okay that?"

"I don't give a frigging shit what he okays. I'll go AWOL if I have to and he can throw me in the frigging brig after we kill 'em all."

"Kill them all?"

"Damn right, Mennonite. No prisoners. Just like Tarawa. Every Jap a cold corpse. Bullets, neck breaks, flame throwers, snapped backs, choked off throats, a grenade down the hatch, whatever it takes. Maybe I'll scoop up a collection of ears or scalps or cook me a head into a skull. I don't know. But my war is never gonna be over. I'll haunt those bastards to the ends of the earth for what they've done."

He broke down, still trying to scrub his fatigues clean, snot running down his face along with the tears, big sobs making his tall body lurch. I knew better than to touch him or say a word. Johnny had come over and he knew better too. We let him be. In a few minutes, Billy angrily splashed seawater into his face and wiped it off with the back of his arm. Then he laid his fatigues out to dry.

"You can keep the BAR," Johnny said, smoking a Craven A.

Billy looked at him. "You sure?"

"Sure, I'm sure. I'll keep Garwoski's. You and I will be the BAR men. And I'll go AWOL with you too. So long as it means deep-sixing Japs."

"That's all it means. That's all that matters to me."

Chamorra swam back to shore. When she touched sand, she began to walk. The water was up to her chest. She took her time. Proud, straight, strong. The ocean shone like steel. She emerged from it naked, like some deity. Like Pallas Athene, the Greek goddess of war, who fought alongside the Greek warriors at Troy.

Every Marine on the beach had his eyes riveted to her. She had washed the yellow dye out of her hair and scrubbed the black paint off her teeth. Her long dark hair was unbound and fell over her chest and waist and down past her knees. It was like a shining garment that covered her skin. The first word that came into my mind was *Amazon*.

She walked directly towards Billy and stood over him, tall, fierce, and defiant, daring him to speak to her. He said nothing. Water glistened over her arms and face and dripped from her body onto the pebbles and sand. As much as I loved Kalasia, and had taken a shine to Kalamia, I had never seen a more beautiful woman in my life. She was magnificent. She was divinity. And she turned to gold in front of our eyes as the sun sank lower and lower into the western seas.

"Sergeant," she said to Billy in her perfect English with its lovely Chamorro accent. "I need you to come with me and help bury Amista. It is important that we do it together."

Billy squinted up at her as the sunlight flashed over the sky and over her body. "I want to see Amista buried properly. But why do we have to do it together?"

Chamorra held her head higher. "Because that is what she told me she wanted."

TO HELL AND BACK

JOHNNY STRANGE

Johnny Strange packed BAR mags. And more mags, and then some more. He wanted the pictures in his head to stop their parade: Billy, kneeling over Amista as she bled out and died, the grinning face of Harold Jenkins as he shot his brains out, the big Jap he beat to death in the bunker on Tarawa, Marjean, all heat, cornsilk hair, green eyes and little wolf teeth, the civilians in the caves, screaming as they burned, the bombs, the noise, the death. Like a friggin' Movietone reel, round and round in his head. So he packed BAR mags.

He knew he was going with Billy; he knew his friend had a vast hole in his chest where Amista used to live; he knew they would kill Japs until there were no more Japs to kill. He knew they would become death angels, the destroyers. No matter how much blood the Japs smeared on their doorposts, the destroyers would find them, kill them. There would be no Passover for the little Shinto bastards.

"God, I hate this frickin' war!"

"Yeah, me too."

Johnny looked up. Billy Martens stood there. Not the cowboy Johnny met on the train to Dago. A different Billy, dark, distant, almost unreachable. And Johnny knew he wanted Billy to live, and he wanted Bud to live, and he wanted to go home to the US of A with his friends, because he knew that for the rest of his life he would need someone to call in the middle of a sweat-filled night with the friggin' Movietone running over and over in his head. Someone who knew, someone who cared, someone who had been to hell and back with him.

"Chamorra's gone."

"What? Where?"

"After we buried Amista, she told me she had unfinished business. When I went looking for her a while ago, she was gone. Didn't take any of her team."

"She's gone after Saito, Billy."

"Yeah, I figure."

"We gonna go get her?"

"Bet your ass, Strange. I'm not losing another one, ever."

"You'll need a medic."

They both turned. Bud was standing there with his kit.

Billy grinned. "I don't know, Bud, this will be tough. I wouldn't want you to be a gold star in your Mama's window."

"Yeah, well listen here, Sniper-boy. You may not know it, but *I've* been your Mama ever since boot camp. You and crazy-boy Strange here. I've been watching over you guys like some damned guardian angel and it's been hard work, believe me. And I'm sure as hell not gonna let you guys get all shot to rag dolls out in the dark somewhere. Not without a Medic handy. I'm gonna make damn sure you get your butts home."

Johnny snickered. "Philo Parmalee, such language. What would your mother say?"

"At this point, Strange, I couldn't give a flying rat's ass."

Billy slapped Bud on the shoulder. "All right, you're coming. Tape your gear so it doesn't clank in the dark."

Johnny kept packing mags. "So are we gonna be corner turners, Billy?"

"No AWOL here, Strange. I already talked to Rudy. K Company and 2nd Div are going behind the lines for some R&R. We're out of the fight as of July 4. He knows what's up. He gave us his blessing."

"So where is Saito hiding?"

Billy pulled out a map. He put his finger down where Chamorra had pointed a few days before. "He's not here anymore. Her people told her he's in another cave south of the Village of Makunsha." He moved his finger north. "We have pushed the Japs to the north end of the island. They've formed a line across from this gulch to the beach on our side of the island. Chamorra has to get around the line to get at Saito. She will go here."

Billy drew a line with his finger.

Johnny nodded. "So we will go through the 27th lines to get there?"

"Right. Everybody is confident the Japs are done, so we shouldn't have to take too much shit to get through."

"Ready?"

Billy nodded. "Let's go."

They went.

JULY 6, 1944. Johnny, Billy, Bud. Alone on the rocky side of a hill, looking down on the Jap lines. It is dawn. Rosy tinges light the red flame trees that cling to the barren hills. Debris litters the landscape. Bloated black Jap bodies split open and putrid. Billy points.

"I figure it's right down there, Johnny. Ready?"

Johnny nodded, checked his BAR. "Locked and loaded, Cowboy."

"Bud, watch your ass, it's gonna get hot."

They move down the hill like ghosts. Billy tracking a bull elk in a cold Montana dawn. Johnny follows, the mantle of hate now carried on Billy's strong shoulders. Bud behind, praying. Three friends, the end of the road, the last chance café, the non-refundable offer.

Hand raised. Stop. Four fingers up, signal left and right. Billy's Katana snicks out, the broken blade now a killing knife, Johnny's KA-BAR glints in the predawn light. Bud packing mags right behind them. Quick, noiseless, four careless Japs sent to hell. The nights with the Chamorros making their bodies automatons. Kill quick, kill silent, the destroyer angels come. Death in khaki.

Again, silent, a wolf pack. A Jap raises his head, looks for the sound made by the moving rock. Too late. Dead. Moving closer, mouth of the cave. Voices. Billy slips up, Looks in. Motions Johnny to the other side.

Chamorra is standing in front of a little Jap with a big uniform, her face swollen and bloody. Seated on a rock, watching, another Jap who looks like a bulldog.

Saito! Nagumo!

Three attendants at attention, waiting for the General's orders. Saito stands in front of Chamorra.

"So you thought to kill me? Me? General Saito? The prodigal daughter returns to claim revenge?" Saito slaps Chamorra, Johnny sees Billy stiffen.

"You Chamorros, such putrid pieces of garbage. I should have rounded every one of you up and shot you when I came. Now I will finish the job I started with your family. Kneel before me."

Chamorra raises her head, spits in the General's face. Saito's aide rushes forward, hands him a cloth. Saito wipes his face. "I said kneel."

Chamorra's voice, low, like the hiss of a serpent. "My father did not kneel to you, my brother did not kneel. I am my father's daughter. Kill me, but I will not kneel."

Saito punches Chamorra in the face, knocking her to the ground. The sword whips out, raises. "Now you are kneeling."

"I wouldn't do that, General." Billy steps into the cave. Johnny right behind. Bud stands in the entrance, watching, looking out for his guys, praying. The BARS point into the room, right at the Japs. Saito steps back, the sword comes down. Nagumo stands.

"Chamorra, move over here."

Chamorra stands. Her face is a mask of blood, her hair yellow, the black teeth bared. Hands tied behind her. Blood runs from a wound in her shoulder. She steps behind Billy, leans against him. Johnny cuts her hands free. Billy hands her the broken Katanga. "Do what you came to do, Sergeant."

Chamorra steps close to the General. Gliding. The Serpent. His eyes widen in fear. "You are a coward. You hoped to commit *Hari-Kari*. I will not give you the honor. You will come before your ancestors in shame, killed by a woman."

The Katanga goes back, thrusts. Hiss. "For my brother." The General gasps. Thrusts again. Hiss. "For my mother." Two quick stokes. Hiss. "For my sisters." Saito stumbles to his knees. The Katanga at his throat. Hiss. "For my father, who will always be a better man than you." The Katanga slides across the neck. There is no noise from the mouth that opens there. Just blood. A river of blood. The General tries to speak. The aides step forward, but the BARS move them back. Blood rushes from the gaping neck. Chamorra's fist goes back, smashes into the face. The General goes backward, his knees bent. Chamorra spits in his face.

"Now who is kneeling?"

"Dear Jesus." Softly, from Bud.

The aides crab sideways toward Nagumo, hands raised. Chamorra hands him the Katanga. "Goodbye, Admiral. May you roast in hell with your general." Nagumo looks around then jams the blade into his gut. Chamorra steps back. The BARS bark three times in the cave, and the Japs tumble into a heap.

Chamorra collapses at Billy's feet.

It is finished.

"She's lost a lot of blood, Billy. We can't move her." Bud was bending over Chamorra, bathing her face, the compress taped to her shoulder. "Give her a chance to rest."

Billy nodded. "We'll hole up here. I'll take first watch. Johnny, catch some shuteye."

The Saipan sun outside was hot, but it was cooler in the cave. Billy had piled the Japs up at the back of the cave. "There's some gasoline over there. We'll burn these bastards when we go."

The three friends watched and waited throughout the day. Billy was asleep when Johnny came and woke him up. It was dark outside.

"There's something going on out there, Billy. The Japs are making a lot of noise, like they are singing or something."

"They are preparing for *gyokusai*—honorable suicide."

The three friends looked around. Chamorra was sitting up. "I heard Saito order it after they caught me. They are massing all the troops they can find and they are heading right down the center of the valley."

Billy knelt beside the woman. "How many are there, Sergeant?"

"Probably four thousand."

Johnny shook his head. "That's right where the 27th is. I don't think the Dogfaces can take it."

"We need to warn them."

Bud came over and touched the compress on Chamorra's shoulder. "Let me look." He gently peeled the bandage off. The bullet hole was high on Chamorra's shoulder. "Went right through, closed up. She's good to go. Can you walk?"

Chamorra nodded. "I feel much better, Bud. The sleep helped me. And killing the General, that too."

Billy grinned at Chamorra. "Say, Sergeant, how did you get captured?"

She smiled and dropped her eyes. "I did not have a man to protect me. My man."

Johnny gave Billy a light boot in the butt. "You're done for now, Cowboy."

Billy looked around. "No time for that, Corporal. We have to warn those GIs."

"But Colonel O'Brien, you have got to get some help up here. There are four thousand Japs coming right down your pipe." The diminutive O'Brien looked up. "Don't shout, son. We are aware of the buildup. Headquarters doesn't think it's such a big deal. Maybe a few hundred Japs at the most."

"I'm telling you, we saw them. Every Jap that's left on the north end of Saipan has armed themselves with whatever they can find; swords, sticks, pitchforks, pieces of broken sugar cane. These bastards are crazy. And they are coming."

"Listen, Sergeant, we have been hearing the yells and screams going on for hours. The artillery and our mortars have been pounding in their direction. Our boys are waiting in their foxholes. They have ammo and fixed bayonets. Contrary to what that jerk Howlin' Mad Smith says about the Army, we are ready to fight."

Just then an officer burst into the tent. "Sir, you have got to hear this."

O'Brien stood and went out of the tent. Billy followed. Johnny, Bud, and Chamorra waited.

O'Brien looked around. "Hear what, Captain?"

"That's just it, Colonel. Nothing. The bastards have been screaming for hours. Now they've gone quiet."

Johnny looked over at Billy. "Lock and load, Sergeant. I think the shit is about to hit the fan."

Suddenly there was a horrible sound, like the buzzing of bees. Bud cocked his head. "What the hell is that?"

Johnny ratcheted a shell into the chamber of his BAR. "It's men, Bud. And they are all screaming the same thing."

"Banzai!"

The Japs came running out of the dark. A nightmare of drawn swords, bayonets, pitchforks, machine guns. Bullets whizzed around the GIs like angry bees. Death came in a cloud. Billy pointed and shouted. "We've got to get under cover."

The four of them ran toward a pile of equipment. As they were running, Johnny looked up. Something was flying toward them.

"Grenade!"

Then Johnny felt Bud's powerful arms grab the three of them and shove them over the pile. There was a tremendous explosion.

Is this it, Lord? Is this the end?

"MARJEAN!"

Then everything faded away.

DAY 22 — BANZAI

JULY 7, 1944

36

THE ROCKET'S RED GLARE

BILLY MARTENS

Billy was stunned by the explosion.

The screaming and yelling made no sense to him. Stabs of fire from gun barrels made his confusion worse.

Flares burst overhead.

A million faces suddenly appeared out of the dark—white, green, black.

A body hurtled into him and knocked him flat.

Strong fingers crushed his throat.

A fierce and exultant Japanese cry pierced his ears.

Billy groped for the Ka-Bar on his web belt, tugged it free, and plunged it into the man's ear and skull. His second blow sliced into the neck and severed the artery. So much blood gushed over his face he was blinded, even choking from what he swallowed. He was moving purely on instinct, still disoriented from the grenade blast. One of his hands shoved the body off him. The other hand continued to grip the knife while he used the back of his arm to wipe his eyes clear. The first thing he saw in the gun flashes and burning flares was hundreds of men charging at him.

Billy still had not had a rational thought. Now, he had even less than that. He panicked and left America and Montana ranchlands and Sunday dinners farther behind than he already had on Guadalcanal and Tarawa. His free hand yanked grenades off his belt, he unpinned them with his teeth, and he threw them at the horde rushing to swallow him up. Billy knew somewhere in his head he had seven grenades on his body. He hurled them all, the first exploding by the time he was launching his fifth. He saw two men break apart into chunks of skin and bone, their shrieking heads spinning off into the dark, orange flames ripping up the blackness. Then there was another explosion. And another.

By that time, Billy was pulling grenades off the body of the man he'd killed with his knife. He primed them by slamming them against the helmet of the dead soldier. He had no idea where his own helmet was. He pitched the Jap grenades into the tumble of attacking men. The whole night exploded.

A part of his brain remembered Bud and Johnny and Chamorra. He looked behind him and saw them sprawled in the dirt. He had no idea if they were dead or alive. He threw himself over all three, reaching out and tucking Chamorra in under his chest, his legs over Bud, his stomach over Johnny. Grenades roared to life all around them, red and yellow and white. Some were Jap grenades. Some were American. Shrapnel bit into his back. He saw dogfaces smashing heads with rifle butts as the enemy swarmed over them. Then it was all Japanese troops again, a stream that had no end, trampling their own men and dead Americans as they surged past, howling.

Billy spotted a Nambu. He remembered a Japanese general and a cave. He saw a second Nambu. Both pointed away from the cave. Part of their defense. He crawled to the first and hoped it was ready to go. War oozed back into his mind and his fingers. He sighted and squeezed the trigger. The machine gun erupted.

Bodies jerked and heaved and flew. Billy did not smile or grunt with satisfaction as tracers gleamed from the barrel and tore the enemy up. He was just glad he knew where he was again and what he was doing. Soldiers changed direction and came right at him and his machine gun. He felt nothing except the solidness of being in control. The enemy fell in heaps in front of the Nambu. He knew the barrel would overheat soon. It didn't matter. There was the second Nambu he could turn to.

Japs raced past Billy, yelling, and fell on his friends. All three were struggling to get up, still groggy from the explosion that had knocked Billy senseless. Now they were helpless to fend off the sudden attack of the Japanese soldiers who gripped *Tantos*. Even Chamorra was trapped in a death choke from behind. An officer had leaped on her. He suspected who she was. Billy heard him use her serpent name in Japanese. He understood from the Jap's shouts that he was swearing to kill her for the Emperor with his bare hands. Just as she had killed many soldiers with hers. She fought back, but the officer only smiled at her efforts, cried out in victory, and squeezed harder, his arms tight around Chamorra's neck. He knew he had defeated her. Chamorra's eyes rolled up white.

Billy went berserk. Something others had seen before several times. But not like this. Johnny, wrestling with two Japs, watched in astonishment as Billy ripped the soldiers off him and smashed their heads into rocks as if they'd been toys. Then he turned on the Jap choking Chamorra, yanked the officer's pistol from his holster, pushed the barrel into the man's temple, and emptied the entire clip into the Jap's head within seconds. The two trying to carve up Bud, who was barely fighting back, Billy tackled headlong, knocking both men to the ground. He pinned them, grabbing one of their *tantos* and swiftly and fiercely slitting their throats. Jumping back to his feet, he ran to Chamorra.

"Are you all right?" he demanded

She stared into a face that had wild eyes, black with dried blood.

"I am now," she said.

He suddenly flashed a grin. His teeth, like his eyes, were black with blood too. Billy bore the grotesque face of a gargoyle in a morning lit only by grenade blasts, muzzle flames, and green flares, and despite her normally unflinching resolve, she pulled back.

He laughed at her fear. "It's just me, Cham. Your soft Marine."

The sun lifted itself into a brass and bronze sky. Billy leaped behind the second Nambu. He began pouring a blistering fire into the Jap soldiers who were still rushing past and over-whelming American troops who tried to make a stand. When the barrel overheated, he throttled an officer swinging a samurai sword, seized the weapon, and began slicing off heads and arms and slashing open stomachs with the *katana.* Johnny was suddenly there, his BAR smashing bullets into Jap bodies. Billy and Johnny saw the contorted faces of American soldiers and their enemy fighting to the death with knives, bayonets, shovels and bloody fingers that were scraped to the bone. They were all desperate men killing other desperate men in the lowest pit of hell. The screaming was so loud Billy scarcely heard the gunshots.

The bombs from 81mm mortars began to hit. Billy used the chaos to plunge into Jap ranks with his sword flying. "Banzai! Banzai! You bastards!" In the midst of the slaughter, Billy had fished his Jap bandana from a pocket, his Rising Sun *hachimaki* and twisted it around his head. Now he thrust his face into those of the men he ran through with Japanese steel. "Here's to your g'damn Land of the Rising Sun and your g'damn Emperor!" Many of the Jap's eyes went huge when they saw the *hachimaki* on a Marine's head as the sword swept across their stomachs or pierced their chests. He smiled grimly. "You wanted to die, didn't you? Now here it is. In the rocket's red glare."

THE KILLING WENT on all day. Jap units were everywhere. Even their wounded with broken heads and bandaged arms and legs fought, even those on crutches. By rights, Billy knew, the four of them shouldn't be there. They should have been safe behind the lines with the rest of the platoon and K Company and the 2nd Division. This was the dogfaces' fight. This was the 105th Infantry Regiment's day in hell. Them and the 10th Marine Artillery Regiment. Billy saw the shoulder flashes for both among the dead as the battle swept all around him that Friday in July. But fate or God had put them here so that Chamorra, like Deborah and Jael, could have her revenge on the Japanese general. The Good Book said that vengeance was the Lord's. And God had deployed three men and a woman to carry it out.

Billy wasn't keeping track, but Chamorra took crazy risks with her *tanto,* her M1 carbine, and her strong, life-ending hands, running all over the battlefield in her Marine uniform. Ever since she had walked out of the sea after washing the yellow dye out of her hair and the black off her teeth, her beauty had mesmerized him. He knew he'd been attracted to her before that, admiring her strength and courage. Now it was something more. Billy watched her like a hawk over the Rockies kept an eye on the terrain below its wings. He saved her ass over and over again. Some of that she noticed, turning to see a Jap cut in half by his bullets at her back. But Chamorra said nothing. Just went on fighting.

"She said she blessed our union," Chamorra had told Billy at Amista's graveside.

"What union?" Billy had snapped back. "You hate my guts."

"I don't. I admit I know more about killing men than loving them. In fact, I don't want to love them. But the day we were in the LVT and heading for Saipan, you told one of your men you were here to free my people. It was hard for me to forget that or to stop having feelings for you. It frightened me. So, I was hard on you. I spurned you, rejected you. Especially after you saved the lives of Amista and her sister at that pillbox. I saw how brave you were, Sergeant. My heart leaped for you. And that made me push back even harder. I was glad when you fell in love with Amista. I felt safe then."

"You were glad?"

"Some of me. Not all of me. But I swear to the heavens, I wanted you and Amista to stay together. I did not want you. I did not want to love a man and be trapped by that. But she saw through me. She said, *I know you love my man, Chamorra. It's all right. I know you would never come between Billy and me. But if I die, you must take him to your heart and to your body. You must. Promise me that. I don't want him with any other woman but you if I am gone.*"

Billy had stared. "She told you all that?"

Chamorra had given him a small smile. "You know she liked to talk."

"So, is that what you're going to do? Take me to your heart and your body?"

"I already have. Weeks ago. I resisted it. But I knew my heart had yielded, and that my flesh was eager for your strength and courage. As a woman yearns for her husband on their first night."

"Aren't you jumping the gun?"

"Am I? If you want me to go, tell me."

Billy's response had been to take her into his arms and kiss her as fiercely as a firestorm lit by lightning. He had no idea what the hell had happened. How could he move from grief to passion like that? But in his head, it was as if Amista was encouraging him. *This is who I want for you. Put your arms around her. Love her. Serve her. Even though she says she doesn't need protection, she needs yours. You must cherish her the same way you would cherish me.*

Billy felt like he was caught up in an ancient biblical drama, something right out of King Saul, or King David, or Daniel, or Jeremiah. Now, here was a wild battle on the plains of Jezreel to go with it. A battle that only ended with a tropical sunset, the red lingering over the western seas like a dying sky. There were bodies strewn everywhere. He half expected to see spears sticking out of chests, arrows out of backs, shields lying by dead men's sides. Where were the horses? Where was the bronze body armor? The smashed chariots? The shattered shafts of the battle standards?

The warring, he prayed, *it never ends, God, it never ends. From generation to generation since the beginning of man.*

Small fires flickered everywhere in the night, and a white smoke lay over the mountains and valleys. Billy wandered away from the others for a few minutes. They were with a platoon from the 10th Marine Artillery Regiment. Casualties had been high. Bud had been busy. He'd pulled the scraps of metal out of Billy's back too. The fighting had lasted fifteen hours. Billy's head felt scrambled. But not just by the banzai and the long battle that followed.

Chamorra's hand suddenly slipped into his. Her skin was warm.

Warm as blood. Warm as sunlight. Warm as the jungle at noonday.

"Are you trying to get away from me?" she asked.

"I'm trying not to think of you. Is that the same thing?"

"Am I that much of a burden to you?"

"You're that much of a mystery to me. I'm just a simple cowboy."

She tried to lean her head on his shoulder. Then she took it away. Then put it back.

"I'm not very good at this," she said. "But I remember Yale."

"Did you go out with guys?"

"Go out? Not at all. I watched others do that. Now here I am trying to imitate them."

"You don't have to do that."

She pulled her head away again. "Well, I have to do something."

"Just hold my hand and we'll keep walking."

"That's enough for you? You like my touch so much?"

"I like it a lot."

She gave a small laugh in the dark. "I don't think any man has ever liked the touches I've given."

"This one does."

"That's because the ones I've given you are different from any I've ever given before. But I still don't know what I'm doing or what I'm supposed to do. I don't like that."

"What do you want to do right now, Chamorra?"

"Honestly?"

"Yes. Honestly."

"With the dead all around, I want to give life for the first time in a long time. I want to give it to you. It feels so strange to say that. But the feeling I have is overpowering, and I'm going to give in to it."

They had kissed at Amista's graveside. As if they wanted Amista to witness it. To witness their surrender to her will. This kiss was something different. In a way, it was Chamorra's first kiss. She gripped Billy's face in her hands—his bloody, bearded, battle-scarred face—and her long, strong fingers were not gentle, but fierce, as if this were combat. Her kiss was fire, and it was powerful.

"Surrender yourself to me, Sergeant," she said, breaking off a moment before kissing him again. "End the war for me. Give me another life. Take me into your heart and your soul and give me another life."

37

THE LAST ROUNDUP

THE CORPSMAN

When that grenade came flying out of the dark, I thought we all bought the big one, the one-way ticket out on Charon's barge. I just remember grabbing my buddies and shoving them over a pile of equipment into a ditch or a hole and then it went black so Philo Parmalee kisses his ass goodbye. But I woke up and Billy was lying on top of all of us— me, Johnny and Chamorra and Grenades are going off all around us and I remember the zip and patter of fragments of steel, like a hard rain falling, biting the dirt, biting flesh. I heard Billy curse as he took some shrapnel in his back covering for us—then he was up and gone and Johnny groaned and got up to his knees and I remember some parts of the rest of the fight, like someone took the pieces of a film off the cutting room floor and stitched them back together in the wrong order and I'm in and out of this strange reality like one of those weird Picasso paintings and there are a hell of a lot of Japs and I have my troubles just trying to stay alive.

Then there's Billy on a Nambu he took off a dead Jap and he's mowing them down like combines taking down summer wheat on the dry plains of the Inland Empire. Johnny's up and he found his BAR somewhere and the two of them are making a wall of steel and I'm still behind it shaking off the numbness in my head and then a couple of Japs are on me and then they are flying away and Billy and Johnny and Chamorra are making a damn British Square out of our little hole and the Japs keep coming and it's like one of those Buffalo stampedes I read about where you shoot the leaders and the rest of them split around you, and the herd goes from horizon to horizon raising such a cloud of dust that it's dark in the middle of the day.

***

SUN'S SETTING on the backside of Tapotchau. We have been at it since daybreak. There are dead Japs everywhere, I mean piles. This must have been the last hurrah, the last roundup for them, because if there is one Jap left alive on Saipan, they gotta be hiding in a hole somewhere crapping in their jeans.

Once I got my head back together, I patched up Billy's back, and a couple of nasty cuts I got wrestling with a Jap officer armed with one of those Samurai swords. Can you believe the guy wanted to cut my head off? I'll tell you this—there are no pacifists in foxholes and I killed that yellow bastard with my bare hands. I'm glad I did because otherwise my pals would be sending my head back to my mom in a cardboard box.

Johnny Strange, he didn't get a scratch, nothing but a big ringing in his ears that's still there from the first grenade. But that's not surprising. Johnny's got a date with a beautiful gal back in Sandpoint, Idaho, and I got the inside word that he's going to make it home.

Chamorra's compress came off in the fight and her wound opened up but she kept at it, although Billy had to pull her out of trouble heaps of times, cause she was a little off her feed from being shot up there in Saito's cave. And you know what?. I was right all along. Billy and Chamorra are a woo-some twosome.

Yeah, I know Billy fell for Amista, but I think that was more of a first-love-oh-wow-a-girl-likes-me kinda deal. But I always knew there was something deep going on between Chamorra and Billy, even though she treated him like dog squat. Amista was a sweet gal, a genuine beauty, but she wasn't for Billy. He's older than that now. He's not the skinny kid I met in Boot, nor is he the guy who wandered around Cactus trying to figure out how to get the bones home. No, he's a genuine guy, a grownup man, and he needs a woman, a grownup woman, and that's Cham. After this war is over, I can see them starting an outfitting company back in Montana and taking city people way into the back country and wrestling grizzlies and swimming naked in ice cold lakes and Chamorra laughing at the cold and using an axe like a sword on a big pine tree. I bet they build themselves a log cabin way back in and Billy will grow a beard and they'll have kids and Billy will teach them how to take down dinner at 800 yards with an iron sight. Yeah, I got a real clear picture in my mind. Course I won't be freezing my ass off in three feet of snow. Nope. Ol' Bud is headed for Tonga. Oh, I guess I'll take a wide swing through Ritzville, say hello and goodbye to Mom and Dad, but then, straight and as fast as I can get there, I'm heading for the South Sea Islands. And you know what? After what we just went through, I'm pretty damn sure that's going to happen. I mean, it can't get any worse than this.

IT'S July 10 and we are moving up to the north end of the Island. Our mortuary system was almost overwhelmed by the number of dead Marines in the *gyokusai's wake*. They had a lot of trouble separating the GIs from the Japs, recovering bodies from shell holes, trying to put together pieces of meat mortars had blown apart. They recorded lots of the guys dead three days after they died because they didn't find them until then. What Americans they recovered they put into amphibious tractors, took them offshore and hauled them down to Yellow Beach 3 and then directly to the cemetery. I guess that was so they would not bring the rest of our guys down, seeing all the dead Gyrenes and Doggies. The Japs? Well, the Seabee's just bulldozed out some big pits, pushed the dead Japs in and covered them over. I guess if any mama-sans come looking for their baby boys, they will have to weep over the entire island.

We heard that some guys from 4th Div found Saito's cave up in Paradise Valley. The Jap who led them there said that Saito and Nagumo committed *hari-kari,* and then their staff finished them with a shot to the head. Then they burned the bodies. When Billy and Cham heard that, they just shook their heads. I don't think it mattered to Cham because no matter what the Jap press says, the real deal is Saito standing before his ancestors telling them a woman killed him. But then, I don't think that will be his biggest worry since he'll be roasting in hell for all eternity.

But the worst part of this entire story was not over, not by a long shot. Only this time it had nothing to do with soldiers killing each other in the heat of battle. This part was senseless, and it's something I'll never forget watching happen. All the remaining Japs were up at Marpai point—that's the extreme north end of Saipan and the land ends in a series of two hundred to three hundred foot high cliffs. In fact, there's one that's eight hundred feet high. There are a lot of caves there, too, and we were back with K Company as a reserve for the 4th, cleaning out the last holdouts. We had just watched a bunch of Japs in a cave blow themselves up when I hear a shout. "There goes another one."

Well, we head up a trail and we come out on the edge of a three hundred foot drop. Down below us, the surf is pounding on the rocks. Someone yells, "There he goes." I see a body plummet off the cliff about a hundred yards away. It fell down and down and then hit the rocks. The man hung up there for a minute, and then a big wave comes in and takes him off. As I look, I can see that the water all around the rocks is full of bodies. It looks like the lagoon at Betio. There are bodies in the water and on the rocks, but no military uniforms.

I grab a Sergeant from the 4th. "What the hell is this, Sarge?"

"These are Jap civilians. They believed the propaganda that we would rape the women and kill the babies so they are all committing suicide. There must be a hundred babies down there, floating in the water. And it's the same all over this end of the Island. I was up by the big cliff an hour ago. A woman comes up the trail with two kids. We were taking sniper fire, so we are down in the brush beside the trail. We yell at this woman, but she just kept going. She looked like she was asleep. She just walked to the edge, threw the kids off and then jumped."

"Are you kidding me, Sarge?"

"Nope, these people are nuts. Right now there are hundreds of them down on the beach, right down there. They're changing clothes, washing up and getting ready to die. There are some soldiers down their with guns, so we got a guy who could speak Japanese and set him up on the cliff with a loudspeaker. He's begging them to surrender, telling them we won't hurt them, but they don't listen."

I'm looking over the cliff and I see this point right below me. It's crowded with hundreds of civilians and soldiers. I hear a strange sound and then I realize they are singing. Singing! What the hell is this, a freaking Japanese "some bright morning when this life is over, I'll fly away" church service? What is with these people?

There are families with kids, men in g-strings with spotless white headbands and women washing themselves. Then they jump into the sea. Entire families are jumping off the rocks holding hands. Some women have babies strapped to their backs. Black heads dot the water. Some of them are swimming slowly out to sea. It looks like a summer day down at Lyons Ferry on the

Snake, water filled with swimmers, scorching sun beating down, but these heads are going down and not coming up.

I see one of our guys down on the beach jump in and drag out three women who changed their minds. Some women try to turn around, but all the men and boys just keep swimming out into the ocean until they disappear. Meanwhile, the rain of bodies off the tall cliff doesn't stop. Bodies like flocks of birds wheeling around the cliffs, plummeting down, down, women with long hair streaming out behind them, like angels, held up by the wind until they smash on the rocks below.

I look over at Johnny. He's white as a sheet.

"Bud, what are they doing?"

"They got no hope, Johnny. And that's the difference between them and us. No matter what happens in this life, there is always a better day, something to look forward to."

Billy turns away. "I keep seeing my mom and my sisters up there, Bud." He shook his head.

And I'm thinking, what did these Japs bring into this world. Murder, rape, butchery, torture, savagery, but worst of all, they brought their stinking religion, a faith with no hope. What did Paul say? "If Christ is not risen, then we are the most wretched of men." And right here, right now, I'm seeing the truth of that. Because Christ is not risen for these folks and they are the most wretched of people. They are jumping into the ocean, jumping off cliffs, because they got no hope. And right now, right this minute, I am as glad as I have ever been that I know a God who gives me hope. Hope in the Resurrection, Christ in me, the hope of glory. And strange as it may seem, as I watch these Jap-birds plunge down and down, my soul is lifted and a song of praise is in my heart.

I only wish I could have gotten here sooner to tell these poor fools what I know.

3 8

IF I HAD WINGS

JOHNNY STRANGE

"Okay, here's the deal." Captain Rudebaker looked around at what was left of his company leaders. "We got one more job to do and then we can wrap this turkey up and go home."

Johnny cocked his head and turned it a bit to the right so he could hear what Rudy was saying. His head was still ringing and the hearing in his left ear sounded like he was underwater. Bud said the first grenade that went off over their heads in the *gyokusai* might have ruptured his eardrum.

"You should get it back in another week," Bud said while shining a flashlight in the ear. "Ears heal up pretty good."

"Strange, you with me?"

Johnny nodded. "Yes, Sir. It just sounds like you're talking through a bowl of pea soup."

Chuckles all around. Crandall pulled out a Havana. Zarate looked surprised.

"Hey, Crandall, you been holding out on me?"

"That's right, Bake, I got this one and two more. I won 'em from an artillery guy in a poker game."

"Stop beating your gums, you guys, and listen up."

"Yes, Sir."

Rudy went back to the map. "The Japs have everything they own in trenches on the beach and behind Tinian Town. That's the only place they think is wide enough for us to land. They have nine thousand troops in those trenches just waiting for us to come ashore. And the Brass has finally figured out that they don't want another Tarawa on their hands so they came up with a different plan."

Johnny glanced over at Billy, who was staring out the window. Johnny grinned.

My pal looks like a mule kicked him.

"Sergeant Martens!"

"Yes, Sir."

"You're not married yet!"

The Captain looked around the room.

"Dammit, I might as well send you guys to the beach and conduct this briefing for myself. Now get in the room, all of you! This is serious business. Yes, they have declared Saipan secured. But three and a half miles north is another Island and the Japs there are just as fanatical as the ones on this Island."

Crandall stood. "You're right, Sir." He turned to the men in the room. "All right, you mud-suckers. The Captain is right. We are not done here. Stop your wool gathering and listen up. You're not safe from a bullet until you're in your baby's arms and even then, if you're with the wrong baby..."

This time the room exploded with laughter. Rudy looked at his watch and shook his head. "Oh, for shit's sake, you guys..."

Just then the door swung open. "TEN-HUT!"

Everybody jumped. To their surprise, Red Mike Edson walked through the door. Salutes snapped, and Edson smiled. "Well, here you are, my tough guys from Cactus. As you were, men."

The General stepped up to Rudy, shook his hand. "Rudy, how are you?"

"Just great, General. Good to see you."

Edson looked around the room. "I see some familiar faces, faces I remember from our fight on Bloody Ridge. I am damn proud of 2nd Div, and I am especially proud of K Company. You have always been the tip of the spear, and I've been counting on you since you bailed my butt out on Tulagi."

His eyes stopped on the men of X-ray. "Lieutenant Crandall, good to see you."

"Sir!"

"There's a face I know. A sergeant now, eh, Sniper? Congratulations."

"Yes, Sir. Thank you, Sir."

"For you new guys, I once watched Sergeant Martens shoot the balls off a Jap Colonel at 800 yards with his 30.06, and I ain't lying." Edson grinned. His eyes stopped on Johnny. "Strange, good to see you, son—Corporal, no less. I heard how you beat the crap out of those Kiwis back in Wellington when you were on the boxing team. You made the Corps proud. You still wound as tight?"

Johnny felt himself blush at the General's words.

I haven't blushed since Marjean and I...

"Well, Sir, probably, but in a different way, Sir. I have a girl back stateside and I think if I could see her for about a week, I might fix that."

Johnny didn't expect the whoops and hollers that filled the room. He blushed again.

Oh, Lord, why did I say that?

The General laughed with the rest.

"Okay, fellas, I just stopped by to tell you I got a problem. Have you all heard about General LeMay? He's the big honcho flyboy and I'm telling you he's been tearing me a new one."

"Sir?" Rudy asked.

"Well, he's got this big new plane, the B-29, and they can fly 5,000 miles without stopping. LeMay thinks he can win the war with this plane because he can get all the way to Tokyo and back from somewhere in the Marianas. But he needs an airstrip with 1000 more feet than anything around here, except for the one right over on Tinian at Ushi Point. So to get the bastard off my back, I need you boys to go get me that island. You're going in behind the 4th, but your role is no less important. Have you briefed them on this mission, Rudy?"

Rudy glared at his men. "Well, Sir, I was just about to do that."

Edson smiled. "You boys have a special place in my heart. Get your orders and get over there and kick some Jap ass, okay."

The entire room stood back to attention and shouted as one, "SIR, YES, SIR!"

"Good. Make me proud. Rudy, carry on. I'll see you when I see you."

JULY 24. Johnny looked over the side of the landing craft as they headed for Tinian Town. The brass had warned them that the Japs were fully expecting Marines to come ashore here on Orange, Red, Green and Blue Beaches. But the actual plan would not be to the Japs' liking. He and Billy talked it over.

"The Navy and now the artillery over on Saipan have been softening up the Japs for fifty days. As soon as we look like we are going to land at Tinian Town, we are going to do a hard left and steam up to the north end of the island. There're some beaches there, White 1 and 2. The Japs will never expect us there, Johnny, because the beach is only 200 yards wide. Tinian Town is the only place with a beach wide enough to get an entire division ashore, so they are sitting there, waiting. We'll beat them to White Beach by hours. There are some coral cliffs, but the Seabees built some extended landing ramps to attach to the LVT ramps. We will have 5,000 men ashore before the Japs even wake up."

"So, when do we get to go?"

"4th Div goes first, and then we follow as soon as they have their perimeter locked down. When the Japs figure out what's going on, they will rush a bunch of guys north. But we'll be waiting."

IT WORKED out exactly like the Brass had planned. The 2nd Div boys watched 4th Div swarm ashore on Jig day and set up their perimeter and artillery. Soon they were pounding the Japs that were trying to move up-island from Tinian Town. Dusk closed down and Johnny watched from the landing ship as the onshore Marines surrounded their perimeter with barbed wire.

Crandall stood next to him, the ubiquitous Havana unlit and chewed, hanging from his mouth.

"Smoking lamp not lit, Lieutenant?"

"I got this one and one more, Strange. Gotta make them last."

Around midnight, machine-gun and mortar fire awakened the off-shore reserves. All around the perimeter they could see tracers going out into the dark.

Johnny and Billy watched as the heavy fighting continued.

"The Japs are up to their old tricks, Billy. They high-tailed it up here as soon as they could. They are trying to sweep our boys off the beach, but they didn't expect the barbed wire, I'm guessing."

"Yeah, when we go in tomorrow, I bet we'll see a bunch of those little bastards hanging there. Buzzard bait."

After two hours, the firing died down. Rudy came and stood with them. "Looks like we whipped them good, fellas. Now why don't you hit the sack. We've got some butt kicking of our own to do in a few hours."

THE 2ND DIV began coming ashore in force on Jig plus 1. When the LVT got to the beach, it opened its ramp onto an assault ramp. The Seabees were directing traffic as the tanks and mobile artillery streamed ashore.

Johnny stopped one of the Seabees. "Where did you get these ramps?"

"Hell, we made 'em. Tore apart that abandoned sugar mill on Saipan and used the steel to build these. We call them Doodlebugs."

Johnny looked at Billy. "These would have been nice at Tarawa."

"Well, you live and you learn."

Johnny shifted his BAR on his shoulder. "For the Marines, it's more like you die and you learn."

THE NEXT MORNING K Company was pushing eastward, supported by Shermans of the 2nd Tank Battalion. They made excellent progress and by the afternoon they were swinging south to sweep the Island. Casualties were minimal, and they established a perimeter before dark.

That night the Japs lashed back. Johnny and Billy were in the same foxhole when the attack came. They could hear the screams of "Banzai" first, and then the wave came. Suddenly the night was lit by artillery flares and starbursts. They could see the wave coming and the two BARs went into action.

"Like friggin' ducks on a pond, eh, Johnny?"

Wave after wave, like the tide moving up the beach, but they could not overcome the massive firepower the Marines put on them. Soon they were retreating. Johnny and Billy had just settled in when they heard the cry.

"Corpsman! Corpsman. Get your ass over here on the double."

Billy looked out of their hole. "That was Crandall. Wonder what's up."

Ricky Garowski appeared out of the darkness. "You guys better come."

"What, Ricky?"

"It's Rudy."

Johnny and Billy followed Ricky on the run. When they got to the right side of the perimeter, they found a group of their guys standing around a figure on the ground. Rudy! Bud was working frantically, but they could see an enormous hole in Rudy's chest where the bright blood was pumping out. He was pale, too pale. Bud looked up, smiled that sad smile and shook his head. Crandall dropped to his knees beside his captain.

"Rudy, Rudy, hang in there. Bud'll fix you up. Stay with us."

Rudy smiled. "Bud's damn good, Jamison, but not that good. Have you got a cigar?"

"I got two left, Captain. You want me to light one up?"

"That would be good."

Crandall lit the cigar and placed it in Rudy's mouth. He took a deep drag and coughed. Then he looked around at his men. "Fella's we've come a long way together." He coughed again. "I have been proud to serve as your Captain, from Cactus to Helen and now here. I'm gonna head out before you all now, a little scouting mission. Jamison, make sure my wife gets my things and my boy gets my ribbons."

"Will do, Rudy."

Rudy took another drag. "Not only have you been my men, but you've been my friends. Don't worry about me. I've got my faith and I'm sure where I'm going. I hope I see you all there when it's your time." Rudy was quiet for a minute, then he turned his head to Billy. "Sergeant Martens, you marry that Chamorra. Corporal Strange, you make sure you get home. The rest of you guys, keep a tight asshole and remember me well." Rudy took a

deep breath. "Jamison, you're in charge. Get them home...
Semper Fi."

Rudy's eyes closed. The cigar fell from his lips. Gone.

Johnny Strange stared down at his captain.

I hate this friggin' war.

SEVERAL DAYS LATER, the men of King Company stood at attention
at the Saipan Marine Graveyard while Red Mike Edson read a
eulogy for Rudy.

"Rudy Rudebaker was a great captain and a good friend. He
graduated in the top third of his class at West Point and came
from a long line of Marines and soldiers who served their country. He's taken flight for a distant shore. Every one of us here
today will have an empty place in his heart that only Rudy could
fill. As we prosecute this war and bring the Japanese Empire to its
knees, we will remember the men who gave their lives to bring
our victory about. For me, Rudy Rudebaker will always remain at
the top of that list. I have something I want to read. It's a poem
that Walt Whitman wrote after the death of Abraham Lincoln. I
think it's appropriate for today." He pulled a piece of paper and
some glasses out of his pocket. Adjusting the glasses on his face,
he read.

O CAPTAIN! My Captain! Our fearful trip is done,
   The ship has weather'd every rack, the prize we sought
is won,
   The port is near, the bells I hear, the people all exulting,
   While follow eyes the steady keel, the vessel grim and daring;
         But O heart! Heart! Heart!
          O the bleeding drops of red,
            Where on the deck my Captain lies,

Fallen cold and dead.

O Captain! My Captain! Rise up and hear the bells;
    Rise up—for you the flag is flung—for you the bugle trills,
    For you bouquets and ribbon'd wreaths—for you the shores
a-crowding,
        For you they call the swaying mass, their eager faces turning;
            Here Captain! Dear father!
                This arm beneath your head!
                It is some dream that on the deck,
                You've fallen cold and dead.

My Captain does not answer, his lips are pale and still,
    My father does not feel my arm, he has no pulse nor will,
    The ship is anchor'd safe and sound, its voyage closed
and done,
        From fearful trip, the victor ship comes in with object won;
            Exult O shores and ring O bells!
                But I with mournful tread,
                Walk the deck my Captain lies,
                Fallen cold and dead.

Johnny turned his head to wipe his eyes. He saw that many were doing the same thing. Edson continued. "Captain Rudy Rudebaker, we salute you."

The cry rang out. "PRESENT HARRMMMS!"

Slowly the men of King Company lifted the slow salute, the mark of greatest respect. They stood silent for a long time while the lonely notes of the bugle rang out. Johnny couldn't keep the tears out of his eyes, but he ignored them. He knew he was not alone.

I sure wish Big Band was here.

The notes ended and echoed away.

"ORDERRRR HARRRMMMS!"

Every arm lowered slowly in unison.

Edson leaned forward and dropped the poem into the open grave. "So long, Rudy. I'll see ya when I see ya."

Lieutenant Crandall stepped forward, pulled a well-chewed cigar from his pocket, dropped it beside the note.

"It's my last one, Rudy."

Edson turned to the men. "By order of the General Staff I am honored to inform you of the promotion of Lieutenant Jamison Crandall to Captain. As of today, he is now your Company Commander. Good luck, Captain Crandall. Do what Rudy said and get these men home."

"Sir. Yes, Sir."

Just then they heard a noise, like the droning of bees far away in the distance. Closer and closer it came, louder and louder. They all looked up. Shining in the bright sunlight high above them, headed north, was a squadron of the biggest planes any of them had ever seen. Long, big, beautiful. They stood in amazement.

Edson grinned. "Well, LeMay got his damned B-29s. And every bomb they drop on those little yellow bastards will have Rudy Rudebaker's name on it. Sergeant, dismiss the company."

Bakar Zarate stood forward. "COMPANY! DISMISSED!"

Johnny stood watching the planes as the men slowly began drifting away. Finally, only Billy and Bud stood with him.

"One day, will we know that all this was worth it, Bud?"

"I don't know, Johnny. All I know is that we gotta get home. We'll have time later to talk about it. Don't know what's next, but we need to stay alive. That's all we have left."

Johnny Strange looked at his two friends.

Yeah, God. We gotta stay alive.

39

THE WEIGHT ON HIS BACK

BILLY MARTENS

"Will you leave soon?" Chamorra asked.

Billy nodded. "Probably."

"Where will you go?"

"After the Solomons, they sent us to New Zealand. After Tarawa, it was Hawaii. I don't know where we'll go now."

"You know I can't leave Saipan, Billy. You know that."

"Yeah, I know it."

"I've fought so long for it to be free. So many of my people have died. So many of your people. I have to stay here and be free with my island. Be free with my people. You understand that."

"I understand it, Chamorra. It's okay. It's not as if they're going to let you go wherever the Marines are going. Your war was here. Your war is over. It's mine that doesn't stop. One damn island after another."

"How many more?"

"No idea. But eventually we'll wind up on the granddaddy of them all, Japan. And however hard they fought for Saipan, they'll fight a thousand times harder for Tokyo and their Emperor and Mount Fujiyama."

"Will you come back to Saipan? Will it matter to you to return to me?"

"Of course, it will matter."

"Then I will see you again on Saipan? I won't be forgotten? You truly do love me?"

"Chamorra, that is not something you should worry about. You have to know how much I care for you. Nothing and no one will stop me from coming back to you."

Billy found he didn't have much to give her now that the battle was over. Inside, he was gray and flat. There was no spark. No fire. Nothing like he had felt when they'd been fighting together. He drifted his way to the tent of the Protestant chaplain, Ty Jackson.

"Cigarette, Sergeant?" Jackson asked.

"I've got lots, padre, thanks."

"What's on your mind?"

"I never felt this tired after the Canal or Tarawa. But now I feel about ready to drop dead."

"On Guadalcanal, you didn't have anything else on your back. On Tarawa, you only had Guadalcanal. Now you have three islands on your shoulders. And everything that comes with them. The fighting. The killing. Your dead buddies. It's different in 1944 than it was in 1942. There's weight on you now."

Billy lit a cigarette, but never put it in his mouth. "I met an island girl here. One of the Chamorro. For weeks, I couldn't stop thinking about her. Now we have the chance to be together as much as we want. And I don't feel anything."

"Give yourself some time, Sergeant."

"She told me she loved me an hour ago. I couldn't say the same words back to her."

"Do you love her?"

"I thought I did. Now my brain is scrambled." Billy looked down at the cigarette burning between his fingers. "When it's war, I don't think much, I just feel stuff. Once the fighting stops, I think too much and I don't feel anything at all. You know, I start thinking about my father. If he knew how I've killed with knives or shovels or my bare hands, he'd despise me more than he already does."

"I think we've talked before. Maybe on Guadalcanal. But I'm pretty certain we spoke on Tarawa too. You're from a Mennonite background. You were raised never to bear arms."

"That's right." Billy stubbed out his cigarette without ever smoking it. "Yeah, we've talked before, padre. The first time was on Canal. Two years later, I still don't have anything figured out."

"What do you want to figure out?"

"How I can kill so easy. Fight so hard. Go wild during combat. Do crazy Superman comic book things. Then when it's over, I want someone to tell me who I really am. That I'm not that guy. That guy is a fiction. A story someone made up. A comic strip. I want someone to tell me I'm really a good Mennonite boy at heart."

"Is that what you think you are?"

"Hell, Chaplain. I don't have any idea who I am anymore. I'm not anyone I know. But there will be another island in six or seven months, and I'll do what I always do. I'll destroy. How the heck am I gonna make it in peacetime? If I ever make it to peacetime."

"You can't untangle all this. You can eat and sleep and that's about it. One day you'll tell her you love her. One day you'll write a letter to your father. One day you won't have any reason or inclination to kill. Right now, you could use a prayer and a long, long sleep with no thinking involved. I can provide the prayer."

"You think that'll do it? A prayer and a nap?"

"It'll do something. There's no magic making the rounds, Sergeant. Some faith and some hope. But the supply ships didn't bring us any wizard's wands with the ammo and dried plasma and C rations."

Billy made his way back to the 2nd Division camp and the

tent he shared with Johnny Strange and Jesus Navarro, both corporals. Johnny was there, stretched out on his cot, hands clasped behind his head.

"Were you with Chamorra?" Johnny asked.

"Nah." Billy sat on the edge of his cot and took off his helmet. "You could fry an egg on my head."

"Where is she?"

"She's gone back to her village."

"For how long?"

"Who knows? She's not allowed to go in and out of our camp anymore now that the fighting's over on Saipan. I have to request leave."

"No shit."

"Crandall says it won't be a problem."

"So?"

"That's not the problem."

Johnny stared at him. "Okay. What is the problem?"

Billy shrugged. "I'm outta gas. Got nothing left, Johnny. I don't even know if I've got feelings for her."

"You got 'em or you don't. You feel it or you don't."

"I don't feel anything."

"You're just coming down from all the combat. Scuttlebutt has three times as many men lost here as cashed in their chips on Tarawa. You felt crappy after Canal too."

"This is worse. This is Chamorra saying she loves me and me telling her I care for her. That's all. *I care for you.* Why didn't I just tell her I loved her?"

"We're all wiped out. Bud calls it combat fatigue. Chow and your pillow are your best friends right now."

"That's what the padre said."

"You go to one of the chaplains?"

"Jackson. Yeah."

"Well, hell, Billy. He's right. Take his advice. Grab forty right now."

Billy stretched out. "The dreams are bad too, Johnny. You have shitty dreams?"

"Nah. I don't dream. Not lately."

"Makes a man not want to close his eyes."

Jesus Navarro came into the tent. "*Hola.*"

Johnny nodded. "Anything exciting going on in camp?"

Jesus sat on the last cot. "The word going the rounds is we stay on Saipan."

"What?" responded Johnny.

"What?" Billy propped himself up on his elbows. "You're shitting me."

Jesus put his hand over his heart. "On my mother's garden. Which by the grace of the Blessed Virgin she manages to keep flourishing in an American desert. Everybody's jawing about it. No Hawaii. No New Zealand. No Tonga. We stay put on Saipan."

"Till when?" Billy demanded.

"Till we fight again next year."

"We could be here as long as six months." Billy lay back down with a groan. "Probably longer."

Jesus looked at Johnny, and Johnny shrugged.

"But," Jesus said, "that's a very good thing, right? *Muy bueno.*"

Billy's arm was over his eyes. "It should've been a *muy bueno.* But I don't have a scrap of emotion in me. Of any kind. Sad. Happy. Angry. Romantic. Chamorra might as well go find a flat rock to kiss."

Garowski stuck his head in the tent. "Hey. Sarge, good news. We're staying on Saipan."

Billy grunted. "So I've heard."

"Isn't that something?"

"It is something."

"You lucky dog. Stuck on a tropical island with a beautiful woman."

"I'm stuck all right, Garowski. Where's your buddy?"

"Levy's with the rabbi, Sol Davids. He'll be by." Garowski

stepped into the tent. "Also heard that there's brew coming our way."

Johnny perked up. "There is? Who told you that? What kind?"

"I don't know what to call it, Corporal. It's islander brew. Juice that the Chamorro cooked up for us. Traditional. Like the Irish giving us Guinness."

"Or Kentucky giving us moonshine." Johnny fished out a pack of Player's. "I sure hope you're giving us the straight dope."

"As straight as scuttlebutt can make it."

"Yeah, well, that ain't saying a lot."

"No, it's God's truth." Red O'Brien, crimson beard thick and wooly, came into the tent with Sammy Crown, who towered over all of them. "We actually saw the stuff coming into camp in a Marine Corps truck."

Crown nodded. "It's here. First round gets served to K Company and Platoon X-Ray. Crandall is handling it. I think the idea is we line up with our tin mugs. Everybody gets a refill. You won't get more than that. Crandall will be watching like a hawk."

O'Brien began passing out cigars. "Some colonel gave Crandall a box. But, you know, he swore he wouldn't smoke no more when Rudy got killed. So, here you go. And something else." O'Brien looked at Billy, who was still on his back with his arm over his eyes. "The Chamorro cooked us up more than home brew. I don't know how they did it. The fighting on Saipan's only been over for ... what the hell is the date today?"

"It's the 9th, Red," Crown told him.

Johnny snorted. "The hell. It's Friday the 11th of August. Want the year too?"

O'Brien threw Johnny a cigar. "I'm just saying, the fighting on Saipan's only been over for a month. Yet they pulled this feast together. How'd they do that? So, when we line up for the liquor, bring your mess kit for some hot chow. And speaking of heat, Sergeant Martens, guess who's helping dish it up?"

"Tokyo Rose," Billy mumbled.

"Oh, someone much, much better than Rose. *Mucho mejor.* It's your gal, Chamorra. In some kind of island dress and looking out of this world. If I were you, Sarge, I'd be first in line before somebody better looking catches her eye."

"That's not gonna be hard." Skillet showed up. "Sergeant Martens is uglier than sin with that chewed up beard and all his cuts and bruises and scabs."

"All proudly earned and proudly displayed," said Billy.

"You ever gonna shave?"

"When Red does."

O'Brien laughed. "That will never happen. Not until the last shot is fired. A pirate's life for me."

Billy actually smiled, which startled Johnny and Jesus. "Me too."

"What the frig are you yard birds doing crammed up in this hot stinking tent?" Gunnery Sergeant Zarate barked, thrusting past O'Brien and Crown. "Didn't you get the word? Chow and whiskey, courtesy our Chamorran allies." He loomed over Billy's cot. "And shit, Sergeant Martens, I'd have thought you'd be the first in line. The goddess even asked for you."

"Count me out."

"What the hell are you talking about?"

"Maybe I'll check into sick bay. Maybe I won't. But I'm not in a line-up-like-a-good-Marine mood."

"You're not in the mood? For liquor and hot chow? And a beautiful woman who thinks the sun rises, shines, and sets on that godawful puss of yours? Are you *loco*?"

"I am *loco*, Gunnery Sergeant."

"Damn rights. All the combat must've shaken your gears loose." He looked around the tent, hands on his hips. "Did I mention they're all there in their island dresses? Flowers in their hair? Latasi? Sirena? And that big old tough Hudana looks closer to forty than seventy-seven right now. I don't know how she does it." He clapped his hands together. "Mess kits. Tin mugs. Chow line. On the double."

The men charged out of the tent, Zarate right behind them. Only Johnny lingered.

"You okay, buddy?" he asked Billy.

"Yeah. Don't worry about me. I'll catch up."

"You sure?"

"I'm sure. Go get some grub and home brew."

Billy waited a while after Johnny had left. Then he got up and went in the opposite direction of the mess tent and Chamorra. He walked to the beach. Marines swept past him, headed the other way. When he got to the shoreline he sat down in the sand, put his Zippo to a cigarette, smoked the Lucky Strike and watched the sea. He watched it for a long time. Even after the stars came out and lit up the sky.

40

THE THINGS WE LEAVE BEHIND

THE CORPSMAN

I don't know if it was a good idea to linger over Rudy's grave or not.

But my feet took me there.

My head and heart too, I guess.

I wasn't just thinking of him. I was thinking of all the guys we'd left behind on Guadalcanal and Tarawa. Yeah, and now Saipan. Every island, we left some. We left ourselves too. I wasn't the guy who left the States when I left the Canal. I wasn't the guy who left New Zealand when I left Tarawa. And I sure as hell wasn't the guy who left Tarawa now that I was about to leave Saipan.

Pieces of me were gone. They were gone for good. New stuff had been crammed into me. Wounds in the body that would leave scars I'd look at when I was somebody's grandfather. Cuts in the mind that would trouble me till they shoveled me under like Rudy. Dark thoughts that a noonday sun would never burn away.

I'd saved a cigar for Rudy's graveside. I smoked it slowly. I had no idea when I'd be back on Saipan again. A bunch of guys were going home for good. Johnny and I were heading home too, but we'd be back to the Pacific. I wasn't sure if that meant Saipan. It could be they'd just bring us to the next island in line. Scuttlebutt was rife about that. Iwo Jima? Okinawa? Japan?

I was pretty sure Johnny would marry his woman once we were in America. He'd asked about me standing for him. Hell, yes. Billy should've been in the wedding party too. But there was no way he'd be leaving Saipan when Saipan had Chamorra.

I inhaled and held it and looked down at Rudy's white cross. I wondered what advice he'd have for his Silver Star winner. Billy was in the dumps and Chamorra was waiting and watching in the wings while he struggled to pull himself together. But she wouldn't wait forever. With peace and liberty had come a new world for the Chamorro. Marriage, children, grandchildren. She wanted to be part of that. The warrior wanted to lay down her sword and hold an infant in her arms. If Billy didn't want to make her his wife and join her, she'd move on. It's not as if he didn't notice the Chamorran guys who were suddenly hanging around her now that the war on Saipan was over. I was pretty sure part of his heart was still with Chamorra. But I was also pretty sure part of his heart wasn't.

He was too tired and worn out to care. At twenty-one, he was an old man. He couldn't un-see what he'd seen. He had to live with it. He'd watched others do terrible things. He'd done terrible things too. Either he'd bury it and live his life out or it would bury him. I had no idea which way he'd go.

There had been other guys who cracked under the strain. Hundreds of them. The poor buggers fell apart. Billy might too. My biggest fear, one I didn't voice to Johnny or anyone, was that we'd return from leave in a couple of months, and Crandall would pull us aside and tell us Billy was gone. Used a Colt 45 and put the barrel in his mouth.

No one talked about the suicides. It was all hush-hush. But I knew about them. Every island we'd fought on had them. Chamorra could save Billy from that. Her and God. It's what I prayed. But one thing I'd learned about prayer since I'd left home. You had to work with God to make it work. You could say no to God. You could say no all your life. And then one day, that would be it. Life over and done. No more opportunity to pray. No more need.

I felt I was being pushed towards Billy. The ship was leaving for Pearl in a couple of hours and we'd start boarding soon. But I had to go to him. Maybe Rudy pushed me. Along with the good Lord. Who knows? Billy wasn't in camp. Johnny was pretty sure he'd taken off for the beach after the morning drill. No, he hadn't headed toward Chamorra's village, even though Crandall had given him leave to do just that.

I found Billy swimming in the sea. Not close to shore. Far out. I sat down and waited. I still had some cigar left. He was a speck on a sheet of shining silver. Over time, he swam closer and I could make out his face and beard. He called to me. "Something up, Bud?"

"Nothing's up. Just wanted to say *adios*. Johnny and I will be getting on board ship soon."

"I said goodbye to Johnny already."

"Yeah, well, I'm Bud."

He treaded water. "What's to say?"

"Not much, I guess. You gonna be okay?"

"Yeah, I'll be okay."

"You plan on tying the knot with Cham while we're gone?"

"What? Tying the knot?" Billy started swimming away from shore again. "You guys have a good trip, Bud. Say hello to FDR for me."

"Will do. We can drop by Montana if you want."

"Don't."

"Anything you'd like us to bring back?"

He was stroking hard and didn't answer. Pretty soon he was a speck again. Even less than a speck. The sun and sea combined to dissolve his head with light. Nothing of him was left. All I saw were slow-moving ocean swells. No one would have any idea a man was swimming far out of sight of shore. If he disappeared, Crandall would type up a casualty report. MISSING PRESUMED DEAD.

On my back to camp, I ran into Chamorra. The craziest thing. No more black pajamas for her. She was in a pretty incredible red dress. Red as sunset. And she wasn't alone. A tall, dark, good-looking island man was with her. They'd been holding hands, but I saw her drop his, the moment the three of us met.

"Hello, Bud," she sang out, as if I wouldn't have seen anything that might have made me look twice. "I hear you are leaving us."

"That's right. For a few months, anyway."

"How long have you been away from America?"

"A couple of years."

"Won't it feel strange?"

I nodded. "Probably. We've had our quiet times in New Zealand and Hawaii, but seeing the States again? That will be something completely different. I think it will rattle our brains."

She laughed. "Oh, by the way, let me introduce my friend, Napo."

He extended his hand, and I took it.

Chamorra glanced over my shoulder. "Were you swimming?"

"No. Just went out to look at the sea."

"Alone?"

I hesitated. "Yeah. I went alone."

She turned her eyes back to me and smiled. There was something different in her look, but I couldn't read it. "So, when will you be back with us, Bud?"

"Two months. Maybe more. Maybe less."

"It's just Johnny going with you?"

"That's right."

"Could ... um ... your friend have gone with you?"

"Billy? Sure. If he'd wanted."

She waited. I waited too. I was going to force her to ask. Okay, to be honest, her hand-holding with Napo pissed me off. Finally, she gave in.

"So, there's no one he wishes to see back in America, Bud?"

"Not really."

"What's on Saipan for him now that the fighting has ended?"

"Peace and quiet. Good grub. Coffee and chocolate. The ocean. He loves to swim in the ocean with no one shooting at him."

"Is that all, Bud?"

I put a cigarette between my lips and offered them the pack. They both shook their heads. I lit up. God forgive me, but I had to get in a dig. "What else does a man need, Chamorra?"

She swung her head away. "Well, perhaps you'll get in a swim yourself before you sail away."

"The ocean's been taken." I gave the pair of them a half-salute. "Take it easy. I'll see you when I get back."

I hadn't been fair. I knew I hadn't been fair. Chamorra had every right to take another man. Billy wanted nothing to do with her. But I guess I wanted more out of her. More compassion. More commitment. More love. I really did want her to be a goddess. Who was I kidding? She was as human and as weak as anyone else. The war was over and she wanted arms around her. So did I. So did everyone. I couldn't fault her for that.

Johnny was squared away when I reached camp. "Where have you been hiding, Bud? We're outta here in an hour. Crandall was cussing."

"Let him cuss. I was saying goodbye to a friend."

Johnny was checking over his sea bag and stopped. "How's he doing?"

"If you mean Rudy, heck, he's fine. He's outta here and at peace. If you mean Billy, not where I'd want him to be."

"Where do you want him to be?"

"Back on Saipan. With Chamorra. With her kisses. In the moonlight. It's the Mennonite romantic in me."

"Where the hell do you think he is if he's not on Saipan, Bud?"

"Lost at sea."

Johnny stared. "Give me the straight shit. Is he gonna be here when we get back?"

"I don't know."

"No. I mean it. I want to know."

"I mean it too, Johnny. I don't know."

"Well, hell, you say he's down at the beach?" Johnny got up.

"Don't bother," I told him. "There's nothing you can say that will amount to a hill of beans. He's wherever he is in his head and you can't pull him out of it. This is his fight. It's totally his fight."

"He'll listen to me."

"He won't."

"I'll make him listen."

I put my hand on his chest. A dangerous thing to do with Johnny Strange, but I did it. I even pushed him back a little. "This isn't Bloody Ridge, Johnny. It's not wading through the surf for a frigging mile at Tarawa while the Jap guns are chewing us up. It's not that wild banzai on Saipan with three or four thousand Japs pounding over our heads. It's another war, another island, another fight. And Billy's in it on his own. We're not there. We're still on the beachhead. He's gone in first. He's gunned his way deep into the jungle. Now he's trapped. We're not there. He's going to have to get himself out of the hole. It's up to him."

"How is it up to him?" Johnny snapped.

"He has to want it bad enough."

"Does he want it bad enough?"

"Not yet. Maybe he never will."

Crandall thrust his head into the tent. "Quit the goldbricking and move your butts. Time to go to sea."

"Aye, aye, skipper," I said quietly.

He glanced from me to Johnny. "Everything okay here?"

I nodded. So did Johnny.

"Everything squared away?" Crandall asked again, aware of the tension.

"We're squared away, skipper," Johnny told him.

"Grab your sea bags."

They drove us to the pier along with hundreds of Marines. Got in line. Did our slow walk up the gangway. Found bunks. Went back topside as the ship's horn sounded. Watched Saipan fall astern. The sun was at our backs as we steered east for the Hawaiian Islands.

"I don't see him," Johnny muttered.

I was scanning sea and shore. "He could have gone back to camp."

"Or be diving."

"Or lying on the beach."

Johnny glanced up at a cluster of seagulls. "Hell of a thing if I come back here a married man."

"Oh, you'll come back a married man, all right. I know how much you love her. What I don't know is if you're going to be able to handle leaving her a second time."

"I'll have to. The job's not done. I need to be with my buddies. I gotta see as many of them back safe to the States as I can. I can't leave that to anyone else."

Three or four dolphins shot out of the blue water and dived under again in a spray of crystal.

"No, neither can I," I said.

Murray Andrew Pura writes in a number of genres for a variety of publishers including HarperCollins, Harlequin, Harvest House, Islands, Elk Lake, Baker, Barbour and MillerWords. He is the author of the award-winning series The Zoya Septet which includes the novels Zo, The White Birds of Morning, Beautiful Skin and A Sun Drenched Elsewhere. He makes his home in southwestern Alberta by the Montana border and Waterton-Glacier Peace Park.

Patrick E. Craig is a lifelong writer and musician. After retiring from the ministry in 2007 he concentrated on writing and publishing fiction books. He has published six Amish novels, two YA mystery books, two World War II historical novels, a Civil War novella and two anthologies of Amish stories. He lives in Idaho with his wife Judy.